MW01407441

THE MILLS OF THE GODS

BOOKS by TIM POWERS

The Mills of the Gods

My Brother's Keeper

Vickery and Castine Series
Alternate Routes
Forced Perspectives
Stolen Skies

The Skies Discrowned
An Epitaph in Rust
The Drawing of the Dark
The Anubis Gates
Dinner at Deviant's Palace
On Stranger Tides
The Stress of Her Regard

Fault Lines Series
Last Call
Expiration Date
Earthquake Weather

Declare
Three Days to Never
Hide Me Among the Graves
Medusa's Web

Short Story Collections
Night Moves and Other Stories • *Strange Itineraries*
The Bible Repairman and Other Stories
Down and Out in Purgatory: The Collected Stories of Tim Powers

To purchase Baen Books titles in e-book form, please go to www.baen.com.

THE MILLS OF THE GODS

TIM POWERS

BAEN

THE MILLS OF THE GODS

This is a work of fiction. All the characters and events portrayed in this book are fictional, and any resemblance to real people or incidents is purely coincidental.

Copyright © 2025 Tim Powers

All rights reserved, including the right to reproduce this book or portions thereof in any form.

A Baen Books Original

Baen Publishing Enterprises
P.O. Box 1403
Riverdale, NY 10471
www.baen.com

ISBN: 978-1-6680-7301-8

Cover art by Kieran Yanner

First printing, December 2025

Distributed by Simon & Schuster
1230 Avenue of the Americas
New York, NY 10020

Library of Congress Cataloging-in-Publication Data

Names: Powers, Tim, 1952- author
Title: The mills of the gods / Tim Powers.
Description: Riverdale, NY : Baen, 2025.
Identifiers: LCCN 2025028878 (print) | LCCN 2025028879 (ebook) | ISBN
   9781668073018 hardcover | ISBN 9781964856438 ebook
Subjects: LCGFT: Fantasy fiction | Paranormal fiction | Historical fiction
Classification: LCC PS3566.O95 M55 2025 (print) | LCC PS3566.O95 (ebook)
   | DDC 813/.54—dc23/eng/20250717
LC record available at https://lccn.loc.gov/2025028878
LC ebook record available at https://lccn.loc.gov/2025028879

Printed in the United States of America

10 9 8 7 6 5 4 3 2 1

To Bob and Karen Silverberg
and with thanks to: Joy Freeman, Russell Galen,
Steve Malk, Joe and Liz Stefko, Toni Weisskopf—
and especially to Serena Powers

The mills of the gods grind slowly;
But this mill
Chatters in mechanical staccato.
    —Ernest Hemingway

PART ONE:
An Intrusive Weed

CHAPTER ONE:
Death at Midnight Goes A-Dancing

The electric streetlights glittered on passing automobiles and bicycles and horse-drawn cabs in the wide lanes of the Boulevard Saint-Michel, and signs still glowed even in the windows of the closed shops, but in the narrower Rue Saint-Séverin the old gas streetlamps shone no brighter than the lamps under the awning of the Café Lepovre a dozen yards ahead.

A couple of iron chairs and tables still sat out on the brick pavement, but Harry Nolan had already been in there today to pick up his mail, and he opened the gate of the dark courtyard across the street. His flat was on the third floor of the hotel on the far side of the courtyard, and he stepped carefully around the potted lilacs to the front door. The concierge had long since retired to her back room, and he crossed the dimly lit lobby to the stairs. The uncarpeted treads creaked and the landings were drafty.

He unlocked the door of his flat and swung it open, starting to unbutton his coat, then stopped. The gas jet was lit in his room, though he had shut it off when he'd left an hour earlier, and in its yellow glow a young woman was standing beside his drafting table, blinking at him in evident surprise and holding a pistol—his own Army-issued .45-caliber semiautomatic—in her left hand. She was wearing the same long corduroy skirt and baggy flannel blouse she had been wearing this morning, and the remembered tweed cap and cloth purse now lay on the floor by the open window. The cold breeze from the window tossed her unconfined straw-colored hair around her pale gamin face.

She didn't raise the gun, but she didn't put it down either, and she gave him a defiant look. Her eyes were hazel—green with a tint of amber. This morning he had guessed her to be in her mid-twenties, but in this light she seemed younger.

"It will never be published now," she said. "You *will* let me read it."

"Yes," he agreed quickly, raising his empty hands. She probably wouldn't know how to disengage the safety lever on the pistol in her hand, but her finger was carelessly inside the trigger guard. "Yes, you can read it. And you could throw that on the bed."

She stepped to the side and laid the pistol on the blanket. He exhaled and pushed back the comma of dark hair that had fallen across his forehead.

"I had no intention of shooting you," she said. "Where is the story, the article?"

She had knocked on his door this morning, shortly after he had come back from breakfast at the café across the street, and she had asked to see a manuscript that had been sent to him by the editor of *La Prosodie* for an illustration. Her accent was vaguely British and her clothes were resolutely bohemian, and he had assumed that she was another of the tiresome literary expatriates who seemed to throng the Latin Quarter in these postwar years, probably a poet; when he had impatiently told her that it would be published in a few days, and she could wait and read it in print, she had nodded and walked away to the stairs.

He crossed to the bedside table now, and slid open the drawer in which he customarily kept the pistol; his passport document and a sheaf of francs lay undisturbed.

"I didn't come to steal from you, either," she said. Her tone was matter-of-fact, not indignant or defensive.

"Huh." After a moment he shrugged and stepped to the drafting table; he looked from his uninvited visitor to the pistol on the bed and back, then pulled out a shallow drawer below the table's hinged top.

"You can read it here, then go," he said as he lifted out the ten pages of typescript. "Why do you say it won't be published?"

She was staring past him at the drawing board. Clipped to it was a sheet of heavy paper on which he had done a preliminary pencil sketch of an implausibly winged bull charging down from the sky.

"Tonight," she said softly without looking away from the picture, "the office of *La Prosodie,* and the whole building, caught fire. It's just a flaming shell now. Monsieur Barbier and the typesetter did not escape."

Nolan automatically looked past her out the window, in the direction of the old Marais district across the river.

"I'm sorry," she said. "Were you and he friends?"

"Acquaintances, at least."

Nolan had met Claude Barbier only a couple of times at the *Prosodie* editorial office on the Rue du Trésor, and the man still owed him for the last three illustrations Nolan had done for the journal.

He rubbed his free hand across his mouth. "They're dead? Burned?"

"That's what the *gendarmes* are saying. The fire was sudden, and comprehensive. I came straight here."

"Jesus." It might have been something like a prayer.

Nolan glanced down at the pages in his hand. *La Prosodie* was a low-paying and ill-regarded journal, known to local writers and artists as *Leprosy*. Barbier, the editor, had in the past sent Nolan proof pages for illustration, but this time had sent an actual typed manuscript, with instruction that it be returned in good condition along with an appropriate half-page pen-and-ink drawing.

The pages had been dog-eared and smudged when Nolan received them, and on the top page the writer's name and address had been heavily crossed out in pencil, with *Anonyme* scrawled below the title: "A Parisian Bullfighter."

He shrugged and handed her the pages. "I should have let you see it this morning. It's not much."

She took them and nodded toward the drawing on his drafting table. "It's much to me."

She was already reading the typescript as she stepped to the room's one chair and sat down. Nolan picked up his pistol and sniffed the barrel; it had not been fired, and when he slid the magazine out of the grip he saw that all seven rounds were still present. He clicked the magazine back in place, looked around the flat, then tucked the pistol behind his belt.

The young woman showed no expression as she read, but after a couple of pages her lower lip pulled in, and he guessed that she was gently biting it.

He wondered why she was so anxious to read the article. It was about an old Spanish drunkard who claimed to have been a bullfighter in Spain, and after some apparently prefatory remarks about a motion picture—an Italian historical epic—the old man had recounted a fable about a goddess who destroyed a winged golden bull. To kill the bull, the old man had said, the goddess had to lure it down from the sky, and for a decoy the goddess used a straw effigy of a child with a mirror for a face. The bull became its mirror image, and died when the goddess broke the mirror. The article's writer had asked the old man why the bull would descend on a child, and the reply had been, "To kill it, and grow bigger."

The article dwelt on the old man's penurious situation, but Nolan had been struck by the image of the winged bull—enough so that this afternoon he had walked the half mile south to the café where the interview had taken place, hoping to find the old Spaniard and perhaps get a detail or two that would make his illustration more striking. But it had been a wasted hike, as the old man had died some years earlier.

The girl had reached the last page when the black alley cat Nolan called Lejeune scrambled up onto the windowsill. Nolan started toward the sink, where he customarily saved bits of cheese to give to the cat when it appeared, but the girl said, "Marechal!" and the cat sprang into her lap, yowling and tearing the page she'd been reading.

"Now see what you've done, *mauvais garçon*," she said to it, holding the pages away with one hand and stroking the cat with the other.

"He lives here," remarked Nolan. "Sometimes. I give him things to eat, if I have anything."

The girl was staring into the cat's eyes. "He follows me sometimes."

"I was supposed to keep that manuscript in good condition."

"For Monsieur Barbier at *La Prosodie*?"

Nolan shrugged, acknowledging her implicit point.

A moment later, the cat leaped back to the windowsill.

"I can't remember," Nolan remarked, "whether I locked my door before I went out this evening."

"You did," she said, watching the cat. "I picked the lock. No damage. I locked it again after I came in."

"Ah." He blinked at her, annoyed with himself for being more amused than angry. "What were you going to do with my gun?"

"See if it was loaded, but I didn't know how."

"You don't even know how to hold it safely. You never—"

He was interrupted by a yowl from the cat. It was looking out over the courtyard and street below, its back arched and its tail fluffed wide. Its cry subsided to a low growl.

The girl stood up and gave Nolan an uncertain look. She waved the pages and asked, "Does anyone, anyone alive, know you have this? Besides me?"

"I—yes, I was curious about it. I went to the café that's mentioned in it—the Café des Amateurs, awful little place on the—"

"I know it. In the Rue Mouffetard."

"Right," Nolan said. "Huh. I asked some of the old bums there about the fellow in that article, and they said he's dead—"

"Beltran Iglesias. Yes, he's dead."

The cat jumped away onto some rooftop below.

She picked up her purse and flipped the tweed cap onto her head. "Marechal is capricious—but I might not be the only one to come straight here, after the fire."

Nolan exhaled through his teeth. "What, to read that article? As if anybody even knew—"

"Not to read it. I think we should go to the café across your street for a while."

Nolan preferred to meet people at other cafés than the one out front, where he was known to the staff and could be confident of not being interrupted while sketching or reading a newspaper.

"We can meet somewhere tomorrow," he told her, with in fact no intention of seeing her again. "If anybody else comes here tonight, they can—"

She stepped up close to him, scowling. "Barbier is dead," she rasped. "I'm going to that café. And I'm taking this," she added as she folded the typed pages and stuffed them into her purse. "Trust the cat, at least."

She crossed to the door and pulled it open, but didn't step into the hall until she had leaned out of the doorway and looked left and right.

"You can't take the—" Nolan began, then followed her out the door. "All right then, yes, the café."

"If there are back stairs," she said, "we go that way."

At least for the moment respecting her urgency, he quickly led the way to the back stairs.

✥ ✥ ✥

"We can watch your place from here," she said.

She had hurried to a sidewalk table under the awning at the café, partly hidden from the street by a curbside horse chestnut tree, and now she pulled out one of the white-painted iron chairs. She sat down and he took the chair across from her. The breeze down from the river was cold.

"I'm Harry Nolan," he said.

She shook her head, then said, "Vivi." She was shivering. "You are American."

"Yes." He shifted in his chair so that the pistol grip under his shirt didn't jab him in the stomach, and pulled a pack of Gauloises and a box of matches out of his coat pocket. "And you're not British," he said, laying them beside an ashtray on the table. *"Deux eaux-de-vie, s'il vous plaît, Armand,"* he added to the young white-aproned waiter who had slouched up to the table.

Armand nodded and retreated. The only other patron of the Café Lepovre at this hour was an old man at a far table, who exchanged a customary nod with Nolan.

"No," said Vivi. When Nolan raised his eyebrows she went on, "I suppose I'm French." She tugged the battered typescript out of her purse and unfolded it on the table.

Nolan shook a cigarette out of the pack and struck a match. "So why," he said around a puff of smoke, "should anyone care about that old article?"

Armand walked up from behind them then and set two glasses of brandy on the table, each on a saucer with 2 FRANCS printed on it.

When the waiter had gone back inside, Vivi said, "Maybe no one does. But yesterday Barbier asked me about old Beltran, because he was going to publish this, and wanted to know more about him. I asked to see it, and he said his only copy"—and she tapped the pages—"was in the hands of an artist who was to do an illustration for it."

She slid out one of his cigarettes and lit it. "Beltran was murdered three years ago, near enough. Now Barbier is dead."

Nolan frowned and sat back carefully. "I gather you knew this Beltran fellow?" He picked up his glass and took a warming sip of the brandy.

Instead of answering, Vivi pulled back the left sleeve of her flannel shirt to look at a wristwatch. It was the size of a silver dollar, and the crystal was a shallow, scratched dome. Nolan saw that it was a pocket watch pinned at both sides to a leather band.

He wasn't able to see what time it was, but the hour must have been getting late. "I should really—" he began.

Vivi caught his hand, looking past him. "Hold on," she said softly.

Nolan looked around to see what had caught her attention, and saw six children, none apparently more than twelve years old and several a good deal younger, skipping up the dark street into the glow of the nearest streetlamp. Windblown capes clung around their knees.

Turning back to Vivi, he saw a look of alarm on her pale face. Her cold fingers tightened on his hand, then released it.

One of the children crouched and straightened, then threw a pebble at a low black shape racing across the street toward the café. The pebble missed its target, which proved to be the cat Nolan still thought of as Lejeune, and it jumped up onto their table.

Vivi stroked the cat's bristling fur with her free hand. "Oh, I don't like this at all."

Nolan could think of nothing to say but, "They shouldn't be out at this hour." He nodded toward the cat. "Uh—I gather you and the cat are old pals."

She was watching the children, who had pulled open the courtyard gate across the street. Absently she said, "I know all the *matagots* in Paris."

"The . . . ?"

"*Matagots*. Magical cats." She drew on her cigarette and exhaled a fluttering stream of smoke. "Be quiet."

Nolan was regretting having left his comparatively warm flat to come out here with this clearly delusional girl. He drank the last of the brandy in his glass and slid his chair back, looking across the street.

The children had moved out of sight into the hotel courtyard, and Vivi lowered her head and whispered to the cat in rapid French. It sounded like a question, and Nolan was only able to catch *"l'Inconnue"* because she said it more slowly. She stubbed out her cigarette and looked up at Nolan. "I'm sorry, I should have told you to take away your drawing. They will be sure of you now."

"What, you mean those children? I'm not—"

"Children!" Vivi pushed her own chair back and stood up. "Some of those *children* remember when Trochu was president!" She started toward the street, paused, and stepped back to snatch up her glass and gulp the brandy. "Thank you," she said, clanking it down. "Goodbye and God be with you."

She hurried away in the direction from which the children had come, and the cat went loping after her.

After a few seconds, Nolan crushed out his cigarette and lit another, and when Armand stepped into view with a questioning look, Nolan nodded. He picked up the battered manuscript of "A Parisian Bullfighter" and shuffled the pages back into their original order, flattening the wrinkled pages and closing the section torn by the cat's claw. The heavily pencilled-out lines at the top-right corner of the first page caught his eye, and he began patting the pockets of his shirt and coat.

Trochu, he thought. Trochu was president when? A good fifty years ago, anyway. And Mademoiselle Vivi knows all the magical cats in Paris? I daresay.

Armand delivered the fresh glass just as Nolan found what he had been looking for, among the coins and pencil-stubs in his coat pockets: an eraser. For the next couple of minutes, as he alternated between puffs on his cigarette and sips of brandy and glances toward the gate in front of his hotel, he carefully rubbed the eraser across the heavy pencil lines.

He looked up when a little girl came scampering out of the darkness down the street into the streetlamp's glow. She too hurried through the courtyard gate.

Nolan returned his attention to the pages on the table. He had rubbed out enough of the pencil marks to read the name and address at the top corner of the page, and he blew eraser shreds away to peer at it.

Ernest Hemingway, he read. *Hotel Jacob et L'Angleterre, 44 Rue Jacob, Paris France.*

He had heard of Ernest Hemingway—a young writer with several small-press books to his credit. And Hemingway evidently lived in Paris, unless he had moved since writing the article; it must be at least three years old, since Vivi had said that the old bullfighter's death had been that long ago.

The children all emerged from the courtyard now, and went

skipping away down the street in the same direction Vivi had taken, toward the river.

He picked up the girl's empty brandy glass. *I should have told you to bring away your drawing,* she had said, clearly implying that those children should not find it. *They will be sure of you now.* And, certainly talking to herself more than to the cat, she had said something about *l'Inconnue.*

He took another sip from his glass and set his cigarette in the ashtray; and he flexed the hand she had caught hold of when she had first seen the children appear.

Nolan had heard the old story of *L'Inconnue de la Seine*—an anonymous girl found drowned in the river, whose enigmatic smile, so entranced a pathologist at the morgue that he made a death mask of her face. The cast was widely reproduced, and Nolan had seen plaster copies of it in shops. It occurred to him that he had not once seen Vivi smile, and he tried to imagine what a death mask of her would look like, if she too were to end up in the river.

The thought chilled him. She had seemed delusional, but—though it was an absurd consideration—the cat *had* been agitated about *something.*

He dropped seven francs beside the saucers on the table, gulped the remainder of his brandy, and got to his feet. Stepping out of the lamplight under the café's awning, he hurried in the direction opposite to that taken by Vivi and the children, up the street to the Boulevard Saint-Michel; a cab would get him to the river more quickly than even rapid walking.

The cabdriver reined in his horse behind a truck and an automobile that had collided in the crowded and brightly lit Quai Saint-Michel, just short of the bridge to the Île de la Cite, and Nolan handed the man some coins and hopped down to the pavement. He threaded his way between stopped and slow-moving vehicles to the gap in the low riverside wall, and tapped quickly down two switchback sets of stone stairs to the embankment beside the river.

The six-foot-wide embankment was a shadowed, brick-paved track that extended away into utter darkness under the high southernmost arch of the bridge. He touched the grip of his pistol, then sighed and groped his way forward, careful to crowd the masonry on his right, away from the echoing ripple and splash of the invisible river to his left. When he emerged on the far side of the bridge, the narrow pavement underfoot was still only dimly visible, for a concrete roof extended out as far as the riverside coping, and the moon was down. But his night vision was good, and soon by the faint paleness of the low clouds he could make out the shifting, empty expanse of the river on his left. Spots of light on the far side were probably office windows in the Préfecture de Police.

He hurried up two short sets of steps, and the shadowed embankment stretched ahead for a good hundred yards, with recessed alcoves along the stone wall on his right.

The night wind was cold down here, smelling of fish and smoke. The thought of the long walk back to his flat had just begun to slow his steps when he saw a figure crouched beside the low coping a dozen yards ahead, and he stopped.

For perhaps half a minute the figure didn't move. Then the sudden flare of a match lit the figure's face under a tweed cap, and he recognized Vivi's profile; a moment later another flame appeared—a candle wick—and the match was shaken out. Vivi raised her head and looked out over the rippling dark water.

A signal? thought Nolan. He peered across at the far embankment, but saw no answering light.

Above the lapping of the water a few feet below where Vivi crouched, Nolan heard a whisper of sound behind him. Without moving his feet he turned to look back, but could make out nothing in the blackness below the bridge.

He breathed a curse and stepped silently back into the nearest recessed alcove. He didn't want to leave the evidently demented girl alone down here, but he hesitated to interrupt whatever she was doing.

After what he judged to be a minute, he was about to discreetly scrape a shoe on the pavement when he heard water sluice and splash below her.

He took several steps forward to see over her shoulder—then rocked back in surprise.

A head had risen out of the water. It shook wetly clinging hair away, exposing a white porcelain face gleaming in the candlelight; and now two hands rose from the water to grip the stone coping.

The hands were bare bones, draped with tendrils of weed.

The breath stopped in Nolan's throat, but old training kept him from focusing exclusively on the shocking sight. He touched the grip of his pistol, and paid attention to his peripheral views of the river and the embankment in both directions. He reminded himself that he had seen terrible injuries during the war...

But there had been no swimmer in the river for at least the last several minutes, and the skeletal fingers were flexing now on the stone. This thing was dead, but moving. This was nightmare.

Vivi was speaking to the eyeless porcelain face, and when she paused, a voice like a stroked violin replied from the horizontal slit of a mouth. The wind and the rippling of the water kept Nolan from catching any words, or even recognizing a language.

The dead thing's reply seemed to have shocked Vivi. She sat back on the stone pavement and said something that sounded like *L'apash?* and then more words too quiet for Nolan to make out.

Now he heard definite footsteps on the embankment from the direction of the bridge; he hesitated, then cautiously retreated into the alcove. He saw Vivi look back, and then she quickly got to her feet. The head and the skeletal hands sank out of sight with a quiet ripple.

"Beltran's daughter, sure enough!" piped up a child's voice. "It's been a long time, *enfant*. Hurrying away from us down Saint-Séverin tonight—confess, you were visiting the artist!"

"Talking about the goddess and the bull," said another, "without a doubt!" The accent sounded incongruously American.

"Who do you hope will see your candle?" asked a third.

Vivi took a step back, clearly ready to run away along the embankment to the next set of stairs, then stood still, staring toward the children Nolan couldn't see.

Vivi seemed to be afraid of them, or possibly of someone with them, so he sidled around the alcove corner into the candlelight. Six feet away, blocking the way back to the bridge, stood only a cluster of children in dresses and short pants and flapping capes. Certainly this was the same group that had been in the courtyard of his hotel, though there seemed to be a few more of them now.

Abruptly his gaze sharpened.

A girl in front was holding a Derringer pistol; a pocket gun, but in the candlelight the twin muzzles looked like a big caliber, possibly .45.

It was aimed at Vivi, but in an instant the girl swiveled on her toes to point it at Nolan.

For several seconds, no one at all moved, nor even seemed to breathe. The wind along the embankment was the only sound.

Then Vivi abruptly yelled, *"Sauteur chienne!"* The girl turned toward her, and in one movement Nolan drew his semiautomatic, clicked off the safety, and leveled it. To his horror, the sights were now squarely lined up on the girl's face.

His hand was steady, but his face was cold with sudden sweat. His finger was only a fraction of an inch away from the trigger. Could this little girl have any comprehension of what a .45 bullet would do, to him or herself?

"This," he said, in as calm a voice as he could muster, "would blow your head to pieces. Neither of us wants that."

The little girl stared at him thoughtfully. "There are more of us than you've got rounds in that."

"They're small," Vivi called to him, her voice tight with bravado. "You could probably shish-kebab several with each shot."

The children commenced whispering among themselves. The girl in front kept her little gun pointed at Nolan but, without taking her eyes off him, leaned back to join in the conference.

"Death at midnight goes a-dancing," she said finally, "but we're hardly dressed for it." She turned away, and a moment later all the children were skipping back toward the bridge and the stairs beyond it.

Nolan stared after them for several seconds, then turned sharply when he heard a splash in the river and the candlelight was extinguished. Vivi was racing away down the embankment in the direction away from the bridge.

The footsteps receded in both directions, and when all he could hear was the wind and the river, Nolan sat down on the damp brick. His hands were shaking now as he clicked his pistol's safety back into engagement, and he breathed deeply till his heartbeat slowed down.

After a minute he got to his feet, tucked the pistol behind his belt, and pulled his shirt out to hide it. He walked to the edge of the embankment and looked down at the dark water.

He had been living in Paris for four years now, but at this moment he felt that he knew no more about the ancient city than the most frivolous tourist. Had he really been menaced at gunpoint by a group of children? Come close to *killing* one of them? *Sauteur chienne,* Vivi had called the girl with the Derringer; some sort of dog?

And had he truly seen—already it seemed doubtful!—a *corpse* rise out of the river and speak to the girl who spoke to cats?

He began trudging back toward the Pont Saint-Michel. The idea of walking to a friend's flat, waking him or her up and asking to sleep there, simply didn't present itself as something that would happen. He knew he would make his way back to his own flat and go to bed—albeit with the door bolted and his pistol on the bedside table. Those eerie children, he assured himself, would not be able to break in and...*exchange gunfire* with him.

Besides, he thought, they're not dressed for it tonight.

CHAPTER TWO:
He Travels the Fastest

At his customary table under the awning of the Café Lepovre next morning, sipping coffee and absently taking bites of a warm brioche, Harry Nolan had made some progress in concluding that nothing of lasting consequence had actually happened the previous night.

He still quailed at the memory of having had to point his service .45 at a little girl, down on the embankment—but a child that young couldn't have understood what her gun, or his, could do, and the admittedly dreadful moment had passed, and the girl and her chums had run away. When he'd got back to his flat last night, the sketch of the flying bull had been gone; but no one at all had come to his door during the remainder of the night. The only interruption of his sleep had been the tolling of a distant bell in the small hours, more of a bass vibration than a sound. And no one, of any age, had been waiting for him outside this morning.

He shivered in the chilly breeze and tugged the sleeves of his sweater down over his wrists.

Sparrows were chirping in the sunlit roof gutters along the familiar length of the Rue Saint-Séverin, and anyone could see that the real world had no place for things like skeletons that swam in the river and spoke like violins through porcelain masks! In nightmares he had often seen things as grotesque as that, things morbidly and fantastically synthesized from scenes he had actually witnessed in the fighting at Château-Thierry and Belleau Wood and Saint-Mihiel seven years ago.

Along with the coffee and the brioches, the morning waiter had brought him the pack of cigarettes and the pages of the Hemingway manuscript he had left on the table last night, when he had set out after the girl Vivi. Nolan caught the man's eye and raised his emptied cup, and the man stepped to the table and refilled it. Nolan nodded and shook a cigarette out of the pack.

The sudden clarity of Vivi's face in the candlelight, down there next to the black river—after her enigmatic talk about implausibly aged children and magical cats, and her mention of *l'Inconnue,* together with his own fatigue and two fast brandies on an empty stomach—and probably some actual piece of floating litter briefly snagged at the edge of the river!—had simply triggered a few seconds of hallucination: a momentary waking nightmare, already indistinct in his memory. He believed that such things were not uncommon in men who had been in combat.

Probably that little girl's gun had not even been real. In fact it was very likely, he told himself, that Barbier was fine, and the *La Prosodie* office had not burned at all.

And the Vivi girl was just some kind of eccentric occultist whose father was mentioned in the Hemingway article, and who had made enemies of some of the street urchins of Paris.

He was hopeful that he had seen the last of her. Since the war, and since a brief and alienating return to his boyhood home in Oklahoma, he had found it easy to avoid close involvements with people, and he certainly didn't want to get acquainted with this Vivi person.

He quoted to himself a favorite line from Kipling: *He travels the fastest who travels alone.*

He was sure that these thoughts over breakfast had cheered him, or would soon. He picked up the battered typescript pages and tapped them even. He really should take the manuscript back to Ernest Hemingway, since it didn't seem that Hemingway was the one who had brought it to *La Prosodie,* and Hemingway might object to it having been submitted to that second-rate journal.

And, Nolan admitted to himself, he did want to know something more about the old bullfighter, Beltran Iglesias, who had told Hemingway the story about the winged bull.

Nolan ate the last brioche and chased it with the rest of his coffee, then got to his feet. Sylvia Beach would know where Hemingway was these days. It seemed that every writer and painter in Paris frequented

Beach's bookshop, Shakespeare and Company, and many of them used the shop as their mailing address.

He folded the typescript pages lengthwise and tucked them into his back pocket.

Bicycles angled between slow-moving automobiles and horse-drawn wagons in the lanes of the Boulevard Saint-Michel this morning, and crowds thronged the sidewalks—men in suits and white straw hats clustered by news kiosks, moustached *gendarmes* strode purposefully or paused to get their boots shined, men in bowler hats and young women in long, loose dresses sat shoulder to shoulder at the little tables in front of the cafés. The cool June breeze carried reassuringly familiar smells of dew-damp stone and automobile exhaust and horse droppings.

At the intersection with the Boulevard Saint-Germain, Nolan walked west, past tall old hotels with scrollwork above the windows and tiny dormers on high slanted roofs, and after a few minutes of weaving around busy pedestrians he turned his steps south into the Rue de l'Odéon.

Soon he could see the green shopfront and display window of the bookshop, with a sign bearing a picture of Shakespeare swinging on a bar over the door, and after a few hurried steps he was pulling open the door to a puff of warm air and the scents of wood and paper and tobacco smoke.

The bookshop was small, with several tables and armchairs between the fireplace and the street-facing shelves at the front window, but the walls were high, either fretted with crowded bookshelves or nearly paneled with framed photographs and letters. The books were a mix of leather-bound, gold-stamped volumes, current American bestsellers, and new French books still in their glassine dust jackets.

Sylvia Beach was probably in her late thirties, slim and studious-looking, with short chestnut hair brushing the collar of her brown velvet jacket. She had been conversing in French with an elderly man by the fireplace when Nolan entered, but looked up and then hurried around one of the tables.

"Mr. Nolan," she said, and gently touched his arm. "You've heard about *La Prosodie*?"

For a moment Nolan just stood with his mouth open; then, "Someone told me the building burned," he said. "Last night."

"Yes. It was a—it seems so inadequate just to say it was a terrible thing. Evidently Mr. Barbier and an employee didn't survive."

Nolan looked past her at the photographs framed on the wall: D. H. Lawrence, Ezra Pound, André Gide. He didn't bother to look for Claude Barbier. Poor old *Leprosy*, he thought. "I'm sorry to hear it confirmed."

"Do sit down. Would you like a cup of tea? Brandy? It's a cold morning."

"Yes. No. Thank you." He rubbed a hand across his chin. "The reason I came—I was hoping you might be able to tell me how to get in touch with a writer. Ernest Hemingway? I know at one time he was living in the Rue Jacob. I have something of his that I'm—anxious to return."

"He hasn't lived there in years. You could leave it here, he's in practically every day."

"Ah. I'd like to talk to him about it, actually."

She peered up at him. "Well, at this hour... I believe he likes to work at the Closerie des Lilas, on Rue du Montparnasse... but that's a good kilometer south of here, and he might be anywhere. Why don't you leave a note, and I can pass it on to him."

Best not to push it, Nolan thought. He nodded reluctantly. "That would be fine, thanks."

Beach walked to another table and picked up a pencil and a notecard. "Did Genevieve Chastain find you yesterday? I told her you were the artist who did most of the illustrations for *La Prosodie*."

Genevieve, he thought. Vivi. "Yes," he said in a neutral tone.

"I'm sorry. She does take some getting used to."

"Yes." In spite of himself he asked, "Who... *is* she?"

"Oh—" Beach leaned against the table. "I suppose she's a poet, as much as anything. She's done several translations of English verse into French." She wrinkled her nose. "Unreliably, I'm afraid."

I guessed she was a poet right off, though Nolan. "Oh?"

"I shouldn't tell tales out of school..." Beach rocked her head judiciously. "They're very *freehand* translations. *The Waste Land* as a minstrel show dialogue! Browning's 'My Last Duchess' from the point of view of the Duchess's ghost!" The pencil danced in her hand as she listed Vivi's transgressions. "She was once paid a substantial fee to do a translation of Tennyson's *In Memoriam,* but it was rejected; she made it about a *woman* who drowned, not Tennyson's friend Arthur Hallam, and she grafted in some lines from *Hamlet* about Ophelia."

Nolan's face had gone cold. He made himself speak casually: "Really. Gertrude's description of Ophelia drowning, I suppose."

Beach nodded and handed him the card and the pencil. As he bent over the table, he was hardly aware of his hand writing his name and address.

Coincidence! he told himself. Just because she buggered up the Tennyson poem to focus on a drowned woman is not—emphatically is not!—any sort of *validation* of what I thought I saw last night down there on the embankment.

He travels the fastest who travels alone.

But, damn it, I can't just let it go.

He straightened, leaving the card and pencil on the table. "Uh... do you know how to get in touch with her?"

"I suppose that's only fair. Sometimes she works at the Taverne Olympia on the Boul' des Capucines, across the river by the big opera house."

Nolan had seen posters for the place, and he tried to imagine the laconic, carelessly dressed girl he'd met last night working in that gaudy and expensive-looking place. "As a waitress? A *dancer*?"

Beach smiled and shook her head. "In the *carambole* billiard parlor upstairs. Apparently she's an expert player, except for the times when she's a terrible one."

"Huh." Nolan had seen the French *carambole* style of billiards, which seemed to be just interminably nudging three balls around in one spot on a pocketless table. He much preferred the 8-ball pool style of billiards he had played in pool halls in New York.

"Characteristic, I'm sure," he said.

He thanked her and walked out of the shop.

Standing on the windswept pavement, he squinted up and down the narrow street at recessed shop doorways, and up at the low stone balustrades fronting open windows, and smiled wryly at his relief not to see the faces of feral children peering at him.

After a moment, his smile unkinked.

Gertrude's description of Ophelia drowning, he thought. *L'Inconnue.* A thing glimpsed by candlelight in the river.

A story about a winged bull plunging out of the sky. *I should have told you to bring away your drawing,* Vivi had said. *They will be sure of you now.*

Beltran's daughter, sure enough, one of the children had said last night.

Barbier was dead. *La Prosodie* was eradicated.

He would really have to ask Vivi some questions, and get clear answers. Sylvia Beach had said that the Taverne Olympia was by the Opera Garnier, across the river in the 9th arrondissement. Well, that wasn't far.

It occurred to him that the only times he had crossed the river in the last several months had been to visit the *Prosodie* editorial office in the Rue du Trésor, and for those occasions he had got a haircut and worn a hat and a jacket. Today his dark hair was tossing around his collar in the wind, and his sweater and khaki trousers were, he had to admit, a bit threadbare. Altogether, his appearance was adequate for the bohemian Latin Quarter, but a bit shabby for the establishments on the Right Bank.

He trudged back up the Rue de l'Odéon toward the Boulevard Saint-Germain, and he considered walking back to his flat and putting on a coat and hat and a better pair of trousers.

He cast one look back over his shoulder, and saw two little boys on bicycles a hundred feet away, riding in a tight circle in the middle of the street. They were not looking at him.

Whoever those children last night had been, they had apparently known Vivi only as *Beltran's daughter* and that one little girl had at least *seemed* to be ready to shoot her. The children had backed down only after Nolan had intervened with a gun of his own, and Vivi had fled, unpursued.

They had lost her, and it seemed they did not know her name. Might they have followed him, from the embankment back to his flat? The only chance they'd have of finding her now, he mused, would be to follow him today, in the hope that he might meet Vivi again.

Nolan quickened his pace, even as he assured himself that the suspicion was as delusional as Vivi's talk of impossibly aged children. Children—even, for the sake of argument, children who were somehow old enough to remember long-dead French presidents—could hardly track a man across Paris, a man who might at any moment get into a cab. They could, at most, serve as . . . scouts, errand runners.

Yes? he thought. For whom?

The display windows of a tobacco shop a few yards ahead were angled inward, and he sidled up to the shop. On the other side of the glass was a stepped array of cigarette cartons and cans of tobacco and open cigar boxes, but Nolan shifted on the pavement until he was able to see the street behind him in the glass's reflection.

The two boys were still riding in circles in the middle of the street, still only about a hundred feet behind him.

He jumped when something tugged at his pants cuff over his left ankle, and when he looked down he saw a black cat staring up at him. He nearly shook his leg to nudge it away, then looked again at the reflection in the window. There they were, pedaling their bicycles in the same circular pattern.

Nolan sighed and bent down to looked into the cat's slit-pupil eyes.

Really? he thought.

The cat stared intently back up at him.

... Okay.

He resumed walking, moving slowly and watching shop fronts and doorways. Ahead of him, one of a pair of tall, green-painted doors swung open, and an old woman in a black shawl shuffled out into the street; Nolan sprinted to the door and caught the edge of it before she was able to close it. He bowed hastily, as if he had meant to hold it for her, then stepped through and pulled the door closed behind him.

He was in a small cobblestone-paved square with a low open arch ahead of him. Ivy-bordered doors and windows were inset in the brick walls to right and left, and window boxes on upper-floor windows spilled tendrils of bougainvillea vines. Nolan sprinted to the arch and ducked through it, and found himself in an alley so narrow between high walls that he doubted sunlight ever touched the wet cobblestones under his shoes. Wooden boxes draped with wilted cabbage stood beside an open doorway a few yards to his left, and the smells of garlic and onions and a clatter of metal pans told him that it was the back door of a restaurant. He hurried to it and ducked inside. He sidled past steaming pots on stoves and startled men in gray aprons, then through a pair of swinging doors. He stepped around half a dozen tables and pushed open an exterior door, and then he was facing a wide courtyard fronted with shops, opening onto the next street over.

He crossed the courtyard to the street, and five minutes of brisk walking brought him to the wide sunlit lanes of the Boulevard Saint-Germain. He let his pace slow to a normal pedestrian walk then, and grinned self-consciously at the memory of the insistent cat and his own energetic response.

Nolan watched the automobiles and carriages in the lanes till he spied the white top hat of a *cocher*; he waved, and the man reined in his horse and stopped his cab, with the air of being imposed upon that seemed habitual in all Paris cabmen.

"Le Taverne Olympia, dans la Boul' des Capuchins, s'il vous plaît," Nolan called up to the cabman as he pulled open the door, and then had to repeat it twice as the cabman pretended not to understand Nolan's pronunciation. At last the man mimed sudden comprehension and nodded, and Nolan climbed in and pulled the door closed as the cab got underway.

He snagged the crumpled pack of Gauloises and a matchbox out of the thigh pocket of his khaki trousers, and got a cigarette lit in spite of the headwind. He was sure the cabman had understood him the first time; though he had to admit that his French was still far from perfect, even after four years of living in Paris.

He hitched around to look out the back window, irritated with himself now for having fled from two little boys on bicycles—but he watched the shifting cars and cabs behind him until his cab turned north into the heavy traffic on the Boulevard Saint-Michel. No vehicles stayed in sight among the wide, churning cluster of horses and fenders and windscreens.

Nolan shifted to face forward, and he let himself relax to the jiggling of the cab on its springs.

Within minutes the cab was rattling over the Pont Saint-Michel, and he leaned forward to peer at the river below. He couldn't see the embankment under the concrete shelf that roofed it from this bridge east to the next one, and in any case there would have been nothing to indicate the spot where Vivi had lit her candle.

Soon the cab had passed the embankment on the other side, and within minutes it was rolling past the Conciergerie at the far end of the Île de la Cite. Nolan bent to look up at the ornate Horloge clock in its inset arch—two o'clock. He wondered if he would have to buy Vivi lunch. With her odd ways, she was probably a vegetarian.

After ten minutes of weaving among shifting cars and bicycles north of the river, the cab was moving west along the Boulevard des Capucines. Nolan was surprised to see figures in shabby hats and overcoats shambling along the sidewalks in front of the big clothing and jewelry shops: several carried hand-lettered signs, at least a couple hobbled on crutches, and Nolan saw one legless man on a wheeled cart, propelling himself along with his hands. They were clearly beggars, and it occurred to him that he had seldom seen beggars on the streets of Paris—and hoped his own well-worn clothing wouldn't get him mistaken for a *mendiant*.

The front of the Olympia Taverne took up sixty feet of a block-long building, and its garish facade was three stories tall, with dozens of electric bulbs framing the big letters OLYMPIA. Above the lights, smaller letters spelled out CAFE 10 BILLIARDS. Nolan stepped down from the cab, paid the driver, then walked into the establishment with as much assurance as he could muster.

Past an ornately mirrored foyer he stepped through an arch and then just blinked around. The air in the long room shook with laughter and conversation, and smelled of anise and cigarette smoke. Lamps on a dozen closely set tables shone on the faces of men in neckties and women with cloches over short-cropped hair. On a stage against the far wall a girl in a harlequin costume, apparently ignored by all, was dancing while playing a flute.

A hand gripped Nolan's elbow, and he was turned around to face a heavyset bald waiter in a black vest and long white apron. The man spoke French too rapidly, but Nolan understood that he was being told to leave.

He pointed at the ceiling and said loudly over the noise, "*Excusez moi, je souhaitre voir,* uh, *Genevieve Chastain.*"

The waiter snorted and asked some question that seemed to involve horses. Nolan nodded as if he had understood, and the man pointed to a stairway along the street-side wall. Nolan walked unhurriedly to the stairs and started up the carpeted treads.

On the next floor, double doors stood open on a scene that was almost familiar to him—men in shirtsleeves leaning over wide green tables with pool cues poised in their hands. But though they worked the cues and straightened to move around the tables, Nolan didn't hear the sharp click of billiard balls striking each other. *Carambole* billiards, he thought sourly.

He saw the familiar slight figure of Vivi at a farther table, in a loose white linen blouse and the same corduroy skirt and tweed cap as yesterday, and he stepped quietly across the polished wooden floor to watch her. On the table in front of her, three balls—red, yellow, and white—lay nearly touching one another on a line down the middle of the green felt; Vivi bent over them, shifting a cue in her hands, and she gave the white ball the gentlest nudge. It touched the yellow one so softly that the ball could scarcely be seen to move as it in turn touched the red one.

A couple of men who had been watching applauded quietly.

She walked around to the other side of the table and again tapped the white ball with the tip of her cue. The balls moved fractionally, the white one again nudging the yellow to touch the red. Ignoring the further approval of the two men watching, she picked up a little cloth bag from the rail and hurried away from the table to set her cue in a rack on the wall.

"*Perdre?*" asked one of the men in evident surprise. Nolan knew the word meant *forfeit*.

"*Oui, désolé,*" she told them. *Yes, sorry.*

When she turned around she saw Nolan, and her eyes widened in alarm.

He hurried to her and whispered, "I made sure I wasn't followed. Do you understand? *Certain.*"

True enough, he thought, though surely pointless.

She leaned back to look into his face. "You own a...a serious-looking gun," she said quietly. "You know about such things?"

"Yes."

Vivi's shoulders relaxed and she looked back at the two men, who had resumed play at the table. She tossed the cloth bag from hand to hand. "Sylvia Beach," she said with certainty, and when Nolan nodded she went on, "How did you get past the doorman, dressed like that?"

"I don't know. I mentioned your name, and he said something about horses."

"Ah. I win money at the races sometimes. You're too tall for a jockey—he must have thought you're a tout." She looked up at him again, squinting. "What do you want?"

"I know the name of the man who wrote that article about your father, Mademoiselle Chastain," Nolan told her, "and I think I know where he is. I'm going to go talk to him. Want to come along?"

"He wasn't my father." Nolan followed her to the door, where she lifted a woolen coat down from a hook and stuffed the little cloth bag into a pocket. "But," she said, turning to look back at him, "yes."

"The writer's name is Ernest Hemingway," Nolan said when they were on the sidewalk in front of the building, "and I'm told he's likely to be at the Closerie des Lilas, in the Rue du Montparnasse." He saw the roof sign of an approaching motor cab among the vehicles maneuvering down the wide lanes, and waved.

The cab slowed and squeaked to a halt in front of them. It was an old two-cylinder Renault AG, probably left over from the mass transport of soldiers during the war. Nolan opened the door and Vivi stepped up on the running board and slid onto the seat, leaving him to convey their destination to the white-haired driver perched on the open seat between the engine and the windscreen. After only a couple of repetitions from Nolan, the man nodded and tromped the little engine into gear, and Nolan hurriedly climbed in beside Vivi and pulled the door shut. The leather seat smelled like old shoes.

The cab lurched into motion, pressing Vivi's shoulder against his, and she shifted away and pulled off her cap. "You want me to thank you?" she said, and bobbed her head. "For saving my life last night? Thank you. I can pay the fare for this." Nolan saw several blue ten-franc bills in her cap.

He took a deep breath, then began, "Sylvia Beach told me—"

He paused, unsure how to proceed. Vivi's face and throat in profile looked very young, but in the flickering sunlight through the window at his elbow he saw a forbidding tightness in the set of her jaw. He exhaled, and after a few seconds just remarked, "I never saw so many beggars in Paris."

She tensed at the apparently innocuous statement. "Because the *jalon* bell was rung last night," she said through her teeth. "A month early! January first and July fourteenth it rings, and by tradition the beggars may come down from Montmartre into the city on those days. But something must have *happened* last night."

From his Army service in France, Nolan recalled that *jalon* meant *milestone*. He thought of the bell he had heard, very late last night, deep and far away; but all the way from Montmartre across the river?

Their driver made a chirping U-turn virtually under the hooves of an oncoming horse-drawn cab, and was now getting the most out of the two-cylinder engine as he drove east along the boulevard: only perhaps twenty-five miles per hour, but a risky speed in the crowded lanes. Vivi had fallen against Nolan again, and she pushed herself back against the window on her side.

"Where is it?" Nolan asked. She gave him a distracted look from under a tangled fringe of fair hair, and he added, "This milestone bell?"

"You heard it? It's several bells in several places, but never the same places two years running. And they don't ring for long—no use trying to find them." From her coat pocket she pulled the cloth bag that had sat on the billiard table rail, then shrugged and put it away again. "At least the billiard balls did nothing."

"They never do much," Nolan said impatiently, "in that French style of pool. Listen—last night—"

She shifted as much as possible in the narrow cab to face him. "Sylvia Beach told you what? Besides my name?"

Here we go, he thought. "You translated Tennyson's *In Memoriam* to refer to a drowned woman. And last night on the embankment—damn it, it really looked as if you were talking to a drowned woman! And earlier you mentioned *l'Inconnue*, which was—"

"I was talking to the cat."

She does take some getting used to, Sylvia Beach had said. He closed his eyes for a moment, then asked, "Was that *l'Inconnue*?"

"Of course not! *L'Inconnue* was a nameless girl who drowned forty years ago. They buried her. I use the term as...an anonymity." Vivi scowled at him. "Call me mad, after what you saw! The woman I spoke with—you saw that she is dead. She was killed nine years ago."

Nolan grimaced. "She certainly appeared to be dead. The hands—"

"Her name is Elodie," Vivi interrupted angrily. "She found me on the streets when I was a six-year-old runaway orphan. She was a child herself, then, only twelve—but she was a mother and a sister to me."

Nolan sighed, and finally admitted to himself that he really had seen the thing move, really heard it produce something like speech. He kept his voice level as he went on, "How is it that such a—that she...spoke, after a fashion, and held onto the embankment?" With hands that were bare bones, he added to himself.

"I never take these motor-cabs," Vivi said, peering ahead through the windscreen. "The drivers always imagine that they're in a race.

Elodie was a *sauteur*—they're reincarnated, and they can remember their previous lives, completely." She touched her oversized wristwatch and seemed about to say something, then shook her head. "And they have some way of learning future events too—it has to do with the *jalon* bell."

Nolan murmured a noncommittal "Ah," but Vivi wasn't listening.

"Elodie was murdered," she went on, "stabbed and thrown into the river, but she has chosen not to be reincarnated into a new body this time—she says she is through with repetitions of life. She has chosen instead to stay in her dead body just for as long as she can sustain it in the river." Vivi put her cap back on and turned away, toward the window beside her. "Probably not much longer."

Nolan earnestly hoped the unnatural thing would fall apart soon. "Who murdered her?"

"She says it was the *apaches*."

She pronounced it *apash*, and Nolan recalled that she had used that word last night when she had been speaking to the drowned woman; and he realized that she was referring to the *apaches*, the particularly vicious street gangs that were responsible for countless brazen thefts and murders in the city.

The driver made a sharp turn south onto the Boulevard de Sébastopol, almost capsizing the vehicle. Nolan pushed himself off of Vivi and wondered if they might wind up in the river themselves.

A faint scent of anise lingered in his nostrils for a moment. He settled himself on the seat, cleared his throat and said, carefully, "Those children last night, who followed you to the river and pointed a gun at you. At us. You said some of them can remember when Trochu was president. I suppose they're some of these, uh, *sauteurs*?" He believed the word meant *leapers*.

"Of course." When he opened his mouth to ask another question, she raised a hand to stop him.

Nolan sat back and looked out the window by his elbow. The cab was passing over the Pont au Change, and several small boats were set like chess pieces on the glittering face of the Seine below. Dizzily he imagined Vivi's drowned friend swaying in the weeds on the river floor, among rusting bicycles and broken bottles.

Vivi didn't speak while the cab crossed the Île de la Cité in the dappled shade of the trees fronting the long Palais de Justice, but when the view opened up as the cab roared out onto the Pont Saint-Michel, she sighed and said, "The *sauteurs* killed Beltran Iglesias. I'm sure of it. I heard that it was a boy who stabbed him three years ago, and now it's the *sauteurs* who want to erase every trace of the story he told to Mr. Hemingway. They burned the *La Prosodie* office, and they went to your flat looking for the manuscript."

Again she raised her hand to forestall any interruption. "No, he wasn't my father, not by blood. But... as Elodie became my mother in the streets, so old Beltran became a sort of father to me... in the Rue Mouffetard, after Elodie was killed."

Nolan shook his head. "What's the big significance of the winged bull anyway?"

The question seemed to anger her. "Who are *you* anyway? Why did you have to do work for that trashy journal? Bad enough that those *sauteurs* knew who I am, but their lookouts saw me *leaving your street*."

"Well, I won't be doing any more work for it, will I? Seems to me your old friend Beltran started it all, by telling the story to Hemingway." He rubbed his eyes, then dropped his hands and scowled at her. "Barbier and his typesetter *killed*? And you and me stalked by little boys and girls with guns!"

She returned his frown for several seconds, then looked away. "He drank too much," she allowed. "And he loved an audience, such as Mr. Hemingway."

The cabdriver was vigorously steering his little vehicle through traffic on the Boulevard Saint-Michel now, and Nolan glanced past Vivi's head as they passed the narrow Rue Saint-Séverin, but a motorbus blocked the momentary chance of a view down his own street.

A couple of times during the next ten minutes each of them turned to the other as if to speak, then sighed and resumed looking out a window at the passing shops and cafés. At last the cab swerved to a curb and braked beside a little elm-shaded square. Nolan opened his door and stepped down to the paving stones.

A bronze statue stood on a pedestal in the center of the square, and beyond it was a cluster of tables below a green awning partly visible through tree branches. Nolan could make out the words CLOSERIE DES in white capitals on the awning. Vivi slid out of the cab after him, and when she had paid the driver she stood beside Nolan and blinked at the people sitting at the many tables.

Nolan was relieved to see a mix of what appeared to be elderly pensioners and students who had walked down from the Sorbonne, lingering over cigarettes and coffee. No one looked particularly affluent.

Vivi took off her cap, tucked some bills into it, and settled it back on her disordered blonde hair. "I don't much like crowds," she said. "Do you know what he looks like?"

Nolan shook his head. "I should have asked Miss Beach."

"I've read a book of his. It had an engraving of his face on the cover." She blew out a breath through pursed lips and began to walk forward. "I may not know him when I see him, but I'll know who isn't him."

Nolan followed her as she threaded her way between the tables. Around a low hedge were more tables, and Vivi sidled among them. Finally she glanced back at Nolan, shrugged, and stepped through the café's front door.

She halted in the entry, alternately stretching her fingers and closing her fists as she looked left and right in the relative dimness. Nolan caught up with her and took her elbow. Ahead of them the bar stretched the length of the room, with framed pictures and shelves of bottles on the wall behind it, while to their left, up a step and beyond a rail, half a dozen tables and their occupants were silhouetted against long windows in the opposite wall. Nolan could see that at least a couple of tables were empty, and he led Vivi to the one closest to the window. Beyond the glass the street was hidden by a shoulder-high hedge.

When they had sat down, Vivi whispered, "The chap at the corner table is about the right age, and he's writing in a notebook."

Nolan looked across an unoccupied table at the man. He looked a few years older than Nolan, perhaps thirty, square-jawed, with a moustache and dark hair that was carelessly combed back from his forehead. He wore a tan sweater with the sleeves rolled halfway up his forearms, and a glass of beer stood on the table near the hand that was scratching a pencil across a page of the notebook.

A white-aproned waiter walked up to their table, and Nolan ordered two calvados brandies. He sat back and dug the battered matchbox and pack of Gauloises out of his thigh pocket. Vivi carefully shook two cigarettes out of the pack and took one. She struck a match to it and exhaled smoke at the window.

"Interrupt him," she said.

"Right," Nolan said, shifting back his chair. He got to his feet and pulled the typescript pages from his back pocket. The man at the other table didn't look up until Nolan was standing beside his chair.

"Mr. Hemingway?"

The man gave him a cautious, tight-lipped smile. "Yes."

"Uh... this is yours." Nolan laid the smudged and wrinkled pages on the table.

Hemingway looked down, and slowly let go of the pencil to touch the top page. Just as slowly, he leafed through all ten pages, then raised his head to stare intently at Nolan. "Where," he said in a level tone, "did you get this?"

"I'll explain, but it'll take a while." Nolan waved back at his table, where Vivi was watching wide-eyed. "Could you join us?"

CHAPTER THREE:
Tied up with Witchy Stuff?

Hemingway carefully tucked the pages and his pencil into his notebook and stood up. He nodded and carried his beer and notebook to their table. When he had set them down and pulled out a chair, he paused, squinting at Vivi. "I've seen you at the races, at Auteuil." His accent was American, Midwestern.

She tapped ash from her cigarette. "You may have seen me in the Rue Mouffetard. I believe you were one of the last people to talk to Beltran Iglesias."

Hemingway sat down just as the waiter brought the two glasses of calvados and set them down on saucers marked 2 FRANCS. He waved toward the table he had vacated, and the waiter nodded and fetched two saucers from there and laid them beside Hemingway's beer glass.

"Iglesias," said Hemingway. "That was the name of the old Spanish bullfighter." He slid the typescript out of his notebook. "Tell me how you come to have this."

Nolan had taken a chair next to Vivi. He spoke quickly, before she could start talking about magical cats or billiard balls. "Claude Barbier at *La Prosodie* was going to publish it, and he sent it to me for an illustration. I'm Harry Nolan, and this is Vivi Chastain."

"*Leprosy!* I'd never have—I hear Barbier is dead."

Vivi leaned forward. "Murdered, because he was going to publish this! The story of the winged bull and the goddess!" She snatched up her glass and gulped a mouthful of brandy.

Hemingway stared at her for a moment, then turned to Nolan. "How did Barbier get it?"

"I don't know. I—"

"This," Hemingway interrupted, "was written for the *Toronto Star Weekly*. But it never got sent, because all my articles and stories were stolen, or lost, several years ago." He was breathing deeply. "Now this one has reappeared, though someone crossed out my name—"

"To protect you, without a doubt!" said Vivi. "When were your pieces stolen? Do you remember the date?"

Hemingway's mouth turned down at the corners in a bitter smile. "I sure do. December third, 1922."

"Beltran Iglesias," said Vivi, "was stabbed to death by a street boy on December second of that year. Until today I thought the boy who killed him was a random pickpocket. Beltran *would* have got in a fight with one such."

Hemingway sat back. "You think," he said, peering closely at her, "that Iglesias was killed because... because what, because he told me that story? And then whoever killed him stole all my papers?"

Vivi spread her hands. "Yes. And then evidently somebody stole this article from them, crossed out your name, and delivered it to *La Prosodie*."

Hemingway took a long sip of his beer, looking from Vivi to Nolan and back. It was clear that he thought Vivi's theory was nonsense. "I want the rest of my stuff. It was everything—everything I had written. Who are you two? What do you do? Where are you from?"

"Mr. Nolan told you my name," said Vivi. "I work sometimes at the Olympia Taverne, in the upstairs billiard hall, and sometimes I make winning bets on horses. I'm an orphan, but I believe I was born here in Paris."

"You speak English with a British accent."

"I learned it from an English girl. Named Elodie," she added, with a glance at Nolan.

"You were in Paris during the war?" Hemingway asked her.

"I was." After a pause, she went on, "Elodie and I hid in the Metro stations when zeppelins and airplanes bombed the city." She took another big sip of her brandy, and shuddered. "It was a bad time altogether—the Spanish flu killed more people than the German bombs ever did."

Hemingway turned to Nolan and raised his eyebrows. "You're American."

"Right, from Norman, Oklahoma." Nolan picked up the other cigarette that Vivi had shaken out of the pack and lit it. "I was in France during the war, and after I was discharged there was... nothing back home to hold me, so I decided to come back here." He shrugged. "Now I do illustrations and book covers."

It seemed to him that Hemingway was trying to estimate their reliability, if any. "I was a Red Cross ambulance driver," Hemingway said, "in Italy, in 1918. Couldn't get into the U.S. Army because of my eyesight."

"Well," Nolan said, "I was in the army, in the Second Engineers Regiment in Company C." Hemingway didn't say anything, so he added, "I laid a lot of rail for the trains, repaired roads, put up barbed wire in some places and cut it in others."

"Where?"

"Château-Thierry, Saint-Mihiel. Lots of places."

Hemingway nodded. "If you were cutting barbed wire at Saint-Mihiel, you were on the front line, cutting German wire so the infantry could advance."

That was true. Nolan picked up his own glass and took a sip of the apple brandy. "As to this business," he said, with a cautioning glance at Vivi, "it does seem likely that there are people who want to suppress the story the Iglesias fellow told you. My flat was apparently searched last night, but I was out, and had that manuscript with me."

"And who told you to get out?" said Vivi indignantly. "Besides the *matagot* cat?"

Nolan clenched his teeth and looked down at the table.

"Okay," said Hemingway, "okay. That's the magical cats they talk about in Gascony, right? You folks are tied up with witchy stuff?"

"No," Nolan began, but Vivi cut him off.

"You're a writer in Paris," she said to Hemingway, "a reporter. I read your little book, *In Our Time*—you're not afraid to look at things as they really are. Perhaps you've heard of the *sauteurs*?"

"Remind me," said Hemingway, looking tired now.

Vivi reached across the table and flipped open his notebook, quickly riffling through the scrawled pages till she found a blank one. She picked up his pencil and drew something; then pushed the notebook toward Hemingway.

"Have you ever seen that mark?"

Nolan peered at it upside down. It seemed to be a horned head with three circles like eyes arranged in an upright triangle on the face.

Hemingway took the pencil from her and drew random squiggles across the image, then blacked it out with tight back-and-forth strokes.

"Here and there, maybe," he said. "Graffiti, like the woman-and-lion one you see sometimes." He shrugged.

"I'm told it's the sign," Vivi said, "the sigil, of this group. The *sauteurs*."

Hemingway sighed and picked up the manuscript pages. He tapped them even and slid them back between the pages of his notebook. "And they want this, you say. Well, I've got it again, haven't I? I do thank you for it." He frowned and shook his head. "It was sent to *La Prosodie*? And there's no way to ask Barbier about it now. A cold trail." He looked from Vivi to Nolan. "But if you get a line on any others of my lost manuscripts, or hear anything that seems to be related to them, I'd be grateful if you'd leave word at a bookshop called Shakespeare and Company, you can remember that, right? It's in the Rue—"

"We know," said Nolan. "I was there this morning. I left you a note, with my name and address. It was Sylvia Beach who told me we might find you here."

"Did she." Hemingway was clearly about to leave, so Nolan went on quickly, "I don't know anything about any magical cats and all that, but Vivi and I *were,* uh, followed last night, and at one point I found myself looking down the barrel of a gun. What did Iglesias talk about, besides this damned goddess-and-bull story?" He had nearly said *cock-and-bull.*

Hemingway squinted at him for a moment. "What gauge track did you lay?"

"What—oh, some broad gauge, and a lot of the narrower *soixante*—sixty millimeter." After a few seconds of silence, he added, "For steam locomotives at first, but the smoke trails were a target for the German artillery. Later it was for gas-mechanical locomotives."

"Okay." Hemingway picked up his nearly empty beer glass. "Who aimed a gun at you?"

Nolan closed his eyes for a moment. "It was a little girl." He opened his eyes and shrugged. "Street thugs often use children to do errands and crimes for them." Hemingway hadn't stood up, so Nolan repeated, "What else did Iglesias talk about?"

"A little girl? If you say so." Hemingway sat back. "Oh—he talked about his days as a bullfighter, mostly in the little *capeas* on the east coast of Spain, around Valencia and Tarragona—"

Vivi nodded, but Nolan raised a spread hand; so Hemingway explained, "*Capeas*. Illegal bullfights in the provinces, especially provinces on the Mediterranean coast. Small villages set up makeshift arenas in the town square, and amateurs, anybody, can jump in and fight the bulls."

Vivi seemed to bristle at the suggestion that Iglesias had been an amateur, but Nolan asked, "Illegal?"

Hemingway nodded. "They're illegal because it's *used* bulls, experienced bulls, that the people fight, in the *capeas*—bulls that have fought men before. They've learned men's tricks." He relaxed in his chair, clearly talking about a subject that interested him. "The legitimate bullfights, like in Madrid and Cádiz, use bulls only once, and kill them, but the remote villages are too poor to kill their bulls. Some of their bulls have fought men dozens of times—killed and maimed a lot of them."

"Huh," said Nolan. "It seems fairer that way."

"It is," Hemingway agreed. "The man and the bull are more evenly matched in the *capeas*. It's more genuinely a sport, a fair competition. The legitimate bullfights, with inexperienced bulls—it's like a ritual. A sacrifice, enacted over and over again."

"Did he talk about anything else?" persisted Vivi. "Ordinarily, it was hard to get him to *stop* talking."

"That's how I remember him. Sure, he talked about the war, and buildings that got destroyed in the bombings, and movies—there was one movie he said was important, I remember." He paused, and Vivi made an impatient beckoning gesture. "Let's see," Hemingway said. "Oh, it was that Italian epic about ancient Rome, the Punic Wars..."

"*Cabiria*," said Nolan. "I saw it." He looked at Vivi. "This girl, Cabiria, survives the destruction of Pompeii and gets kidnapped and taken to the Phoenician city of Carthage, and nearly sacrificed to their god Moloch, and has all sorts of adventures."

Hemingway moved Nolan's and Vivi's glasses to the side and stacked their saucers on top of his. Nolan gathered that he was paying for their brandies. Only fair, he thought, after we returned his manuscript. Hemingway picked up his notebook with the typescript in it and got to his feet.

"Thanks again," he said, "I'll keep this somewhere safe, and look over my shoulder for a while."

"Be wary of children!" said Vivi.

"Yes, ma'am." He laid some coins on the table. "Shakespeare and Company, remember." With a smile, he added, "I'd rather you didn't visit me here again."

He nodded and started to walk away, but paused. He looked back and said to Nolan, "You're an artist?" For a moment he seemed to consider, then went on, "You might look up a woman named Gertrude Stein, she likes artists. Sylvia Beach can tell you how to get in touch with her. Uh," he added with a dismissive wave, "both of you."

He looked away and walked out of the café.

Vivi watched him leave, then turned to Nolan. "He's seen that symbol before."

"Graffiti, he said."

"Sure. And he crossed it out, thoroughly." She finished her brandy and set her glass down. "You want to know why Elodie took me under her wing—me a six-year-old scavenger orphan?"

When Nolan raised his eyebrows, she pulled back the left sleeves of her coat and blouse and unbuckled her big wristwatch. It fell to the table and she extended her hand.

"She saw this."

Visible now on the back of her wrist was a quarter-sized tattoo. The lines were faded and blurred, but it was recognizably the symbol she had drawn in Hemingway's notebook—a horned head with three circles in a triangle on the face.

Nolan look up. "What's *this* now? You're a ... a *sauteur* yourself?"

She pulled her hand back and picked up her watch. "Apparently I am. Keep your damn voice down. Iglesias gave me this watch to hide the mark. Before that, Elodie had me tie a scarf around it."

Nolan's cigarette had gone out, and he carefully struck a match and relit it. "Reincarnated, you said?"

"The *sauteurs*? Yes."

"And you said they can totally remember their previous lives. So," he said in a neutral tone, "who were you before?"

"Did that girl with the gun last night talk like a child?" Vivi rebuckled her wristwatch and pulled her sleeves down over it. "Mr. Hemingway paid for our first round, it's your turn."

Nolan looked around till he spotted their waiter. He caught the man's eye and raised both their glasses. The waiter nodded and Nolan turned back to Vivi.

"I was a man in my last life," Vivi said quietly, looking down at her restored wrist watch, "who must have died in 1905 or '06, since I was born sometime in 1906. But the return of that old life hasn't happened, fully, with me."

She was silent for several seconds, then went on, "In dreams, even once in a while when I'm awake, I get memories that aren't mine, aren't *this* body's—they're in a man's body. Sometimes I remember walking in a long twisting tunnel, or looking out across Paris from some very high-up place, or speaking in a man's voice in a language that sounds like Spanish, though I can never catch the words—but that previous-life version of *me* hasn't... come back very far, waked all the way up." Vivi raised her head, and her narrow face was taut. "Hasn't pushed *this* me aside. Sometimes my hands do things without me willing it—but I can control that when it happens. And if he gets *too* close, there's a bit of music I whistle. It pushes him back."

Nolan kept his expression blank. A few months ago he had illustrated an article on *dédoublement*, a mental condition in which one imagined another personality, or several, existing in one's own head.

"The terrible thing," she went on, "is that he's *supposed* to have this body." She touched her face. "This is rightfully his reincarnation—there wasn't supposed to be such a long delay in him taking this body that a spurious personality—Genevieve Chastain!—could grow up in it.

"You and Elodie," Vivi added, "are the only ones I've talked to about all this, now that old Beltran is gone."

Nolan shifted uncomfortably in his chair and looked around for the waiter. "So when did you get the tattoo?"

"I don't know. As an infant. Elodie told me that the orphanage I ran away from was a nursery for reincarnated *sauteur* babies, and they all get the tattoo somewhere on their bodies. Elodie had it on her leg."

The fresh brandies arrived, and Nolan wished Vivi had not pulled her sleeve down over her watch. It must be getting late, and he wanted to check his mail at the Café Lepovre. He could use a new assignment, and a couple of publishers owed him checks, and *La Prosodie* was no longer a market.

"A nursery for *sauteur* babies," he said, trying to gauge the daylight past the hedge outside the window. "How's that supposed to work? They all get reborn... what, in the same place?"

"Elodie told me that there's a grid of lines—*heilige linien*, holy lines—all over the Earth, and a lot of them cross at the Louvre, which is why a French king built the Louvre Castle there in the twelfth century. The *sauteurs* tether their souls to that tangle of lines, and when they die, no matter where, their souls are reborn within a kilometer or so of it." She shrugged. "And their fellows find the newborn babies and take them to one of the nurseries."

Nolan frowned, wondering if there could be any truth at all to this story, this secondhand fairy tale: if some such obscure group might actually have been, or still be, kidnapping babies. "Where's the nursery you came from?"

"I've never been able to find it."

"Do these *sauteurs* have any sort of... organization?" he asked, waving a hand. "Meeting places, membership lists?"

"I suppose so. Elodie said she used to get checks."

Nolan reminded himself that this Elodie person was supposedly the drowned creature he had briefly seen by candlelight in the Seine last night.

It seemed unlikely that a little girl would be sent checks. "Did she say from which bank?"

"If she did, I don't recall it."

Nolan relaxed. Altogether, this fantasy was nothing that he ought to take to the *Sûreté* police.

Staring into her drink, Vivi said, "You've got a gun."

"Not on me." *He travels the fastest who travels alone,* he thought. "And," he added, pushing his chair back and standing up, "I hope I have some work to do. It's certainly been exciting knowing you, Vivi—and I'll steer clear of any street children I run across. I expect I might see you at Shakespeare and Company sometime." He dug a handful of coins out of his pocket.

"Wait. Sit, please."

He sighed and resumed his seat.

"Last night," she said, "by the river, I told Elodie that an old story of Beltran's had turned up—the bull-and-goddess thing—and that the *sauteurs* were killing people to suppress it. She said, *It's known that*

Beltran adopted you, they'll soon come for you too. You must ask the apaches."

Five more minutes, Nolan told himself. "You said it was the *apaches* who killed her. Stabbed her, you said."

"That's right. I don't know why Elodie thinks they wouldn't kill me too. If there is some reason, those monstrous children interrupted her before she could say what it is."

Vivi picked up her glass and took a sip of the brandy. "Elodie has the idea that the *apaches*—if they have any aims besides rape and theft and murder—are fiercely opposed to the *sauteurs*. They killed her because she was one."

"And she decided not to be reborn, you said. Maybe she's opposed to the *sauteurs* too."

"I think she has been, the whole time I've known her. I think that's why she took charge of me, to keep me from them. She was...her body was only twelve years old then. She was sixteen when the *apaches* killed her."

Nolan rubbed his eyes. "It sounds like you should leave Paris."

"And abandon her. No. Listen." She hunched forward and spoke quietly. "You've *seen* her, and you've seen the old souls who appear to be children. Wait! Tell me—you haven't touched your brandy—tell me about that movie Beltran spoke of."

"*Cabiria*." Nolan had seen the movie in 1919 at the Cinéma du Panthéon, not half a mile from where he and Vivi now sat, during the two-week wait for a ship back to the States after his discharge from the Army. "Like I said, it was about this Roman girl who gets sold into slavery, and then in Carthage she's nearly sacrificed to Moloch..." He paused, remembering that scene in the movie.

Vivi nodded impatiently.

"Moloch," he said slowly, "the image of the god, was a hollow bronze statue, thirty feet high, with a furnace burning inside it, and children were laid on a platform that lifted and dumped them into the thing's furnace belly. Fire would burst out of the statue's mouth then...but its head..."

He hesitated, then reluctantly reached across and touched the sleeve of her coat over her wrist. "Its head had horns, and three eyes in a triangle."

Vivi shivered and pulled her arm away to grip her elbows. "I have to approach the *apaches* somehow. Alone, it seems!" She slid her legs out to the side and stood up. "Will you come with me to meet Gertrude Stein? I read a book of hers, and I believe she must be insane."

"What do you want to meet insane people for?"

"Damn it, Mr. Hemingway said we should, didn't he? After we told him these things? And," she added, "this woeful business mimics insanity."

"It *is* insanity."

He stared up at her. Her hazel eyes were wide under the fringe of straw-colored hair, and to his annoyance he found himself thinking of her life as she had described it—a six-year-old runaway from some orphanage—and her two haphazard protectors: this Elodie, a twelve-year-old fellow runaway, and Beltran, the alcoholic ex-bullfighter in the unsavory Rue Mouffetard. And he was reminded of a girl he had noticed among the French refugees on the long road from Meaux to Paris in 1918, after a heavy German bombing. There had been many families in horse-drawn, two-wheeled carts in the exodus, but this girl had simply been trudging along by herself, with a heavy-looking rucksack on her back. There had been nothing he could do for her, and in any case the 2nd Engineers had been moving forward to Montreuil-aux-Lions, away from Paris.

That was seven years ago. Had that girl made it all the way to Paris—was she still alive, or had her body been one of the many left along the side of that road? Certainly she had had a name. Had *she* found any help?

He travels the fastest...?

He gulped his brandy now and got to his feet. "I suppose Sylvia Beach can tell us how to find Gertrude Stein."

Back to the bookshop, he thought. At least I know a quick shortcut to Boulevard Saint-Germain now, if we see any scary children.

Vivi smiled in evident relief. It was the first time he had seen her smile. She snatched off her cap and pulled a ten-franc note out of it. "A horse-drawn cab this time."

The remaining two cigarettes in Nolan's battered pack of Gauloises broke up in dry dust that blew away across his trousers. He hiked himself up on the rocking cab seat and shoved the empty pack into his pocket. It would have been tricky in any case to get a cigarette lit in the breezy open cab.

Already he was regretting having agreed to go with Vivi to meet this Stein woman. He had heard of her—in addition to being the author of reputedly impenetrable stories, she was said to host a salon frequented by avant-garde writers and painters, and to be a collector of contemporary paintings. His own opinion was that painting had reached its peak thirty or forty years ago, with the Impressionists like Claude Monet and Alfred Sisley. He saw no merit in the new, Cubist works of Braque and Gris and Picasso, if those were even still fashionable. He imagined that Stein would be contemptuous of the sort of artwork he did—fast illustrations for magazines.

And he hoped Stein would not know anything having to do with *sauteurs* or Moloch or magical *matagot* cats.

He shifted on the leather seat, turning away from the view of well-dressed and apparently carefree Parisians strolling along the afternoon-shaded sidewalk—the beggars from Montmartre didn't seem to have crossed the river—and squinted at Vivi. Her cap was in her lap, and in spite of the headwind she was sorting banknotes. She had insisted on paying for this ride too, which was fortunate, since Nolan had only a few francs left in his pocket.

"The Olympia Taverne must pay well," he said, speaking loudly over the clatter of hooves and the roar of passing automobile exhausts. He wondered if it had been an ungracious remark.

She didn't look up. "A few francs a week, when they remember. Just as a shill, to provide a player when needed." She tucked her hair back and carefully pulled the cap over it. "I make money betting on horse races."

"Yes, you said. You study that, do you—odds, jockeys, trainers?"

"I just find out the colors the jockeys wear." She turned to face him, and for several seconds while the cab rocked over the pavement she said nothing. Finally she tapped her sleeve over her watch and tattoo. "I've told you I'm a sort of failed *sauteur*. The memories, the personality, of my previous life have not... *manifested* in me in the way they should have, the way they do for the others."

Nolan nodded, just to indicate that he remembered her saying that.

She slumped lower on the seat. "You believe I'm deluded," she said, "but the person I was before, a man, *can* sometimes break through this identity." She touched her chest. "I do worry that he—I!—will one day reawaken completely, and push *this* person—*me*—into the dust bin! But... like a bullfighter who must risk his life to earn sustenance!... I call him up sometimes, briefly, to make money. And so far I can whistle him away if he gets too... immanent." She looked up at Nolan from under the bill of her cap. "Elodie does not approve."

"He—what, he tells you which horses are going to win?"

"After a fashion. He never," she went on with a shudder, "*speaks*, through my throat! And in any case he wouldn't see the horses' names. But I put scraps of colored cloth or paper in a bag, the colors which some horse will run under in the next couple of days at Auteuil or Enghien, and I lay the bag on the rail of a billiard table. Then, God help me, I open my mind to the man I once was, and *ask*. If the horse with those colors will be in the winner's circle after the race, he strikes the cue ball too forcefully. If the horse doesn't win, he does nothing and I take a normal shot myself."

"He, uh, can see the future, you mean." Nolan kept his voice level.

"I told you before that the *sauteurs* can do that."

"So you did." Nolan suppressed a restless yawn. "You had a little cloth bag on the table railing this morning, and when you cued the balls they hardly moved at all. Your horse won't win?"

She shook her head. "*I* will, at least for now. I think." She dug a hand into the pocket of her coat and pulled out the bag. She loosened the drawstring and reached into the bag with two fingers. What she pulled out was a folded square of white cloth with blotted brown stains on it.

"Your blood," Nolan guessed, and his heart sank when she nodded. Is she cutting herself, he thought, for this fantasy?

"I asked if my blood is to be spilled in the next two days," she said, "which is about as far as he can perceive. And I think his inaction meant no." She straightened up and looked out the window on her side of the cab. "Unless my old self wasn't listening. Sometimes he's not, and the horse with my colors wins and I didn't have a bet on it."

Their cab rattled in a shaky turn to the left, into the narrow Rue Racine. Vivi shivered in the chilly breeze through the open front of the cab, and peered up and down the street.

"The *sauteur* children were certainly watching you this morning," Vivi said, "but you are sure you evaded pursuit. Right?"

"Certain." *One of your cats advised it*, he thought.

Rue Racine soon opened out at the wide circle of the Place de l'Odéon. Bookstalls and tables were clustered around the shaded colonnade of the Odeon Theatre, and scents of horse chestnut blossoms and automobile exhaust mingled in the fresh breeze. The cabdriver reined in his horse so as not to trample any of the pedestrians milling in both directions across the street.

Vivi sat back and crossed her arms. "You were in France in the war," she remarked. "Cutting barbed wire."

"And building cantonments and repairing roads. And," he added, remembering, "walking across the countryside with other soldiers, for miles! Through mud, often as not, in the rain. All over France, it felt like."

"I've never been outside Paris. The Enghien hippodrome is as far as I've ever been from the Seine."

The cab was moving again, slowly. Vivi was looking past Nolan at the crowded tables in the square in front of the theater. Nolan looked down at her right hand clasping her left elbow. The nails were short and ragged.

He opened his mouth to tell her that she could certainly find a job that wouldn't involve an imagined risk to her identity; but he closed it and looked ahead as the cab angled into the Rue de l'Odéon, down which waited Shakespeare and Company. Perhaps she didn't really want to be entirely separated from the personality she imagined to be her older, male self.

She tucked the cloth bag back into her pocket.

After a minute the cab squeaked to a halt in front of the green shopfront. The bookshop was on the right side of the little street, and Vivi climbed out first but waited for Nolan to get out and step around the rear of the cab. Late afternoon sunlight gleamed in dormer windows on the roofs of the buildings on the other side of the street.

"I don't think she likes me," she whispered to him as he pushed open the door and led the way in.

CHAPTER FOUR:
The Lady or the Tiger

Several men stood in front of tall bookshelves on the far wall, an elderly woman sat reading a magazine in one of the armchairs by the fire, and a gray-and-white cat lay curled around a kitten on a shelf below a framed William Blake print on the wall to Nolan's left. The chilly breeze from outside riffled the pages of a magazine on the central table until Nolan closed the door.

"Genevieve!" came Sylvia Beach's voice, and a moment later she appeared from a back room, carrying a stack of paperbound chapbooks. "And Mr. Nolan. Mr. Hemingway hasn't been in, I'm afraid."

"We found him," Nolan said, "and returned the ... thing."

"Ah, good. And I was hoping to see you, Genevieve," Beach said as she set the chapbooks on the table. "Gertrude Stein was in today." She said it as if a visit from Stein was a novelty, which seemed odd since Beach's bookshop was the literary hub of Paris, and Stein was one of the city's most prominent literary figures. "She asked," Beach went on, "that you call on her right away."

For several seconds Vivi just blinked at her. Then, "Gertrude Stein," she said. "Me? Did she say ... why, what about?"

Beach brushed back her short chestnut hair and smiled uncertainly. "No. I gathered you know her?"

Vivi shook her head. "I've never met her."

"Oh! Perhaps she's read some of your work, then." Beach avoided meeting Nolan's eye. "Her *atelier* is just a trot down the Rue de Vaugirard from here—I'll write out the address for you."

"*Atelier?*" said Nolan. He believed the word referred to a painter's studio. "She paints?"

Beach shook her head. "She collects paintings—and painters."

She found an index card on the table and scribbled on it, then straightened and held it out toward Vivi, who hesitated a moment before taking it.

"She's very nice, really," Beach assured her, "not at all intimidating."

Vivi cleared her throat. "Do you have a copy of her book *Tender Buttons* for sale?"

"None for sale so you could get it signed, I'm afraid—but I believe I have two copies to lend, and you're a subscriber to the bookshop. Shall I fetch one?"

"Yes, please." As Beach moved away toward the bookshelves on the far wall, Vivi squinted at Nolan. "You'll see what I mean."

Beach returned shortly carrying a small yellow-bound book, and laid it on the table while she pulled a sheet of brown paper from a roller. She wrapped the book neatly and handed it to Vivi.

Vivi took it with a nod of thanks.

"I'll, uh, escort her," Nolan said. He took Vivi's elbow and steered her around the table and back toward the door.

The mother cat on the William Blake shelf reached out a paw to snag Vivi's coat as she walked past. Vivi paused and stared at the cat for a moment, then nodded and let Nolan lead her outside.

He thought of the black cat that had caught at his pants cuff a couple of hours ago, only a few dozen paces down this street.

Out on the windy pavement, he looked up and down the narrow street for a cab, but Vivi clearly read his intention, and shook her head. "Better we walk," she said, stepping forward in the direction of the Odeon Theatre. "Take time to *consider*." She looked up at him. "They'd watch your flat, but they wouldn't be hanging about all this time watching the bookshop."

Nolan walked along beside her with his hands in his pockets, and he remembered that he probably didn't have enough money for a cab in any case. "If you'd loan me a few francs," he said, "we could stop to eat somewhere. I can pay you back as soon as we—"

"After," she interrupted. "I couldn't eat anything right now. Hemingway told us to see Stein after I showed him the *sauteur* symbol—and now, independently, she wants to see me! What can she know of me?"

"Your work," Nolan suggested, "your poetry?"

"Hah."

Clearly Beach's suggestion had sounded farfetched even to her. Nolan pulled several one-franc coins out of his pocket. "On my own I can afford a pack of cigarettes. After?"

"No."

Ten minutes later they were walking west along the Rue de Vaugirard, past the segmented pillars and clustered tricolor flags of the Senate building. The wind was at their backs and the sun was silhouetting the high roof of the Petit Luxembourg, where the President of the Senate lived. They were still on the Left Bank, but the pedestrians on the broad flagstone pavement here all seemed to be dressed as if for office work, and Nolan wished more than ever that he had put on a coat and hat, and a better pair of trousers.

Vivi tossed aside the last inch of her third cigarette and began unfolding the brown paper from the book Sylvia Beach had given her. She crumpled the paper into a pocket, flipped the book open, and began reading as she walked along: *"A can containing a curtain is a solid sentimental usage. The trouble in both eyes does not come from the same symmetrical carpet, it comes from there being no more disturbance than in little paper."*

She looked up at Nolan. "Have you ever known a crazy person? That's how they talk."

"Serious people take her seriously."

Vivi shook her head. "The *matagot* in Sylvia's shop warned me that the sun will be down soon."

Nolan flicked his own cigarette away and looked around the street. "Cats do that all the time," he said, insisting on it to himself as much as to her, "snag you as you pass them." They had walked out of the shade, and he nodded ahead. "And we didn't need the cat to tell us anyway."

"She didn't mean the literal sun."

That's how they talk, Nolan told himself sourly.

Soon they were walking past the iron fence bordering the Luxembourg Gardens, its pickets looking like upright gold-tipped spears. Beyond the fence, leafy boughs of tall trees blocked any view of the gardens.

Vivi looked up at Nolan. "Elodie and I used to spend many days in the *jardin*, when she was around thirteen years old, in that incarnation, and I'd have been just six or seven. It was another world." She walked backward for a few paces, facing Nolan. "You've seen it?"

"Yes. It's very beautiful."

She nodded and turned to face forward as he caught up to her.

"It was the widest spaces I'd ever seen," she said quietly. "Lawns and fountains and the enormous *bassin* with toy sailboats jigging back and forth on the water, and lots of tables for chess games!" She was silent for several steps, then added, "I wish Elodie could still come there with me. She showed me a statue of Saint Genevieve by the *bassin*. She's the patron saint of Paris, you know, Saint Genevieve."

"I didn't know."

"And she took a lifelong vow of virginity."

Considering Vivi's rootless and neurotic life, Nolan thought she would be wise to follow her namesake's example.

For at least a full minute neither of them spoke; several times Nolan glanced down at the short skinny girl in oversize clothes pacing along beside him, and he found himself mimicking the practiced way she stepped around oncoming or slower-moving pedestrians. Speaker to cats, he thought, eccentric poet, consulter of billiard balls—who are you, Genevieve Chastain?

But *he travels the fastest* . . . !

They turned their steps south on the Rue Guynemer, walking now in the shadow of ornate old apartment buildings on their right, while the iron fence marched along uninterrupted on their left.

"Maybe someday," Vivi said at last, peering ahead, "I can show you the statue."

"Maybe someday," he said.

She went on quickly. "During the war we feared that the Germans would bomb *le Jardin du Luxembourg*, though they never did. Elodie was not taken in by the . . . optimism! . . . in 1914. People believed for a while that Paris could hold out against the Germans—cannons were mounted in the Eiffel Tower, cattle were brought in and kept in the Parc de Belleville and the Bois de Boulogne. As it happened, we could have stayed here—but in the bombings we hid in the Metro tunnels."

She gripped her elbows and shook her head sharply. "Were you often frightened? During the war?"

He glanced at her. She was looking up at him through the fringe of fair hair, and her hazel eyes were narrowed.

"Sure," he said. When she didn't look away, he rocked his head back and stared at the trees crowding up against the fence on their left. "Oh—one night in the La Rochette woods, German shells were striking all around us, shaking the earth, exploding in the trees, spraying shrapnel and throwing down broken limbs, and our own machine guns were firing from behind us. The sky was...a roaring, fiery hell. All I could do was lie flat in a bomb crater and try to pray louder than the guns and the bombs."

"You're religious?"

He laughed shortly. "I was that night."

She nodded and faced forward. "In summer, Elodie and I sometimes slept in the triforium gallery at Notre Dame cathedral, way up high, closer to the arched cross-vault ceiling than the floor below." She skipped ahead a few steps. "The cathedral is such a vast, holy place, standing up there on the Île de la Cite, immune from bombs! I've wished I could be Catholic, but the Church is wrong about reincarnation. They says it can't happen, but, ah—I know it does."

They had reached the corner of Rue de Fleurus, the street Sylvia Beach's card specified. It was another very narrow street between high walls fretted with rows of window balustrades.

"I wonder," Vivi said, not skipping now but still walking rapidly so that Nolan had to hurry to keep up, "if I'll go along." She looked back and gave him a strained grin. "After this body dies, and my real self gets reincarnated again. Will he carry this frivolous Vivi self into his next body? Will you look us up?"

They were passing a *boulangerie,* and Nolan deliberately looked to the side at ranked loaves of bread on display in the window—for he had suddenly imagined himself crouching at midnight on the Seine embankment, and lighting a candle.

"You'll outlive me," he said gruffly.

Vivi might have guessed his thought, for she sprinted on ahead, weaving expertly between startled old men in overcoats and students on bicycles, and Nolan had to follow as best he could, sidestepping and muttering apologies. Vivi finally stopped some distance ahead, and when Nolan stepped up beside her he saw that she was standing in front of a glass-and-wrought-iron door, staring at a street number—Twenty-seven—beside a stone head of Bacchus above it.

She glanced up at him. "The lady or the tiger," she said, and reached for the iron door handle.

But two women had come bustling up from the other direction, and the taller of them caught the handle first and gave Vivi a stern look from a long bony face. She had black hair bound up, and wore a long dress of blue and brown printed silk, but it was her companion who caught Nolan's attention.

She was scarcely five feet tall and bulky, wearing a suit jacket and long skirt of brown corduroy, and her iron-gray hair under an embroidered straw cap was cut very short, much shorter than his own. Her broad, seamed face, dewed with perspiration, would have looked forbiddingly stern if her eyes had not been bright with lively interest.

"I might be either one," she said, and after a moment Nolan realized that she was replying to Vivi's remark. "Depending," she added. "And who are you?"

Vivi was just staring at the woman, so Nolan said, "This is Genevieve Chastain, ma'am, and my name is Harry Nolan. We're hoping to find Gertrude Stein."

"Ah!" the woman said, "Beltran's waif, grown up! Somewhat," she added, peering more closely. "And a friend—from Oklahoma, unless my ears deceive me."

Nolan nodded, and the woman said, "You've succeeded in finding me, and my companion is Alice Toklas. Come in, pilgrims."

Nolan was surprised at her own accent, which seemed to be more American than anything else. She pulled open the door and started down a walkway bordered on the left by a small garden and on the right by windows in a high wall, closely followed by her taciturn companion. Nolan and Vivi exchanged a cautious glance and then walked through the doorway. Nolan closed the street door behind them.

"You're carrying a copy of one of my books," Gertrude Stein said as she unlocked a door on the right side of the walkway.

"I borrowed it from Sylvia Beach," said Vivi hastily, "just before coming here."

"Oh, she's a good soul, really," Stein allowed with a sigh, "even if she did publish Joyce's silly *Ulysses*."

Her companion sniffed in evident disapproval, and Nolan wondered if Beach had declined to publish something of theirs.

Stein and her companion led Nolan and Vivi into a long, high-ceilinged room with a fireplace in the far wall. Nolan was reminded of Sylvia Beach's shop, but here it was paintings that crowded the walls, from the waist-high wainscotting all the way to the ceiling. Below the paintings, dark cabinets of various styles stood against the walls, and leather-backed chairs were clustered on the wide rug as if from several recent conversational gatherings. Candlesticks and little sculptures and stacks of books stood on the mantel and several polished oak tables. The fireplace was dark, but heat and a smell of hot metal radiated from a small iron stove against one wall; a fencing foil had been stuck behind the stove pipe that extended to the ceiling.

Alice Toklas had stepped away to the side, into a kitchen, and Stein walked into the room and waved at a couple of chairs near a couch and table against the left-side wall. "Do sit," she said to Nolan and Vivi. "Alice will bring fruit brandies."

Stein crossed to the couch and sat down heavily. She exhaled, and tugged her skirt away from her legs and unbuttoned her jacket. "I didn't hope to see you this soon—Alice and I were having supper at Lipp's."

Her breath carried the aroma of *cervelas* sausage and onions, and Nolan was reminded that he hadn't eaten since the brioches at breakfast.

Vivi sat down in one of the chairs facing the couch and dropped her cap on the floor. Nolan took the chair next to hers.

He looked around at the paintings, most of which struck him as unskilled at best, but his attention was caught by a large canvas on the wall behind Stein—it was clearly a portrait of her, pictured seated and leaning forward, possibly on the same couch, looking off to her left with her hands on her knees. Her face in the portrait, though almost as stylized as a Byzantine rendering of a saint, showed a degree of intelligence and firmness that he could now detect in the woman who sat below it.

"Mr. Nolan," Stein said as Alice Toklas came into the room carrying a tray bearing a carafe of clear liquor and four small glasses, "how has a lad from the Sooner State found his way to the Latin Quarter?"

In other words, *Who are you?* thought Nolan. "I was in France with the Army during the war," he said, "and after I was discharged I came back."

"He's an artist," Vivi put in. "I met him last night."

Toklas set the tray on the low table and sat down beside Stein. She gave Nolan a censorious look as she lifted the carafe and poured the liqueur into the glasses.

"Vivi ran off shortly after we met," he said, not wanting these women to think he had spent the night with the neurotic girl. "I found her again this morning."

"He saved my life last night," added Vivi. "He knows my history. Entirely."

"Ah?" Stein picked up one of the glasses and waved toward the remaining glasses on the tray. "Artist?"

"Illustrations," he said shortly. "For magazines."

"*La Prosodie*," said Vivi. Nolan suppressed a wince.

Stein only nodded, then said to Toklas, "Would you bring Mr. Nolan a pad and pencil, my dear." She turned her bright eyes on Nolan and said, "Do me a portrait of Genevieve."

Toklas stepped to a cabinet by the fireplace and returned with a large pad of textured paper and a blunt-tipped charcoal pencil. Wondering if this was a test, Nolan rested the pad on his knee and looked sideways at Vivi.

"I'm generally called Vivi these days," she told Stein, as Nolan lightly sketched the shape of her face.

"I don't recall what name Beltran Iglesias called you by," said Stein, "though he told me your real name, and I've remembered it. I met him eight years ago, during the terrible winter of '17. You were a young girl."

Vivi looked at her curiously. "I was eleven," she said. "I remember that winter. We were allowed a fifty-kilogram sack of coal every forty days, but he was often able to get more."

"Yes indeed." Stein took a swallow of the liqueur and exhaled. "Alice and I were driving everywhere in those days, delivering medical supplies for the American Fund for French Wounded, and by the time of the armistice I had lost track of him. And then I heard he was killed three years ago, and I wondered what had become of you, until I saw your translations being published." Her weathered face crinkled in a smile. "Baudelaire's translations of Poe were better than Poe's English-language originals; I think your translations are improvements too."

With a stroke of the pencil Nolan caught the startled look in Vivi's eye.

"How did you come to know him?" Vivi asked.

Toklas had picked up a glass of her own. "This cordial is distilled from wild raspberries," she noted.

Nolan sketched Vivi's jawline, and was mildly surprised at his accuracy. Not wanting to spoil the picture now, he put down the pencil and picked up a glass.

"A common interest in bullfighting," Stein said. "The thing is, child, that I may be the only one—well, aside from Alice, and Mr. Nolan—who knows that Genevieve Chastain is the orphan child Beltran Iglesias took in. And a friend told me today that there's a sort of cult in the city that harbors some old resentment against Beltran and has decided to... well, *get* that child."

Nolan sipped the fiery liqueur, which did carry a fragrance of raspberries. Vivi lowered her eyes, and Nolan put the glass down and picked up the pencil again.

"*You* got the extra coal for us," said Vivi.

After a moment's pause, Stein said, "It was no hardship, for a fellow afficionado."

"A sort of cult." Vivi nodded, seeming to have come to a decision. "You're talking about the *sauteurs*."

Toklas gave Stein a sharp look.

"Yes," Stein said, and Nolan conceded that Vivi hadn't simply made up the term. "What do you know about them?"

Vivi picked up a glass and bolted the contents.

"Vivi!" Nolan exclaimed. To Gertrude Stein he said, "We haven't eaten all day."

"Ach! Alice, would you be so kind as to...?"

Toklas stood up and crossed the long room to the kitchen doorway.

"I know," said Vivi unsteadily, "that the *sauteurs* offer a kind of immortality."

"Beltran told you about them?"

"Just enough to be sure I'd stay away from them." Vivi put the empty glass down and rubbed her mouth. "Mostly I was told about them by one of them, a woman who died before I was born."

Stein stared at her. "How old is she now?"

Nolan looked up in surprise. It seemed that Gertrude Stein shared Vivi's belief that these *sauteurs* were routinely reincarnated.

Vivi opened her mouth, then just shook her head.

Nolan repressed a shudder at the memory of the thing in the river—the porcelain mask and the skeletal hands.

Stein went on, "Do you know why they want to... silence you? My friend didn't say. In any case, you should certainly leave Paris for a while. I can give you some traveling money, for Beltran's sake."

"I can't," said Vivi. Toklas hurried back into the room and set a tray of small sandwiches on the table. Vivi picked one up and took a bite. "The woman who told me about the *sauteurs*," she said around a mouthful, "refused reincarnation when she was killed by the *apaches*. She's in the river, still animating her dead body. I can't abandon her."

Nolan was feeling lightheaded himself, with the liqueur on top of the *calvados* brandies at the Closerie des Lilas an hour ago, and he caught the aromas of ham and mustard from the tray Toklas had brought; but the only moments when he took his eyes from Vivi's haunted face were when he glanced down to add a line or a bit of shading to his portrait of her.

He heard Toklas say, "Others have seen her, from the bridges, by moonlight. She is nearly gone."

"It doesn't matter," said Vivi, still hungrily chewing. "I can't flee *every one* of them." She put down the sandwich and turned her left hand palm-up. With her right hand she unfastened the buckle.

Nolan leaned forward and dropped the pencil. "Vivi—" he began, but she gave him a defiant look.

"I've trusted you," she said, "and these people helped keep Beltran and me alive in the winter of '17."

The watch strap came free and the watch fell to the table. Vivi took a deep breath, then turned her hand over, exposing the Moloch tattoo on the back of her wrist.

"I can't flee every one of them," she repeated.

Gertrude Stein's eyes were wide, and Toklas had stepped back toward the fireplace.

Toklas spoke sharply to Stein: "What is the answer?"

Stein nodded and said, "There is no answer."

"Then there is no question."

The brief exchange had sounded to Nolan like a ritual.

Stein turned to Vivi. "I don't understand," she said. "Beltran told you to avoid them, but... you're one of them?" She looked up from Vivi's wrist to stare intently into her eyes. "Who *were* you?"

Nolan repressed a sigh and resumed his drawing—from Vivi's varied positions and expressions he had managed to synthesize a good three-quarter-view likeness of her.

"I don't know!" cried Vivi. "I was born in 1906, so in my previous life I must have died then, or the year before—but that old identity, *my old* identity, hasn't surfaced. He still hasn't displaced me, *this* me." She was hugging herself and rocking back and forth in her chair. "He's close—I have dreams of his life, his memories. And sometimes," she added with a glance at Nolan, "sometimes I even let him work my hands. But really this person you're talking to is just a—like a weed! Like an intrusive nineteen-year-old weed that happened to sprout in a plot where a tree is trying to grow."

After a pause, Stein said, "He?"

Vivi waved as if in apology, then picked up her sandwich. "I'm in a man's body, in the dreams and the memories. In boats, in long tunnels. When I speak, in the dreams, it's in Spanish—though I can never quite understand it."

Stein was frowning, and picked up one of the glasses herself. "Why do they want to silence you?"

Vivi's mouth was full, and she waved to Nolan.

He sighed, and shifted in his chair. "Ernest Hemingway interviewed Beltran Iglesias three years ago—"

"And," Vivi mumbled, "Beltran was killed the next day!"

Nolan nodded, and went on to explain how the manuscript had come to him by way of the *Prosodie* editor. He paused after recounting Vivi's first visit to his flat, yesterday morning, when she had asked to see the manuscript and he had told her to wait and read the story in print.

Vivi swallowed. "But I went back again last night, after the *Prosodie* office burned down, and then Harry let me read it." She summarized the article, then gave Stein an account of her summoning Elodie on the Seine embankment. She paused for a few moments, then went on to describe the *sauteur* children menacing her, and Nolan intervening with his gun.

Stein shifted on the couch to look at Nolan. "Where is your drawing of the winged bull?"

"It was gone when I got back to my flat. Apparently the children took it."

Nolan was surprised when Toklas's only response to the whole outlandish story was, "You may be sure they destroyed it." To Vivi she said, "And they didn't ... don't know that in fact you're one of them?"

Vivi shook her head.

Toklas was frowning. "*Something* made a considerable change last night. Something outside their view. Whatever it was, the deviation made them decide to ring the *jalon* bells, off schedule! I think one of the *sauteurs*—you—did something, made a move that wasn't in their charted future, and disrupted it."

Vivi was looking at the high ceiling, clearly calling to mind all the things she had done last night.

Toklas squinted at her. After several seconds she said, "You went *twice*, to ask to see the manuscript? And you weren't able to, on your first visit. You only *saw* it on your second visit, after the fire at *La Prosodie*?" When Vivi nodded, Toklas said to Stein, "Perhaps no such second, impulsive visit figured in the timeline the *sauteurs* perceive. It was a counter-likelihood enacted by one of their own, namely this girl—and it made the change." She picked up one of the little glasses.

Stein tilted her head as if considering. She looked at Vivi. "Did you ... how shall I say, *confirm* it? Did you *touch* each other, during that second visit, last night?"

Vivi frowned and looked at Nolan.

"For God's sake," he muttered, then said, "Yes, you grabbed my hand. At the café table, when the children first appeared. You touched the cat too, if that counts for anything."

"The cat warned us," said Vivi, ignoring his derisive tone. "And on that second visit I picked up your gun. That might be another ... counter-likelihood."

Stein raised an eyebrow. "Part of the same one, I daresay."

To Vivi, Toklas said sternly, "Trust the cats, the *matagots*. They see past fate."

Stein smiled at Nolan, whose skepticism was evident. "Abandon nineteenth-century ideas of time, beginnings and middles and ends! It's all present, a complete picture ... but the picture is unexpectedly nudged into new lines sometimes." She looked around at all the paintings on the walls, then lowered her gaze to the pad on Nolan's lap. "Can I see what you've drawn?"

Nolan passed the pad over to her. She tore off the sheet on which he had drawn Vivi's face.

"That's good!" Stein said. She laid the pad and the loose sheet on the table. "You've captured her."

"Meanwhile," said Toklas impatiently, "the *sauteurs* are clearly frightened by the story of the goddess and the winged bull."

"Yes," Stein said, putting down her glass and then getting to her feet in stages. "I think we need to ask some questions of my friend who told me about you, Vivi. He knows about the *sauteurs*—more than he should. I can drive us in my auto." She pulled her skirt straight and added, "He lives on the other side of the river, in Montmartre." She waved at the painting that hung on the wall above the couch. "That portrait of me is his work."

"Who is he?" Vivi asked.

"You may have heard of him—Pablo Picasso."

CHAPTER FIVE:
That Buys Me

Vivi didn't stir. "I won't," she said. "Beltran told me to stay away from him. He said Picasso sold his soul to be able to paint." She turned to Nolan. "I can buy dinner for us."

Nolan had concluded that Gertrude Stein and this Alice woman were as crazy as Vivi had predicted—reincarnation, changing timelines!—but he didn't want to prolong his association with Vivi either.

"That's not true, child," said Stein.

Vivi turned toward her. "I could tell when he was spinning tales," she insisted, "and when he was telling the truth. Beltran knew Picasso in Barcelona"—she cocked an eyebrow at Stein—"because of a common interest in bullfighting! And one night Picasso got drunk and weeping, and told him he sacrificed his sister's life for his art, but the devil's gift became only ugliness."

Stein paused in buttoning her jacket. "Beltran was unkind," she said. "Pablo has told me about this." She sat down again. "You must understand that Pablo was thirteen, and his little sister was dying. He made a pact with God, not the Devil! He vowed that if God would spare his sister, Pablo would give up painting forever. But...he so needed to paint that he began, helplessly, to hope that his sister would die, and free him from his vow. She did, and he paints."

"Ugliness," said Vivi. She looked at the portrait of Stein on the wall and amended, "When he paints from his own soul, rather than from life."

Stein was silent for a moment, and Toklas said, "Say nihilism, rather."

Stein nodded. "Deliberate annihilation of the gift of art, in a sense."

Vivi picked up her tweed cap and put it on, and got to her feet. "I'm away. Thank you for the drink and sandwiches." She started toward the door.

Nolan stood up too. "Yes, thank you."

Stein called, "Vivi." She picked up Vivi's wristwatch and held it out. Vivi pursed her lips and hurried back to the table. She took the watch with a murmured thanks and flipped the strap around her wrist.

"You've trusted us," Stein said. "Come back when you can."

"I . . . will," said Vivi, fastening the buckle. She walked to the door.

Nolan followed her out onto the paved path and led the way past the garden to the street door. The sky between the surrounding roofs had dimmed to twilight, and the breeze carried the fragrance of white lily blossoms.

He sighed, then said to Vivi, "Nobody bothered me last night after that confrontation with the children by the river, and if they followed me today, hoping I'd lead them to you, I evaded them after I went to Sylvia Beach's bookshop. I'm going to go back to my rooms now, and . . ."

"And we shouldn't meet again," said Vivi flatly. "Because they might always be following you, to find me."

He took hold of the street-door lever and lifted it. "Well, yes, if they're as . . . determined as you'd have me believe. You can always leave me a note at the bookshop."

He pushed the door open and stepped out into the street, and Vivi was close behind.

"We split up, then?" said Vivi, closing the door.

He travels the fastest who travels alone, thought Nolan, and he forced out of his mind the memory of the fugitive girl he had seen, and been powerless to help, on the road to Paris in 1918.

"Looks like it."

Lights glowed white and amber in windows in the high close walls. Nolan began walking up the street toward the broader and more brightly lit lanes of the Rue de Vaugirard.

"We could have dinner someplace first," said Vivi, catching up. "I can pay for it. And," she added quickly, "if you don't want to owe me, you can leave money for me at the bookshop."

He looked down at her, and her upturned, anxious face was briefly lit by a window they were passing; and he recalled the drawing of her he had done at Gertrude Stein's. *You've captured her.*

"Sure," he said. "Thanks. There's a place up here—"

All at once, Vivi kicked against the wall and slammed sideways into him, knocking him off his feet; in nearly the same instant he heard the loud, hard knock of a big-caliber gunshot, and for an instant the pavement under his stinging elbow was lit by the flash. A moment later, a second shot battered echoes from the close walls.

Nolan was rolling to his feet when a harsh voice began speaking directly above him, and then Vivi had stepped forward, past him, and he realized that it was *her* voice booming over the ringing in his ears. She was shouting in Spanish at a familiar-looking little girl on the pavement ahead of them.

Nolan was crouched, hesitant to interrupt Vivi. If the gun the little girl was holding was the Derringer she'd pointed at them last night, two rounds was all it could hold. Beyond her he could see half a dozen short figures silhouetted against the lights of the Rue de Vaugirard. Capes flapped around the legs of a couple of them.

Vivi's voice ground to an angry, contemptuous halt, and the *sauteur* children turned and ran away toward the boulevard.

Vivi gave Nolan an incurious glance, then looked at her hands, and patted her face and breasts. She gave a grunt of evident surprise—then sagged. Nolan straightened up and caught her under her arms before she could fall to the pavement.

He shuffled to the wide sill of a ground-floor window and sat her down on it. A couple of people were leaning out of doorways, and one elderly fellow called, *"Était-ce un coup de feu? Est-ce qu'elle va bien?"* which Nolan understood to be asking if the noise had been gunshots and if Vivi was all right.

"Elle va bien," he said shortly. He looked down into Vivi's face; her eyes wandered for a moment, then fixed on him.

"Harry," she whispered. Her left hand drifted up to touch her throat, and when she lowered it he saw blood on her fingers.

Quickly he tilted her chin up, and he exhaled in relief to see only a shallow two-inch cut in the side of her neck above the trapezius muscle; but it was bleeding freely, and he pressed one hand against it and hoisted her to her feet with the other.

"Back to Gertrude Stein's place," he said, and she looked toward the boulevard and then nodded against his blood-slick hand.

"They're gone?" she asked as Nolan hurried her back the way they'd come.

"You shouted something at them," he said breathlessly, "and they ran away."

"*I* didn't." He felt her shiver. "I saw the gun and knocked you down—and her shot hit me in the neck—and next thing, I was sitting by that window." She sighed deeply. "The *matagot* tried to warn us."

In only a few more steps they reached the street door that led to Gertrude Stein's studio, and it proved to be unlocked. Nolan opened it and led Vivi through to the paved walkway by the garden, and after a few hurried steps he was knocking on the familiar door.

Alice Toklas pulled it open and regarded the returning pair with concern but no evident surprise.

"How badly is she hurt?" she asked. "We heard gunshots."

"The first one grazed her neck, second one missed. If you've got a bandage..."

"Yes, come in." Toklas hurried through the kitchen doorway as Nolan led Vivi inside.

Gertrude Stein had been standing behind Toklas, and now stepped forward and looked from Nolan's bloody hand on Vivi's neck into Vivi's eyes.

She nodded and said, "Sit down, both of you." And when Nolan had guided Vivi across the carpet and nudged one of their previous chairs closer to the other, he and Vivi sat down. His hand was still pressed to her neck.

Toklas strode back into the room with a bottle of peroxide and a cylindrical paper packet that Nolan recognized as a French military field dressing.

"You can wash your hands in the kitchen," she told Nolan with a nod in that direction.

Nolan got up and crossed to the doorway. The kitchen was small. Toklas had turned on an electric light in the ceiling, and Nolan stepped to the sink below a window facing the garden. He rinsed his hands thoroughly before drying them on a towel.

When he walked back into the big room, Vivi had a

professional-looking bandage on her neck. She shifted in her chair to face him and said, tensely, "Tell them what happened. Tell *me*."

Nolan described Vivi knocking him down a moment before the first gunshot, and then her shouting at the *sauteur* children in Spanish. "They simply fled." To Vivi he added, "You touched your face and your chest after that, then collapsed."

"What did you say to them?" asked Stein.

Vivi's hands, one of them streaked with blood, were clasped tightly in her lap. "*I* don't know! *I* wasn't there! It wasn't *me* who shouted at them—it was...myself, from my last life! The *wound* must have awakened him fully!" She turned to Nolan. "Of *course* my hands touched my face, my breasts!"

Stein started to speak, but Vivi interrupted her. "I always believed I'd be uprooted one day to make room for *him*, but—I never thought it would happen!—on a *particular* day!"

She looked around, possibly for the now-gone glasses of wild raspberry liqueur. "Ah, God," she muttered, and ran her bloodstained fingers through her hair, dislodging her cap. She looked up at Stein. "You said Picasso knows about the *sauteurs*? How they work?"

"Yes, child."

"Then I think," said Vivi, and she exhaled, "I need to see him after all. Devil or no Devil." She looked at Nolan. "You were going back to your flat, you said?"

"Not now." He looked at the picture he had drawn of her, which still lay on the table. *You've captured her.* "That first bullet would have hit me instead of you," he said, "if you hadn't knocked me down and got in the way of it. That buys me."

She gave him a startled look, and smiled for a moment before shaking her head. "You saved my life last night, by the river. We're square."

"They don't cancel," he said.

"Come along," said Stein. "My auto is parked in the back."

Gertrude Stein's automobile was a 1923 Model-T Ford. Nolan and Vivi got in the back seat and Toklas took the passenger seat.

Nolan had driven Ford trucks during the war, and when Stein had climbed into the driver's seat he watched as she turned the dashboard switch to the magneto position, adjusted the two levers on the steering column to retard the spark and set the throttle, then stepped on the starter button on the floor. The four-cylinder engine started smoothly, and Nolan recalled having had to get out and rotate the crank below the radiator to start older Army trucks, often in the rain. In a moment, Stein had advanced the spark and throttle levers, the headlights were switched on, and the vehicle was rolling forward down an alley that led to the next street north.

Stein was soon motoring up Boulevard Raspail, and Nolan was impressed with her skill at working the gear pedal and the hand lever to weave around the evening traffic at a fairly steady thirty miles per hour. In the intermittent glow of passing shop and café lights, Vivi was frowning in evident concentration, and twice she gripped Nolan's hand—as one might grip the railing of a pitching ship in a storm, he thought, to keep from being thrown overboard.

"Excuse me," she whispered after she released his hand the second time.

He nodded, though she might not have seen, and he cleared his throat. "Where does Picasso live?" he asked Stein.

"He has an apartment in the 16th arrondissement, a dozen steps from the Arc de Triomphe," she said without taking her eyes off the cabs and bicycles ahead of her, "but he's likely to be found at his old shabby studio—called the Bateau Lavoir, the washhouse boat, though it's not a boat —in Montmartre, halfway between the cemetery and the basilica."

That was at the top of the highest hill in Paris. "I hope you have a full tank of gas," Nolan said, recalling that gasoline couldn't flow to the carburetor if the gas tank were half full and the automobile were tilted backward.

"I won't have to go up the hill in reverse," she assured him.

Vivi spoke up. "Please say nothing to Picasso about my tattoo. I only want to know"—Nolan felt her shiver—"if there's some way to halt a ... a legitimate *sauteur* reincarnation."

"You're not a weed, child," said Stein. "Old Beltran nurtured a flower, which should not be uprooted."

Under Stein's practiced control, the Ford sped nimbly down one brightly lit boulevard after another and across the Pont Saint-Michel, and then it chugged sturdily up the increasing slope of the boulevards on the Right Bank. At last she trod on the low-gear pedal and worked the throttle lever to slow the vehicle beside a long, low building whose level roof necessitated that the downhill end of the structure was considerably taller than the uphill end. Several doors and shuttered windows interrupted the mottled wall, and lamplight shone through gaps in the shutters. It was a run-down-looking structure, and Nolan was surprised when Stein trod on the brake pedal to bring the vehicle to a final halt beside the uphill door of the place. *Old shabby studio,* he reminded himself. And *nihilism.*

Stein switched off the motor and the headlights, and the narrow, steeply curving street was dark and silent.

"He works," said Stein as she opened the driver's side door and stepped carefully down to the brick pavement, "halfway between the cemetery to the west and the church to the east."

"He faces west," said Toklas dryly, getting out on her side, "but fears it."

Nolan edged out past the front seat and stepped to the running board and the street, closely followed by Vivi. The breeze was chilly, smelling of cabbage and woodsmoke, and the moon was halfway up the eastern sky.

Stein had already rapped on the door. Vivi gripped Nolan's hand again, briefly, then walked forward to stand beside the short, stout old woman. Toklas and Nolan hurried up to join them.

Shoes sounded on a wood floor within, and then the door was pulled open by a middle-aged man in worn blue overalls. He was nearly as short as Gertrude Stein, but compact and muscular; under a fringe of graying hair his close-set dark eyes focused on each of his visitors in turn, then fixed on Stein. He didn't speak, and Vivi shifted closer to Nolan.

"This," said Stein, nodding toward her, "is the young woman the *sauteurs* are trying to find."

"Iglesias's orphan," the man said. "You bring this dangerous person here." He spoke with a heavy Spanish accent.

"You've driven with me," said Stein easily, stepping forward so that he had to retreat or physically block her. "And I hurried."

"We weren't followed," clarified Toklas, following Stein into the wide, dimly lit studio as Picasso moved back.

Picasso scowled at Vivi, but said nothing as Nolan took her elbow and led her inside. The room was lit by three oil lamps on shelves, and ran nearly the whole length of the building. A row of doors in various stages of disrepair lined the far wall, and a door in the high-ceilinged downhill end couldn't have led to more than a couple of small rooms. Big canvases, their subjects indistinguishable, hung or leaned on the plaster walls. The air was nearly as cold in here as outside, and Vivi wrinkled her nose at the aromas of fried onions and turpentine.

Gertrude Stein made her way across the paper-strewn floor to a table on which stood a wine bottle, a half-full glass, and a lit candle, and she pulled out a chair and sat down. "Glasses!" she called to Picasso. "And another bottle, I think." Several chairs and a stool stood not far from the table, and she waved at them and beckoned to her companions.

Toklas quickly found a chair and dragged it to the table, and Nolan and Vivi followed her example.

Not caring if he was being rude, for he had not even had one of Toklas's sandwiches, Nolan said, "And something to eat, *si es possible, por favor!*"

Vivi nodded emphatically.

Picasso disappeared through one of the tall downhill doors, and soon reappeared carrying three tumblers in one hand and a bottle with a fourth tumbler upended over the neck. He set it all down on the table, gave Nolan a glowering look, then strode again to the back room.

Stein muttered, "God knows what you'll get, if anything."

This time Picasso came shuffling back to the table with a wooden plate, on which were half a dozen thick slices of ham and half a loaf of bread. After he set it on the table he looked around, then pulled up the stool and sat down.

"*Muchas gracias, señor*," said Nolan sincerely, tearing the loaf in half and passing one half to Vivi.

"*Oui, merci beaucoup*," said Vivi.

Picasso watched Vivi gobble a slice of ham. "She must be got out of Paris," he said abruptly to Stein. "Out of France."

"Not possible," Stein told him cheerfully, taking the upended glass. The cork had already been pulled from the bottle, and she filled the three new glasses. "Why do the *sauteurs* want to silence her?"

Picasso just brushed stray locks of silvery hair back from his forehead and stared at Stein. After a few seconds he picked up the half-full glass of wine and took a sip.

"You advised me not to join them," Stein went on, "when Adrien Achard offered me membership—the tattoo. You didn't say why. Why?"

Nolan paused in reaching for a second slice of ham. He was not surprised to hear that Stein was acquainted with Adrien Achard; the man was the wealthy scion of an old family, and his social circle included many artists and writers and composers. But belonging to an occult group like these mysterious *sauteurs* was at odds with Achard's popular image as a worldly cosmopolitan.

Picasso shrugged irritably and spoke. "They would only have killed you. You are too ... mundane, by nature. This girl of Iglesias's, she would be killed, if they find her. Claude Barbier has been killed, did you hear of that? And *La Prosodie* with him!" He squinted at Nolan. "And this fellow too, if he is the ... artist to illustrate the damned story of Iglesias! It was a mad day when I involved myself."

"What did you do?" Stein asked quietly.

"I have not ... had the tattoo," Picasso said, and after a glance at Nolan and Vivi he went on defiantly, "I will not be one day appearing in a child's body! But Achard courts me still, and he pays *desmesurado* for my paintings. I was at his villa at Cap d'Antibes in April, and in his library I found the typewritten story—which his people had stolen, years ago! I crossed out the name of the writer, and gave it to Barbier."

"And now he's dead," spoke up Toklas.

"It was right," insisted Picasso, "that the story be published, as Iglesias intended. The defeat of the Phoenician god, the Moloch bull, soon. Already there are devils in *les carriéres* from excavations last year to make the Exhibition at Les Invalides." He rubbed a hand across his mouth and looked down into his glass. "But," he added softly, "the story is not published."

Devils in the ... careers? thought Nolan sourly, taking another piece of the ham, which was dry and salty but very good. Digging to make the Exhibition?

Nolan had spent a day walking through the new International Exhibition of Modern Decorative and Industrial Arts—it occupied both sides of the Seine from the Invalides gardens on the Left Bank to the Grand Palais museum on the Right, and he had been more intimidated than impressed by the geometrical pavilions and modernist towers ... but any devils there would have been metaphorical ones.

Picasso slumped and shook his head. "There are *sauteurs* among my patrons," he went on more quietly, "and they imagine I will soon... get the tattoo. And because I know many Spaniards in Paris, one of them asked me today if I know how to find Iglesias's daughter. He told me she was meaning to reveal something dangerous, and she was seriously to be stopped.

"You," he said, turning to Nolan, "have the story?"

"I gave it back to its author today."

"They will assume you read it. You should leave France too—and not for London or New York. And," he said, standing up, "you should all go away from here. Now. I cannot be connected with your troubles."

Which you started, thought Nolan, by giving that manuscript to Barbier.

"Moloch?" said Toklas. Her usually unexpressive face was now tense in the candle-light. "Yes, the fools! It fits." She gave Picasso an intense stare. "You must interfere, decisively."

"I have done what I can do," Picasso said sullenly. "More than you know! It is for others now. I cannot dare pray—perhaps you can."

Vivi put down her wineglass and burst out, "Can a *sauteur* reincarnation be halted? Can the returning person be pushed back from his new body?"

Picasso blinked in evident incomprehension; then he stared at Vivi more closely. Nolan shifted in his chair and noted the tense compression of Vivi's lips, the intensity in her narrowed eyes. And Picasso reeled back, a look of sudden horror on his long face.

"*What?*" he said loudly. "Do you carry one? Is it close, is it listening now? Get out!"

Vivi yelled, "But can he be stopped?"

"Drown yourself in the river! Actually! This very night!"

Gertrude Stein got to her feet. "Pablo," she said, "come see me tomorrow. Tell me what you haven't told me." Picasso just stared at the floor, breathing deeply, as she and Toklas started toward the door.

Vivi and Nolan had got up too, and Vivi hurried around the two women but stopped in front of a huge square canvas—it was sitting on the floor, but was several feet taller than she was—and a lamp on a shelf by the door behind her made her shadow one of the figures on it.

Nolan stared over her shoulder at the painting. It was a monstrosity in garish pink and dull blue: four awkwardly stylized naked female figures stood in the foreground, and some kind of broken-faced crimson devil squatted in the lower right corner. All five figures were painted with no concessions to perspective or anatomy. Two of the women's faces, rendered in the fewest possible black lines, were blankly expressionless, while the faces of the other two were crude gray masks. Vivi's shadow stood between one of the women and the crouched devil.

She reflexively brushed at the canvas as if to dislodge her shadow, and in an instant Picasso was beside her, catching her by the shoulder and spinning her away from the canvas.

His face was taut with anger. Vivi was motionless for a moment, staring at his face in the lamplight, then she recoiled and ran to the door. She pushed past Stein and Toklas, out onto the dark street.

Nolan followed her outside, and then had to sprint to catch up with her. Over the slap of her shoes on the cobblestones he could hear that she was jerkily whistling as she ran. The street was steep and unlighted between close walls, and they were around a curve and out of sight of the studio when Nolan caught her elbow.

Her labored whistling choked to a halt as she whirled on him, and he stopped her fist with the palm of his free hand. "Vivi!" he whispered. "It's me, Harry!"

"Harry!" she said breathlessly, also whispering. She tugged against his hand that gripped her arm. "Come away from them, quickly!"

"Stein and Toklas are leaving. Come on back."

"Picasso might be at the door." She was panting, and choking out her words, but she took a breath and said clearly, "I'll be lost if I see his face again, I know it. Come away with me, please!"

He released her arm and then fell into step beside her as she walked rapidly up the street.

After hurrying past a succession of level walls that each diminished in height as Nolan and Vivi ascended the slope, he remarked, "I'm on the wrong side of the river."

"You no longer have a side," Vivi told him. "Stay at my place for tonight." In the dimness he saw her cap turn toward him. "Keeping Saint Genevieve in mind."

"Thank you, but my...money, my passport, my pistol..."

"Are all gone, rely on it."

They walked in silence after that, Nolan reflecting that what she said might be true. Those damnable lethal children were apparently well organized. In the morning, sober, he could go back to his flat, very cautiously, and see for himself.

At last they were pacing downhill on the brick-paved street, and after a couple of hundred feet the street curved south and was wider, and they were passing occasional glowing cafés and more frequent lighted windows. Vivi was shivering in the night wind, but didn't pause.

He could see her face clearly now when she looked up at him; her jaw was tight, and her young eyes glittered with tumbling thoughts. "We can talk in the Square Louise-Michel," she said. "It's quiet at this hour, and by then I will know what I think."

After another turn to the south there were no more buildings close to them on either side. They were walking beside a railing beyond which all of Paris sloped away below them in curls and squares of distant lights. Nolan looked to his left, and up several broad sets of stairs stood the domes and arches of the Basilica du Sacré-Coeur, white in the moonlight.

A similar stairway soon opened up on their right, descending, and halfway down Vivi led Nolan to the side, into a narrower set of stone steps that curved between rough rock walls. Leafy boughs overhead blocked the moonlight here, except for fleeting spots of lesser dimness on the stone surfaces around their scuffling shoes. After half a dozen careful downhill paces, Vivi sat down on one of the steps and Nolan seated himself one step lower.

"How's your neck—" he began, but she interrupted him.

"We need to talk to Elodie," she said breathlessly, "tonight." Nolan started to protest, but she nudged his shoulder with her knee in the darkness. "Be quiet and listen! I've told you that I sometimes have memories that don't properly belong to me."

He nodded, but it was unlikely that she could see it. "Yes."

"Tonight," she said with a shiver that he felt through her knee, "back there in Picasso's studio, I had the most...vivid memory yet! It was when he glared at me after I touched that terrible painting."

Her voice was tight with strain, but she went on steadily. "It was a memory of looking at Picasso, at a time when he had that same expression on his face. I—well, it was only for that moment, but I didn't dare look at him again, for fear my other self would...extend the memory—come up *again* tonight!—and push me away forever."

Nolan cast about for something to say. "You were whistling something, or trying to, when—"

"Listen!" she said in a fierce whisper. "The memory was as clear as if it were my own. Picasso was a young man, of course, but it was him. He was facing me in daylight from about two meters away—glaring at me as he did just now—holding a gun, a pistol—and he raised it and shot me! In the chest! I lost consciousness—died!"

"I'm sorry..."

"But where we were, in the memory! We were on the Quai de Passy, I could see the Eiffel Tower behind him—and we were standing on a raised walkway made of planks, over wide water! On the quai!" After a moment she said, "It was certainly the great flood of 1910! I remember it, I do—I was four years old, and I remember looking out a second-floor window in the nursery at *gendarmes* in boats on the flooded street. I was four years old," she repeated.

"So Picasso killed your previous self," Nolan began, then stopped. "But whoever he was," he went on slowly, "this Spanish-speaking fellow whose memories you've got, he was killed four years after you were born? Then you're not—you can't be—his reincarnation."

"I can't be," she breathed, confirming it to herself. "I am *not* the—what did I tell Miss Stein?—the weed that sprung up where a tree was supposed to grow. *He* is the stranger, the... trespasser!" She stood up and touched the bandage on her throat. "My neck is not bleeding. We can find dinner on the way."

CHAPTER SIX:
Je T'Aime!

Nolan was embarrassed to have to be shaken awake. He and Vivi had found an open café in the Rue Livingstone and devoured a charcuterie plate of cheese and garlicky sausage and crusty bread, along with a carafe of the house burgundy.

When they had finished and Vivi had paid, she had extinguished the stumpy candle that sat in a glass jar on their table, then slipped the jar into her coat pocket as they walked out of the café. The waiter was impatient to close, and either didn't notice the theft or chose not to bother with it.

They had then walked south for only a few minutes before Vivi spotted a cab and waved it to a stop. She told the driver to take them to the stairs by the Quai du Louvre—and Nolan had fallen asleep beside her on the cab seat sometime during the long, rocking drive down the Boulevard de Strasbourg.

"Harry!" she was saying now. "Out." Her voice was hoarse with exhaustion.

She let go of his shoulder and stepped down to a broad moonlit sidewalk, beside a low wall with a row of tall trees beyond it. Through their branches Nolan could see the broad expanse of the Seine.

He slid across the seat and jumped down to the pavement. The wind that shook the tree branches was cold. Vivi turned away from the driver and put her cap back on, and Nolan followed her across the sidewalk to a walled cobblestone ramp that led down to the embankment.

Money, passport, pistol, he thought, *all gone, rely on it.* And, *We need to talk to Elodie, tonight.*

He travels the fastest, he thought dully as he followed her down the little descending lane, *who travels with Genevieve Chastain.* But God knows where he winds up.

The wall on the right grew taller as they trudged down the incline to level pavement, and after a dozen yards they stepped out onto the embankment. Nolan had no idea what time it was, but he could see no one else on the long riverbank course in either direction.

He followed Vivi to the river edge and looked down when she did, and he saw that a short wooden platform was bolted to the embankment wall here, its surface only a foot or so above the water.

Vivi hopped down onto it, and Nolan sat and carefully lowered himself onto the creaking boards. He crouched on the platform beside Vivi, who was now sitting and untying her right shoe.

"Are you going to swim?" he asked.

She looked up at him impatiently. "Last night I used one of my socks, with a thread pulled out. It got lost in the commotion."

She tugged the shoe off, then shifted her legs and untied the other shoe; this time she pulled the lace completely out through all the grommets. She tied it to the half-undone lace of the shoe she had taken off, and lifted the free end. Her shoe now hung like a pendulum from the yard-long length of shoestring.

She eyed it critically, then dropped the shoe into the water, holding onto the end of the long string.

With her free hand, Vivi pulled from her coat pocket the candle she had stolen from the cafe, and she set it on the edge of the platform. "If you would light it, please."

Nolan dug the matchbox out of his pants pocket and struck a match to the candle wick in the glass jar. The light certainly didn't extend very far across the water.

Nolan recalled that Vivi had summoned Elodie on the opposite side of the river last night. "She'll come to the Right Bank?"

"If she can still swim at all. But she has come to me at lots of places on the river, from up by the Jardin des Plantes to the Pont de la Concorde in the west. Mostly I've called her beside the Pont de la Tournelle—on that bridge there's a statue of Saint Genevieve standing over a little girl. Protectively. No disrespect to the saint, but I pretend it's Elodie and me."

Nolan sat down beside Vivi and looked out at bending tree boughs on the western end of the Île de la Cite, halfway across the river. At the eastern end of that island, not visible from here, stood Notre Dame cathedral, where Vivi had said she and Elodie had sometimes slept in the high triforium gallery. She had told him that he could sleep "at her place" tonight, and he wondered glumly what it might consist of.

He caught a flicker of motion from the corner of his eye and whipped his head around, but it was only the flexing tail of a black cat sitting on the stone embankment. Nolan wondered if it were Marechal.

After ten minutes his attention was drawn to a small turbulence in the water close to the embankment, and Vivi stiffened beside him. She began singing softly, in English; the melody was in a minor key and unknown to Nolan, but he recognized the lyrics as an old nursery rhyme:

> *How many miles to Babylon?*
> *Three-score miles and ten.*
> *Can I get there by candlelight?*

Nolan recalled that one of the biblical psalms specified three-score and ten as the years of a lifetime and, sitting here with his young necromancer companion, he shivered.

Now something swirled in the water only a few feet out. He leaned forward.

The white porcelain face swam up into refracted moonlight and then broke the surface; from only a yard away, Nolan could see that the face was webbed with fine cracks. He was braced for the appearance of Elodie's hands, but still nearly flinched when the bare finger bones rose dripping from the water and hooked onto the planks of the platform. For the space of six fast heartbeats, Nolan gritted his teeth and stared into the empty eye holes of the mask while it bobbed in the water and made no sound.

Then the remembered violinlike notes skirled from the mouth slit, blowing out drops of river water. Nolan was able to distinguish rapid variations like syllables, but not anything like words.

Vivi was nodding, and when the thing fell silent she said, "Yes, a month early, and the beggars came down from Montmartre. A woman says it was because I met this chap," she said with a nod toward Nolan, "and simply *touched* him! She says our meeting changed—"

Again the singing notes shook the cold air.

"Much more strongly than ever," said Vivi, "but tonight—oh, Elodie!—I remembered his death"—she took a deep breath—"and it was during the great flood of 1910."

A brief series of choppy sounds was the reply, ending on a raised note as if it were a question. Nolan thought the expressionless white face almost flexed in anxiety.

"That's right," said Vivi. "It was never reincarnation."

Several seconds passed, and then a loud wail sounded from the mouth-slit in the mask. One of the cracks in the gleaming white cheek widened. The eyeless face turned toward Nolan—for a moment he was looking directly into the empty eye holes, and he shivered at the perception of a still-feminine intelligence there.

The candle blew out, and Nolan expected the necrotic thing to withdraw; but the white face didn't sink and the skeletal hands only flexed on the planks. The eerie strains vibrated out of the mask more insistently than before.

Vivi was nodding rapidly. "Yes, expel him...*l'apaches*...the lion of—?" She started to say something more, but was again interrupted by the scarcely organic voice of Elodie.

Nolan could see that Vivi's shoulders were shaking now. "Oh, Elodie, will you leave me again?"

More of the cracks in the face widened; a coin-sized piece of the forehead fell away inward. One of the skeletal hands rose out of the water, exposing the two forearm bones, and a finger bone extended to touch Vivi's cheek.

"Je t'aime!" Vivi wailed. *"Merci—pour ma vie!"*

I love you! Nolan translated mentally. *Thank you—for my life!*

A last musical phrase shivered out of the mouth slit before the face came entirely apart and the pieces sank, followed by the now-disattached bones of the hands and forearm. All of it quickly sank out of sight in the dark water.

Vivi turned and buried her face in Nolan's sweater. He sat down on the planks, with her half across his lap, and he caught the end of the shoestring as she let go of it. With his free hand he gently patted her shoulder.

She quickly sat back, away from him, and shifted to stare out across the water. Nolan could hear her slow, deep breaths over the sigh of the wind. At last she thumped her fist once, gently, against the planks. She took the shoestring from Nolan and pulled her shoe out of the water. She shook it out, then set about untying the knot that tied the two shoelaces together.

For a while she picked at the knot and tugged at the laces. At last she simply slid her feet into both shoes: one now had a long, extended lace trailing from it and the other had no lace at all. "I'll fix it when we get to my place." She sighed deeply. "It's not far."

She stood up, and Nolan wearily got to his feet. The black cat was gone. They climbed back up onto the embankment pavement and began walking east. Vivi's right shoe left wet footprints for the first dozen steps, and her left shoe, though dry, tended to flop half off her foot.

"Only about a mile," she said.

Nolan fell into step beside her. His hands were shoved into his empty pockets. "I'm sorry," he said.

"I shouldn't have told her." She looked up at Nolan. "That the *sauteur* immortality is not reincarnation—that it is simply people who cannot accept death, pushing babies' souls out of their bodies, to take the bodies for themselves. It made her think of the girl whose life she herself must have stolen, and it tormented her into...finally letting go of the body that was never rightfully hers."

Nolan nodded, and after a few more steps ventured to ask, "The lion of—?"

"The Lion of Cybele." Vivi didn't elaborate.

A Roman goddess, Nolan recalled; he couldn't remember more than that.

"It's that other graffiti Hemingway mentioned," Vivi said. "The woman and lion."

"Okay. What about it?"

"Oh, Harry, be quiet for a while, can't you? The person I loved most in the world is gone. I'll tell you what she said...later."

She was lost in private thought as they trudged past the arches of Pont Neuf receding across the river, and then she led the way around the Place du Châtelet with its towering Napoleonic spire and up the Boulevard de Sébastopol. Soon their course turned east, through streets so narrow that the rooftops on one side nearly touched the rooftops on the other, and only an occasional streetlamp or lighted window made the cobblestones visible. Scents of coal smoke and rotted fruit tainted the wind that funneled between the close buildings. Nolan wished he had brought his pistol along when he'd left his flat this morning.

Vivi indicated turns by lightly pushing or tugging at his sweater sleeve, and even in the darkness he could see that she frequently looked around and behind. Somehow she was keeping her shoes from making noise.

At last she turned into a narrow court and began scuffing up a set of wooden stairs. Several cats jumped out of her way onto the railing, which after one touch Nolan decided could take no more than the cats' weight, and then he heard the scrape and click of a bolt being retracted.

He followed Vivi through a dark doorway and paused on an unseen rug until she struck a match and lit a gas jet on the wall to his right. Nolan was relieved to see that the bandage on her neck showed no blood—Alice Toklas had done a good field dressing.

Vivi stepped to a window in the far wall and pulled a paper shade down over it. "Sit," she said, kicking off her shoes and waving at a battered armchair beside a bookcase.

Nolan sank into the chair and looked around the room, which smelled only of dust and old wood. The upper reaches of the ceiling were netted with cobwebs, and the walls were unpainted gray plaster. A small iron stove and chimney-pipe were attached to the wall beside the window. A few clothes hung in a doorless recess on one side of the bookcase, and a steel basin and military canteen stood on a table on the other side. Nolan wasn't surprised to see a couple of cats perched on the bookcase and another on the narrow bed against the opposite wall. The books all appeared to be new American editions, largely novels by Zane Grey and Rafael Sabatini.

"American tourists leave them behind in the hotels," Vivi explained, seeing his attention on the books. "The hotel maids mostly can't read English, and sell them cheap." She walked to the open closet and crouched to tug free a couple of rolled blankets, which she kicked out into the middle of the floor.

"You can sleep on those," she told him.

"Okay." He had many times slept less comfortably during the war.

She pulled a wooden chair out from the table and sat down facing him. She waved around at the room. "Obviously I haven't settled in, here. It's temporary." She touched her throat below the bandage. "I never settled in *here*, either."

Nolan nodded cautiously. "But the flood of 1910."

"Yes. I wanted to keep on being Genevieve Chastain even when I thought she—I—had no right to me." She looked at her hands and wiggled her fingers. "But it turns out I belong to me after all."

She stood up and took off her coat and hung it in the open closet.

Nolan knew she was thinking of Elodie, and he cast his mind back to the things they had heard tonight.

"What's *carriéres*?" he asked. "I thought it meant careers." Vivi gave him a blank look. "Picasso said there's devils in *les carriéres* because of digging for the Exhibition."

"Oh. It also means mines. There are lots of old limestone mines, tunnels, under Paris. A hundred years ago the city moved the bodies from all the old cemeteries down there. I think some of *his* memories, when they appear in my dreams, are of those tunnels."

"No devils?"

She hiccupped one syllable of a laugh, and shook her head. "Just a lot of old bones."

"You were whistling something," he went on, "when I caught up with you tonight. That was the tune that you said repels the . . . other?" It had sounded to Nolan like random unrelated notes, but after all she had been running.

Tugging down the cuffs of her white linen blouse, she said, "Yes— I remember it from when I was a child in the nursery." She whistled the half dozen notes again, more slowly, and now there did seem to be a melody to them. "I whistle it when I feel his—yes, otherness—getting close to the surface of my mind. But last night he was just *there*, after I was shot." She ran the fingers of one hand through her hair. "No warning."

Nolan recalled the personality that had shouted at the *sauteur* children, in Spanish, out of Vivi's mouth, and he knew he did not want it to erase this girl he'd known for twenty-four hours.

"Elodie," Vivi began. She paused, then went on, "She said tonight that I might banish him, for good. Perhaps I'll get a clue how to do that tomorrow, from the *apaches*."

Nolan sat up straight. "Good Lord, Vivi, you can't go to the *apaches*! They'd kill you—right?—if they knew what you are. Hell, from what I've heard about them, they'd probably kill you even if they didn't know." He yawned. "Forget it. Write 'em a letter or something."

"The hands of my... my parasite!... did not strike the billiard balls energetically this morning. My blood won't be spilled in the next day or two."

"If he was paying attention. You told me sometimes he isn't."

She waved the objection aside. "Elodie said—oh, bear with me now, Harry! She said that when I find the *apaches* I should cite my allegiance to the Lion of Cybele."

Nolan closed his eyes for a moment. "Lion of Cybele," he said, his voice hoarse with weariness and irritation. "What's *this* now, you've got some—"

"I don't know! All I can think of is the graffiti Hemingway mentioned—it's an outline of a woman standing beside a lion. I've seen it on walls up in the 20th arrondissement, around Ménilmontant. That's a dodgy area, and in fact it's fair *apache* stomping grounds." She yawned too. "I—beg pardon—I remember the graffiti. I could paint it on my hand."

"The Lion of Cybele," Nolan repeated flatly.

"The defeat of the Moloch bull," countered Vivi, and Nolan remembered that Picasso had used that phrase. She managed a smile and raised her eyebrows. "Allegiance. You're a friend of Marechal yourself—you've given him hospitality, scraps of food, with no thought of recompense. He was at the embankment tonight, did you see him?"

"Yes." Nolan got out of the chair and sat down on the blankets on the floor. He began to untie his shoes. "So that cat is the Lion of Cybele?"

Vivi stood up and crossed to the gas jet. "The *matagots* all together might be," she said as she started to unbutton her skirt, "or at least avatars. Alice said we should trust the *matagots*." She paused and looked up sternly. "Saint Genevieve, remember."

Nolan pulled off his shoes, and since she had not lit the little stove, he decided to sleep in his trousers and sweater. "The priestess of Cybele," he mumbled as he stretched out, "is safe from me."

She turned off the gas jet, and the room was dark. He heard her bare feet walk to the bed, then heard the bed frame creak. He had nearly fallen asleep when he became aware of Vivi's hitching but resolutely muffled sobbing. After a minute or so it subsided, and sleep took him.

PART TWO:
The Priestess of Cybele

CHAPTER SEVEN:
A Very Exclusive Group

Nolan leaned against a tree by the steps and the arched entrance of the Banque Transatlantique, and squinted through cigarette smoke at the glass doors. He had walked the three miles from Vivi's flat in the old Marais district, and the sunlight and fresh morning air had dispelled his hangover, but he was unshaven and wearing yesterday's clothes; he was afraid that even if one of the tellers who knew him were on duty, in that imposing glass-and-marble establishment, the man would not let him withdraw any cash in his present disreputable state.

"My poor man!" said a woman's voice at his elbow, and he turned to see a woman of about thirty smiling at him. Her dark hair was cut short in a bob and capped with a blue velvet cloche, and she wore a loose blue wool coat with tan fur at the collar and cuffs. One white-gloved hand held the hand of a red-haired little boy in baggy knickerbocker trousers and a short collarless jacket, and the other held a purse that seemed to be all beads and sequins.

Nolan dropped his cigarette and stepped on it. "I, uh, beg your pardon?"

The woman let go of the boy's hand and reached into the purse. "You must be missing this," she said kindly, and lifted out a folded document that he at once recognized as his passport.

Nolan quickly stepped back and looked up and down the street, but none of the pedestrians were paying attention to this quiet meeting, nor seemed likely to try to stop him if he began running. He hesitated and looked back at the woman.

She laughed softly and slid the passport back where it had been. The little boy clapped his hands.

"And this," the woman said, reaching into the purse again and this time holding up a bundle of franc notes secured now with a string. She dropped it back into the purse. "Not to mention this," she added, tipping the purse toward him so that he could look into it.

On top of a handkerchief lay his semiautomatic pistol. The slide was locked back and the gun was tilted to show that the magazine well in the grip was empty.

"Will you snatch the purse from me and run?" she asked, smiling. "That would only embarrass both of us—though briefly." She turned and pointed a white-gloved finger up at a second-floor wrought-iron balcony on the building across the street. "An important man has today taken an office there. He will be a friend of yours. Come and meet him." She took the child's hand again and said, "Come along, Robin."

Nolan looked into the woman's slate-gray eyes, then looked down at the child by her side. His heart was pounding.

The little boy grinned. "Cheer up, pal," he piped. "Nobody wants to shoot you today. Play your cards right and this could be your big break."

Nolan was sure now that the woman was right—trying to run here would be a brief and embarrassing tactic. Clearly these were representatives of the *sauteurs,* and in this moment he didn't doubt that the child remembered when Trochu was president. Thank God, he thought, that Vivi chose not to come along on this long walk to the bank!

He hesitated for another moment, then nodded. "Okay."

The woman tucked her purse under her elbow and clapped her gloved hands.

She and the child escorted him between trundling carriages to the other side of the street, and when the woman held open a polished wooden door for him, he found himself in a wide paneled hall with chandeliers hanging from the high coffered ceiling. A stairway on the right led them up to a carpeted corridor and, after a few steps, to a tall open door. The woman waved Nolan in as she and the child stood back.

Nolan exhaled, then stepped through the doorway into a broad white room. A long table surrounded by six leather-upholstered chairs shone in the bright daylight streaming through high windows in the far wall, and his shoes knocked on gleaming hardwood. He wasn't aware that he was sweating until the breeze through the open windows chilled his forehead.

A man stepped out of the shadows beside the windows. He was dressed—a bit frivolously for his surroundings, Nolan thought—in a red-and-cream striped blazer and white trousers, with a red bow tie at the collar of his white shirt. He had a trim athletic build, with short blond curls around his tanned face, and he appeared to be no older than the woman who had led Nolan up here. Like her, he wore white gloves.

Nolan recognized him from photographs in magazines and newspapers. This was Adrien Achard, wealthy patron of lots of avant-garde composers and artists. Nolan recalled that last night Gertrude Stein had said that Achard had offered her membership in the *sauteurs*, and that Picasso had advised her to decline the offer: *They would only have killed you,* Picasso had told her. *You are too... mundane, by nature.*

Achard took a silver tray from a shelf and stepped to the table. "Sit, sit, Harry!" he said as he set the tray down. A carafe of amber liquor and two squat glasses stood on the tray. "Hair of the dog?" he said jovially. He peered at Nolan and added, "Tuft, rather, perhaps." His accent was vaguely British.

Nolan looked back at the doorway and didn't see the woman or the child.

"Oh!" said Achard. "Gabrielle, Mr. Nolan's bits and bobs."

The woman immediately stepped into the room and, with theatrical flourishes and a smile, took from her purse and laid on the table Nolan's passport, his money, and his pistol, along with its visibly empty magazine. She bowed and left the room.

With raised eyebrows Achard waved toward the chairs. Nolan walked to the one in front of his belongings and sat down. Achard took a chair across from him and poured a couple inches of liquor into each glass.

"Opening hour at your bank!" he said as he slid one of the glasses to Nolan. "We guessed you would appear." He leaned back and smiled. "Harry," he went on, "what it is is, you've got yourself will-ye-nill-ye introduced to a very exclusive group. Haphazardly. Rudely! But here you are, and I really do apologize for the way our youngsters treated you last night and the night before." He laughed softly. "You've spent a day with our strayed sheep Genevieve Chastain, which must have been baffling. And then you had a right old chin-wag with Gertrude Stein too, didn't you, and she took you on a drive worthy of Mr. Toad—if you get the reference."

"*The Wind in the Willows*," Nolan said. He watched Achard pick up the other glass and swallow a mouthful of the liquor, then took a sip himself. It was very good brandy, not one of the postwar blended products.

Some of the children must in fact have waited at Shakespeare and Company after I eluded them yesterday, he thought, on the chance that I'd go back there, with Vivi—which I did. And Sylvia Beach probably gave them Vivi's name.

Achard nodded. "We offered Gertrude *gratis* membership in this group of ours, but she told us she'd rather accept the roll of the dice on"—he spoke distinctly—"reincarnation, hm?"

After a pause of several seconds in which he watched Nolan's face, Achard went on, "You know what we call ourselves?"

"*Sauteurs* is the term I've heard."

"Right." Achard frowned for a moment and clapped his white-gloved hands. "Leapers, jumpers. A hundred years ago it was *sauterelles*, grasshoppers, but the insect image was judged unattractive." Achard had another sip of brandy and cleared his throat. "When our bodies die, we leap into a new conception, always within about a mile of the Louvre. Our maturer fellows use...certain direction-finders to locate the infants who are us, and bring us to special nurseries, where our reincarnated identities can fully emerge."

He sat back and cocked an eyebrow at Nolan. "I hope you don't find all this as entirely mad, today, as you would have two days ago."

"Not as entirely," Nolan allowed. "The examples of your *children* that I've met are certainly not...childlike."

Achard rolled his eyes. "They're old souls, but their physical brains aren't yet developed enough to fully contain their intellects! They got upset because of a silly old manuscript that was stolen from my house in Cap d'Antibes a couple of months ago. It's of no special importance, but they took it on themselves to get it back, and," he added with an indulgent smile, "*deal with* anybody who got in their way! Again, I apologize." He took another sip of brandy. "Do you have it, the manuscript?"

"No. It was sent to me by the editor of *La Prosodie*, for illustration, but"—he flipped one hand—"he's dead and the magazine's office burned down. I threw it away. What," he went on, "is the story on Genevieve Chastain? I did find her baffling."

"Yes." Achard leaned forward, frowning. "She's a case of arrested development, you see. She ran away from the nursery before the person she really *is* had time to fully awaken. Her real self hasn't been able to experience his new life. We can take her back and let her old, genuine self take its rightful place." He clapped his hands again. "It will kindly assimilate the Genevieve personality, which will then be a part, an aspect, of the true, whole self."

Nolan suppressed a shudder. *Kindly,* is it? He thought of Vivi's brave, fugitive life, and it occurred to him that he had never until now, even in the war, encountered true evil.

"For thirteen years," said Achard, "we didn't know what had become of Genevieve. We never detected her proper identity being born *again,* which would have indicated that she had died, freeing it, but neither did it get in touch with us as a teenager. We knew it wasn't simply lost—over the years our direction-finding wallahs have detected moments of its activity, but never long enough for us to track it. So we could only assume what clearly is the case: that Genevieve was still alive somewhere, with her real identity hysterically suppressed, like an impacted tooth— a sure recipe for insanity. We even monitored the various asylums, with no luck. But now, blessedly, she has reappeared!"

"Are you sure," said Nolan carefully, "that you've got the right girl? It's true that she's pretty eccentric, but—"

"Oh yes. Ironically, we've been aware of her all along, but only as an orphan adopted by an old alcoholic whom we've kept track of. It wasn't until last night, when Genevieve's real personality broke through and berated the children, that it became evident. The children, imperfectly wise as yet, simply fled."

Achard got to his feet and stepped up beside Nolan, who caught a whiff of some woodsy cologne. "Our society of immortals is necessarily secretive," he said, more quietly, "and ordinarily membership is, well, *totally* expensive—that is, we entrust to the *sauteurs'* treasury the entirety of our fortunes, which generally must be substantial.

Eventually we die, and are reborn; and after ten years in our new bodies, we have access to the society's pooled wealth, which is...just about infinite, trust me, and growing with every generation. And we've learned things from Indian yogis to extend our various lives, near-total control of our bodily energies and processes! Many of us can go without sleep for a week, slow the heartbeat to a virtual standstill, run flat-out for a mile without getting out of breath."

Nolan started to speak, but Achard continued: "Think of it, Harry! To be assured of seeing the twenty-first century—the twenty-second! Always young again, healthier than you've ever been, and rich! When ordinary people—such as yourself, you know—are reincarnated, they're statistically sure to be reborn into stinking poverty in some place like Africa or India, with no memory of their previous life!"

"And," Nolan interjected, looking up at him, "you can see the future."

Achard walked back to his chair and sat down. "You must have heard that from chatty old Gertrude, right?" When Nolan just returned his stare, Achard went on, "It's true. Every year we ring a particular group of bells, to punctuate yearly intervals. Their tollings are sequential milestones, letting our seers orient themselves in the landscape of time to come. So we can predict...wars, financial crises, new technologies, even individual deaths."

He rocked his head. "Some don't want to know. We occasionally offer membership *gratis,* to certain sorts of genius whose perspectives would be valuable, but such people are often foolishly independent. Gertrude is to die in 1946, after some surgery, but she has refused the gift that would have included that knowledge. We happen to know that a certain local writer will become a very influential figure on the world stage in decades to come—he'll die in a plane crash in Africa in 1954— but he has so far shied away from even our most oblique approaches." He slid his glass across the table as if it were a chess piece. "We still have hopes."

Achard leaned forward, clearly excited now. "I'm telling you secrets, Harry! But it's because I'm confident that you'd be told them soon anyway. You see, I'm offering you membership—immortality, wealth!—for only a token payment."

Nolan guessed what that payment was, and wondered how he might get away from Achard even after pretending to agree.

"Yes," Achard said, "lead us to poor Genevieve so that we can heal her."

Nolan cocked his head. "Just that? In exchange for immortality?"

Achard took a breath, and held it; then he said in a rush, "Okay, Harry, two nights ago something happened that's got our psychics all over the shop. Their *dementia precog* sight, their *ajna chakra* vision, is stalled, the lines of probability are frozen in the configuration of two days ago, not developing as they should do. Our canny lads had the bells rung out of schedule, to try to reset, with no result except that the Montmartre beggars all thought it was *bonne chance* day and came down the hill."

He clapped his hands again, harder.

"We believe Genevieve *did* something, at your flat or by the river that night, that has made a... substantial change in the maths. We need someone she trusts to join us in *coaxing* her into a full explanation, while she's still dominant. *After* that we will complete the delayed reincarnation of her true self."

Achard was staring across the table at Nolan with such obvious sincerity that Nolan was sure it was false. You must know it's *both* of us, he thought, who in all likelihood *will* cause whatever this drastic change is in your calculations of the future. Your best bet is to force the eviction of Vivi's identity and kill me.

As if sensing Nolan's thoughts, Achard closed his eyes and shook his head. "To kill you might be to confirm the change, whatever it is. We have to tread carefully. My offer is genuine. We want you with us." His hands twitched as if he were restraining himself from clapping them yet again.

Nolan sat back and forced a smile as he picked up his glass. "The promise of being reborn into wealth and security after I die. That'll mean a lot to me when I'm dying, but right now—a cash advance?"

"Harry, of course. As soon as we have her safely in hand. Can you take us to her now?"

Nolan hesitated, as if testing his conscience. "Yes," he said finally. "She's in a flat south of the river in the Latin Quarter, waiting for me."

Achard stood up. "I can give you five thousand francs today, that's about a thousand dollars. Gabrielle!"

The young woman who had approached Nolan on the street and

escorted him here stepped into the room. She glanced from Nolan to Achard, and smiled when Achard nodded.

Nolan got to his feet and slid his passport and money into his pockets. Then, without looking at the other two, he slid the pistol's magazine back into the grip till it clicked, tucked it into the waistband of his pants, and pulled his sweater down over it.

He looked up at Achard. "You'll have the cash on hand when we meet her?"

"Gabrielle," said Achard, "would you fetch five thousand francs and have the automobile brought round. Tell Andre we're ready to move."

Nolan stood up and followed Gabrielle out of the room.

Achard's automobile was a big Stutz coupe, its long black hood looking to Nolan like an enormous gleaming cannon barrel. The polished black fenders and the chrome wheel spokes threw needles of reflected sunlight, and though glare on the low windscreen blocked any view of the interior, he could see that a man with sunglasses and a leather helmet sat in the open rumble seat at the back.

Gabrielle and the little boy in the knickerbockers and short jacket stepped up beside Nolan as he paused on the sidewalk, and Gabrielle opened the right-side door and worked a buckle to fold the right seat forward. She waved at the black leather interior, and Nolan crawled into the back seat. The interior smelled faintly of peppermint. His knees were up by his chin, and the grip of his unloaded pistol pressed uncomfortably into his stomach. A moment later he had to hike himself to the left, for the boy crowded right in beside him. He recalled that Gabrielle had called the boy Robin.

The steering wheel was on the left, American style, and Achard opened the door on that side and got in, while Gabrielle righted the passenger seat and slid in and closed her door. Achard started the engine. Nolan nervously tried to hitch around to look through the narrow back window at the man in the rumble seat, but Robin elbowed him.

"Sit still," he said. Leaning forward, he asked, "Are we crossing the river?"

"Yes," said Achard, steering out from the curb. "We'll slant down the Montaigne to avoid the Exhibition. Shouldn't be excessive traffic on the Pont de l'Alma at this hour."

Robin clapped his hands twice, then folded his arms and slumped in the seat. "Careful you don't drive off the bridge."

"You won't die in the water," Gabrielle assured him.

Through the low windshield Nolan could see that Achard was skillfully weaving his way through traffic. "But," Achard said over the roar of the engine, "do be ready to close this chapter."

Robin twisted around beside Nolan, and he looked down at the boy. Robin was grinning impishly at him, and in his chubby fist he gripped a little Derringer pistol, possibly the same gun that had been pointed at him and Vivi two nights ago and fired at them last night.

In this cramped, rocking space Nolan couldn't hope to knock the two-inch barrel out of line before Robin could pull the trigger. The .45 slug would punch under his ribs straight through his abdomen.

"Mr. Achard," Nolan said, speaking loudly enough to be heard in the front seat.

"*I* trust you, Harry," said Achard without looking back, "but Robin isn't being unreasonable. From his point of view, and objectively there's something to be said for it, any duplicity from you at this stage is best met by preemptively taking you out of the maths."

Nolan wished he could straighten his arms or legs. He was leading this party away from Vivi, certainly, but he had no idea how he was to get away from them. He suspected that the creature Robin would be quick with the little gun. And the man in the rumble seat might even have a rifle.

The Stutz sped across the spacious, tree-lined intersection with the Champs-Élysées. Nolan eyed all the cars and cabs and carriages bustling across the expansive pavement, and he was claustrophobically aware of his constricted posture and the gun four inches away from his side.

Then they were out on the lanes of the Pont de l'Alma, and over Robin's head Nolan could see the sweep of the river below.

He took a deep breath, pursed his lips, and quickly whistled the remembered six notes Vivi had whistled last night.

Robin screeched and clutched at his face, and Nolan instinctively ducked as the boy's hand clenched and the Derringer went off—the shot was a deafening hammer-blow in the confined interior of the car. Nolan lunged forward and reached past Achard's right hand, and in one movement he pulled the steering wheel sharply to the right and yanked the throttle lever all the way down.

Robin was thrown across his lap as the Stutz accelerated and swerved to the right, and Nolan pulled his hand back to beat at the boy's scalp, for his hair was on fire from the flare of the gunshot. The car's right tire skipped up the curb, and pedestrians leaped out of the cars path in the moment before the front end crashed into the concrete stanchions of the bridge railing. Nolan glimpsed the man who had been in the jump seat tumble onto the long hood and roll off to the left.

Nolan shoved Achard sideways onto Gabrielle and then climbed right over the seat. The door handle was just within his reach, and he levered the door open and crawled out onto the wide bridge sidewalk.

Achard rolled out after him, and the man from the rumble seat, lying on the pavement now, was tugging at a pistol of his own under his disarranged jacket. Robin had got the driver's seat folded forward and was scrambling out—his hair was still smoldering and he was still clutching the little Derringer, which presumably had one more round in it.

Nolan got to his feet and sprinted between moving automobiles to the far railing. He leaped, got one foot on the top of the railing and kicked off. Then he was whirling his arms to stay upright as he fell through thirty feet of rushing air, and he filled his lungs in the second before he struck the water.

He plunged through the luminous green depths to darker, colder currents, and he paused before kicking his way back up to the surface, wondering which direction to take. He was aware of the dragging weight of the pistol in his belt, but he didn't discard it.

Then a shred of something, river weed perhaps, brushed his hand, and for a moment he found himself imagining Vivi in sunlight—in detail, her eyes downcast and her yellow hair blowing around her face—but she was younger, scarcely ten, wearing a plain blue cotton dress. She looked up with a hesitant smile, and the image dissolved. Nolan caught a close impression that was something like nostalgic music and something like the scent of lilacs, and then he was again quite alone in the depths of the river.

He flexed his arms and legs to hold his position in the dark water, but no other perceptions followed, so he swam strongly upward, and the underside of the bridge echoed when he broke the shadowed surface of the water, gasping. He trod water for several seconds, catching his breath.

Had Elodie's ghost given him that vision of the child Vivi, before drifting away into oblivion? He shook the thought away, then ducked his head and swam underwater upstream, at a leftward slant.

He didn't break the surface again until his lungs were heaving in his chest, for he could imagine the man from the rumble seat having crawled across the lanes to the east railing, hanging on it now with his gun ready.

But he heard no shots, and a low-riding barge was handily moored at the north embankment. He swam toward it, still swimming mostly underwater—both for concealment and in the faint hope that he might sense Elodie one more time, if he had indeed sensed her a couple of minutes ago.

He rounded the flat bow of the barge, and behind its hull the water lapped at the lowest of a set of stone stairs. He clambered up them to a service lane, and hurried along it behind rows of stacked crates until it sloped up toward the quai street. He paused to straighten the .45 in his belt and tug his sopping sweater down so that the outline of it didn't show, then squared his shoulders and walked up to the street.

Ignoring the stares of pedestrians, he looked back over his shoulder at the bridge—but none of the four with whom he had shared the ride in the Stutz were visible.

He dug his fingers into his pockets to be sure he still had his money and passport, now sodden, then began trudging east, back toward Vivi's little flat in the Marais.

CHAPTER EIGHT:
The Dance of Loud Noise

Nolan's bedraggled passport and banknotes lay on Vivi's bed. His clothes and shoes had dried well enough on the long walk back in clear sunshine.

He was sitting on the floor below the still unlit little stove by the window, and his disassembled .45 lay on the rug in front of him. Vivi had found a half bottle of olive oil on a shelf, and he was now lubricating the gun's parts.

"I'm glad she was able to touch you," Vivi said, "deep in the river, before she was quite gone." She had opened the window and was standing beside him, looking out at an alley and a rooftop. Today she was wearing a pair of men's brown twill trousers and a white cotton blouse.

She sighed. "Poor little soul." When Nolan glanced up at her, she said, "That Robin. I wonder what his life would be, if a *sauteur* hadn't taken him."

Nolan pushed away the memory of Robin, his genuine personality restored for a moment after Nolan had whistled the six notes, screaming and unwittingly firing the little pistol in front of his own face. "What *is* that music?"

Vivi whistled the six notes. "At the nursery they just called it 'Scriabin.' I don't remember any more of it than those notes. They played a long version of it as the start of our fitness curriculum."

Nolan looked up from the disattached barrel of the gun, which presently had a pencil stuck in the muzzle. "Oh?"

"It was the first thing with my group, and went on for a whole day, and then they never played it again. Now I think it was a preliminary step, to have a clean slate, drive away any stray spirits that might have been hanging about the place."

"Preliminary," said Nolan.

Vivi nodded. "After that they moved on to other things, like drawing some of our blood, and giving us doses of a liquor they called *kykeon*, that made us see visions and forget which of us was which. Then they made us look for hours at a mirror that only showed half of your face..." Vivi shuddered and sat down beside him. "And none of it ever really worked, with me! Over and over they had me—four years old!—sitting in front of that bloody mirror, even giving me electric shocks... I think sometimes my parasite did take the wheel, and probably spoke to them out of my body, briefly, but they couldn't get it all the way... *revived*, as they put it." She blew out a breath and looked around the room. "So I ran away."

Nolan shook his head, staring at her. "It's lucky you remembered that musical phrase."

"Too right." She whistled the six notes again. "Later I found out that Alexander Scriabin was a composer. I've heard some of his music." She wrinkled her nose. "It's like Gertrude Stein's book that I showed you."

Nolan nodded and pushed on the pencil, and an oil-soaked shred torn from his shirttail fell out of the barrel's breech.

"If you shoot that," observed Vivi, "it'll smell like someone is cooking." She peered sidelong at him. "Five thousand francs?"

"I think he meant to kill me, actually, after I'd led him to you."

"Still, you might have got the money and got clear. And you told him the wrong side of the river." She gave him a small smile that reminded him of the vision he'd recently had of her as a child. "You saved my life again, I think. Saved *me*, anyway. Thank you."

He touched his forehead in acknowledgment, leaving a spot of olive oil.

"While you were away swimming and wrecking cars," she went on quickly, "I bought a bottle of India ink, and a brush." She stood up and crossed to the bookshelf, and came back with a sheet of paper.

She showed it to Nolan. On it was a simple outline of a lion lying beside a standing woman.

"That's the graffiti Hemingway spoke of," she said. "I think it's an *apache* symbol—I think it's the Lion of Cybele. And Cybele, there. And," she said, "I'm going to paint it on my palm and go to the cafés around Ménilmontant. Today. Now."

She didn't say anything else, and didn't look at him. Nolan carefully reassembled the gun and pulled the slide partway back against the resistance of the recoil spring, then eased it forward. He had oiled the rails, and the slide moved smoothly.

He thought again of the young woman he had seen trudging along among the refugees on the long road from Meaux to Paris in 1918. There had been nothing he could do for her, and once again he wondered if she were still alive.

And he thought of the Kipling line that had long been his motto: *He travels the fastest who travels alone.* Yes, he thought, and arrives alone.

"Maybe you know of a shop somewhere," he said now, "where we can buy a box of .45-caliber rounds? Uh, bullets? And some fresh clothes, and someplace I can get a shave."

She was still looking away from him. She frowned for a few seconds and then nodded. "Why?"

"Because I'm going with you," he said, "of course."

Vivi exhaled and leaned back against the wall. "Thank you. Elodie said it should be both of us, but it would have been too much to ask."

She sat still for a moment, then stood up briskly and made herself busy replacing the olive oil bottle on the shelf and fetching her coat.

"And that's enough," she said quietly, perhaps to herself. "I had Elodie and Beltran when I was a child, but I'm nineteen now."

Nolan got up too. He slid the oiled gun under his belt and wiped his hands on his shirt, glad that he'd shortly be buying fresh clothes.

"Enough?" he said.

She slid her arms into her coat sleeves and pocketed a bottle of ink and a short paintbrush. "I don't need a protector anymore."

Nolan recalled again the brief view of Vivi as a child, which, perhaps, Elodie's ghost had shown him. "What did Elodie say?"

"Her concern for me was fanciful. Put on your shoes."

Nolan sat down on the bed and bent to pull his shoes toward him. He slid them on, and as he was tying the laces he said, "What did she say?"

"She thinks of me still as a child—the little girl with Saint Genevieve on the statue at the Pont de la Tournelle." She straightened her coat and patted her hair. "Later I'll show you where there's a bath. It costs two francs. Oh—she said I would find a new protector."

Nolan stood up. "Did she... suggest anybody?"

"Yes." Vivi faced him. "She said it was to be you. But that's plainly a ridiculous fantasy. I only met you twenty-four hours ago." She laughed. "I don't even know where Oklahoma is."

"Right above Texas." He picked up his sweater and pulled it on over his head. When he had tugged it down straight he said, "I'm twenty-seven, but I find I sometimes need somebody to shove me out of the way of a bullet."

She frowned thoughtfully, then extended her right hand, and when they had solemnly shaken hands she stepped back and looked at his wilted money and passport on the blanket.

She pronounced it all dry enough, and as he stuffed them into his trouser pockets she insisted that they leave by the window instead of by the door. Nolan didn't object to the precaution. It was a short drop from the sill to a roof, and a wide-topped slanted wall led them down to an alley.

It was late afternoon when, after a couple of hours walking up twisting, climbing, ever-narrower streets, and having lunch at a promisingly disreputable-looking café and noting several of the goddess-and-lion graffiti but no overtly evident *apaches*, they found their way to a little square off the Rue Henri Poincaré. A weathered and dry marble fountain stood in the center of it, and they wearily sat down on the coping. Some sort of festival seemed to have ended here recently, for the old paving stones were littered with scraps of red paper, and banners with illegible inscriptions flapped from the balconies of the closely surrounding buildings. In the far corner, three young men in colorful shirts were crouched around an automobile engine sitting on the cobblestones; judging by the noise, they were either trying to fix it or break it to pieces.

Nolan was clean-shaven and wearing gray woolen trousers, a white long-sleeved shirt, and a khaki jacket, all secondhand but clean, and his old clothes and gun were in a canvas bag slung over his shoulder. The gun sat on top of the clothes, and was newly loaded, cocked, and with a round in the chamber.

Vivi yawned, then said, "We can ask the mechanics yonder."

She had painted the goddess-and-lion image on the palms of both their left hands, and they had made a point of exposing them at the café and in the streets, but none of the people they had passed had remarked on the symbol; perhaps none had noticed it. The only criminal activity the two of them had seen was a girl pickpocket who had scampered down an alley when Nolan slapped her hand away from his bag.

Nolan had been tense when they had first ventured into the maze of hilltop lanes and alleys reputed to be the territory of the infamous *apache* gangs, but the expedition had come to seem like simply a long and pointless uphill walk.

"What," he said now, "like, 'Excuse me, lads, but we're looking for the *apaches*'?"

Vivi shook her head without answering. The hammering at the automobile engine had become louder and rhythmic, and now the young men were all barking some syllable in time to it. Their short cries echoed back from the close surrounding walls. Somewhere nearby, synchronous banging of perhaps pots and pans had started up.

The young men in the corner now stood up in a line, holding a long driveshaft over their heads and stamping their feet in the same rhythm as their staccato shouts. There was a savagery about the ritual, as if they had dismembered some animal, not an automobile engine.

Nolan stood up. "Let's move on."

But more figures were marching up through the alley by which Nolan and Vivi had entered the little square: more young men in garish shirts, drumming on kettles with ladles and knives.

When the foremost of them stepped out into the square, Nolan saw streaks of blood on the knife blades, and when he looked down to take Vivi's hand he noticed spattered drops of drying blood among the red paper scraps on the pavement.

He drew his pistol from the bag and thumbed down the safety lever.

A heavy clank of metal on stone made him look up. The three on the other side of the fountain had tossed aside the driveshaft and were bobbing forward, their rhythmic shouts in very rapid counterpoint now; they seemed to be performing a dance, but each of them now held a knife.

There were too many altogether for him to hope to shoot a way clear for himself and Vivi.

"Give me the gun," said Vivi urgently. "Our only hope, *trust me!*"

He grimaced but quickly passed it to her—"Just point and pull the trigger!" he said—and she leaped up onto the fountain's coping. She raised her left hand, and stamped her feet rapidly in time to the young men's shouted cadence. Then—to Nolan's dismayed astonishment—she fired all eight rounds into the empty fountain in the same rhythm.

It was an entirely unlikely thing for her to do—unforeseeable.

The gun's slide was now visibly locked back, indicating that it was empty. She tossed it to him and slowly turned all the way around on the coping, still holding up her left hand, palm out.

When the echoes of the gunshots had rung away, all the racket and shouting had subsided, and the only sound, not even noticeable for several seconds, was a waterfall susurration that was all the young men snapping their fingers.

"Hold up your hand," said Vivi. Nolan dropped the gun into his canvas bag and then raised his own left hand, palm out to show the symbol Vivi had painted on it.

"*Par le lion de Cybele!*" she shouted. Then, an apparent afterthought, "*Et les matagots de Paris.*"

A call from overhead made Nolan look up—on the rooftop of the three-story building on the other side of the square, the top half of some person was visible leaning over a wall. The figure waved and shouted again, then stepped back out of sight.

One of the original three young men resumed moving forward, only walking now. He stopped beside Nolan, looking up at where Vivi stood, and he spat out a string of French too rapidly for Nolan to follow.

Vivi answered, scornfully and just as fast. Nolan caught the words *sauteurs* and *matagots* and *cloche de jalon*.

When Vivi finished speaking, the young *apache*—for Nolan was sure these eccentric hooligans were members of that tribe—waved for Vivi to hop down from the coping. As soon as she did, the *apaches* closed in around her and Nolan, pummeling them, and rough hands firmly gripped their upper arms. A knife tore the sleeve of Nolan's jacket as he twisted away from the thrusting hand; but the intention of the crowd as a whole didn't seem to be homicidal, and with one hand he clung to the bag slung over his shoulder. He and Vivi were marched and dragged across the square and through a low stone arch. Nolan glimpsed the words MAGNA MATER painted elaborately and with little skill over the keystone.

An ascending stairway opened on the right, and Nolan's feet barely clipped the edges of the stone risers as he and Vivi were carried over them. Their breathless course changed direction at two landings, and after a few more scarcely noticed steps he and Vivi were shoved stumbling out into slanting sunlight on a rooftop garden. Their violent escorts remained behind in the stairwell.

Nolan was panting and rubbing a rib where a fortunately knifeless fist had caught him. He looked at Vivi, who had somehow held onto her cap and now put it back on. Toklas's bandage was gone, exposing the cut in her neck, and she thoughtfully poked a finger through a new rent in her coat. Nolan shifted the strap of his canvas bag on his shoulder.

Under their feet was a wooden deck. Lush flowering plants that Nolan didn't recognize waved and trailed from stone troughs on three sides of the roof.

A woman stepped away from the wall overlooking the square, and faced them. The rooftop breeze blew her long gray hair around the collar of her heavily embroidered coat, and, like the young men below, she was holding a knife.

She asked a question in a French dialect that Nolan had no hope of understanding. Even Vivi seemed to have trouble with it. Vivi asked, *"Pourriez-vous parler anglais, s'il vous plaît?"*

The woman closed her wrinkled eyelids for a moment, then opened her eyes and reached out to take Vivi's hand and turn it palm-up, revealing the symbol painted on it. "You come," she said in a voice like nails being pried from wood, "in the name of the Lion of Cybele, and you join-deh in the dance of... of loud noise. The *Korybantes*," she went on, with a nod toward the square below, "have gone mad in this time. They like to kill you in their *rosalia* festival." Seeing Vivi's blank look, she added, *"Apaches,* many call them. This festival of them should not be in this season, like the beggars down from Montmartre."

The old woman sighed. "You know of these young men down there—the *Korybantes*? Ah, wine on the pavements, in days ago. Blood now. Rose petals in the *rosalia*, now red paper of fireworks." She shook her head. "Long ago they made clashing noise, dance, so cries of baby god Zeus not be heard by father Cronus, who would eat him. Protect the baby, see? Good—they protect babies now, killing *sauteurs* and throw them in the river—stop their souls, good, still—but also they kill anyone, now, and rape and steal."

Nolan wondered if throwing freshly killed *sauteurs* in the river somehow shorted-out their ability to move on and steal babies' bodies—in which case Elodie had had no choice in refraining from doing it. He recalled little Robin expressing concern about Achard driving across the bridge, and Gabrielle assuring him that he would not die in the water.

The old woman shook her head. "But you spoke—the *sauteurs*, who are in...confusion, today, and their *jalon* bell, which they have rung at this wrong time of year in *desespoir*—in desperation." She released Vivi's hand. "And you spoke—*les matagots. Qui es-tu?*"

Vivi took a deep breath and gripped Nolan's shoulder. "This man and I broke the *sauteur* prophecies two nights ago—and we can kill the Moloch bull."

Nolan kept his face expressionless, waiting to see how Vivi's wild guesswork bluff would be taken.

The woman looked out over the rooftops, frowning, then turned on Nolan. "The Moloch bull, kill it? *Comment?*"

How?

Nolan had no idea what the Moloch bull might even be, much less what would sound plausible as a way to kill such a thing. All he could think of was the story Beltran Iglesias had told to Hemingway. "A trap," he said, trying to sound confident. "A baby made of straw, with a mirror—*un miroir*—for a face."

"Ah! For Cybele you fight." The woman wrung her hands. "You must to the temple, I think," she said. "If you have truth, no harm to you, maybe."

She stepped back to the wall and called something down to the youths in the square, then walked slowly around the walled rooftop, bending to pluck a leaf from one plant, then a leaf from another, and then another, seven times. The selection was clearly deliberate. She carefully folded one and then tucked all seven down between the petals of a big red trumpetlike flower. She nodded to herself and stepped away, and rapped her knife on the top of the wall. The sound was slight, but four of the colorfully dressed young men hurried out of the stairwell onto the roof.

The old woman cut the stem of the red flower and carefully handed it to one of them, then spoke some words that didn't seem to be any sort of French. The one now holding the flower stepped back, but the other three again seized Nolan and Vivi and marched them back down the stairs and into the courtyard. The windows of the building on the east side gleamed in apricot sunlight.

The group hurried past the fountain into which Vivi had emptied Nolan's gun, and then the two of them were prodded down the alley to the street, where an open horse-drawn carriage was rocking to a halt, clearly awaiting them. Several of their rough escorts stood by watchfully while Nolan and Vivi climbed into the front seat, and the one still carrying the flower got into the narrower seat right behind them; in his free hand he was carrying a long-bladed dagger. Another man, contrastingly dressed in worn overalls and a dirty neckerchief, stepped up to the driver's bench.

As the cab began rolling forward, Nolan shifted around on the seat and said to the young man behind them, "We'll be getting out at the bottom of the hill. Do I pay you or the driver?"

The young *apache* had looked irritably at Nolan when he'd begun speaking, but within a few seconds his gaze had shifted to the driver in front of her.

Nolan sat back. "I don't think they speak English."

"Be careful anyway," said Vivi. Her lips were compressed, but she seemed more excited than frightened.

After the carriage had crossed several streets on a staggered downhill course, Nolan said quietly, "We can kill the Moloch bull?"

"If we knew what Picasso meant by that," said Vivi, "maybe we could. Maybe we *will*." She turned to glare at him. "Elodie *chose* not to be reborn! It wasn't just because some damned *apache*—some sort of Korybante—threw her in the river after he stabbed her."

The man behind them shifted on his narrow seat, clearly recognizing a couple of Vivi's words and perhaps the name Picasso.

"You'd know best," Nolan said. He lowered his voice again. "I just hope we don't get stabbed and thrown in the river ourselves." He leaned toward her and whispered, "Whoever we're being taken to, at this temple—do *not* mention your psychic parasite."

"I suppose not," Vivi murmured, "but Elodie thought these people would know how I may get *rid* of him. How am I to learn that?" Nolan opened his mouth to say something vague, but she went on, "What *can* we tell them? We've fairly promised revelations."

Nolan's gun and a nearly full box of .45 cartridges were in the bag he had been permitted to hold onto, but he could hardly eject the magazine, push cartridges into it, and slide it back into the gun, under the eye of the man behind them. "Gun's out," he said quietly, "but we can still run. This contraption has got to stop sometime, and I bet I can block this fellow's knife with my bag."

"Jump if you want. I need to talk to them ... unless you want to soon find yourself talking to a man who was killed in 1910."

Nolan sighed and sat back. "I don't think we'd get along." He spoke lightly, but his mouth was dry and his chest felt hollow. *If you have truth, no harm to you, maybe,* the old woman on the rooftop had said. He wondered now, do we have any truth?

The carriage made its clopping, rocking way down the crowded Boulevard Beaumarchais, passing within a few streets of Vivi's flat, and on to the Quai de la Rapée below the Pont d'Austerlitz. The Canal Saint-Martin flowed under the narrow Morland bridge into the Seine only a dozen yards to the west, and several boats were moored at the embankment. On the far shore of the river Nolan could see only trees, vividly green in the westering sunlight.

A series of shrill whistle blasts made him jump and look behind him—their guard was lowering his dagger hilt from his mouth, and Nolan noticed a mouthpiece in the pommel, and several holes along the ridge of the blade. The *apache*'s face had no expression.

Nolan looked back to the river.

A broad-beamed houseboat was moored on this side, close by the bottom of the embankment stairs, and a door in the cabin bulkhead now swung open. Nolan could see a hooded woman in a long, multicolored coat peering up at them from the doorway.

With a squeal of wooden brake-shoes, the carriage slowed and then halted on the quai pavement. "*Se retirer,*" growled the *apache* behind Nolan, holding his dagger at the ready again. Vivi and Nolan obediently climbed down from the carriage, and the *apache* with the flower and the flute dagger was right behind them.

The concrete stairs led them down to the embankment, and at a beckoning gesture from the woman in the houseboat's doorway, Nolan and Vivi exchanged an apprehensive glance, then stepped over the gunwale onto the boat's deck. They were closely followed by their *apache* escort, who handed the big red flower to the woman and then stepped back onto the embankment, watching and fingering his blade.

The woman looked down at the flower; in one moment her hood-shaded face seemed younger than Vivi's, and in the next it seemed older than the woman's who had sent them here. At last she pinched out one of the leaves from the throat of the flower. It was the one the old woman on the rooftop had folded. She opened it and stared at it carefully, then without looking up waved behind her toward the open doorway.

Nolan and Vivi sidled past her into a low-ceilinged cabin that extended the length of the boat, lit by four portholes and half a dozen oil lamps in brackets on the paneled bulkheads. There was no one else in the cabin. Padded benches ran along both long sides, but Nolan stood just inside the open doorway and watched as the woman freed the aft mooring lines from bollards set in the embankment; she moved away forward along a narrow side deck, and after a few moments he felt the bow shift to port, out into the river.

"We're away," he said over his shoulder to Vivi, who had sat down on one of the benches. "And drifting—no motor."

"We might go aground on the Île Saint-Louis."

The Île Saint-Louis was the smaller island in the Seine, just upstream from the Île de la Cite, and Nolan tried to remember what was at the narrow upstream end of it. A triangular park, he thought.

"Well," he said, "the current's only carrying us along at about three miles per hour. It shouldn't be much of a crash."

He walked back into the cabin and sat down beside Vivi, and after a cautious look around he shifted his canvas bag onto his lap, and lifted out the pistol and the box of cartridges. He set the box beside him and ejected the pistol's empty magazine.

"These people are our allies," Vivi told him as he opened the box and began pushing cartridges one by one into the magazine. "Probably," she added.

Nolan slid the filled magazine back into the gun's grip. "Maybe they'll have a fountain you can shoot up." He stood and tucked the pistol into the waistband of his trousers. He buttoned his khaki jacket over it as he crossed to the door.

"That saved us," called Vivi, also standing up. "I participated in their dance of loud noise."

Nolan walked out onto the aft deck, closely followed by Vivi. The woman was nowhere in sight, presumably up by the bow. The breeze was from the north, bending the boughs of trees along the near shore.

"I gotta look," Nolan said, stepping to the corner of the cabin.

"I'm right behind you."

Remembering the knives these people all seemed to carry, and the rips in Vivi's coat and his jacket, it was with caution that Nolan edged his way along the side deck toward the bow. There was no railing, and his left elbow bumped across the portholes.

You must to the temple, the old woman on the rooftop had said. Temple? All he could think of was the Panthéon, the columned Greek neoclassical building a few streets south of his flat, but in spite of its name—*all gods*—it was mainly a secular mausoleum, not any sort of temple to pagan gods.

He glanced back, and Vivi nodded impatiently.

There did seem to be some degree of organization among these... Cybele worshippers? *Apaches*? Nolan wondered what message the leaves in the flower carried. He and Vivi could easily jump off this boat right now and swim to any point on the north embankment—but they were in effect prisoners because of Vivi's determination to go through with this.

The hooded woman was sitting cross-legged on the foredeck, her left arm raised, holding the red flower like a torch.

Looking past her, Nolan saw that they were indeed heading straight toward the eastern point of the Île Saint-Louis, and would probably scrape the boat's port side against the island's short stone point. As he had thought, this end of the island seemed to be a park, with trees shading two marble pillars that might support an arch hidden by green boughs.

"That's not—" Vivi began, then looked left and right as if for another island. "The tip of it is gone," she said. She hugged herself and shook her head. "There should be an open paved area. Not just trees like this. Not pillars."

The woman in the bow lowered the big flower to the deck, and, to Nolan's surprise, the boat gently slowed to a halt just past the apparently anomalous wooded headland. Only a foot beyond the port gunwale, between the river's edge and a high ivied wall, a narrow, tree-shaded path bordered this side of the island.

The hooded woman stood up all at once and turned to Vivi, holding out the red trumpet flower. When Vivi took it from her, the woman moved back and waved peremptorily toward the walled path.

Possibly to steady herself, Vivi held Nolan's hand with her free hand as the two of them took a long step over the gunwale onto the path.

Nolan immediately had to step sideways on the path to catch his balance, and he saw Vivi crouch slightly for a moment. He had never had a particularly good sense of direction—he had always relied on compasses and the stars—but now he had none. He *knew* that north was behind him, toward the Right Bank shore, but for the first time in his life he didn't *feel* it at all.

He looked back, and was reassured to see the familiar gabled rooftops behind the riverside trees. The hooded woman wasn't visible on the deck—had she jumped into the river?—and the boat had already drifted away from the island's edge and was slowly moving downstream.

Still holding his hand, Vivi leaned close to him. "This isn't the Île Saint-Louis," she whispered. "Not entirely."

The scents on the cold breeze sweeping down the river were only of woods and rich loam.

Nolan tried to speak confidently: "I guess it's where the temple is."

He led the way along the path toward the upstream point of the island, where he had seen the two pillars; and when they rounded the point, where the river splashed and swirled against the stone, he saw that the pillars did indeed support an arch—and now two women stepped out from behind a row of pine trees on the far side of it. They were dark-haired and slim, draped in robes or togas that left their arms bare.

One of them smiled and spoke; her voice was musical, but Nolan didn't recognize the language. A quick glance to the side told him that Vivi didn't understand it either.

But the woman who had spoken moved forward and held out a hand, clearly asking for the flower. Vivi handed it to her, and the woman picked out several of the leaves, then returned to her companion. She sorted through the leaves as if they were playing cards, then tucked them back between the long petals of the flower.

She looked back at Nolan and Vivi, still smiling, and beckoned.

Now Vivi led Nolan by the hand. The two robed women glided along a pebbled path that wound between aromatic juniper and pine trees, to a clearing that Nolan thought was too broad for the Île Saint-Louis—and across a grassy sward stood what certainly appeared to be a temple.

It was entirely of marble. Wide stairs led up to a floor on which pillars thirty feet tall supported a pediment with bas-relief figures carved in the tympanum below it. A dome was visible above the pediment's crest.

This was no place in Paris, or possibly even in the twentieth-century world. Vivi cast a glance back at Nolan as they followed their guides across the grass, and Nolan knew that his own face must mirror the look of plain awe and wonder that he saw on hers.

He could almost believe this was a hallucination, but the grass flattened with mundane ordinariness under their pacing shoes, and when they reached the first of the damp marble steps, the white stone was slickly solid.

The two women reached the top of the steps, and one of them stood aside while the other continued forward. After a moment's hesitation, Nolan and Vivi followed her under an arch, and found themselves in a wide round space lit by open casements in the walls and a circular opening in the center of the dome high overhead. Tapestries hung between the casements, and the floor was a mosaic of dark and light marble. A waist-high white marble wall encircled the central ten yards of the chamber, interrupted by six regularly spaced gaps, and the wall's inward-facing surfaces projected at knee height in six semicircular benches. Wind whistled across the opening at the top of the dome.

A dark woman in an incongruously modern cinnamon-colored frock now stood up from the farthest marble bench. Her black hair was cut in a fashionable short bob, and in perfect Parisian French she called to them to leave their bag and *chapeau* in the doorway.

Vivi took off her cap and dropped it by the wall, and Nolan reluctantly unslung his bag and laid it beside her cap. The woman beckoned them forward.

Nolan followed Vivi as she walked out across the gleaming floor and stepped through one of the gaps into the central ring. Vivi hesitated, then walked the rest of the way to where the woman stood, and held the big flower toward her.

The woman took it from her and asked, *"Qu'est-ce qui vous amène ici?"*

Nolan translated it in his head: *What brings you here?*

"La femme des apaches," Vivi answered, *"uh, des Korybantes."* She glanced back at Nolan and added, *"Peut-on parler anglais?"*

The woman smiled and took the flower from her. "Certainly. You may call me Kirenli. And who are you?" Her English accent was what Nolan thought of as *university*.

"A couple of pilgrims—" Nolan began, but Vivi interrupted him: "Harry Nolan and Genevieve Chastain."

"You are welcome here. Do please sit while I read her message."

Vivi walked quickly back to where Nolan stood, and both of them sat down on one of the crescent marble benches while the woman pulled the leaves out of the flower one by one and examined each before dropping it. The breeze from the open archway behind them sent the leaves scattering across the marble floor.

At last Kirenli raised her head and gave her two visitors a quizzical look. Nolan thought she might be part Arab, or North African. "I note what you claim to have done," she said, "and what you claim to intend. Let's take it in segments, shall we? How did you break the *sauteurs'* prophecies?"

She was smiling, but Nolan wondered if these women too carried knives, and he wished his .45 weren't in his bag back by the archway. He reminded himself that Vivi had said that the *apaches*—who were apparently quasi-allies of this lot—were "fiercely opposed" to the *sauteurs*.

He chose his words carefully. "The *sauteurs* can apparently see the future, track it as it changes, day to day. Like weather forecasting. Their annual *jalon* bells are rung to orient their seers, mark the span between one year and the next—"

"Yes," Kirenli said, not impatiently, "but what happened, two nights ago?"

"Their view froze. No longer incorporating changes. Like a train switched off the main line onto a dead-end siding."

"And you two did this."

"I visited Harry two days ago," said Vivi, "just for a few moments. Inconsequential! But later there was an emergency, a fire and deaths, and I went to him again, that night. One of the *matagots* was there. It seems the view of the future that the *sauteurs* work from didn't include our second meeting, you see. And I touched him, which confirmed it. It made a change, a deviation."

Nolan made himself nod. This was the fancy that had been spun by Gertrude Stein's friend, Alice Toklas, and it didn't sound any better here than it had in Stein's studio.

The woman's smile didn't change, and Vivi added, a bit defensively, "And later that night the *jalon* bell was rung. Off schedule."

"I see." Kirenli looked past Nolan and Vivi, toward the two women still standing by the doorway arch, and Nolan wondered if he and Vivi would be allowed to leave if Kirenli came to the understandable and perhaps valid conclusion that they were delusional. Could he sprint to his bag before being stopped?

"So the *sauteur* auguries didn't include you two getting together," Kirenli said. "But now you have. And together you mean to kill the Moloch bull. How would you do that?" Her smile showed even white teeth.

"The method was described," said Vivi sturdily, "in a story told by an old bullfighter, Beltran Iglesias, who was my adoptive father. The winged bull must be lured to earth by a straw effigy: the image of a baby with a mirror for a face. Oh—and the bull would descend on a child in order to kill it, and grow bigger."

Kirenli stepped back from them, evidently satisfied with Vivi's answer. "A valuable allegory," she said. "And where is this to happen?"

It seemed to be an important question—a test—and Nolan hoped it was not as evident to the woman as it was to him that Vivi was guessing when she answered, "In one of the *capeas*—unsanctioned bullfights in the little villages in eastern Spain—around Tarragona and—"

"Yes, Tarragona," Kirenli interrupted. It seemed that Vivi had stumbled on the right answer.

"A Phoenician city," Kirenli said. She gave her visitors a direct look. "Do you know why the Phoenician empire was so wealthy and powerful, two thousand years ago? It was because the priests of Moloch, like the *sauteurs* today, were able to see the lines of the future, the most imperative likelihoods. The Phoenician merchant princes thrived, with that advantage. The Phoenician empire was at war with Rome, and their victory was assured. But an *unlikelihood* occurred."

Nolan heard faint scuffing behind him, and shifted on the marble bench to look back. A dozen more robed women had filed into the temple, and now stood along the curved wall on both sides of the entry arch.

"Rome," Kirenli said, "as the Phoenicians' view of the future had foretold, was effectively defeated. But the Roman Senate sent ambassadors to the Oracle at Delphi, who gave them outrageous counsel: to invite to Rome the Phrygian goddess Cybele." It occurred to Nolan that the woman was reciting a sort of creed. "The Roman Senate," Kirenli went on, "stepped out of all probability, and followed the Oracle's counsel. They enshrined and worshipped Cybele, who became known in Rome as the Magna Mater, the Great Mother. She arose and ensured Rome's defeat of the Phoenician power, and Moloch. Carthage, the great Phoenician city, was burned, leveled, its soil sown with salt."

The women alongside the archway began singing a single sustained note, rising and falling in volume as if advancing and retreating. It made Nolan dizzy.

"And now," Kirenli said, "Cybele is poised to defeat Moloch in this century—at Tarragona, on Midsummer Day, which for the Romans was the festival of the goddess Fortuna, and which Christians call St. John's Day. The *sauteurs* use the tools of Moloch, but they cheat the god of his demanded sustenance, and so their power is wavering—was wavering even before you two met." She raised a hand. "And touched."

Vivi stirred on the bench beside Nolan. "The *sauteurs*," she ventured, speaking more loudly over the waxing and waning sung note, "claim that they are reincarnated after their deaths—in a controlled way, so that when they're reborn they're gathered together and sequestered, and can . . . resume their interrupted lives, with full memory."

"Do you doubt it?"

Careful, Nolan thought.

"It seems unlikely."

Kirenli nodded. "It is a lie. When one of them dies he simply displaces the natural soul of some young child, and takes the child's body for his own. It's how they can see the future."

Vivi cocked her head. "That's how?"

"You mentioned the *matagots*. Are you friends of the Lion of Cybele?"

"If the *matagots* are the lion's avatars, yes," said Vivi. "Both Harry and I have given them hospitality, and followed their guidance."

Kirenli turned to Nolan.

He thought of Marechal and the cat outside Sylvia Beach's bookstore, which had advised him to evade the surveillance of the *sauteur* children.

"Yes," he said readily.

"Will you give your allegiance to Cybele?" asked Kirenli. She waved down at the leaves scattered on the floor, and the singing increased in volume and held there.

Vivi hesitated and bit her lip; and Nolan remembered her saying that she wished she could be Catholic, which this definitely was not. But she swallowed and said, "Yes."

"Will you?" Kirenli asked Nolan.

He looked at Vivi beside him. *That buys me,* he had told her last night. For better or worse.

"Yes," he said.

"Good." Kirenli walked back to the bench on the far side of the ring and sat down. She looked across the center of it at Vivi. "Yes, that's how. Long ago in Carthage, the priests of Moloch arranged for the god to consume very young children, whose minds are not yet fibrous with memories and experiences—not yet fixed into time's pavement."

Nolan repressed a shudder as recalled the thirty-foot-tall bronze Moloch statue in the movie *Cabiria,* with little children being dropped into the blazing furnace that was the idol's belly. And he recalled the tattoo on Vivi's wrist.

"Such children," Kirenli went on, "have not yet lost what Hindus call the *ajna chakra,* the third eye, which can see the bright and dim branches of the future, though they would soon lose it as they accumulated perceptions of the present.

"Killing these children," Kirenli went on, "had two effects: When a child's soul was forcibly split from its killed body, a burst of life-energy was released, which sustained Moloch. As in your fable, Moloch broke the child, and grew bigger.

"Then the third eye function radiated away in all directions, lost above ground in the tumult of fears and daydreams of the population, but was caught pure by *magi* in tunnels under the Moloch temple. Rome put a stop to it all."

The sustained sung note hadn't faltered, and Nolan wondered if the women were breathing in shifts.

Vivi started to speak, but Kirenli did not stop. "What the *sauteurs* have done," Kirenli said, "is cheat Moloch of his sustenance, for their own gain. They separate a child's soul from its body *without* killing the body; no surge of life-energy is released for Moloch's sustenance. But the *ajna chakra*, the third eye which can see the patterns of the future, is still released at the moment of separation, and is detected and read by *sauteur magi* in *les carriéres* under Paris."

Kirenli stood up and walked across the ring floor and around behind the low wall at their backs. "We will have questions, and work for you to do, in the name of the lion. It may be that your meeting has been the cause of the alarm among the *sauteurs*; that's as may prove itself. But in the meantime there are people to watch, messages to carry, excursions above and below ground. You'll find the service of the goddess—"

"Is there a way," Vivi interrupted, "to halt a deceased *sauteur* from fully taking the body of a child?"

Here we go, thought Nolan, tensing on the marble bench.

"Halt?" said Kirenli. "Slow, perhaps, but no—once the parasite soul has attached to the child, there is virtually no way to prevent that child's body being forfeit."

She had been moving away from Vivi and Nolan, back toward the entry arch, as she spoke; now from under the arch she said, "The parasite can be excluded from further pirated lifetimes—can fall away at last to judgment in the afterlife—if the host body is killed and quickly deposited in the flowing river before the parasite soul has left it. That too closely mimics Christian baptism, and is thus a blind spot in Moloch's field of empowerment."

"What are the ways," Vivi pressed on, "of *slowing* it?"

Perhaps at a gesture from Kirenli, the singing abruptly stopped, and for several seconds there was silence.

Then, "Genevieve Chastain," Kirenli said in a hollow tone that echoed in the big chamber, "you are not wearing gloves, and I have seen that your fingers are all intact. Nevertheless I must ask you to take off your clothes."

Both Vivi and Nolan stood up and looked around. Kirenli was striding back toward them, and she was now holding Nolan's pistol.

CHAPTER NINE:
The Taurobolium

"I know how to fire this sort of gun," Kirenli called to Nolan. When she was a few steps closer she said to Vivi, "We must see if you are marked with the Moloch tattoo—see if we have admitted a *sauteur* in among us." The dozen women who had stood by the arch were advancing on either side of Kirenli, and each held a bared knife.

Vivi took off her coat and dropped it on the marble floor. "It's right here," she said, pulling back the left sleeve of her shirt and unbuckling her watch, which fell onto her coat. She held up her hand with the tattooed wrist toward the women, then reversed it to show the Lion of Cybele inked on her palm.

"The tattoo was involuntary, administered when I was a small child," she said loudly. "The mark on my palm is deliberate and sincere."

"Sit, both of you," said Kirenli, walking quickly through one of the gaps in the circular wall to stand ten feet away from Vivi and Nolan with the pistol raised. When they hesitated, she said to Nolan, "Sit, or I will shatter one of Miss Chastain's kneecaps." The woman was standing too far away for him to hope to spring at her and knock the barrel aside; he sat down. To Vivi, Kirenli said, "Sit, or I will shatter one of your kneecaps."

Vivi sank onto the marble bench. Nolan saw that her face was paler than usual, but her lips were set in a tight line.

Kirenli stared hard at Vivi, who rocked her head back as if the woman had touched her forehead. After a few seconds Kirenli looked away. "I believe you are sincere," she said softly, then looked past Vivi and nodded.

Nolan heard sandals scuff behind him, and then he felt the scrapingly sharp edge of a knife blade press the skin below the hinge of his jaw. To move forward at all would slide the edge into his throat. Peering to the side without moving his head, he saw that Vivi was being held the same way. The knife was at the right side of her throat, opposite the cut from last night's gunshot.

"Are you a virgin?" Kirenli asked Vivi.

"What has that—" Vivi began, but at an apparent twitch of the knife at her throat, she answered, "Yes."

"Good," said Kirenli to Vivi, not lowering the barrel of the .45. "We can consecrate you, make you a priestess of Cybele. You will be ours."

The woman turned to Nolan with, he thought, a faint trace of a smile. "There is no need for you to be initiated," she told him. "The ceremony would involve a sacrifice which must be voluntary, and to which you would almost certainly object."

The breeze from behind was now heady with an incense of aromatic resins and oils, calling up images of camel caravans and desert oases and terraced Babylonian pyramids. Nolan exhaled sharply through his nose, but the intrusive aromas filled his head.

For nearly a minute Kirenli simply stood in front of them without speaking, Nolan's gun steady in her hand. He could hear Vivi's regular breathing, and more shuffling of sandals behind them.

Then he jumped in surprise, causing the blade at his throat to nick the skin, for loud percussive music had suddenly shaken the air, accompanied by rapid notes wrung from stringed instruments; and now a dozen of the women in togas spun out barefoot across the central floor in a wild dance. Long hair whipped back and forth, feet slapped the marble, and long bare legs flexed as the togas whirled. Behind the fast pace of the barbaric music intruded a deep, jarringly slow drumbeat. Nolan's thudding pulse seemed to leap between the two tempos, and he felt a drop of sweat roll down his jaw and stop at the blade of the knife.

Another woman came bobbing around the low wall behind Nolan and Vivi, holding a brass urn that she alternately clasped and held at arm's length, and when she was facing Vivi she stood on tiptoe and reached one hand into the urn—then flicked a scatter of red drops onto Vivi's face.

Vivi blinked and reached up to brush them away, but the woman shook her head vigorously, and Vivi let her hand drop.

The dancers were now bounding and whirling faster than Nolan would have thought possible, and momentary streaks in the air followed their whipcrack motions.

The background drumming increased its pace, loud enough now that it was no longer background. It was the thunder of men marching, an army—

—the smell of resinous incense was stronger, dizzying and choking him—

Then all at once the whole chamber seemed to tilt and rotate sharply, and Nolan clawed upward with both hands and flexed the cords of his neck, for he was sure he would be pitched against the knife at his throat. But the blade held steady except for a quick warning tap, and the chamber realigned, slowed to a halt and fell back to level.

He lowered his hands. The dancers whirled away to the sides and even overhead, and in the instant before they were lost to sight they were curls and wisps like white smoke, graceful but without solid form any longer.

And as if the dancers had been a curtain, now whisked away, Nolan squinted against sudden brightness. The temple was gone, and he was looking across a landscape of low dry hills under a glaring southern sun, with mountains at the horizon. As he watched helplessly, a pinnacle separated itself from the highest of the distant mountains; it didn't fall, but began to grow taller and wider. No, it was approaching with unthinkable speed through the bright air, and Nolan tensed on the marble bench that he could still feel under himself. The fast-approaching column of stone was changing its shape as it came, becoming the crudely formed image of a rotund woman, enormous, and though it was still miles distant it already loomed over him. The sun shone on its blunt, weathered face far overhead, but when Nolan closed his eyes and opened them again, the vast face had assumed the smooth planes of human forehead and nose and cheek and jaw. Its luminous eyes were turned to the sky. If there was anything comparable to an entity behind that monolithic face, it surely partook more of earthquakes and storms than of flesh and blood.

Nolan cringed, for he knew this was a goddess—was in fact the Phrygian goddess Cybele, the Magna Mater—and her recognizing full-on gaze would surely unmake him.

The perspective changed, and the goddess now stood astride the world, towering over mountains and turreted cities. For a moment a gigantic black lion stood beside her, and at her feet Nolan glimpsed ships bristling with oars on a sunlit sapphire sea, and armies advancing under streaming banners...

The vast head of the goddess began to sweep downward, and Nolan held his breath and clenched his eyes shut. Something like an electric shock flexed his arms and arched his back, and again the world seemed to spin and tilt, realigning... and then it was still, and he slumped limp on the marble bench.

The music had stopped, and after perhaps half a minute he dared to open his eyes; and around a red retinal glare he was profoundly relieved to see the floor and walls and dome of the temple. The daylight through the casements had taken on an amber tint, and he wondered dazedly how much time had passed.

He could hear Vivi's panting breath over his own. When he turned toward her, the glare spot in his eyes had faded enough for him to see that her eyes were closed and her lips were pulled back from her teeth. After several seconds she exhaled sharply, then opened her eyes and blinked around without seeming to focus on anything.

I closed my eyes when the goddess looked down at us, Nolan thought. Vivi apparently didn't.

At some point the knives at their throats had been lifted away, and when she turned her head he saw that her neck too had been nicked by the restraining knife of one of the women.

At last Vivi blinked and looked directly at Nolan with bewildered recognition. She reached up and wiped some of the spots of blood from her face, then licked her sleeve to get rid of the taste.

From behind them, Kirenli's voice seemed muted after the battering music: "Bull's blood and vinegar, Genevieve." She stepped around in front of them again. "You did see *her*, didn't you?" Kirenli gave Vivi a look of sympathy or envy. "I did too, once. If we could have done this in Rome, at leisure, we would have done the taurobolium in the traditional manner. You would have stood in a trench with a grating laid over it, and we would have killed a bull with the goddess's sacred spear on the grating, showering you with its blood. But you are now ours, in any case—a priestess of Cybele."

Vivi's panting had subsided. She inhaled deeply, then just exhaled without saying anything. She looked from side to side, and her eyes were again alert.

Nolan looked past her, and wondered if the dancers he had seen fly away and dissolve had resumed human form, for a dozen women indistinguishable from the others, again or still in togas, now walked into the circle and stood around him and Vivi. Nolan was not surprised to see that they all carried the apparently customary knives.

This ritual had been an ordeal, with knives to their throats and either a drug-induced hallucination or an actual vision of the goddess Cybele—but surely it was finished, or nearly so; and these women could hardly mean to kill Vivi and himself, after consecrating Vivi as a priestess. Nolan longed to be away from this unnatural place; he was ready to swim, if necessary, to the Left Bank, and find a café that served strong drink.

To Vivi, Kirenli said, "Cybele did not reject you. How is it that you harbor a *sauteur* soul in addition to your own?"

Vivi rolled her head and touched the far side of her neck. When she lowered her hand there was blood on her fingertips.

"You'd have," she said hoarsely, "cut our throats, both of us, if the goddess had rejected me?"

Kirenli shook her head and waved Nolan's gun at the ceiling. "This, and the knives at your throats, were simply restraint. So...?"

"Huh." Vivi wiped more of the bull's blood spots from her face. "Well, then." She cleared her throat. "I grew up in a *sauteur* nursery, but I ran away in 1912, when I was six years old." She sighed and rubbed her face. "They had started the exercises that—I now know—would have let my *sauteur* parasite fully take me, push me out, but I was difficult, and they hadn't succeeded before I escaped them."

Kirenli nodded—sadly, Nolan thought.

"That's why you still have all your finger joints," Kirenli said. "You escaped them while you were too young for preparations to be made for your *next* life."

"Cutting off finger joints...?"

"A finger bone from a deceased *sauteur*," Kirenli said, "is a direction finder. It acts as a compass, pointing to where the bone's onetime owner has found a young child, and occupied that child's body. When possible, the *sauteurs* retrieve their dead comrade's skull too, which is a better compass, having once held his mind." Kirenli pursed her lips in evident distaste. "We're told that it turns to *face* the direction of the unnaturally relocated soul."

"And there's *no way*," asked Vivi desperately, "to expel him from me?"

"No. Nothing you could have any remote chance of doing, sister." For several seconds Kirenli didn't speak. Then, "Him? You know it's a man?" she said.

"Yes. I've seen a lot of his memories in my dreams. He speaks Spanish. Last night I even saw his memory of his own death—he was shot in the chest."

Again Kirenli paused before speaking. "Ah! He is very close to the surface of your mind. Do you know where he was killed?"

"Here in Paris," said Vivi, "on the Quai de Passy." She shivered, then repeated, "On the Quai de Passy..."

She exhaled and looked around the temple.

"Surely the *sauteurs* have tried to find you," said Kirenli.

Vivi gave her a tight smile and for several seconds didn't speak; then in an accent that was not her own, said, "I can speak English, if you like."

Nolan's face was suddenly cold. Kirenli stepped back and gave a warning look to the women surrounding Vivi and Nolan; the women gripped their knives more firmly.

She turned her gaze back to Vivi. "What was your name, before you died?"

The voice from Vivi's mouth said, "We can negotiate." Her hands raised from her lap and clapped. "What year is it now?"

"1925," Kirenli answered.

Vivi's head rocked back. "I knew some long time passed. Fifteen years! All just dreams, and sometimes observing horseraces for this child!" Again her eyes swept the wide space under the dome. "This would be the temple of Cybele, once again on the Île Saint-Louis, yes?"

No one answered.

"Will you kill this body?" said Vivi's voice. Her right hand touched her chest. "I would only be reincarnated."

"Reincarnated?" said Kirenli scornfully. "You mean you would find a child whose body you can steal."

For several seconds Vivi's blue eyes stared at her. "Who says so?" her voice finally replied.

Nolan spoke up: "And cheat Moloch of his... horrible dividend. Already there are," and he quoted Picasso's phrase, "devils in *les carriéres*."

"Ah?" Vivi's brow tensed in a frown, and her hands clapped loudly. "Do you know if... Have you heard of a man called Charles-Édouard Jeanneret? He was a draftsman in the Paris office of an *arquitecto,* an architect."

Again, neither Nolan nor Kirenli answered. Both simply stared at Vivi's unrecognizably taut face under the familiar tangle of blonde bangs, Kirenli without expression and Nolan with narrowed eyes and clenched jaw.

Nolan said, "Your Adrien Achard claps his hands frequently. So do his associates. Is that to... reassert your possession of the stolen body? Is it so insecure?"

"Achard!" said Vivi's newly harsh voice. "I remember when he was a boy in the old nursery—does he lead now?" After several seconds of silence, her face turned toward Nolan and the voice said, "What are you, a friend of this girl? I'll wager these women did the whole ceremony, and consecrated her as one of their own. A *priestess*." Vivi's eyebrows raised in question.

Nolan hesitated, then nodded.

"Ah, *verdad*. You must know that they intend to kill this body. Drown it." Again her hands clapped. "It's a sin for them to cause the death of ordinary people, but they have absolute power over their own priestesses." Her head turned back toward Kirenli.

Nolan shifted on the marble bench, and a woman stepped close to him on his left, the point of her upright knife touching his shoulder, while Kirenli aimed his own pistol at him.

"It's true that we may not kill ordinary people," she told him, "but at any moment you may have a useless right arm and a ruined leg."

"She came to you voluntarily!" Nolan protested. "She opposes the *sauteurs,* she brought you the story of how to kill the Moloch bull! It was our meeting two nights ago that broke the *sauteurs'* view of the future, and made them ring their damn bell!" He didn't dare move his head, but he waved toward Vivi. "Obviously she and I are... *destined*... to *do* something, something decisive, in all this! We are your *allies*!"

Kirenli shrugged. "The story of killing Moloch is good. And the unforeseen effect of you two meeting may have been that you have brought this man to us. It may be that decisive things will be learned from him."

"Vivi's face had shown momentary surprise at Nolan's statements, but quickly lost all expression, and turned to Kirenli. "Let me take this girl and go—one more *sauteur* free in Paris changes nothing. In return I will explain much, freely answer many questions."

Nolan glanced at Kirenli, hoping that she would agree. Once he and Vivi were free of this unnatural place and its weird sisterhood, he could surely whistle the Scriabin phrase and restore Vivi's personality—at least for a while. But the woman shook her head.

"I won't lie," she said to the seated figure of Vivi, "even to such as you. Yes, you will answer many questions. There are many things we need to know about the *sauteurs,* the duplicitous devotees of Moloch."

Kirenli looked directly into Vivi's face. "And that body will die today," she said, "or possibly tomorrow, if the questioning is difficult—but we do not dishonor our hands. Yes, that body will be bound and heavily weighted and sunk in the Seine—the river will drown it in mimic baptism, and *you* will drop out of Moloch's web—to judgment."

Nolan shifted to set his heels against the base of the marble bench, and at the movement the knife-point at his shoulder punctured his jacket and shirt and the skin over his collar bone.

In the same moment, Vivi's body jackknifed forward off the bench and knocked her head hard against the marble floor; the quick knife of the woman behind her had cut a long rent in the back of her blouse, and Nolan saw blood quickly blotting the fabric.

He dove forward onto his hands, expecting a slash across his own back, but the woman who had held a knife to his shoulder was running around the corner of the marble bench.

One of the women was already crouched between him and where Vivi lay, and he shoved her out of the way and knelt beside Vivi.

She was lying prostrate on the floor, motionless. He was hesitant to roll her over onto her back but took hold of her slack wrist. The women were crowding around him—"The cut in her back isn't bleeding!" one cried—and he had to punch a couple of them aside to be able to feel Vivi's pulse for several seconds.

There was no pulse.

Kirenli's voice rang out over the exclamations of the others: "If she is dead, there is no call for weights—we must get her into the river."

"She's not dead!" Nolan shouted. "Get away from her!"

Vivi's face on the floor was turned toward him, her eyes open but vacant. He bent down and pressed his ear to her open mouth, but could feel no breathing.

Sweat stung his eyes as he straightened up.

"Stay away!" he commanded, and the women hung back.

He straddled Vivi's thighs and leaned forward to lay her limp arms up past her head, then gripped the slashed edges of her blouse and tore them entirely apart, exposing the pale skin of her back. A streak of blood ran across her ribs from the vertical slash down her shoulder blade, but it was true that the wound didn't seem to still be bleeding.

"Can she be revived?" demanded Kirenli.

Desperately Nolan called to mind the page in the *Cantonment Manual* that described the Schaefer method of reviving a person who had stopped breathing.

Vivi's pelvic bones were easily visible at the base of her back, and he laid his hands above them, on her lowest ribs; he pressed downward with increasing weight for three seconds. He lifted his hands away—but even after ten seconds her ribs didn't rise. Her lungs hadn't refilled, as the manual said they would. There was no point in trying it again.

He got off her and gently rolled her over onto her back. Her forehead was scraped, but also not visibly bleeding. He felt for a pulse in her throat—and found none there either. He bent over and held his ear to her mouth, but still felt no breath.

"She is dead," said Kirenli, "*her* soul is gone. We need to take her body to the river now, before the other succeeds in moving on."

"You'll wait—" Nolan began desperately—

For an instant he glimpsed the rushing butt of his pistol—a stunning blow to the side of his head pitched him sideways off of Vivi's body, and several hands pulled him away.

Then he was sitting on the floor, firmly held at forearms and wrists, with a powerful bare arm crooked so tightly around his throat that he could hardly breathe. His head throbbed like hammer blows on an anvil, and his mouth tasted of copper.

Through the ringing in his ears he dimly heard Kirenli's voice say to him, "She is free from their bondage at last."

His yell of protest was choked off.

The women stood around Vivi now, chanting. Vivi's chest remained horribly still. Nolan let himself confront the idea that she was, indeed, dead. Her parasite had willfully ended her life, to escape.

Angry tears blurred his vision as he stared across the floor at the body of the brave, willful, contrary girl who had pushed him out of the way of a bullet last night. Why had he let her go searching for the *apaches* today?

He exhaled, and sucked in a constricted breath. The air still carried a taint of incense.

But how could he have *stopped* her, she being who she was? He remembered her leaping up onto the fountain coping at the *apaches'* lair, and firing all eight rounds of his pistol into the dry fountain. That had been an inspired move, though at the time it had seemed insane, and it had probably saved the two of them from being thoughtlessly stabbed to death by the *apaches*.

But that had led her inexorably to this temple of Cybele—*Jump if you want,* she had told him in the carriage on the way down from Ménilmontant, *I need to talk to them*—and to her death.

He wondered if she had been relying on her reading of the billiard balls yesterday—*I asked if my blood is to be spilled in the next two days . . . I think his inaction meant no.*

But, *sometimes he's not listening.*

Or, Nolan thought now, he was aware only of the *sauteurs'* stalled timeline, in which Vivi didn't come to my flat a second time, didn't touch me.

The women moved forward now, and crouched to lift Vivi's limp body. Nolan was hoisted dizzily to his feet, his wrists still tightly held, the arm of the unseen woman behind him still clamped around his throat. Despite a new clumsiness and the throbbing pain in his head, he was able to walk, and he and his escorts followed the procession out through one of the gaps in the circular wall toward the entry arch. Vivi's left arm was dangling, and he winced at the momentary sight of the Lion of Cybele symbol that she had carefully painted on her palm.

As they passed under the arch into fresh air and a warm breeze, Nolan looked past the procession and noted that the tops of the pines were no longer in sunlight, and the broad lawn was shadowed.

The women carried Vivi's body along the path that wound

among the waving pine and juniper boughs, and soon they passed between the two pillars at the eastern point of the island. The cloudless vault of the dimming sky arched above them, and only ranks of trees were visible across the wide, flowing water to left and right.

Nolan's escorts led him forward to the group by the water, and stopped a yard away from the two who supported Vivi's narrow shoulders. Her head was down, her chin on her chest and her disheveled blonde hair over her face.

The women carrying Vivi crouched at the narrow stone point, then straightened and stepped aside in pairs as they let go of her shoulders, hips, and legs, and Vivi's body slid without a splash into the water. Nolan watched the limp arms float up as the body sank.

At a word from Kirenli, his escorts finally released him.

For several seconds his mind was empty. Then, Rest in peace, Vivi, he thought, with Elodie, who was sister and mother to you.

And then, Back to America? Paris is finished for me.

He stepped away, with vague thoughts of swimming to one bank or the other, when a startled, dismayed cry from behind him made him turn, and he looked out at the water where the women were pointing.

Vivi's body had bobbed to the surface, her bared back white against the dark water, and her head was lifted. Her right arm, and then her left, rose out of the water and splashed in ahead of her and thrust back, pushing her forward.

She was, impossibly, swimming.

Nolan's legs were still unsteady, but he ran to the edge of the grass and threw himself right over the stone point and into the river.

Under the cold water he shrugged his shoulders free of his jacket and let the current pull it off. A moment later he thrashed to the surface, clumsy in his shoes, and he spat out a mouthful of water—momentarily startled that it tasted brightly fresh, almost intoxicating.

He began swimming after Vivi. The shock of the cold water must somehow have revived her, but it was inconceivable that she could long sustain this muscular effort so soon after her heart and respiration had been stopped for more than a minute. It was inconceivable that she was doing this at all. Within seconds she must lose consciousness, if not die... again. He needed to catch up with her, keep her head above water and tow her the rest of the way to the shore.

But he was the one in difficulty. After the blow to his head, it required concentration to work his arms and legs, and his head itself didn't feel firmly attached to his neck. There was no hope of contorting to untie and shed his shoes. He took a deep breath and tried to call to Vivi, but his voice was a raspy croak, and the effort left him gasping and choking on plain old river water that no longer tasted fresh.

He kicked and pushed down with his hands to thrust his shoulders up out of the water for a moment, and saw that Vivi was still swimming strongly, far ahead of him; it seemed sure that she would shortly get to the embankment, unaided. His heart was hammering, and it occurred to him that he could be in some trouble himself.

He reluctantly abandoned the hopeless goal of catching up to her, and relaxed, simply treading water. When he had got his breath back, he began swimming slowly and carefully toward the north embankment, pausing to tread water every minute or so.

At one point he realized that his vision had darkened, but the momentary panic passed when he raised his head and saw that the slow current was carrying him under the arching span of the Pont de Sully, and a stepped section of the embankment was not far off.

With a final burst of exertion he floundered his way to the steps and pulled himself up onto the blessedly solid concrete surface. Water trickled and puddled around his hands and knees, and his sodden shirt and trousers were an unwelcome weight.

He sprawled flat on his back in the spreading puddle around him and breathed deeply.

A family group picked up their wine bottle and sandwiches and slid a blanket farther away from him along the pavement. Without raising his head, he gave them what he hoped was a reassuring wave.

After a minute he struggled to his feet. He stretched out his arms, and though the left side of his head still ached and throbbed, he was relieved to see that his fingers worked easily and naturally again. He stood on one foot and had no trouble with his balance.

Streetlamps had already been lit along the broad embankment here, and as he began walking back eastward he watched for stairs up to the street, shivering in his clinging wet clothes.

The vision he'd had of Cybele was already retreating in his mind, too far beyond comprehension to consider; and he told himself that it might well have been a hallucination brought on by the heavy aromatic fumes. But again and again, incredulously, he reviewed his vivid memory of seeing Vivi swimming with evident strength toward the embankment, well east of where he was now. Her nameless *sauteur* parasite might still have been occupying her body, but even so—

And then Adrien Achard's words came back to him: *We've learned things from Indian yogis to extend our various lives, near-total control of our bodily energies and processes! Many of us can go without sleep for a week, slow the heartbeat to a virtual standstill, run flat-out for a mile without getting out of breath.*

Nolan was sure now that the parasitic personality had caused Vivi's body to mimic death, just long enough for the Cybeline priestesses to consign the in fact still-living body to the river. The question that tormented Nolan now was how he might find Vivi. Would the parasite have kept control? If so, Vivi's body might be anywhere now on the Right Bank—possibly on the way to find Adrien Achard, who would surely complete the parasite's possession of Vivi's body. Nolan nearly groaned aloud at the thought.

But if Vivi had managed to regain control, would she be on this long embankment somewhere, watching to see if Nolan had followed her?

He had just begun to hurry east along the embankment, peering ahead for a sight of her—he was achingly cold, but he had walked for miles in wet clothes during the war—when a low, dark shape darted in front of him.

He sidestepped it, and it snagged on the right cuff of his wet trousers. He stopped and didn't try to kick the obstacle away, and when he looked down he was not very surprised to see a black cat staring up at him. Its eyes glowed gold in the radiance of a nearby streetlamp.

"Marechal?" he said. Then, "Take me to her."

The cat scampered in the other direction, west along the embankment, and—hoping he wasn't simply chasing a stray cat—Nolan wearily began running after it.

After a dozen fast paces, Nolan settled into the jog that he remembered as "double time" from his Army days, and the cat accommodatingly slowed its bounding progress to a trot. Nolan was panting, but he was able to keep the cat in sight from one cone of lamplight to the next. Across the dark water to his left, the mundane glows of windows on the Île Saint-Louis moved past his view like the lights of a slow-moving ship.

The exercise of jogging at double time was at least taking the sting out of the twilight chill in his wet shirt. Nolan wondered again if the parasite might still be in control of Vivi's abused body, and he hoped, even prayed to Cybele that, if so, he was taking it easy with her.

The cat led him for several hundred yards west along the embankment lane, under the arch of a bridge Nolan didn't remember the name of, and then up a ramp and onto another bridge that he was sure was the Pont Louis-Philippe. He and the cat made their steady way across it to a short street that transected the narrow downstream end of the Île Saint-Louis, and Nolan had to halt, wheezing, and sit down at a table outside a sparsely populated café. A concussion, the swim, and this run had taken a toll.

"Cat!" he called weakly. "Marechal! Give me a—damn—minute!" It would do Vivi no good for him to have a stroke or a heart attack here. Seven years ago he had kept up the double-time pace for much longer than these past minutes, but that, he thought, was many packs of cigarettes ago.

He looked up at the surrounding rooftops as he worked his aching lungs. It had been at the other end of this island, a mile east of where he sat, that he and Vivi had found themselves in the temple of Cybele. He waved off a waiter now, and wondered how long the temple had remained accessible there, and what response the priestesses of Cybele might have to Vivi's unexpected escape.

A black cat, probably the one he had been following, landed on the table in front of him, and only by jerking his head back did Nolan escape a slash across his nose.

"I'm up, I'm up," he said hoarsely as he got to his feet. If I'm beat, he thought, Vivi is probably worse. The cat jumped down from the table, and Nolan began running after it with renewed desperation.

He swiped a damp shirt cuff across his eyes to see what was ahead. Another bridge, a short one, over the strait between the two islands, and when they had crossed it he and the cat were hurrying down the Rue du Cloître-Notre-Dame on the Île de la Cité. The moon was already bright in the darkened sky, and ahead and to the left the flying buttresses of the Notre Dame cathedral stood out like a giant's rib cage.

Trying to keep his eyes fixed on the cat galloping tirelessly a dozen yards ahead of him, Nolan was soon dimly aware of passing the cathedral's tall stained-glass windows, and a quick upward glance showed him the row of towering vertical buttresses and pinnacles. The north tower loomed ahead.

Twenty more fast pounding steps took him past the corner of the tower, but the cat had disappeared among the pedestrians and spottily lit vendors' carts in the open square in front of the cathedral.

Nolan sat down against the tower wall, gasping. The cat had led him here, surely with a purpose, and then vanished. Was Vivi in the cathedral?

He made himself stand up, though his legs were trembling, and he limped to the high recessed arch of the north entrance. By the glow of streetlamps across the square, he could dimly see the intricate carvings in the upper reaches of the arch, and he shuffled under a high row of stone saints into the church.

The only light inside was the muted radiance of moonlight through high stained glass and a red pinpoint up at the remote east end of the nave—probably the candle on the altar indicating that the Eucharist was in the tabernacle. He looked up, but couldn't even see the arches of the triforium gallery far overhead, much less the vaulted ceiling above that. If there were other people in here—in the pews, in the confessionals?—he had no hope of seeing them.

Could Vivi have come in here to pray? He recalled her saying, *I've wished I could be Catholic, but the Church is wrong about reincarnation. They says it can't happen, but ah—I know it does.* Well, she couldn't be sure of that anymore.

He stood there, six steps into the church, for a full minute, peering vainly into the darkness, before he heard a faint sound to his left; it seemed to echo. He groped in that direction, and by the filtered moonlight he was now dimly able to see the outline of an open doorway in the stone wall.

Nolan shuffled carefully to the doorway and peered through it into complete blackness. When he edged inside, his damp shoe struck a stone step; when he lifted it he felt another. His right hand trailed along an unseen iron banister as he slowly ascended what he could feel to be a tight spiral staircase. Wind whistled through some opening in the shaft far overhead.

Nolan's knees stung as he climbed each wedge-shaped stone step, and the noise of his breath rebounded from the close, curved wall at his right. He was ready to sit down on one of the steps when he heard the unmistakable shuffling of shoes above him—descending. Moments later, the stones of the wall were dimly visible in reflected yellow light. The glow bobbed irregularly, and he guessed that the person coming down the stairs was holding a flashlight. He leaned against the central column and peered around it at the stairs mounting in front of him. He tried, with little success, to breathe more quietly.

The steps from above had got louder but now halted, and the beam of the flashlight was directly on the wall to his right. Vivi's voice, very close, said, "The fellow from the Cybeline temple, no?"

After a pause, Nolan answered, "Yes."

The flashlight rounded the pillar and shone in his face. Nolan held up his hand to block the beam; in the ambient glow he could just see the figure of Vivi behind the flashlight.

The flashlight beam swept down Nolan's body, and in the reflected light he was able to see her more clearly. Her cap and coat had been left in the Cybeline temple, and she was now wearing a different woolen coat, long and dark, over her white blouse. A strip of cloth covered her forehead, and her right hand, touching the central pillar, had a new bleeding cut across the knuckles.

Her voice said, "I think you will not oppose me."

For a moment Nolan panicked, thinking he had forgotten the musical phrase she had whistled last night; but in fact it was fresh in his memory, and he drew in as deep a breath as he could, licked his dry lips, and quickly whistled the six notes. They echoed up and down the stairwell, and the flashlight dropped as Vivi collapsed.

Nolan threw himself forward, and his knees knocked against a step as he caught her. The flashlight, still on, had rolled one step down and stopped, and for several seconds Nolan just breathed quickly through clenched teeth until the razory pain in his knees subsided to a bearable intensity.

Vivi's head was against his shoulder, his hands across her back. He looked down at her pale young face, underlit by the dropped flashlight. The white cloth bandage, spotted with blood over her forehead, was wrapped around her head above her ears and eyebrows, and her pale hair was a tangled thatch above it.

She opened her eyes.

"Harry," she said. She shifted in his arms, and they both winced. Her blood-streaked right hand floated up to touch the bandage on her head. "Are we dying here?" Her hand dropped. "Where's here?"

"I think we're not. Dying." He freed one hand and reached down to pick up the flashlight. "Look at me," he said, and when she turned her face to him he shone the flashlight beam on the close wall behind him. He peered at her pupils in the reflected light, and was relieved to see that they were normally wide for this dim light, and the same size.

"Where's here?" she repeated.

He swept the flashlight bean around at the steps and the curved stone wall. "We're in a stairwell in the north tower of Notre Dame."

"On the Quai de Passy," said Vivi softly.

"No," said Nolan, alarmed again about her likely concussion, "the cathedral is—"

"Oh, Harry, my head hurts! I know where the cathedral is. But that's the last thing I remember saying to that priestess in the temple: on the Quai de Passy. Telling her where my parasite was shot." She shook her head. "How long ago was that?"

"I don't know. An hour, hour and a half?"

"What... *happened*?"

Nolan sighed, then recounted her apparent self-inflicted death in the temple—along with his conclusions about *sauteur* breath-and-heartbeat control—and the ceremonial consigning of her body to the river, and their separate swims to shore. "I jumped in after you, but you were swimming like a champion, and one of them had near knocked me out with my gun." He shrugged. "I was just too damn dizzy to catch up with you. I got ashore with no idea where you were—or who you were. But then Marechal, or another just like him, led me here."

Vivi reached up to grip the fabric of his damp shirt. "Harry," she whispered, "did you see her too? The goddess?"

"Yes—though I looked away at the last moment. Unless that was a hallucination...?"

"Hush." She released his shirt. "You know it wasn't. She's real." Nolan felt her shiver. "I'm glad we got to see her—and I hope we never see her again."

Nolan nodded. "It sounded as if even Kirenli only saw her once. At her own consecration, I suppose."

"It's a different world, isn't it, with... gods?"

"I'm afraid it is."

He felt Vivi tense in his arms then; and he knew that both of them had had the same thought: if Cybele was actually a real, huge, powerful entity—and not just an abstract force, like gravity—then Moloch probably was too.

"We were just in a pagan temple," Vivi said. "I'm glad we've wound up in a Catholic church."

She sat back against the central column, and Nolan winced in sympathy. "How's your back?" he asked. She gave him a blank look, and he said, "One of those women cut you. We should get it looked at."

"My back? No strain. My *head* feels like somebody drove a nail into it." Vivi looked over her shoulder, at the ascending stairs. "An hour and a half. Kirenli was really going to kill me?"

Nolan rolled to the side, his back against the close wall, and rubbed his knees. "I'm afraid so."

She shook her head. "I thought we had found a friend." She scratched under the bandage on her head, then dropped her hand. "Did you whistle that Scriabin bit, just now?"

"Yes. Lucky I had the breath for it."

Vivi peered at him. "Where's your gun?"

"Back at that damned temple."

"Huh. After we bought all those bullets for it." She stretched out her left arm, and her tattoo was visible on her wrist. "My watch too. Beltran gave it to me."

Nolan nodded. "My mother gave me that pistol."

"She did not! Really?"

"Just before she died. She said, 'Here, son,' and pitched over."

"Harry!"

He waved and shook his head.

"You liar!" But she coughed out one syllable of a weak laugh.

After a few seconds she sighed and peered around in the glow of the flashlight. "It seems I was coming down the stairs," she said. She flexed her fingers. "And this cut on my hand looks very fresh. I wonder what business my parasite had up in the bell tower."

Nolan was reassured to hear no sounds from above. He shifted and thought about getting to his feet. "Does that stove in your flat work?"

She stretched, then pinched the woolen fabric of the coat she was wearing. "I wonder where he got this." She looked up. "Yes, the stove works, and it'll be nice to get there and get it lit." She stood up, bracing herself on the central pillar. "But I'd like to know what he was doing here."

Nolan closed his eyes for a moment. "You're sure he won't come back on?"

"No, I'm not." She took two steps up the winding stairwell, then looked back. "Thanks for ... restoring me just now. You can go to my flat, and wait for me."

"Don't be ridiculous. We shook hands, remember?" He struggled upright, took a deep breath, and followed her up the stairs. He let the iron banister take a good deal of his weight, while his left hand was braced on the central pillar. Vivi too was content to take the steps slowly.

CHAPTER TEN:
You Should Go to Confession

There were more than three hundred steps in the tightly curled stairwell. Nolan and Vivi kept listening for footsteps from above, but heard only wind through some opening higher up. Eventually they came to the source of it, a barred casement overlooking the moonlit rooftops of Paris. They paused on the steps there to sit down and rest, and Vivi peered out through the bars, inhaling the cold evening air.

"I won't let him have me," she said softly.

"*We* won't let him," Nolan agreed, though he saw no way yet to prevent it.

"Just before I found myself here, I remember asking Kirenli if there really was no way to stop him, and she said... *Nothing you could have any remote chance of doing, child.*"

Nolan cocked his head. "She did say that, didn't she?"

"And! Before that, she said there's *virtually* no way. That's not the same as *absolutely*. So... there must *be* a way, you see, Harry? Something that *could* be done, but which she was sure I have no hope of doing." She turned to him, and her eyes gleamed in a slant of moonlight.

Nolan shifted on the chilly stone step. He was exhausted and cold, but he said, "You're right." And he managed to add, "It may be that she underestimates us."

She clasped his hand. "Thank you for *us,* Harry. Us and the *matagots.*"

"Yes." Nolan thought of the black cat that had led him here. "Gertrude Stein's friend Alice said they see past fate."

"Right! Kirenli may want me dead, but the Lion of Cybele hasn't abandoned us." She peered up the stairwell. "We must be nearly at... someplace."

They got to their feet and resumed climbing the interminable steps.

"Some time I want to take a look at your back," Nolan said over his shoulder.

She managed a breathless laugh. "Remember Saint Genevieve."

"Oh for God's sake..." But he was cautiously reassured that the slash he recalled didn't seem to be troubling her. Still, medical attention soon.

At last they stepped out through an open doorway into gusty open air under the night sky. The moon was bright, and Nolan switched off the flashlight.

They were on a narrow gallery overlooking the Seine. The south bell tower loomed ahead of them, and weathered stone gargoyles crouched on the parapet, staring out and down. Nolan and Vivi peered around among the moon shadows, but saw no one.

Vivi leaned on the parapet, looking out at the Seine and, beyond it, the moving paired pinpoints of automobile headlights on the streets of the Left Bank.

"He's been up here before," she said. "I've had his dream memories of this view, by daylight."

Nolan was shivering in his still-damp clothes and anxious to get back down to street level. "Maybe he just liked Gothic architecture," he said, loudly enough to be heard over the wind between the two bell towers.

Vivi shook her head. "He must have rushed to get here tonight..."

The eroded stone face of a gargoyle beside Nolan's elbow was suddenly clearly lit, and Nolan spun to see that an unnoticed door in the recesses of the stairhead had swung open, spilling lamplight across the gallery paving.

Nolan and Vivi both took a pace back as the silhouette of a wild-haired man in a long coat stepped out of the doorway.

Vivi was behind Nolan, and when the man had moved out enough for the moonlight to show a face under a mane of white hair, his expression was irritated and cautious, but when he looked past Nolan he scowled and stepped back. He barked an angry sentence in Spanish.

"*En Inglese,*" said Vivi.

"*Inglés ahora?*" The old man spat and went on, "This *ruffian*, you had him in reserve? Will you have him to kill me? Conjure my ghost, even, it will tell you nothing." He reached into the pocket of his coat and, after some effort, pulled out a folding knife, and opened the four-inch blade.

"I'm not him!" said Vivi loudly. She slapped her chest. "I'm a girl, the girl he was ... inhabiting!"

Nolan nodded quickly. "It's true—the body is the same, but she is *not* the person who was up here a little while ago!"

The old man moved back to the doorway. He glared at both of his visitors for several breaths, then said, "Come forward, girl if you be."

Vivi sidled around Nolan, into the light, and said, "Do you know about—have you heard of the *sauteurs*? My name is Genevieve Chastain. I don't know the name of the man who was in possession of me a little while ago." She sneezed. "And I'm not insane."

"Ah?" The old man peered at her. "Not that man? You say so!" He rocked on his heels for several seconds, then asked, "Who then is... Charlie Chaplin?"

In spite of her coat, Vivi too was shivering in the wind. "The most famous cinema actor in the world," she said.

"Huh. And what is *Le Canard Enchaîné*?"

Nolan could only translate the phrase as *The Chained Duck,* but Vivi answered, "A newspaper."

Chaplin had certainly become widely known only after 1910, when Vivi's parasite had been killed, and Nolan assumed the newspaper had started after that date.

The old man cocked his head and eyed Vivi suspiciously. "Maybe you are as you say." He waved his knife. "But I'll cut you again if you start on being him."

"No no," said Nolan hastily, "I chased him out of her on the stairs, and I can do it again."

"*Ah, verdad?*" said the old man. "*Seguro?*" He peered at Vivi's face. "*Somrie.*"

She just shivered and blinked at the old man. "Smile? At what?"

"Anything, *chica.*" He waved at the gargoyles. "Smile because my monsters cannot move, but you can. Smile because you are alive at this moment. Smile to show you are not afraid."

"I'll smile because I am afraid," Vivi said, and she gave the old man a trembling grin that reminded Nolan of the glimpse Elodie had shown him in the river, of Vivi as a young girl—uncertain, but ready to meet what might come.

"Ah," said the old man. He relaxed, and there was sympathy in his voice. "That is not a smile *he* could make. Come inside, both of you two." He stepped back to the head of the stairs and waved toward the open doorway. "I think you need a shelter, and brandy."

Nolan and Vivi glanced at each other hesitantly, then followed him into a little room walled on three sides with variously sized wooden cabinets and drawers, lit by an oil lamp hung from the ceiling. A sink and several cluttered shelves and a narrow door occupied the remaining wall, and on the floor was a box full of picture postcards of the cathedral. Two chairs sat beside a small table on a patch of carpet, and the old man waved toward them.

"Even just the stairs," he allowed, "never mind what else efforts of yours, this night."

Nolan and Vivi pulled the chairs out and sat down. Nolan set the flashlight upright on the table. A smell of hot metal proved to be emanating from a little kerosene heater glowing in one corner of the room, and Nolan and Vivi both slid their chairs closer to it.

Vivi looked at the bloody cut on the back of her hand, then at the old man's knife, which he hastily set down on the table beside a couple of chipped ceramic mugs. "Who are you?" she asked.

"I am Fernand Beaufroy, miss, dealer in postcards for tourists... and," he added with a wave at the surrounding cabinets, "sometimes relics." A bottle of Monnet cognac stood on one of the shelves over the sink, and he pulled the cork out of it and set it on the table. "Drink," he said. At an apparent afterthought, he pulled a handkerchief out of a pocket and held it toward Vivi. "I defended myself, when I cut your hand," he said. "Put brandy on this, for a bandage."

After a moment's hesitation, Vivi took the handkerchief, liberally splashed some brandy on it, and wrapped it around her hand. She made a fist and winced briefly, then handed the bottle to Nolan.

Nolan looked around the cramped room. He shrugged and poured brandy into the two mugs and pushed one toward her.

Vivi looked up at Beaufroy. "What did my parasite want here, with you?"

The old man grinned. "*Parasite!* Heh-heh. You know you are not him, reborn?"

"Yes." Vivi picked up her mug with her unencumbered right hand and took a long sip of brandy. "Whew! *Merci!* He died in 1910, but I was born in 1906. Who is he?"

Beaufroy picked up the bottle and had a drink from the neck of it. "Old days he would come here, tall and moustache, to bring me bones. Today he wants to know where is *his* finger bone, or maybe his skull, if it was saved in one of the many repositories. He thinks he will put blood from you on his skull, and finish, complete, him becoming you."

Vivi choked and spat some brandy back into her mug. "Would that *work*?"

Beaufroy shrugged. "Who can say? They have always a connection with their lately bones, or the old finger joints would not point to the new body."

Vivi took another mouthful of the brandy, and swallowed it. "Who *is* he?"

Beaufroy set the bottle down and turned toward the shelves. "I do not speak his name to you," he muttered, fumbling around among the bottles and boxes, "lest it wake him." When he faced Nolan and Vivi again he was holding a pencil and a scrap of paper. He leaned down over the table and carefully wrote: THIBAUD CADIEUX.

He dropped the pencil and straightened; then, seeing blank looks on the faces of his two visitors, he said impatiently, "Before he died in 1910? Shot with a gun? He was in the National Assembly, and wealthy, as a *sauteur*. He bought many artworks, paintings—Pablo Picasso is rich, now, from him. But"—he shook his head gravely—"God for him was Moloch."

"That's the god of all the *sauteurs*," Vivi said.

"Such bad worshippers they are! No child is killed—not the same to Carthage in the past days. Now they cheat the god. With stealing the god's power, when they die—they find a child near the lines crossing at the Louvre, and then they take it as their own, not kill it! And Moloch goes hungry for the...the—" Beaufroy waved his hands helplessly.

"The burst of life-energy," said Vivi somberly, "that's released when a child's soul is forcibly split from its killed body." She was exactly quoting what Kirenli had said in Cybele's temple.

"Ah!" said Beaufroy, "you know! But this man"—he bent to tap the name he had written—"his want is to bring back the old way, very much. See? Burning the children again."

"Good God," whispered Nolan, remembering the movie *Cabiria*. Both he and Vivi eyed their host with ill-concealed horror.

Vivi tipped up her mug to get the last of the brandy, then clanked it down. "Why did," she asked, with a nod toward the paper, "*he* imagine that you would know where his bones are?"

"I have no tattoo," the man said. "I am...not yes and not no, you see? They pay me to be one who holds: copies of records, in case of floods or fires, yes sometimes, in the *carriéres*. And," he added with a wave toward a dozen little wooden drawers in the wall beside him, "finger bones, for those which die abroad, or do not trust the repositories. There is among the *sauteurs* sometimes jealousy and... pilfering, down there in *les carriéres*! But atop this holy place they are not happy to stay long, or be getting attentions of maybe the true God. Moloch and his creatures have *révulsion* to Christianity."

Vivi and Nolan both looked at the rows of little wooden drawers, then looked away. Vivi gingerly slid her hands into the pockets of the coat she had found herself wearing, and sighed in relief to pull her hands out empty.

"You didn't give him his finger bone," she said.

"I threw it in the river in 1910, when I read of his death. And I don't tell him where is kept his skull."

Vivi cleared her throat and said, "But you do know where his skull is."

"I am not yes or no, in this...*activity*...but I see I am no for burning the children. Push them out—bad, yes, but already done, by the time, and none are killed! Okay, they go to Heaven. But *burn* them out? Kill them?—no. Already Cybele is come to Paris, angry. This man in you gets no help from me."

Vivi's hands on the table were fists. "You said the *sauteurs* still have a connection with their old bones. Very well, then—I need to find his skull, and destroy it. That might banish him from me, since his finger bone is already in the river! I need a map."

"Hoo-hoo! You need a...army of Carthusian priests! There are devils loose in the eastern tunnels of *les carriéres*, since digging for the Exhibition. You know the *Shaydim*? No? Ach, Moloch has not sat quiet, being robbed of his due these years."

"A map," persisted Vivi.

"You get up," said Beaufroy to Nolan, "you are rested. I sit now." When Nolan had got to his feet, suppressing a wince at the pains in his knees, the old man sat down in the chair. Nolan took the opportunity to move closer to the little heater.

To Vivi, Beaufroy said, "You would die in *les carriéres*. Yes, that's where the skulls of the *sauteurs* are kept, on shelves in the repositories. But you go there? Hah! At best starve, you, in the miles and miles of tunnel! Water everywhere, no light! And the *Shaydim* are broken out from the salt walls of *sauteur* making."

"A map," Vivi repeated again, as firmly as before.

Beaufroy sighed and picked up Nolan's mug. "You are lost even with a map—and I would not write it on paper for you, because he"—he touched the name he had written—"will come awake and see it." He drank the rest of Nolan's brandy.

Nolan leaned on a cabinet and looked down at Vivi. Her handkerchief-bound left hand was tightly clasping her right; and he knew Thibaud Cadieux would take her again soon, and very possibly forever, if he wasn't exorcised.

They have always a connection with their lately bones. And according to Kirenli, the skull was a better direction-finding compass than a finger bone, having once held the *sauteur's* mind. Destroying Cadieux's skull—burning it, grinding it to powder, and sifting it into the Seine—did seem like the only possible way to drive his spirit away and let Vivi live securely in her own body.

"I'm good at taking directions," he said gruffly. "Tell me where to go, how to find the skull." To Vivi he added, "Don't let me forget the flashlight."

Vivi's eyes were wide as she looked up at him.

"We shook hands on it," he reminded her. "I can't be there at every moment to whistle, so..." He was already beginning to wonder what he was agreeing to this time, but went on resolutely, "Let's go stomp this fellow's skull."

"I tell you nothing," said Beaufroy. "If she even could find the certain repository—which not—being close to that man's skull would wake him up in her."

"He's likely to wake up in any case," said Nolan. "But I drove him out of her on the stairs here. I can do it again."

"And," said Vivi hesitantly, "I'm a priestess of Cybele."

Beaufroy smiled at her. "You heard me say that name."

"Today in a courtyard in the Ménilmontant district," Vivi said, "at the *apaches' rosalia* festival, we went among them in the name of *le Lion de Cybele*, and they did not kill us. You understand? We told an old woman there—a priestess?—that Harry and I knew why the *jalon* bell was rung, and that we know how to kill the Moloch bull. She sent us on a boat to the temple of Cybele, which appeared for us on the Île Saint-Louis."

"Kill the Moloch bull," said Beaufroy flatly. He tried to drink from Nolan's empty mug, then set it down gently. "If this is not a lie, tell me what you saw there."

Vivi refilled her own mug, then told him about the geographically anomalous grove of pines, and the temple, and Kirenli. She described the wild music and dancing, and the apparent transformation of the attendant women, and the baptism with bull blood that had accomplished her consecration to the goddess. And she tried to convey some impression of the vision of Cybele, though her voice trembled as she described it. "After that," she went on more steadily, "Kirenli asked me about *him*." And she pointed at the name on the paper.

She shivered, picked up her mug, and took a deep sip. "After that point I knew nothing until Harry here, as he said, drove *that one* out of me on these stairs here."

Beaufroy cocked his head, staring at her. After a pause, he said, "Consecrate you, so quick? Ah, they knew he was in you." When Vivi nodded, he went on, "Yes, they want to drown you in the river to snuff *his* step-by-step life—for that to be legal in their way, they did make you into one of them." He spread his hands. "But you see you are not dead."

"They *believed* she died," Nolan said, "but *he* knew how to mimic death—when they put her in the river, he revived and swam away. Otherwise—yes, they would have killed her."

"My sisterhood." Vivi looked around, seeming to look through the close walls at all of Paris. "Who are my allies?" she whispered. She turned to Nolan. "I have you, thank God."

Nolan nodded. "And the cats. And I think Gertrude Stein and her friend."

Vivi sat back and touched the cut on her throat where the bullet had grazed her last night. From where he stood, Nolan couldn't see the smaller cut from the Cybele priestess's knife. "And nevertheless," she said, "I *am* now a priestess of Cybele."

Beaufroy stared at her, then rolled his head around and stared at her some more. "Hah!" he said finally. "A priestess of Cybele in my house!"

"So will you tell a priestess of Cybele," asked Nolan, "how to find that man's skull?"

Beaufroy sat back and rocked one hand in the air. "Maybe you *don't* die down there, much."

Neither Nolan nor Vivi spoke.

At last Beaufroy turned to Nolan. "So listen." He sighed and got back to his feet. "*Les carriéres*, the catacombs, are under all of Paris, nearly, left and right of the river." He stepped to a cabinet. "But the most *sauteurs* passages are around under the Jardin du Luxembourg. Many chambers for skulls and bones! That man's skull in in a repository under Boul' Raspail, near Boul' Montparnasse." He gave Nolan a sharp look. "They tell me the *Shaydim* are not yet east of under Rue de Sèvres, still near the Exhibition, so you must stay east of there. I will *tell* you a map, the turns and signs of the way to that chamber."

He opened a drawer and stirred the faintly rattling contents with a finger; then picked out a handful of little objects and turned to Nolan. "Here," he said, bending to lay four angular tan bones on the table. They were each about an inch long, and Nolan realized that they must be human finger bones.

"Take these with you," said Beaufroy. "Two for each of you. They are of four *sauteurs*, and might confuse the bad *magi* who are kept down there. They see very much, and if you are close they can hear your thinking, and pick through your lately memories like children who find box of toys."

He picked up the depleted brandy bottle again. "Still, I think you will die. The bad *magi* also put things in, put sights in your eyes." He waved his free hand toward the floor. "You should go to Confession before."

"How do we get down into the catacombs?" Nolan asked. "Stairs, a drainage pipe, a hole in the street?"

"In these days?" Beaufroy frowned at him. "The entrances change, with building and roadwork and collapses. Many years since I have been, for records. You say Gertrude Stein is an *ally* of you? She can tell you. But I will now say where you go, when you are down in *les carriéres*." Stepping to a shelf, he pulled down one of a dozen big leather-bound volumes. He sat down and opened it, and after riffling through the pages he tapped a particular inked entry.

"Here he is. Skull number one-forty-seven. So listen now..."

PART THREE:
Cybele in the Underworld

CHAPTER ELEVEN:
Speak of the Devil

"My money was left at the temple in my cap," Vivi said as the cab clopped away behind them. Her voice was hoarse, but willfully steady.

"Lucky I was able to peel off a couple of bills." Nolan carefully tucked the rest of his sodden bankroll back into his pocket.

The cab had dropped them off on the street just north of Gertrude Stein's studio on the Rue de Fleurus, and Vivi and Nolan now made their way down a shadowed walk between two buildings to the alley behind Stein's studio. Nolan had tucked the flashlight behind his belt, wishing it was his lost pistol instead.

"Around the Luxembourg Gardens," whispered Vivi, "down Boul' Raspail to Boul' Montparnasse—the catacombs are right under us."

Nolan resisted an impulse to stamp on the pavement. "I want to ask her about this word *Shaydim*," he said quietly. "The old man in the belfry said they've broken out of... salt walls of...?"

"'Of *sauteur* making.' Yes." Vivi paused to cough. "Picasso's devils in *les carriéres*."

She and Nolan edged around Gertrude Stein's automobile and walked up to the back door of her flat. Nolan exhaled and knocked on it.

A moment later it was swung open, releasing a puff of warm air that carried the aroma of chicken chow mein. Nolan recognized Alice Toklas's silhouette in the doorway.

"Well, speak of the devil," she said. "Come in, fugitives."

They shuffled into a hall with a closed door on either side, and as

Toklas pulled the back door shut behind them they walked into the big studio room.

Gertrude Stein was sitting on the couch below her portrait, and Ernest Hemingway was getting to his feet. Nolan thought he looked startled, and not happy with these intruders in an ongoing conversation. He was wearing the same tan sweater that he'd had on yesterday, and in the glare of the several electric lamps his firm jaw and moustache made him look older than he had then. Plates and glasses stood on a couple of nearby tables.

"Good God, child," said Toklas from behind them, "what's happened to you now?" She took Vivi's elbow and steered her to a chair.

"She knocked her head," said Nolan, and when Toklas had pushed Vivi into the chair, he presumed to sit down in the one next to it. He set the flashlight on the floor, and noticed spots of dried blood on the carpet from when Vivi had sat there the night before.

Toklas was carefully unwinding the blood-spotted cloth from around Vivi's head. "Who was it that thought this was an adequate bandage?"

"Thibaud Cadieux," said Vivi. Nolan tensed, ready to whistle the Scriabin notes, but Vivi's expression didn't change.

Toklas nodded, clearly humoring her, and Hemingway and Stein only looked concerned. "Check for concussion," Hemingway said.

"Of course," said Toklas, tipping Vivi's chin back to look into her eyes.

"When did the injury happen?" asked Hemingway.

Vivi couldn't readily open her mouth, so Nolan said, "Maybe three hours ago."

Hemingway gave him a sharp look. "And where were *you*?"

Nolan leaned back and rubbed his eyes. "Sitting right next to her," he said on a long exhalation, "in the temple of Cybele on the Île Saint-Louis." He inhaled and went on, with weary defiance, "And it was Thibaud Cadieux who gave her the blow on the head."

Hemingway shook his head, frowning. "Who do you mean?"

Recalling Hemingway's skeptical disdain yesterday at the Closerie des Lilas, Nolan let go of caution and, though his eyes stung with exhaustion, gave him a direct, unblinking stare. "He was a member of the National Assembly, we're told. And an art collector who made Picasso rich."

Gertrude Stein had stood up and now tried to speak, but the much taller Hemingway waved her back.

"Uh-huh," he said. "And he's been dead since before the war."

"Intermittently," Nolan agreed.

Vivi had twisted her head free of Toklas's hand and looked at Stein. "Do you trust this fellow?"

Stein ran the fingers of one hand over her short-cropped gray hair. Her eyes were brightly alert in her round, wrinkled face. "Yes," she said. "He won't write an article about this." Hemingway shook his head in irritable agreement. Stein went on, "Vivi, right? We've been worried about you ever since you ran away from Picasso's studio last night—"

"1910," interrupted Alice Toklas. "Cadieux was fatally shot in 1910. You said you were born in 1906."

For several seconds nobody spoke. Hemingway looked simply baffled by Toklas's remark, and Stein was shaking her head.

Toklas looked up at Stein. "What is the answer?"

Stein raised her hands and let them drop. "There is no answer."

"Then there is no question," said Toklas.

Nolan recalled that they had said the same three lines the previous night. He was sure now that it was some sort of ritual exchange, and he thought of Catholics making the sign of the cross.

For several seconds no one spoke.

Nolan broke the silence: "She's also got a knife-slash on the back of her right shoulder."

Stein looked from Nolan to Vivi and back. "What *have* you been doing?"

Toklas straightened up and took Vivi's left hand, then saw the dried blood on it. "Ach! Cadieux can't have done all this to you! Come with me."

Vivi stood up, and Toklas led her back down the hall to one of the rooms they had passed. Nolan heard an interior door open and close.

"She'll want another first-aid kit," Stein said, stepping toward the kitchen. She looked back at Nolan and asked, "And stitches?" Seeing his doubtful expression, she added, "I studied at Johns Hopkins School of Medicine—and Alice and I have both assisted in surgeries, during the war."

"Yes," Nolan said, recalling the slash in Vivi's back, "stitches. And lots of Acriflavine." It was the disinfectant the Army had used during the war. And I'll have to keep her sitting still for a few days, he told himself, somehow.

Stein disappeared into the kitchen, and Hemingway sat down on the couch below her portrait.

"Intermittently?" he said; before Nolan could answer he went on, "For an American soldier, you don't seem to take very good care of your girl."

My girl, Nolan thought. "I could have done better," he said. He leaned back and closed his eyes. "At least she still *is*... my girl? She was almost someone else."

"Uh-huh." Almost diffidently, Hemingway asked, "No further word about my stolen manuscripts, I suppose."

"No. Sorry."

Stein came back into the room carrying another French military field dressing packet and a small metal case. She hurried past the two men and trotted down the hall. Again Nolan heard the door open and close.

"I sent you here," said Hemingway, "didn't I, yesterday? And Gertrude and Alice filled you in on the *sauteurs*, along with their mystical reincarnation bullshit." He smiled and picked up a glass from one of the tables. "I never heard of a temple of Cybele on the Île Saint-Louis."

Nolan managed to smile back. "I believe it's seldom there."

"Intermittent."

"Just so."

Toklas came bustling back into the room then, closely followed by Stein and Vivi. Hemingway got up off the couch. Vivi had shed her coat and there was a fresh and smaller bandage around her head, and a cotton pad was taped over the back of her left hand. She resumed her seat next to Nolan. Toklas or Stein had even made some attempt at brushing Vivi's blonde hair.

"You only imagined a cut on her back," Toklas said crossly to Nolan. "Her blouse is torn in half in the back, but her skin is intact."

Hemingway exhaled through pursed lips.

Nolan frowned and reviewed his memory. No, he had seen the long cut down her shoulder blade! He had seen the blood!

He looked at Vivi, who shrugged and shook her head. "I was gone, pushed out," she said apologetically. "In the Notre Dame stairwell you mentioned a cut, but I didn't feel anything."

Nolan was glad he was sitting down. "Is there blood on her blouse?" he asked, and even before Toklas shook her head he thought of Vivi's swim to the embankment through the cold water.

"But," Toklas allowed, "the girl says you got a concussion too. Show me where you were hit and tilt your head back so I can see your pupils."

Nolan complied, willing for the moment to let them all believe that a concussion had left him confused about Vivi's condition, but internally he was scrambling for an explanation. The injury to Vivi's *head* had not vanished, nor the cut on her hand from the old man on top of the cathedral—Bullfrog or whatever his name had been.

Toklas gently probed his scalp and cheek around his left ear, then stepped back. "No palpable fracture or bleeding from ear or nose, and your pupils look fine. Dizziness, nausea?"

"I was dizzy right afterward," he said, "swimming in the river. No nausea."

Hemingway looked as if he wanted to ask why Nolan had been swimming in the river, but Toklas spoke up.

"Likewise three hours ago, the injury?" When he nodded, she said, "Confusion and memory problems should pass." She sat down on the couch beside Stein. "Probably you'll live."

Nolan turned to Vivi and said, carefully, "How's the cut from the gunshot last night?"

She faced him and raised her chin. An angry red line showed where the bullet had grazed her, but the cut on the right side of her neck, where the Cybele priestess's knife had nicked her, was gone.

He sat back, nodding as if reassured.

Hemingway too was peering at Vivi's throat. *"Gunshot?"*

"We didn't tell you about that part yet," said Stein, settling herself back on the couch and tucking her skirt around her thighs. Nolan wasn't paying attention. So it was only the injuries from the knives of the Cybeline priestesses that had vanished. Vivi had been consecrated as one of those—and when they chose to end the life of one of their own, it was by chaining weights to the unfortunate sister and sinking her in the river, letting the deep water do the job and keep the body. Perhaps, as priestesses of Cybele, they were *incapable* of doing lasting damage to one another.

He recalled that the river water immediately around the temple had tasted uncharacteristically, startlingly fresh, though after a few yards of swimming it had had the usual faintly rancid flavor of an old city's river.

Toklas sat down beside Stein. "Cadieux was killed in 1910," she said again, "and you said you were born in 1906."

"It's not reincarnation," Vivi said. "The *sauteurs* are not reborn, they evict the souls of young children and take their bodies for their own. I was four years old when Thibaud Cadieux's soul took possession of me. Partial possession. I hope, with Harry's help—his selflessly generous help!—to free myself from Cadieux altogether."

Hemingway was frowning reprovingly at Nolan. Toklas was peering at Vivi, and Stein was staring at her, open-mouthed.

"I think," Stein said slowly, "this may be true. And I think Achard *would* have had to kill me, if I had accepted his offer, his veiled offer! As Pablo said, I'm too ... mundane? ... to accept the terms."

Hemingway opened his mouth, then waved away whatever he had intended to say or ask, and turned to Vivi. "So who shot you?"

"A *sauteur*," said Vivi. "A little girl—probably the same one Harry told you about yesterday."

"Vivi here shoved me out of the line of fire," said Nolan, "or the bullet would have hit me in the face."

Hemingway cocked his head to one side as if to see Vivi better.

She met his gaze and said, "They're desperate to erase every record or memory of the goddess-and-bull story in that article you wrote."

Hemingway nodded, then returned his attention to Stein. "And Adrien Achard now? *Kill* you? I wish someone would tell me what there was in that damned article..." He paused, staring at the wall to the left of Picasso's portrait of her. "But that's him, isn't it?"

Nolan followed his gaze to a pair of framed pictures that had not been there last night. One was his own drawing of Vivi, and the other, bigger, was a painting of a middle-aged, black-haired man wearing the double-bulbed black hat of a toreador, rendered like a mosaic in what must have been hundreds of little rectangles of variously colored pigments.

Stein shifted on the couch to look up at it. "Yes. Guillaume Cendrebénir painted it some twenty years ago. I moved it in here today."

"My God," said Vivi, standing up and stepping closer to the painting, "it *is* Beltran." Her voice was strained, tight with control. "Younger than when I knew him."

Hemingway was now staring at the charcoal drawing beside the painting. He tilted his head toward Vivi without looking away from the drawing. Hesitantly, he said, "I almost feel I know you, from this." At last he turned toward her. "Who did it?"

Vivi's attention was still fixed on the portrait of Beltran Iglesias. Hemingway touched her shoulder.

"Oh—Harry did," she said. "Yesterday."

Hemingway turned to look at Nolan. "You *do* care for her." He sounded apologetic.

"I try." Nolan stood up too.

Vivi stepped back from the painting. To Stein, she said, "We need to know how to get down into the catacombs. We were told that you would know a way."

"Hah!" exclaimed Toklas, and Stein said, "Told? By whom?"

"What was his name?" Nolan asked Vivi. "Not Bullfrog."

"Fernand Beaufroy," Vivi said. "He lives on the chimera gallery at Notre Dame cathedral."

"Beaufroy!" said Stein. "He must be a hundred years old. No, child, you'd only get lost and die down there. What would you hope to do?"

Vivi looked again at the portrait of Beltran Iglesias, as if for strength. "Cadieux wants to find out," she said in a carefully level tone, "where his vacated skull is, so that he can spill some of my blood on it. He thinks it would finally consummate his possession of me. He doesn't know where it is, though, and Beaufroy told us."

Hemingway had raised his eyebrows at this. "Good God," he said, "I hate to think what sort of novels you read!" He shook his head. "Anyway, Gertrude's right: skull or no skull, those catacombs are supposed to be a real labyrinth—hundreds of miles of them! You'd never find your way out again. But will somebody tell me what it is about my article that—"

"That got Claude Barbier killed," put in Nolan, "and the *Le Prosodie* office burned down, and got Vivi shot."

"Okay," said Hemingway, nodding. "What?"

"*He* told you how," said Vivi, pointing at the painting of Iglesias, "that is, he told you a *parable* about how to catch and kill Moloch."

"Moloch needs killing? I believe the Romans put an end to all that two thousand years ago."

"The *sauteurs* have called him back," Vivi retorted, "and Cadieux wanted—still wants, I'm sure"—she paused and took a deep breath—"to revive the old Carthaginian custom of actually killing the child-sacrifices, instead of just taking the children's bodies for themselves to possess."

Hemingway looked sternly at Nolan. "You keep her out of the catacombs, hear?"

Stein had for several seconds been staring past Nolan and Vivi, and now fixed her gaze on him. "A temple to Cybele, you said." She held up a hand to forestall remarks from Toklas and Hemingway. "She was the goddess opposed to Moloch, in the Punic Wars."

"That's right," Nolan began, but Vivi talked over him: "The *sauteurs* revived Moloch," she said, "and so Cybele came back too. Natural—or unnatural—counterweight. Equal and opposite reaction.

"And," she added, "the only crew in Paris that fits the mold of her worshippers now is the *apaches*!"

"*Korybantes*," put in Nolan, "according to the old woman we met in the Ménilmontant district."

"Who sent us to the temple of Cybele," Vivi continued, "which appeared at the upstream edge of the Île Saint-Louis."

"Yes," mused Stein, "it would be *Korybantes*, wouldn't it? Perverted and murderous now, in this century."

"But hunting *sauteurs*," Vivi said, "and killing them and quickly sinking them in the river, to stop the... the otherwise *migratory* soul. Saving the children from them."

Hemingway was listening with evident interest; possibly gathering material for a story, Nolan thought sourly.

"And killing very many others too," Toklas pointed out. "Amid savage rapes and robberies."

"I'm not defending them," said Vivi. "They came close to killing us, and would have, if I hadn't shouted, *par le Lion de Cybele*."

"Even then we got roughed up," said Nolan, "and both of us nearly got knifed." He turned to face Stein. "What are *Shaydim*? Both Picasso and Beaufroy said there are devils in the catacombs, and Beaufroy called them *Shaydim*."

Toklas answered him. "*Shaydim*? It's in the Book of Psalms in the *Tanakh*, the Old Testament, where they're associated with Moloch. The singular is *shayd*. They're Canaanite demons."

Nolan grimaced. "Why not. He said they've... what was it?"

"Broken from salt walls that the *sauteurs* made," Vivi said. "On account of excavations for the Exhibition."

Toklas stepped back. "Yes. Salt would make sense for barring spirits. Conquered cities used to be leveled and sowed with salt to keep the defeated ghosts at rest—and it would be like the Hebrew *cherem*, something banned, quarantined."

"Not quarantined anymore, evidently," said Nolan.

"And they're active," Vivi said, "because Moloch wants his...burnt offerings." She nodded toward Hemingway. "Which is why he needs to be killed."

Hemingway just frowned at her.

"Driven back, say," said Toklas. "Banished. You can't *kill* a god."

Stein looked up again at the portrait of Beltran Iglesias. "This makes sense—in a sense!—of things Pablo Picasso has told us."

She lowered her gaze, again looking past Nolan and Vivi. "The effigy of a child with a mirror face," she said, "to lure the winged bull..." She shook her head. "For Moloch to descend, again, materially, it would surely have to be in a Phoenician city, in a temple of his."

"There's nothing left of Carthage anymore," noted Toklas.

"They had cities in Spain," said Stein, "on the Mediterranean coast. There might still be the ruins of a Moloch temple."

Hemingway shifted his weight and rubbed a hand across his moustache.

Stein gave him an inquiring look.

"Out by Tarragona," he said gruffly. "About a hundred miles north of Valencia. Ruins of an old pre-Roman arena in a village near there, Sant Salvador. I've been there." He picked up a glass from one of the tables, then hesitated and put it down. He looked at Vivi. "On a wall of the old arena, not quite weathered away, there's that symbol you drew in my notebook—the horned head with three eyes."

"Tarragona," said Nolan. In the Cybeline temple, Kirenli had taken the word as the answer to her question, *And where is this to happen?*

He turned to Vivi. "Yesterday you said Iglesias was a bullfighter around there, in the—what was the word again?"

"*Capeas*," said Vivi and Hemingway together.

"Right," said Nolan. "The illegal village bullfights around the Mediterranean coast."

"Beltran Iglesias fought in those *capeas*." Vivi let her head roll back and yawned, from evident tension as much as from weariness. "I think the Cybeline priestesses would like to know about this ruined Moloch temple."

"If they don't already," said Nolan. "And even if you could find Cybele's temple again, they'd only kill you again."

"Uh," said Stein, "again?"

Vivi gave a shivering sigh. "They made me a priestess of Cybele," she said, "consecrated me to the goddess, so that they could kill me according to their rules. But I appeared to be dead already, and they just threw me in the river."

Hemingway muttered something but didn't comment.

Toklas sat back. "They actually made you a priestess?" she said softly.

"Yes." Vivi turned to Nolan. "And you and I are still fated to *do* something, remember?" She looked at Toklas. "The change in the timeline, and ringing the *jalon* bell? I think..." She was silent then, and nobody else spoke. "I think," Viv went on, "it might be important that I—oh, I'll tell you later, Harry." She fixed her bright hazel eyes on Stein. "So, how do we get into the catacombs? We'll go tomorrow morning."

"*Tomorrow?*" burst out Nolan. "*Morning?* You need a day's rest, at least"—he looked at Toklas—"after a concussion, right?" Turning back to Vivi he went on, "And how about recovering from plain exhaustion? Two days' rest, three! In bed! No, Vivi, you can't—"

"And you'd have been without supplies," put in Hemingway, with a dismissing wave. "Lights, water, a shotgun—"

Vivi rubbed her eyes. "I should wait a day?" She dropped her hands and looked at Nolan. "I *am* tired! So are you, I know. But rest? For two days, three, you think? No, *really* think! He had me for more than an hour this evening! What are the—bloody hell, what are the actual chances that he would not come on, during the day tomorrow? And he knows you have some way of forcing him back—he won't announce his arrival! He'll just kill you, while you still think I'm me."

For several seconds nobody spoke, though Hemingway was scowling.

At last Toklas said, "She's right, given her premises." To Vivi she said, "We can provide you with...a kerosene lantern, a couple of canteens of water...a couple of big tubes of titanium white pigment, to mark your way—unless Matisse took that box?"

Stein opened her mouth to protest, then just closed it and shook her head. It was clear to Nolan that Toklas was the unobtrusive real power in the two women's relationship.

"Thank you," said Vivi, lifting her head. "So how do we get down there?"

Stein looked away, but Toklas said, "Gertrude and I sometimes hid down there during the bombings. The entries appear and disappear, but there's one that will surely still be there."

Stein and Hemingway both protested, but Toklas quieted both of them with a sharp stare. "The entrance," she went on, "is in a church, the Église Saint-Jacques du Haut-Pas, off Rue Gay-Lussac..."

CHAPTER TWELVE:
I Had Not Thought Death Had Undone So Many

Vivi declined Stein's offer to let them stay the night at her studio, and so Stein insisted on driving them back to Vivi's flat across the river in the Marais district. At Vivi's request, Stein dropped the two of them off a couple of narrow streets from her place. After the Ford rattled away, Nolan hefted the rucksack Stein had given them and they made their careful way to the remembered alley and stairs and Vivi's cold room.

In addition to the rucksack and its heavy contents, Stein had insisted on loaning Nolan a tweed coat that was at once too roomy for him and too short in the sleeves. He didn't take it off even when Vivi had lit the gas jet and got the wood chips in the little stove burning and radiating heat.

Vivi sat on the bed as Nolan laid the rucksack against the wall. He carefully extricated his damp passport and banknotes from his trousers pocket, then crouched to separate the pieces of paper and arrange them on the floor near the stove. They were looking distinctly wilted.

At last he straightened, moved the armchair closer to the stove, and sank into it.

He closed his eyes. "As old Bullfrog said, smile because you're alive in this moment."

Vivi didn't smile, but touched her throat. "I had a cut here, from one of their knives, at that temple."

"Yes, you did."

"And I bet I did have a cut on my shoulder, like you said."

"It would have needed stitches."

"Miss Stein was ready for that." She peered across the small room at him. "You got a cut in your neck too. And it's still there."

"I'm," he said without opening his eyes, "not a priestess of Cybele."

"That's right, I am. What I was going to tell you back there—I must be unique among the goddess's priestesses. I'm—my body is virginal, but my mind is not—hasn't been since I was four years old. That could be important. I think Kirenli was too hasty in deciding to kill me."

Nolan was wondering how good a pillow Stein's coat would be. He peered blearily at Vivi in the dim gaslight. Huddled in the long coat Thibaud Cadieux had got somewhere, and with Toklas's bandage around her head, she looked especially young and frail. "How's that?" he asked.

"I'll free myself from Cadieux... but even after that, my mind's lock is broken. The door is ajar." Seeing Nolan's uncomprehending look, she said, clearly enunciating each word, "I can be occupied without the occupier committing the sin of breaking the lock."

"Huh. I don't think any would-be occupiers are likely to care about the *sin* of it."

"I think Kirenli would."

"Forget about her." He looked toward the open closet, trying to recall how many blankets Vivi had. "What did Hemingway say to you, when I was getting in the car?"

"He asked what time we'd be going to that church tomorrow morning."

Nolan yawned. "I guess he really does want to stop you going into the catacombs."

Vivi's voice was quiet: "And you too."

"He's got no objection to me going." He shifted in the chair to look at her. "Vivi." When she looked up, he said, "I should go alone. Beaufroy said your close proximity to the skull might bring *him* back up."

"And you said you could whistle him back down." From where she sat on the bed she glowered at him. "You don't think you might need help from a priestess of Cybele, down there? Harry, I *am* going. Even if you start without me, you couldn't stop me following you."

He met her fierce gaze, then looked away. She certainly *would* follow him, if it came to that. "Okay. Though I wish we were bringing a shotgun, like he said."

"Huh." She stood up. "We've got the things Miss Stein lent us, and that flashlight, and I've got a good British compass here that Elodie gave me." After a yawn she went on, "Are your clothes too damp to sleep in? I have an old flannel nightgown you could wear."

He suppressed a smile. "I'm all dried out now, thanks. And the stove is nice. But any spare blankets—or coats or towels or newspapers—would be welcome."

Alice Toklas had mentioned that the Church of Saint-Jacques du Haut-Pas had originally been outside the city walls, but over the centuries the city had expanded and engulfed it; and as Nolan looked up and down the extent of the Rue Saint-Jacques, he could believe it. The street, still in shadow under the clear early morning sky, was wide enough for only one automobile at a time, and no more than fifty feet of pavement separated the church's present Classical facade from the nineteenth-century apartment building that now crowded up on the other side. Above a couple of steps, four tall pillars framed the church's main doors, but Nolan pulled open a smaller door on the left side of the pillars.

Vivi came up the steps behind him, her unconfined pale hair tossing in the breeze. Under the long wool coat Cadieux had acquired yesterday, she was wearing her flannel shirt and twill trousers, with her British compass strapped to her belt beside Cadieux's flashlight.

Nolan, still wearing Stein's ill-fitting coat over his long-sleeved white shirt, readjusted on his shoulders the straps of the rucksack Stein had given them—olive-green canvas with stenciled French military markings.

When they stepped into the church and Nolan closed the door behind them, the previously unnoticed sounds of birds and wind and distant voices were shut out, and he and Vivi stood staring down the church's long central aisle to the tall altar, gleaming with gold even in the relative dimness. The still air carried hints of old incense. To their left was an iron table with stepped ranks of votive candles, one of which showed a flame, and in the stone wall beyond it was the door Toklas had described.

They glanced at each other and nodded.

The nearby sound of shoes tapping the stone floor was startling, and they both glanced toward one of the back pews, where the stocky figure of a man had stood up. He shuffled into the aisle, hesitated, and then genuflected; when he turned around they saw that it was Ernest Hemingway. He was carrying a paper bag with a long loaf of bread sticking out of the top of it.

He walked back toward them, smiling, and when he was close enough to be heard in a whisper, he said, "I was hoping you'd have had sensible second thoughts, and I could sit here for a while and then go get coffee somewhere. Eat most of this baguette with some cheese. But here you are."

He stepped to the door in the side wall. It had no knob, just a keyhole, and when he pulled the baguette out of the bag and tore the top off of it, Nolan saw the curved, flat-bladed end of a short iron crowbar.

Vivi moved in front of him, and pulled from a pocket the two narrow strips of metal she had taken from a shelf in her flat an hour ago. "I can pick it—no damage."

She crouched beside the door and fitted the two strips into the keyhole, and after a minute of jiggling and twisting them in the lock, the door shifted in its frame.

All three of them looked at the front doors and down the main aisle toward the altar, but there was still no one else in the church.

Vivi straightened and pushed on the door, and it swung inward. The three of them hurried into the room beyond, and Nolan nudged the door back until it was not quite closed. Hemingway set his paper bag on the floor.

By gray daylight from a little window high in the street-side wall, Nolan could see a haphazard collection of dusty old furniture—stacks of wooden chairs, two raised stone bowls that were probably holy water fonts, racks of black robes and white smocks, and what looked like a tall, ornate wooden litter with three doors and no carrying poles.

"A spare confessional!" said Hemingway.

Vivi touched one of the object's doors. "Beaufroy said we should go to Confession before we went down into the catacombs."

"You're Catholic?" asked Hemingway.

"I don't know." She looked over her shoulder at him. "Harry and I seem to spend a lot of time in Catholic churches these days. You?"

Hemingway rubbed his chin. "I suppose I'm Catholic if I'm anything. Certainly can't take any other religion seriously." He rapped on the central door of the confessional. "Nobody home."

Nolan spoke up, a bit impatiently. "Alice Toklas said the main door is in the far wall. It must be behind this thing."

"Right." Hemingway stepped to one side of the big wooden box and Nolan took the other, and between them they were able to slide the confessional several feet away from the wall.

Now they could see a low wooden door, inset into the marble wall. Hemingway brushed cobwebs away from an iron plate at one side of the door, exposing a big rust-rimmed keyhole.

"They apparently want to hide this door," he said.

"I guess they're embarrassed by it," said Vivi. "Miss Toklas said some mad groups had control of this church during the Revolution."

Hemingway pulled the baguette out of the bag and broke bread fragments away from the concealed crowbar. "I don't think your lockpicks will work on that."

He fitted the flat edge into the gap between the door and the stone frame, and pushed on the end of it; and with a crack and a burst of dust, that side of the door creaked forward six inches.

Nolan pulled the straps of the rucksack from his shoulders and set it on the floor. He and Hemingway both took hold of the thick door edge and pulled, and the door slid out across the floor, opening a three-foot gap. They were greeted with a cold draft redolent of stagnant water.

Vivi stepped between them and switched on the flashlight, illuminating a downward-slanting arched brick ceiling. She tilted the light down, and it shone on stone steps extending away below, into darkness beyond the flashlight's reach.

She gave Nolan a smile that was more of a facial tic. "Downstairs this time," she said, with obviously forced lightness.

"Okay," said Hemingway, stepping back. "Are you two ready now to join me for breakfast at the Closerie? Let the priests shove the confessional back."

"We've had breakfast," Vivi told him. "Beer and ham sandwiches on the way here."

Nolan nodded toward the yawning abyss beyond the door. "We've got an errand to run."

Hemingway frowned. "Go by yourself, Harry. You can't take her down there."

Vivi was crouched, unbuckling the rucksack. "I'm taking *him*," she said. She reached in and pulled out two sausage-sized tubes of white pigment and put them in her coat pocket, then lifted out the kerosene lantern. She struck a match and thumbed up the glass chimney to light the wick.

Nolan rebuckled the rucksack and picked it up, then slung it onto his back and put his arms through the straps.

Hemingway clicked his tongue and pulled a book from his back pocket. Nolan recognized it as the copy of Stein's *Tender Buttons* that Vivi had left at Stein's studio yesterday.

"Alice Toklas said I should give this to you, if I saw you this morning. She said it's counter-logic, and it could be an evasion from some kinds of tracking. God knows how, but... she'll want to know if I delivered it."

Vivi took it and slid it too into her coat pocket. "Thanks." She gave Hemingway a curious look. "Could Harry and I have moved the confessional by ourselves?"

"Sure," said Hemingway. "Harry would have slid one end over, then moved around to the other side and slid that end. Walked it out."

"Miss Toklas didn't mention the necessity of a crowbar."

"She told me."

Vivi smiled at him. "So it was up to you whether or not Harry and I go down there."

"No. Just like moving the confessional. You'd have got a crowbar on your own. Half-hour delay."

Vivi nodded. "Then she was just giving you the choice of being complicit, or not."

Hemingway laughed softly. "Yahweh tested Abraham. Miss Toklas tests her friends. I hope I haven't helped get you killed." He stepped back to the door Vivi had unlocked.

"I lit a candle for you," he said, then turned and was gone.

Nolan crossed to the door and pushed it shut. It clicked. "It doesn't look as if anybody comes in here much. You can always pick the lock again."

Vivi gave a jerky nod. "Or we can just clamor and say we thought this was the way to *les toilettes*."

"Heh." Nolan walked back and picked up the lantern. He stood beside the wooden door he and Hemingway had forced open, and Vivi stood beside him as they looked down the old stairs.

Nolan walked down the first few steps and looked back at Vivi. "Turn off the flashlight for now." He raised the lantern and peered down the stairs. "Okay, Bullfrog said that if we go down at any point east of the Luxembourg Gardens, to try to move west to a north-south tunnel with old mining car rails. Follow it north to a tunnel slanting northwest. And those landmarks he said to watch for—we'll pass what he called 'the timekeeper's chamber'—"

Nolan had asked Beaufroy if some timekeeper would be present there. The old man had answered, *Yes, but he can't do anything*, and had dismissed any further questions and quickly moved on to the next landmark.

"—And then to the bridge of sighs..."

"I remember," said Vivi. "'I stood in Venice, on the Bridge of Sighs—'" Seeing Nolan's puzzled look, she added, "Byron, from *Childe Harold's Pilgrimage*." She tucked the flashlight back behind her belt and pulled one of the pigment tubes out of her coat pocket. "Down we go."

"I know who Byron was," said Nolan.

"I should hope so."

The stairs led down only about twenty feet, and when Nolan and Vivi stepped through a doorway at the bottom they found themselves stepping into a narrow passage that extended to left and right beyond the radiance of the lantern. The walls and low flat ceiling were of featureless gray stone blocks, and two inches of gray water flowed from right to left over a stone floor that was gritty underfoot. The passage was not wide enough for them to walk abreast, and Nolan took the lead.

"Left is west." He was whispering, but even the slight sloshing sounds of their footsteps echoed away ahead and behind. The still air smelled of stagnant water and rusty metal.

"Step careful," Nolan added. "Unexpected pits under the water, according to old Crawdad."

"Bullfrog. *Beaufroy*."

Nolan was trying to keep a count of his shuffling steps as they made their careful way along the downward-slanting passage. Beaufroy had said that moving a hundred meters west from almost anywhere would put them in peril of the *Shaydim*.

But the tunnel didn't continue straight west. After two hundred splashing paces it curved to the right and led them up a short flight of stone steps. They had left the flowing gray water behind, and no longer had to shuffle along, though their shoes now leaked water at each step. The tunnel was wider here, the ceiling higher and arched, and Vivi was walking beside Nolan, looking down at her compass in the reflected light of the lantern Nolan carried.

"We're going northwest," she said.

"He said there's a lot of cross-tunnels. We should catch a left-hand turn before long."

They passed several ragged-edged openings at waist or knee height in the walls on either side, but after dutifully peering down the couple of holes in the left wall, neither Nolan nor Vivi had to discourage the other from trying to climb into them. From one of them drifted faint musical notes that might have been singing, and down the other, in darkness far beyond the lantern's radiance, spots of red fire appeared and then vanished, making Nolan think of torches carried in a procession.

At last they came upon an arch in the left wall, leading to a corridor that split into two passages. One appeared to lead directly west, and Nolan led the way along it—pausing while Vivi squeezed a glob of white pigment into the palm of her right hand and smeared it on the side of the arch.

"I should have brought a paint brush," she said.

This corridor was only wide enough for one person, and slanted so steeply downward that both of them braced a free hand against a wall. The walls were again stone blocks, but the passage was widest at shoulder height and the ceiling nearly brushed Nolan's hair. He was reminded uncomfortably of the proportions of a coffin. The passage floor here was dusty and dry—evidently the water flowed away down discrete channels.

Within a few yards they began to see bones lying against the walls, as if kicked aside to clear the floor. Soon they came upon a skull, missing its jaw.

From behind him, Vivi's voice was steady. "Beaufroy said to expect a lot of bones." Nolan just nodded.

Within a hundred more steps, they were placing their feet carefully between angular rolling femurs and forearm bones, careful not to slip on kneecaps and loose vertebrae.

The passage branched again, and again, and both times Nolan chose the west-trending one and Vivi smeared paint on a wall in a spot that would be readily visible when coming back this way.

Now they were bracing themselves against the walls and choosing each step, for they were walking on bones piled to a depth of at least a foot, and ribs and skulls rolled and cracked under their damp shoes. Nolan had to duck his head under the closer ceiling. The smells on the cold air here were of nothing but damp rock and the burning lantern wick; the thousands of forgotten relics underfoot had long since lost any defining odor.

He nearly called to Vivi, *Is it worth it?* when it became necessary to climb on all fours over the tumbled lengths and bumpy globes of yellowed ivory. Holding the lantern above the morbid jumble, he had to lean on his free forearm to pull himself forward, and though he was now virtually crawling, the ceiling scraped the top of his raised head. Behind him he could hear bones snapping and shifting even under Vivi's lesser weight.

"Who the devil," he said through clenched teeth, "*put* all these here?"

"Maybe," came Vivi's whispered answer, "someone who wanted to keep them together, safe."

A pelvis broke in half under Nolan's knee. "Well, we're making a hash of that."

"Hush," said Vivi, and for a moment Nolan thought she was reproving him for disrespect of the dead; then it occurred to him that she was simply telling him to be quiet. He paused in his ruinous crawling to listen, but heard nothing besides their fast breathing.

He took hold of a cluster of separating ankle bones with his free hand, and resumed pulling himself forward.

Soon the lantern showed him the flat stones of a wall blocking the passage ahead. Good God, he thought, now to crawl back—backward!—and take a different passage!

"Dead end," he said hoarsely.

"We're just under the ceiling," came Vivi's strained voice. "A doorway would be lower down."

Nolan had to grip the lantern handle tightly to keep his whole arm from trembling. Dig? he thought. Excavate? Move or break aside the volume of bones below me, and then lower ourselves into the cleared gap in hopes of finding a doorway, which itself would be jammed from bottom to top? And if it were impassable, would they be able to clamber up again, even to this narrow space between the horribly close ceiling and the high-piled extent of tumbled skulls and femurs and ribs?

Had any of the dead people whose remains lay below him made their way here and tried to do that, and been unable to climb out again, and themselves ended up just adding to this endless mortuary accumulation?

How far below the sunlit streets of Paris had they descended?

"Pass the lantern back to me." Vivi's voice was tight with control. "I'll set it back here where it won't get knocked over while we work."

He could hear Vivi's quick breathing behind him.

"Okay," he said, rolling onto his side and extending the lantern back toward her. Her eyes shone through a tangle of fair hair in the moment before her reaching hand blocked his view of her, and the lantern went bumping away across some poor soul's spinal column.

Nolan turned back to the obstructing wall and wiggled both hands down through the tumbled bones, and he hauled up an armful. "Pass them back to me," came Vivi's voice, and he twisted around to push them toward her, dropping several.

After doing it half a dozen more times—and, he noticed, filling the gap below the ceiling behind him, and making a fragmented pattern of the lantern's glow—he drew his knees up to his chest and extended his legs down into the unsteady space he had cleared. He shifted his weight onto his shoes, and he sank a yard into the pile below, to the accompaniment of a staccato racket of snapping and crunching.

He braced his hands against the wall and kicked forward, and he could feel that his foot was past the vertical face of the wall. He had found the top of a doorway, or at least some sort of opening. To continue, he would have to get lower down, almost entirely out of the filtered light, and extend his legs through the opening—whatever it was.

It would be a move that might be impossible to reverse.

"I've found some kind of opening," he called back. "I'd have to sit down and go through it feet first. I think this is the—this is *a* point of no return."

After a long pause in which he believed she was listening for sounds not of their making, she said, "Use your judgment."

Nolan was confident that right now he could still climb back out of this unsteady, loose-sided hole, especially with Vivi to take his hand and pull him up. But this tunnel was probably their best hope—perhaps their only hope—of finding their way west and coming to the north-south passage Beaufroy had described. The old man's directions so far had been of little use—clearly Beaufroy had imagined them getting down into the catacombs at some point far removed from the church Gertrude Stein had directed them to.

"I'll try it," he said.

She answered in a low voice, "Good. Careful but quick—I'm really sure I hear something behind us."

Nolan didn't pause to ask any questions. He squatted on the broken bones, while others tumbled onto his shoulders and head, and thrust his legs through the unseen aperture in the wall. Skulls imploded and ribs scraped against stone, and then his legs were fully extended—and he heard a lot of rattling and clattering on the other side.

Bones rolling away. The next space was *not* filled to the ceiling.

Leaning forward and running his hands down the surface of the wall, he felt the long concrete lintel of a doorway. He slid his hands under it and gripped it by its far edge, and pulled hard. Then the lintel knocked his forehead and he was sliding in an echoing racket into darkness. When he came to a stop he was able to kick unseen bones away and stand up on a stone floor.

The high edges of the doorway through which he had come were dimly outlined by reflections of the lantern's light. He scrambled back up the slope of bones, thrashing to keep from sliding back, and called, "Pass me the lantern!"

He caught one edge of the doorway and was able to pull himself up and fit his head and right arm through the new gap under the lintel. Peering upward, he saw the lantern descending in jerks; when he caught it he saw that Vivi had tied her belt around the handle to lower it.

"Got it," he called, lifting it clear. "Now you."

A sort of voice—shrill, like wet stones rubbed together—echoed from up there. A moment later Vivi's hands and arms were in the lantern's light, and she contorted through the doorway headfirst, colliding with Nolan. Both of them slid down to the floor, Nolan hunching around to keep the lantern upright.

They quickly got to their feet and hurried down this next section of tunnel for half a dozen yards and then paused, panting, and looked back. Now there was a smell in the air—an oily metallic reek that made Nolan think of snakes.

The bones of the slope they had slid down were motionless in the lantern light, but Nolan could hear careful scraping and sliding from the other side of the doorway, and a quieter repetition of the shrill voice. It was vocalizing distinct syllables, in—yes, Nolan thought—a narrow but distinct range of musical notes.

"Some sort of guardian?" he whispered. "Of this forgotten ... what's the word, ossuary?"

"I think that's a lullaby," Vivi whispered back. "We disturbed their rest."

Nolan rubbed a trembling hand across his mouth. "I hope you didn't use up a lot of Miss Stein's paint. We're not going back that way."

"No," agreed Vivi with a shudder. She untied her belt from the lantern and threaded it back through the loops in her trousers.

The passage continued to lead downward, and passed through several more of the open doorways. Nolan was wondering who had built this interminable arch-ceilinged hall, which was reportedly just a tiny segment of the miles of labyrinth under Paris. Nolan began to worry about their supply of lantern oil.

After another hundred yards they came upon an iron ladder bolted to the wall—it led up through a circular iron-ringed hole in the ceiling into darkness. Stenciled in black on the wall beside it was the notation: NID.4.

"Do you suppose it leads up to streets?" Nolan asked.

"Maybe. I'll start marking turns, in case—"

She broke off with a startled hiss and slapped at her coat. She leaned over and pulled the edge of her pocket out away from the rest of the fabric and with her free hand lifted and shook the coat's hem. A couple of small tan objects tumbled out of the pocket and clicked on the floor.

She nudged them with her shoe—both rolled away, but one of them spun around before it stopped. She nudged it again, and again it rotated as it came to rest.

"It's Beaufroy's damned finger bones!" she whispered.

Nolan set down the lantern and crouched over the one that had moved on its own, and with one finger turned it forty-five degrees; it immediately resumed its previous orientation.

"It's pointing," he said as he straightened up. He dug from his trouser pocket the two finger bones Beaufroy had given him, and jiggled them on his palm; they didn't move. "You got a live one."

"What did Beaufroy say, they point to the living body that the soul has moved into, right?"

"Yeah. The fellow's apparently north of us. Probably up on the surface." He put his two finger bones in his coat pocket and picked up the lantern. "Just put 'em back in your pocket, I guess."

Vivi bent and picked up the two finger bones, but only put away the inert one. "I'll keep this Mexican jumping bean out."

Nolan shrugged and resumed walking down the passage, with Vivi shuffling along beside him.

The passage split, a few yards ahead. Both branches were narrow, and led downward, but after glancing at Vivi and getting a nervous nod, he led the way into the left-side one. Vivi paused to smear a blob of white paint on the wall before hurrying to catch up. In this corridor there was again a macabre litter of bones pushed up against the walls; the air now carried a sulfury, stagnant smell.

"So many," said Vivi softly, "I had not thought death had undone so many." When Nolan didn't reply, she added, "That's from Eliot's *The Waste Land*."

"Ah," said Nolan, who hadn't read it.

Soon they passed a pipe from which water trickled in a rusty streak down the wall, and then they were splashing through a sluggish stream. A few skulls bobbed and turned slowly in the weak current. Again Nolan and Vivi passed a ladder leading away upward through a circular hole in the ceiling; stenciled on the wall beside it was NID.3.

"Let's keep it in mind," Nolan said.

When they had been sloshing along for another ten minutes, Vivi halted.

"Wait," she said. Nolan glanced back and saw that she was staring at the bone on her palm. "It just reversed." She looked up. "A moment ago it was pointing more or less ahead."

She splashed her way back a couple of yards and stopped. "Now it's forward again."

Nolan walked back, and when the lantern light illuminated the water around Vivi's ankles she gasped and hurried to stand beside him.

One of the many skulls sat on top of a broken rib cage against the wall, and—perched on it like a pink crab—a fleshy hand was flexing. It was severed at the wrist, but its thumb and one finger were hooked into the skull's empty eye sockets, while the three free fingers waved in the air like antennae.

"Great holy Mother of God!" whispered Vivi.

Nolan's scalp had tightened at the unnatural small spectacle, and his lips had pulled away from his teeth.

Vivi held out her hand. The little bone was visibly shivering on her palm.

"Should I give it back to him?"

Nolan shook himself. "What's he going to do with it? Clasp it?" He was speaking too loudly. He moved farther down the passage away from the thing, and whispered, "Come on."

Vivi followed him, though glancing back. "And he's a *sauteur*, or was." She put the bone back in her pocket. "He deserves whatever *misfortune* this is."

"Or *she* does."

"Oh," said Vivi. "Yes."

Nolan wondered if Vivi was thinking of Elodie, who had at least once, albeit unknowingly, died and then taken the body of a child.

They pressed onward and downward, and after a hundred more steps paused in front of a painting on the right-side wall. It covered the wall from the edge of the ceiling curve to just above the water, and Nolan had to raise the lantern and press himself against the opposite wall, as well as he could with the rucksack on his back, to get a view of it. Patches had fallen away, and mineral deposits obscured the bottom edge, but the picture was clear enough.

"Ah," said Vivi softly, "I remember seeing this in his dreams!"

It was a starkly cubist painting of a chubby nude infant with a wide green sex-concealing ribbon floating around its waist, wielding a flaming sword. The infant's mouth was an off-center red rectangle, and its eyes were just short horizontal black lines. Behind that foreground figure were the crude images of a man and a woman, both apparently smiling, likewise nude except for big leaves at their crotches. In the background was a tree with red globes studding its branches.

"What the hell...?" Nolan muttered.

"It's Adam and Eve," Vivi told him, "in the Garden of Eden." She leaned against the wall beside Nolan and closed her eyes. "I wish we'd find a place where we could sit down. That's a cherub with the sword, and behind them that must be the Tree of Knowledge of Good and Evil."

"Huh. I thought the angel, or cherub, drove them out of the garden. This one looks like he's keeping the *viewer* out."

"Sure. Look at the symbol on that ribbon."

Nolan peered more closely at the painting, and saw that the green ribbon bore a repeated pattern in thin blue lines, much of which had flaked off—but in several places he was able to recognize the horned head with three circles on its face.

"We're on course." said Vivi, straightening up.

A few steps farther, the passage turned sharply to the left, and opened on a wider crossways tunnel. The water swirling around their shoes flowed into a more swiftly moving stream here, its rumble echoing under a higher ceiling, but concrete steps on the right led to a raised walkway that extended away into darkness. The sulfur smell was stronger here.

Nolan saw turbulence down the center of the watercourse. He handed the lantern to Vivi and stepped carefully out into the stream. The water splashed and tugged around his ankles. At the middle of the channel his shoe bumped a long, smooth obstruction, and when he took a few splashing steps to the side he could still feel the extent of it.

"I think I found the mining car track," he said as he made his way back and stepped up beside Vivi on the walkway. "Time for a rest, I think. Then we go north."

She gratefully set the lantern on the concrete pavement and sat down beside it. Just as gratefully, Nolan slid the rucksack off his aching shoulders and laid it against the stone wall. He stretched and sat down beside her.

Without the constant splash or scrape of their footsteps, the rippling sound of the water soon seemed to mask other, fainter sounds—distant laughter, or rapid overlapping voices, or an orchestra.

Vivi touched her bare wrist, then sighed. "How long have we been down here?"

Nolan shrugged. "Hour and a half?" He unbuckled the rucksack and pulled out one of the canteens. He passed it to Vivi, who unscrewed the cap and took a long sip.

When she passed it back to him she asked, "Have we got a lot of lantern oil?"

"The lantern's tank holds ten ounces, and it was full when we started." He took several deep swallows of water. The cap was attached to the canteen with a little chain, and he screwed it back on. "Stein said it burns about an ounce and a half per hour. And there's a couple of six-ounce bottles in the rucksack, so we're good for fourteen or fifteen hours."

"I want some of it, to burn... you-know-whose skull."

Nolan respected her reluctance to say Cadieux's name down here, in his realm, but her idea was impulsive and unrealistic. "If we get good and lost, it might take us fifteen hours to find a way back up to streets. Or more, and we'd need the flashlight too." He tucked the canteen back into the rucksack, wishing they'd thought to bring liquor, or food. "Better we bust up his skull and take the fragments back with us. Then maybe—I don't know, grind him to bone meal and feed him to pigs."

"That's good." She scratched under the bandage on her head and shifted to a more comfortable position. "I hate the delay. Every now and then, if I seem distracted, ask me if I fed the cat."

Nolan understood that this would be a test, to know if she was occupied by Cadieux: an answer of either *Yes* or *No* would show that it was not Vivi speaking. But in fact Cadieux would probably try to kill him immediately upon arrival.

"Okay," he said.

"That—" said Vivi, and Nolan felt her shiver against his shoulder. She went on, "That was a severed hand. Alive."

"Yes."

"Most people don't have to see such things."

"I suppose not."

"Do you think we will ever have a... normal life?"

Nolan reflected that he had been having a fairly normal life before he had met her—nevertheless, he was pleased with her use of *we*.

"Hard to say. But," and he quoted Beaufroy: "Smile because you are alive at this moment."

"I'll smile when we've fed him to pigs."

By unspoken agreement they got to their feet then, and Nolan put on the rucksack and picked up the lantern. Vivi squeezed another curl of white paint onto her palm and spread it on the frame of the passageway that had led them to this point.

"Now we watch for the timekeeper's chamber," Nolan said, "according to Beaufroy."

CHAPTER THIRTEEN:
Fair Enough

The raised pavement beside the stream stretched ahead of them as they walked, its farther extents always beyond the illumination of the lantern. They passed another ladder leading up through an iron-ringed hole in the ceiling, this one with *NID.2* stenciled on the wall beside it. Nolan noted it as a possible eventual exit, and he knew Vivi did too.

When they had trudged north for another ten minutes, Vivi suddenly grunted and reached into her coat pocket with her right hand; when she pulled her hand out, both of the finger bones were wiggling on her palm.

Nolan slid his free hand into the pocket of Stein's coat, and pulled out the two that Beaufroy had given him. They too were twitching.

He rolled them back and forth on his palm, but though they kept jiggling, neither of them seemed to stay pointed in any direction.

"They're acting like static on a radio," he said. "Noise but no signal."

After a few seconds, the bones on both of their hands stopped moving. Nolan was about to put his two back in his pocket when the things began moving again—still directionlessly. He saw that Vivi's were doing the same.

"I think their psychics are aware of an intrusion," Nolan said, "and they're ... scanning back and forth across all their frequencies."

Vivi spoke quickly: "They'll find *us*. We need—"

She stopped and took a step as if to catch her balance, and she was blinking around in bewilderment; then she looked at the lantern, and nodded. "Right," she said firmly. "In *les carriéres*. I know where we are. Ladders, Adam and Eve, severed hand."

Nolan opened his mouth to ask her if she was all right, but the intention was eclipsed by his own voice in his head: *I think we're not. Dying. We're in a stairwell in the north tower of Notre Dame.*

He looked quickly from the wall on his right to the rushing stream on their left below the walkway, momentarily wondering how he and Vivi had got into some sort of subterranean sewer. Was it under the Notre Dame cathedral?

A moment later his memories of the last twelve hours flooded back into his mind. He shook his head to clear it, but he felt dizzy.

"I just now had a hard memory," Vivi said, between fast breaths, "no, a *reexperience* of saying to Hemingway, 'So it was up to you whether or not Harry and I go down there.'"

Nolan rubbed his bruised temple. "I had a sharp memory too. Something I said last night in the cathedral stairwell. Yes, like reexperiencing it."

The finger bones on the palms of their hands were just quivering now.

"Their psychics have got a bearing on us." Vivi's voice was tense. "I can still feel it—like the echo in my head is different."

"Yes," Nolan said, frowning and closing his eyes for a moment, "or as if my forehead's . . . open."

"I think it's time for Miss Stein's book." She reached into her pocket and pulled out the now-battered copy of Stein's *Tender Buttons*.

"We need to . . ." she began, but her eyes drifted from his face, down past the book to her shoes. "Elodie and I used to spend many days in the *jardin*," she said. She hissed and slapped her face. "Another! Ach, they're rummaging in our recent memories, as Beaufroy said!"

Nolan resisted the impulse to put down the lantern and clasp his scalp protectively with both hands. "If they find out what we—"

"Don't think," Vivi said quickly. "We need this book—we need a cloud of confusion, counter-logic— break up their reception." She flipped the book open and ran a finger down one of the pages.

"Repeat this after me, and concentrate on the words," she said, then began reading: "'*A large box is handily made of what is necessary to replace any substance.*'" Nolan echoed the words, and his mind reflexively tried and failed to make sense of them. But Vivi had flipped to another page and now read: "'*What is the use of a violent kind of delightfulness if there is no pleasure in not getting tired of it.*'" Again he repeated the words, again trying, fruitlessly, to grasp their sense.

His thoughts felt once again properly contained—the sense that his head was somehow open was fading.

"Memorize this one," said Vivi. "'*Hope, what is a spectacle, a spectacle is the resemblance between the circular side place and nothing else, nothing else.*'"

He recited the first several words, then faltered, and she had to read it again. After three more tries he had memorized only the first few phrases, but Vivi lowered the book and waved him to silence. She peered at the finger bones on her palm and Nolan's; they had stopped jiggling.

"My head feels as if it's my own again," she said cautiously. "How's yours?"

"Restored, yes." Nolan dropped the bones back into his pocket. "I think they decided we're a null signal, and moved on."

Vivi put hers away too. "I'll keep this book handy. And be ready to recite the bits you remember."

They cautiously made their way farther along the walkway, and after what Nolan estimated to be a quarter of a mile, Vivi gave a start and dug a hand into her pocket, and pulled out one of the two finger bones.

She gingerly rubbed it between her fingers. "I think it's the same one that was pointing before," she whispered. She flipped up the compass on her belt and peered at it. "We're still heading more or less north."

Another doorway was visible ahead. From the section beyond it, Nolan could hear a windy whistling over the perpetual ripple of the watercourse at their left.

"Timekeeper?" Vivi whispered. She raised her closed hand. "The bone's still pointing."

Nolan stepped carefully through the doorway, raising the lantern. The smell here was spicy, like Indian curry. Now there was a wall on the left, blocking out the sound of the flowing water. On that wall was mounted a big clock with Roman numerals on its face and no minute or hour hand.

On the opposite wall was a life-sized painting of a nude male body, and a sloped stack of forearm bones was neatly arranged at the painting's base. Raising the lantern, Nolan was startled to see an actual human head mounted at the top of the painted figure. Looking more closely, he saw that it was stuck onto an upward-curved metal pipe that projected from the wall. The pipe was evidently connected to some other level, or even the far-off surface, for air was whistling out of the slack mouth and nostrils of the head.

"God!" said Nolan, too loudly. More quietly he went on, "The clock can't tell time and the timekeeper's dead."

Vivi had gasped and stepped back. "None of his memories showed me *this*." She shook her head and waved toward the farther extent of the passage. "Onward we, bravely."

Nolan nodded and stepped forward, with Vivi following, but they both rocked to a halt when two things happened: from a shadowed corner a severed hand hunched across the floor into the light, dragging another forearm bone held between its thumb and forefinger; and the head on the pipe opened its eyes and, in a hoarse whisper that echoed in the narrow space, said, *"Je ne suis pas mort."*

The sentence was simple enough for Nolan to instantly understand it: *I am not dead.*

The crawling hand had reached the slope of forearm bones on the floor below the head, and began laboriously climbing, still holding its intended addition to the stack.

The eyes rolled downward at the sound of shifting bones. *"Ma main gauche,"* it whispered, *"Il cherche à grimper et à me libérer."*

Seeing Nolan's frown, Vivi said, "Grimper. The verb *to climb*."

Nolan shuddered when he understood the whole sentence: *My left hand is trying to climb up and free me.*

For several seconds he and Vivi just stood staring in mute horror at the exhaling head on the wall.

The thing rolled its eyes. "English?" it croaked. "My right hand... has gone for help."

Nolan recalled the hand they had seen perched on a skull farther back down the corridors, and he actually winced in sympathy at the thought of its impossible quest. The severed left hand lost its hold on the bone it had carried; the bone and two others rolled down to the floor, and the hand began climbing back down to retrieve them.

"Who are you?" breathed Vivi. *"Qui êtes vous?"*

"*Je m'appelais Gabin Tremblay,*" it said. It was silent when the wind in its neck momentarily slacked; then it went on, speaking slowly enough so that Nolan was able to translate its words in his head: *I am punished here—set undying before a clock that shows no duration.*

In reflexive pity, Nolan thought of lifting the head off the pipe—but then what? Set it on the floor? It would no longer have wind to speak, and its left hand—even aided by its right, if that one should give up and make its way back here—could hardly carry it to any better place.

Vivi's hands were in the pockets of her coat. She raised her eyebrows and glanced sharply at Nolan, then stepped closer to the head and spoke in rapid French. The head replied in the same language, haltingly enough for Nolan to understand: *I stole the bones of one who died—so the* magi *could not locate him. That was—in 1921. Perhaps he is—old enough again now—to find his way to us.*

Vivi shook her head and said, "*Seulement quatre ans—*" *Only four years*—then, speaking hopelessly fast, she asked a question.

Nolan shivered and stepped back.

The head rolled its eyes before answering, and Vivi grunted and pulled the two finger bones from her pocket. Nolan could see that one of them was pointing toward the head.

When the head finally answered her question, it spoke slowly: "*Il essaierait faire une trêve entre... Moloch avec Cybèle—lui et Achard.*" and Nolan was able to follow it: *He would try to make a truce between Moloch and Cybele—he and Achard.*

Nolan was nervously licking his lips in readiness to whistle the remembered notes of Scriabin; for he was sure that this was now Thibaud Cadieux speaking through Vivi's mouth. There was no need to ask if she had fed the cat.

Vivi's voice barked more sentences, and then a question in which Nolan was able only to catch the words *Cybele, Moloch,* and *Tarragona.*

"*Parce que le dieu peut venir là-bas, en chair,*" said the head on the wall. *Because the god can come there, in flesh.* It added, "*Mais Cybele aussi.*" *But so can Cybele.*

Vivi's voice spoke again, twice, but the head's eyes had closed and its jaw again hung slack, the lips vibrating with the air rushing up the pipe and out through its mouth. The right hand resumed trying to drag a bone to the top of its little pile.

Vivi turned away from it and faced Nolan. "You prefer English," said her voice, with an incongruous Spanish accent, "as I recall."

Nolan cleared his throat. "Yes." He went on carefully, "And you are...her original self, partly reincarnated."

The laugh that came in reply was in Vivi's voice, but choppier than a laugh of hers could ever be. "Do not waste our time, *amigo*, we are past that. In that temple you said the truth about me. I am as to taking this girl's body, yes, as you said." Vivi's eyes roved over Nolan from his uncombed hair to his sodden shoes. "Are you and she lovers?"

The incongruous question, in this nightmare chamber, caught Nolan off guard, and he thought of the virginal Saint Genevieve; his mental image of the saint was the statue at the Pont de la Tournelle, sheltering the little stone girl.

Mentally he rehearsed the Scriabin notes. "I won't give you information about her."

Vivi's hand brushed across her small breasts. "I see! But I spoil it, yes? Or do I?" Again the rattling laughter shook out of her mouth. Vivi's eyes moved to the head on the wall and then back to Nolan. "We are in *les carriéres*—south of the bridge. Why?"

Nolan stood tensely, listening to the voice, and didn't reply.

"Tell me *who is this girl,* why she clings—like a barnacle on the hull of a boat!—and I will answer you much. I fell out of her, on the stairs at Notre Dame, while facing you. If you—"

Suddenly afraid that Cadieux would recall Nolan's whistling, and cover Vivi's ears, Nolan pursed his lips and vigorously whistled the six Scriabin notes.

At the first notes, Vivi's head had cocked alertly, and then her eyes had widened in sudden alarm and her right foot had slid forward—but when the last of the notes had echoed away she was halted, staring into Nolan's eyes.

She took a deep, shuddering breath and spoke: "He was here, wasn't he?"

"Yes," Nolan said cautiously, not moving any closer to her. "Did you feed the cat?"

"Right, Harry, feed the cat, it's me, Vivi." She touched the bandage on her forehead and glanced at the now inert head on the wall. "How long was he here?"

"Just for a minute."

"Did you drive him away, with the Scriabin?"

Nolan nodded. "But he seemed to catch on. He started to come at me, to stop me—a moment too late."

"Oh, we've got to find his damned skull! What did he say?"

"He asked that head some questions. What's the last bit you remember?"

She nodded toward the sagging head. "He told us his name, and said he was being punished here."

"Ah. Well, he went on to say that he's being punished this way for stealing the direction-finding bones of somebody who died four years ago, who, along with Achard, wanted to make a truce between Moloch and Cybele."

"What? That's nonsense. You heard Kirenli talk about Moloch!"

"It's what he said. Apparently, Achard liked the idea and this... beheaded gentleman didn't. Your man asked a question—"

"Oh, don't call him my man, down here! Say predator."

"Right. Your predator asked him a question I couldn't follow, but I heard *Cybele, Moloch,* and *Tarragona.* And the head answered, 'Because the god can come there—but so can Cybele.'"

Vivi crossed her arms, gripping her shoulders. "Did he acknowledge *you,* standing here?"

Nolan shifted the rucksack straps on his shoulders. "Yes. He wanted to know who you are, why you cling—to your body, apparently. Then he started talking about losing control of you on the Notre Dame stairs, but I was afraid he would remember me whistling, and cover his ears, your ears, to stop from hearing it, so I...hit him with the Scriabin. And here you are."

"That's all he said to you?"

"No. He, uh, asked if you and I are lovers."

"What did you say?"

"I said I wouldn't give him any information about you."

She bobbed her head. "Fair enough. Come on—we must be getting close."

They had trudged on down the passage for another dozen yards, twice splashing through ankle-deep pools, when Nolan spied two upright figures moving in the passage ahead of them, at the limit of the lantern light. They were advancing, though not quickly.

"I see them," said Vivi quietly. "Get your finger bones out," she added, pulling hers from her pocket. Nolan saw that both of the little bones were jiggling on her palm.

The pair of figures carried no light of their own, and Nolan knew that Vivi and himself must be starkly visible in the glare of his lantern. He dug from his pocket his own pair of finger bones and held them tightly confined in his fist.

He eyed the approaching pair warily. They were now clearly a tall person and a short one, but as they drew closer Nolan had difficulty in making out the details of their appearances. Their clothing and faces altered from moment to moment, as if they moved in and out of variations in light and shadow and were dressed in banners that flapped in a nonexistent breeze.

It made Nolan dizzy, and for a heartbeat he wasn't sure he and Vivi had not turned around, weren't walking back toward the timekeeper.

Vivi had Gertrude Stein's book open in her free hand. "I don't think *they're* changing," she whispered, perhaps sensing his confusion. "Just our perceptions of them. I wonder what they *really* look like." She peered down at the book and read, "'A kind in glass and a cousin, a spectacle and nothing strange a single hurt color.' Here," she said, handing him the book, "you read the next bit there."

For a moment Nolan didn't know what she was talking about, and one of the approaching figures called, in a flat, quacking voice, "I don't even know where Oklahoma is."

A memory of his own voice forced itself into Nolan's mind: *Right above Texas. I'm twenty-seven, but I find I sometimes need somebody to shove me out of the way of a bullet.*

"Read it!" said Vivi urgently, tapping a page.

Though disoriented, Nolan obediently read, "... 'an arrangement in a system to pointing. All this and not ordinary, not unordered in not resembling. The difference is spreading.'"

He lowered the book. He had tried without success to make sense of the words, but the effort had left him fully aware of where he was; his forehead didn't feel open. The two people who had been walking up halted now, and their appearances had stopped changing.

And then Nolan wondered if his mind had cleared after all. The shorter one was a distorted duplicate of Vivi, almost a caricature; the blue eyes were bigger, the slim body smaller in the oversized coat and baggy trousers—but it took him a moment to realize that the taller one was a beanpole image of himself, ludicrous in Gertrude Stein's short-sleeved tweed coat.

Both finger bones twisted in his fist. He dropped them into his pocket, and saw Vivi put hers away too.

The figure resembling himself slapped its chest and said, in a distinctly feminine voice, *"S'agit-il de vos vraies apparences?"* which Nolan took to mean, *Are these your real appearances?*

And the exaggerated replica of Vivi piped up, *"Vous n'êtes pas dans une concentration constante."*—*You are not in consistent focus.*

Both of the caricature figures clapped their hands.

Vivi shook her head sharply, then replied in very Oxford English: "We come veiled, at the bidding of Adrien Achard." She pulled back her left sleeve and held her arm down so that the *sauteur* tattoo on the back of her wrist was visible in the lantern light. "Let us pass." In an aside to Nolan, she added quietly, "I'm okay, never mind feeding the cat."

Nolan relaxed a fraction, and in a stern voice recited a line from his recent reading of Stein's book: "The difference is spreading." It seemed apt.

Remembering the *sauteur* mannerism he had noted, he put down the book and the lantern, and clapped his hands. Vivi quickly followed his example, and Nolan retrieved the book and the lantern.

"Ah?" said the one that was a distortion of himself. In English it said, "Veiled in broken mirrors and corkscrews!" Both figures stepped back, and their forms rippled and flickered in the lantern light—like broken mirrors themselves, thought Nolan—and came back into clarity as a couple of teenage girls, in boots and sweaters and dungarees. They're old souls, Nolan reminded himself, no matter what bodies they're in.

One wore an automobile bulb horn on a ribbon around her neck; she had been holding it, but now let it swing loose. Vivi's tattoo and the name Achard—and Stein's logic-defying sentences—seemed to have deflected suspicion, or at least comprehension.

Nolan carefully led the way past them, and when he and Vivi had taken a dozen long strides he glanced down at her. "Whatever all that was—very good." He slid the book into his coat pocket.

"Thank Miss Stein. Now we watch for the bridge."

✣ ✣ ✣

The ceiling was soon low enough that Nolan had to duck his head, and the close walls were simply chiseled from raw stone; he was resolutely not thinking about the volume of earth over their heads.

After several minutes of trudging in tense, wary silence, he burst out, almost involuntarily, "But what the pure holy *Hell*, anyway?" His voice echoed up and down the passage, and he went on, forcing himself to speak quietly, "For a second I thought those were our ghosts!" He realized that for the last minute or so he had been breathing too rapidly.

Vivi gave him a concerned look. "Psychics, I think," she said, "projectors as well as receivers. Beaufroy said their bad *magi* could put sights in our eyes, remember?"

Take it easy, Nolan told himself. "Sorry. Yes, psychics." He inhaled, held the breath, then let it out. Recalling the agitations in the finger bones in their pockets, he said, "I think they've been aware of us since back by that first ladder we saw, but getting confused signals." He was breathing normally again. You've been in worse situations, he told himself; and he managed to smile as he added, or nearly.

Vivi sniffed sharply and glanced at him with raised eyebrows.

Nolan nodded. He too had caught a brief whiff of fresh air, with a scent of pine.

"Cybele?" said Vivi softly.

They both paused.

"Down here?" Nolan whispered.

"A bit," said Vivi, "maybe." She straightened her shoulders and waved forward.

From ahead now came the irregular sighing of wind, and when they passed through one more doorway they halted—for they were only a few yards from the broad footway of a concrete bridge that arched across a gorge to a dimly visible ledge and doorway on the other side, perhaps twenty yards away. The gorge extended into darkness to right and left, and the ceiling was so high that the lantern light could only hint at faint lines and surfaces up there. A fitful wind sighed through the vast space.

The massive parapets of the bridge stood at about shoulder height—but Nolan blinked and rubbed his eyes, for a moment later the parapets had become low wooden railings. The footway was narrower now, and apparently made of planks.

Vivi pointed at the long ledge on the far side of the gorge, and Nolan saw that half a dozen figures now stood there, shifting among themselves. When one of them lit a lantern, he squinted at them and sighed.

They were more grotesque images of himself and Vivi.

"More projection," Vivi said, clearly struggling to keep her voice steady. "Sights in our eyes! But there does seem to be some sort of bridge."

"The bridge of sighs," murmured Nolan.

"Oh," said Vivi. "Yeah."

The bridge flickered, and then Nolan and Vivi both gasped and stepped back.

Spanning the gulf where the bridge had been, there now stood a huge bamboo-latticework head, its broad chin resting on the precipice edge in front of them.

Looking up along the skeletal structure, past the lashed-together stalks that formed the crude mouth and nose, Nolan saw that the oval eye-openings, twenty feet overhead, were decorated with fluttering ribbons like exaggerated eyelashes. His only thought was, I'm not climbing that.

"It's just *projections*," insisted Vivi, "disguising a real bridge. If we close our eyes and step forward—uh, edge forward, carefully—I bet we can cross it."

Nolan thought the figures on the other side of the abyss might have heard her, or more likely read her thoughts, for the giant bamboo head disappeared, replaced by the shallow downward arc of a simple suspension bridge. The support and handrail ropes were looped through pulleys in a pair of short concrete pillars that now stood a few feet in from the precipice edge. The deck of the bridge was a long row of sturdy-looking interlocked wooden squares.

"I think this is real," said Vivi, stepping forward.

But she rocked to a halt when the bridge thrummed and shook, and a moment later the far end of it detached from its moorings and dropped. The pulleys on this side spun as the ropes raced through them, and the entire length of the bridge tilted down and vanished from sight below the close precipice edge. After several seconds Nolan heard it clatter against the wall of the gorge below them.

Now nothing connected one side of the chasm to the other but a pair of slack cables swinging far below—for pulling it back up again, Nolan thought.

Vivi was staring open-mouthed at the now-impassable gulf. "No," she said after a few seconds. Then she whispered, *"Cybele."*

Again Nolan felt a breath of fresh air brush his cheek, and again he caught the scent of pine.

Vivi's eyes were closed. *"Cybele,"* she said out loud. *"Magna Mater."*

Nolan took a step to catch his balance, and caught Vivi's elbow to pull her farther back from the precipice, because his sense of direction, ordinarily minimal, was now gone altogether.

She shook off his hand and called, *"Cybele!"* The call didn't echo.

Nolan narrowed his eyes then, for a luminous white angular object had appeared at the precipice edge in front of them, a few feet to the right of the collapsed bridge's inert anchor pillars. Peering at it, he saw that it was three six-foot-wide ascending marble steps, glowing as if in daylight.

Even as he glanced up, of course seeing no open sky to account for the reflected light, Vivi had climbed up and was now standing precariously on the third and highest step. She looked back, and her wondering smile was underlit by the impossible sunlight shining on the steps.

Four more incandescent marble steps appeared, and the stone floor of the ledge Nolan stood on was now brightly lit in reflection, as were the wall behind him and even the ledge and doorway on the other side of the chasm.

Vivi quickly moved up, and when four more ascending steps appeared—the bright reflected sunlight now illuminating even the remote, arched ceiling of the concourse—she quickly tapped her way to the new top step.

Nolan's mouth had sagged open at the spectacle, but he closed it and gritted his teeth and followed her.

The steps were as steady as if they stood on stout pillars set in bedrock—but with no railing and an unguessably deep black abyss on either side, he took each step with trembling care. Sweat chilled on his face in the uneven wind. The lantern he carried in his right hand cast no detectable light in the unnatural glare of the marble surfaces underfoot, but the weight of it steadied him as he held his left arm out for balance.

The stairs leveled out in a straight track for about twenty feet, and then Vivi was descending steps on the far side. Nolan began walking carefully across the level section. Though there was no natural source for the light, he could see his shadow on the marble footway under him.

He found himself having to concentrate on what he was doing. Memories of little Robin firing the Derringer in front of his own face, and of last night's run in wet clothes from the embankment by the Pont de Sully to the north tower of Notre Dame, kept intruding into his awareness of the surface he was walking on, and of the drop on either side.

Nolan looked away from his shoes for a moment to glance at the half dozen people on the long ledge he and Vivi were approaching. In the radiance of the miraculous bridge, he saw that each of them now appeared to be a distorted caricature of himself; and a moment later three of them had shifted to a crude simulation of Vivi. They were shuffling closer to the point where the end of the bridge rested, and now he could hear that they were all humming.

Something in the hand of one of them had snagged his veering attention, and he thought to look again; yes, one of them was carrying a revolver. So was another, he noticed.

His mind drifted, and he began to wonder what had become of his own gun . . .

A new, deliberate thought forced its way through the distractions: They're rummaging through your memories again.

He paused midway across the level section, and, though the motion made his abdomen quake, he drew in his left arm to reach into his coat pocket. He pulled out Gertrude Stein's book and shook it open.

Sparing a quick glance ahead, he saw that Vivi's head and shoulders had not descended further, and she was facing the weird replicas of herself. She seemed baffled.

Nolan turned his attention to the open pages of the book in his trembling hand. The letters were blurred at first, but quickly arranged themselves into words. In a booming voice, Nolan read:

"Two plus two is four." His voice faltered. That hadn't seemed right—wasn't this book supposed to be irrational nonsense?—but he went on, "Paris is north of Africa. Dead cats should be buried."

That made him think of Marechal. He hoped the cat was all right. Where am I? he thought. Is this a church? Should I find a pew?

He lowered the lantern, and for a moment the edge of the hot steel ventilator cap rested against the knee of his trousers. The sudden pain made him gasp, and he hopped to his left—and as he teetered on the edge of the marble footway, he looked down.

The radiance of the new bridge lit uneven rock walls descending for hundreds of feet directly below him, and he reflexively swung the lantern to the right and hopped back to the center of the meager footway. His mind was momentarily cleared by the pain in his leg and the fright of his near-fall.

He looked up. The Vivi and Nolan simulations were clustered on the ledge ahead, now only about twenty feet away—and with all his strength Nolan swung the lantern over his head and pitched it.

It sailed through the bright air and exploded against the wall above the milling, humming figures. Nolan couldn't see flames, but the figures began thrashing and running back toward the doorway in that wall. One of them tumbled off the ledge and spun away out of sight below.

Vivi gave him an alert look and hurried down the remaining stairs. Nolan was right behind her.

When they both stood on the northern ledge, the glaring white light behind them vanished, and in the sudden darkness all Nolan could see was spots of burning oil on the ledge's stone floor.

Then he saw a narrow line of luminous curls of smoke, and realized that Vivi had switched on the flashlight. The flashlight beam swept across the ledge surface to the brick-framed doorway.

The doorway was empty, but voices and hurried scuffling footsteps echoed from some distance away in the darkness beyond—the people who had been waiting for them on the ledge were evidently in retreat, probably to a better position. A smell of scorched hair and cotton hung in the air—one of them must have been at least partly set on fire by the shower of burning oil.

Nolan stepped through the doorway as Vivi shined the flashlight past him, but no one was visible in the concrete-walled corridor.

"Advance while they're in confusion," Nolan said.

Vivi swept the flashlight beam across the uneven surface under their feet. For once there were no bones to kick aside.

An arch opened ahead on the right, showing only darkness down the length the flashlight could probe, but he and Vivi pressed straight on northward. A few yards farther the flashlight beam showed the outlines of a second, similar arch, likewise on their right. Nolan caught faint sounds of distant clanking machinery from somewhere along its lightless extent, and he quickly led the way past it. The echoes of retreat from ahead had faded to silence, and the only sounds now were Nolan's and Vivi's fast breathing and the scrape of their shoes.

The flashlight beam, dancing between the walls and floor ahead, was a poor substitute for the radiance of the lost lantern. At one point it swept across another iron ladder bolted to the wall, beside the stenciled notation NID.1. Vivi paused to shine the light up into the vertical tunnel above the ladder, but the beam did nothing to dispel the darkness up there. She and Nolan moved on.

After another ten minutes of trudging, Vivi whispered, "Cybele did that. That bridge."

It seemed too obvious to need a reply.

"I *am* a priestess," she said, clearly confirming it to herself.

After a few more minutes of cautious progress, she said, "Paris is north of Africa? I imagine they forced their own sentences. Uselessly logical ones."

"Yes. The words re-formed on the page."

"Do you still have the book?"

"Oh." Nolan flexed his left hand. "No. I must have let go of it when I threw the lantern." Vivi said nothing, so he added, defensively, "Balance."

"That saved us," she said, "throwing the lantern."

In an unforced memory, he saw again the figure that had tumbled from the ledge. "I knocked one of them into the gorge. Killed one of them."

"But they had guns, did you see? They'd have killed us." Her whisper was insistent, and Nolan believed she was trying to convince herself as much as him. After a few more steps, she added, almost too quietly for him to hear, "Probably."

Nolan pursed his lips, trying not to imagine how far that *sauteur* psychic might have fallen.

He shook the thought away, for he could now see white light glinting on a wall some distance ahead. "I think you could give the flashlight battery a rest," he said.

"In a minute."

As the two of them carefully made their way forward, a ringing voice from ahead called, *"Prêtresse de Cybèle, tu es une intrusion. Retour."*

"We trespass," said Vivi.

"Everywhere we go," agreed Nolan.

They kept walking forward. The light on the wall ahead came from a source around a corner on the left. Vivi played the flashlight beam around on the floor of the passage. "Hoping for loose rocks," she whispered, "or even a couple of long sturdy bones." But the floor was bare, and she switched it off.

They've got guns, Nolan thought. And there's one of those NID ladders not far behind us. He opened his mouth to suggest that they retreat—*retour*, as the *sauteurs* ahead had commanded—but he knew that Vivi wouldn't consider it, having come this far and crossed Cybele's bridge.

Roll the mortal dice, he thought. His voice was tight: "We'll have to wing it. Bluff."

Vivi tucked the flashlight behind her belt, and they walked around the corner.

CHAPTER FOURTEEN:
Try to Clean This Slate

They stepped across a raised concrete threshold into a wide, circular chamber that was lit in glaring blue-white by mercury-vapor lamps hung from the high ceiling. Six young men stood side by side in the center of the chamber, two of them holding revolvers half raised toward Nolan and Vivi. Nolan assumed that this was the group who had fled from the ledge over the gorge, though they no longer projected mimic appearances—they were fit-looking adolescents, several with wispy moustaches. All six of them wore white overalls, a couple of which, sure enough, showed some scorch-blackened spots on the shoulders.

"*Prêtresse de Cybèle, nous ne gardons que les os ici,*" called one; Nolan understood *Priestess of Cybele, we only guard bones here.*

Nolan stood up as straight as he could with the rucksack cramping his shoulders, and glared at them.

"Gabin Tremblay's punishment is to be consummated," he called harshly, "by sinking all his fragments in the Seine. This is the order of Adrien Achard." Turning to Vivi, he muttered, "You take the little lad with the gun on the left when I whistle."

The six young men might not have understood English, but they would have caught the proper names; and Nolan hoped his tone of voice had been authoritative. They were listening, at least, and the two with guns were not yet pointing them. Nolan took the opportunity to dart a glance around the chamber. Much of it, probably including another entrance, was hidden by several tall brick pillars that widened at the tops, but he could see electrical cables strung along the wall to a big fuse box on his left. To the right was a plain concrete wall with an incongruously ornate wooden door at its midpoint. Beaufroy had described it, and said it was the skull repository.

In the tense silence, Vivi raised her left fist, showing the Moloch tattoo on her wrist; the young men looked at one another uncertainly. Vivi yanked her hand downward, and Nolan quickly whistled the six Scriabin notes.

One of the young *sauteurs* convulsively fired his revolver at the floor, and as the others flinched at the bang and ricochet, Vivi sprang forward and tackled him. The other who held a gun swung it toward her, but one of his fellows was momentarily standing in the way, wide-eyed and swatting blindly at the air. Nolan lunged, caught the revolver by the barrel, and shoved it upward just as it was fired.

He wrenched it out of the man's hand as the echoes of the shot batted around the chamber and the bullet whined away among the pillars. Vivi straightened up with the other revolver in her hand, and they both stepped back.

Only two of the young *sauteurs* seemed to have been affected by the Scriabin: the one Vivi had tackled was sitting on the floor weeping, and the wide-eyed air-swatter had backed away to the nearest pillar. The other four, including the one whose gun Nolan had taken, retreated to the door in the concrete wall.

Nolan followed him. "Open it," Nolan said, waving the gun toward the door.

"*Ouvre-le*," clarified Vivi.

One of the youthful *sauteurs* said something in a belligerent tone, and Vivi lifted her revolver and replied, sternly. Nolan believed she had asked him if he wanted to spend the next ten years in one of the nurseries.

Nolan doubted that she would be able to actually shoot someone, but it was a convincing bravura performance.

The *sauteur* thoughtfully brushed the fuzz of his nascent moustache, then shrugged and took a key from an overalls pocket. "Only old skulls, here," he said in English as he unlocked the door. "Achard is crazy, I think."

He pulled the door open, releasing a puff of cinnamon-scented air, then stepped back among his fellows when Vivi waved her gun in their direction.

The room beyond the door was dark. "Turn on a light," Nolan said. And he was able to understand the young man's reply: *There is no light. Light is bad for them.*

It seemed unfeigned. Nolan looked back at Vivi. "I'll need the flashlight," he said. With her free hand she pulled it from behind her belt and handed it to him. The barrel of it was sticky with white paint.

"And," he said reluctantly as he slid it into the pocket of his coat, "I think you've got to give me that gun too. You can shout if they move, and I'll come out and shoot them. Tell them that."

"Why—oh!" Her eyes widened and she quickly handed him the revolver. "Yes. In case of feeding the cat."

She barked out a sentence in French, and all six *sauteurs* were looking at Nolan, who now held both of their guns. Their faces looked cadaverous in the harsh blue-white mercury-vapor light, and they didn't shift their positions.

Nolan gave them all a stern frown—the two who had been stricken by the Scriabin notes just gaped at him—then slid one of the guns into his coat pocket and pulled out the flashlight. He switched it on and stepped into the dark room.

Dozens of skulls sat on shelves on the wall in front of him, and he swept the flashlight's beam across them. Some lacked jawbones, or had holes in their craniums, but a small, numbered brass plate gleamed in front of each.

He leaned back to peer out into the big chamber; Vivi was staring at the *sauteurs,* who had not moved. He returned his attention to the skulls—the numbers on the brass plates were in order, and he quickly found number 147, at waist height. The skull behind the plate was undamaged, and Nolan imagined that the flashlight caught a sardonic look in the empty eye sockets. He was holding the revolver in his right hand, and repressed the impulse to shoot the skull right now.

"Feed the cat?" he called.

"Still all right here, Harry," came Vivi's voice.

Now that he had found the skull, the light from the open doorway behind him was enough. He switched off the flashlight and put it back in his pocket. Then, wincing at the intimacy of what he was doing, he hooked his left thumb into one of the skull's eye sockets and gripped the temple with his fingers.

"Cat still fine?" he called as he lifted it. The jawbone was attached with black tape.

There was no answer, and as he started to turn, Vivi's hand chopped his right wrist. The revolver flew from his fingers, and she snatched it out of the air and hopped back, out into the chamber.

She was pointing the gun at his chest, and the skull in Nolan's left hand twisted forcefully to face her. The six *sauteurs* were all just blinking in evident confusion.

Vivi's face kinked in an unfamiliar smile, and she rolled her head from side to side so that Nolan could see a small ivory object in each of her ears.

Nolan's face was cold. The finger bones! he thought. With his left hand he held the skull up in front of his chest, while he flexed the fingers of his right.

"Whistle the Scriabin passage," suggested Vivi's voice, "try to clean this slate, as they do with new children in the nurseries. I will hear nothing." The gun in her hand rocked downward. "I think that is my old skull, yes? I confess I am embarrassed that it be exposed! Place it on the floor and step away from it."

Nolan's heart was pounding. I could *fling* it to the floor, he thought. It would shatter, but would that banish him from Vivi's mind? If the fragments were gathered together, they would still be his skull.

But Cadieux can't know that the gun in Vivi's hand isn't the only one we have.

Nolan slowly crouched and set the skull down—it shifted a couple of inches to resume facing Vivi—and then he gritted his teeth and threw himself to the concrete floor, pulling the revolver from his pocket.

A bullet exploded a crater in the floor beside his head, but he cocked his gun and leveled it at the big fuse box across the room. A second shot from Vivi's gun punched the rucksack on his back as he forced himself to aim carefully.

He touched the trigger, and as the gun fired he rolled away in the booming racket of echoes. The room had instantly gone dark except for a shower of bright sparks bursting from the far wall.

Nolan quickly got to his feet and tried to peer around the chamber, but within seconds even the sparks from the shattered fuse box had subsided to low flames. Hurrying footsteps sounded from every direction.

He pulled the flashlight out of his pocket and, holding it well out to the side as he'd been taught in the Army, switched it on. The beam of light momentarily caught several of the *sauteurs* blundering around in confusion, but he didn't see Vivi. He swept the light around the room, and noticed that the skull was no longer sitting on the floor by the open repository door.

He sprinted to the arch through which he and Vivi had entered the chamber. The flashlight beam showed only the empty passage beyond, and the ringing in his ears made it impossible to discern any faint hurrying footsteps in that direction.

He was viscerally aware that the flashlight made him a target, but as he began running he had to sweep the beam ahead of him to keep from colliding with the close walls, or stumbling on the uneven floor.

He remembered that he and Vivi had passed the entrances to a couple of side passages and one of the NID ladders on their way to the big electrically lit chamber. So one chance in three—probably one of the side passages, and Cadieux might steer her body down either of them. Nolan hoped the flashlight would show footprints in dust on a side passage's floor, if that were the case.

But as he ran past the iron ladder beside the stenciled NID.1, the flashlight beam caught a spot of white on one of the ladder rungs. He slid to a panting halt and held the light close to the rung while he touched the white smudge. It left a smear on his finger: white paint. Turning the flashlight beam upward, he saw another spot of white, two rungs farther up. The upper extent of the ladder disappeared through an iron ring too narrow for him to fit through with the rucksack on his back.

He shrugged the straps off his shoulders and let it fall to the floor, then shoved the flashlight and the revolver into his coat pockets. At any moment, Cadieux might... shoot Vivi's hand, or foot, or to baptize his skull with her blood.

The thought that it might be happening even now sent him climbing rapidly up the ladder.

He was in total darkness. His fast breath was batted back at him from the brick surface inches in front of his face, and his knees and elbows were soon aching with the restricted movements possible in the shaft's narrow space. The ladder's rungs were about a foot apart, and he estimated that he was taking hold of a higher one every second; at that rate he should climb a hundred feet in about a minute and a half. He lost count, but at what he thought was the hundred-rung point he found, to his fury, that he had to stop. His shoulders and knees were cramping to rigidity, and twice one of his shoes had skidded off a rung. The breath whistled through his clenched teeth and a downdraft cooled the sweat on his face.

He emptied his lungs and filled them, then resumed climbing, fiercely resenting the slower pace that his body forced on him.

Another minute had passed when his upward grasping hand found no rung; he slid the other hand up one of the iron side rails and felt a jagged, twisted end. He could hear that his fast breaths were now echoing in a wider space.

The darkness was still total, and he carefully stepped up two more rungs so that his arm would be free to pull the flashlight out of his pocket.

The flashlight beam sketched a round stone chamber no more than twenty feet across, with a dark archway on his right. The sides of the arch were broken, and with his free hand Nolan could feel fragments of masonry on the smooth paving stones around the top of the ladder shaft. A steady draft of stone-scented air from above contended with a heavy smell like sour milk.

He pointed the flashlight at the ceiling, and saw a couple of feet of the interrupted ladder extending down from an iron-ringed continuation of the shaft. The bottom rungs and side rails of that ladder section were twisted and broken off.

Something violent had happened here. How long ago? He hoped it had not happened when Cadieux had piloted Vivi through this chamber. Sweeping the flashlight beam over the floor, he saw no spots of blood among the broken stone fragments. He turned the flashlight on the broken side rail he was gripping, and sighed with relief to see rust on the sheared end of it.

He climbed up out of the lower shaft and bent to rub his knees and breathe deeply. The lowest of the rungs of the broken ladder overhead were about eight feet above the floor, and though he could certainly jump high enough to catch it, he wondered if Vivi's shorter body could.

He shined the frail flashlight beam through the open arch on his right, but the light was swallowed up in the total darkness. That passage led back south, though, and might connect with chambers of this sort at the other NID ladders, which with luck would not also be broken. Surely Cadieux had steered Vivi that way.

It occurred to him that he might have to shoot Vivi's gun-arm, and with his free hand he reluctantly drew the revolver from his pocket.

He had taken one step toward the arch when a low, bubbling growl echoed out of the depths of the passage beyond—a bigger, deeper sound than could ever issue from human throat and lungs. Then a gust of fetid air was being pushed out through the arch, and he heard stone cracking—something big and solid was rushing with tremendous speed up the passage toward him.

Nolan spun and leaped to the downward-hanging end of the interrupted ladder, and in three seconds he had clawed his way up until his heels bumped against the brick wall of the shaft. He glanced down; he had dropped the revolver and the flashlight, and in a moment the flashlight's diffused glow down there was blocked by some bulk. He could see nothing then, but he was palpably aware of a thing looking up at him.

His mind flinched at the perception of multitudes in the thing's attention, countless alien intelligences, and he got a sense of shared vast age and bottomless hatred that had curdled into one quality.

The aches in his knees and elbows were forgotten and he climbed as fast as he could, and when his laboring lungs and heart forced him to stop, he listened intently for crunching iron or breaking concrete below him—and he sagged with relief on his perch when he heard nothing but his own fast breathing. He looked up—uselessly—and wondered how far below the surface he might be. He thought he must be several hundred feet above the passage where he had left the rucksack.

He began rapidly climbing again, and he was startled when after several minutes one of his metronomically upreaching hands bumped a wooden surface. There was a cover on the shaft.

After a moment of sheer panic, he braced himself and pushed strongly upward on the cover, and he exhaled in relief when it swung upward with a creak of hinges.

He let the cover rest on his shoulders as he stepped up two more rungs and felt to the sides—a wooden floor was under his fingers. And when he turned his head on his aching neck, he saw to his left a yard-long line of bright light at the floor level. Squinting closely at it, he could also make out fainter lines of light that defined a tall rectangle above it.

It was a door. He climbed out of the shaft and quietly lowered the wooden cover back to its previous position. He straightened up, then limped to the door and brushed his fingers across its surface. He felt wood, then a lockplate and a knob. He twisted the knob, and it turned.

He took a deep breath and pushed the door open, and he saw Vivi.

She stood, silhouetted by daylight streaming through a cobwebbed window, on the other side of an empty room; she spun around at the creak of the door hinges. She had at some point lost the bandage on her head; her forehead was darkly bruised, but the cut hadn't started bleeding again.

Nolan called, hoarsely, "Did you feed the cat?"

"Harry!" she cried, and she limped to him and threw her arms around him. "I thought you must be dead!"

She had spoken with her natural British accent, and he sighed in profound relief and let his aching knees buckle. A moment later he and Vivi were sitting on the wooden floor, and he could see a line of blood down her cheek from one ear.

The revolver she had taken from a *sauteur*, he saw, was lying on the floor by the window.

"That door was always locked," she said. He gave her a puzzled look, and she went on, "Harry, this is the place! This is the nursery I lived in till I was six years old!" She pointed at a wall, on which Nolan saw faded images of camels and a pyramid under a rainbow. "I helped paint that mural, after the big flood wrecked this room."

She got to her feet and slowly walked to the wall. Brushing her fingers over the faded figures on the mural, she said, "This is the first thing I saw, after that big chamber with the electric lights down there. The sight of this—the memories, *my* memories! *I* painted that rainbow!—it brought me back, pushed him out."

She turned to him. "Harry, how did we get here? Did we climb one of those ladders?"

He nodded. "NID point 1."

"And *nid* is *nest,* in French. I should have guessed." She touched one ear. "My ears are scraped."

"He shoved Beaufroy's finger bones in them, so he wouldn't hear the Scriabin. I guess he tossed them after he was away from me."

"That was clever." She shook her head sharply. "But he could have been more gentle with a body he hopes to take."

Still sitting, Nolan looked past her. For a moment he thought the dusty floor was littered with fragments of broken pottery; then he recognized half of a jawbone. Other fragments were pieces of a cranium.

"Oh," she said, "yes, when I came to myself here, a few minutes ago, I found I was holding a skull! Is it his? I broke it, to start with."

"It's his, all right. He shot at me and took it away with him. I—"

"*Shot* at you?" Her eyes darted from his head to his crossed legs.

"He hit Gertrude Stein's rucksack. Which is gone. But I ran after him—after you—and luckily I saw a streak of your white paint on that first ladder." He looked around at the dusty room. "This place is empty?"

"Yes. They have others. We should—" She peered at him. "You look absolutely knackered."

"So do you. It was a long climb. I—" He shivered and went on carefully: "I believe I saw one of the *Shaydim*. Or many—it seemed to be a lot of them in one. Farther west than Beaufroy said they'd be." He rubbed his face with both hands, then looked over his shoulder at the door to the shaft. "Well, I didn't *see* it. But it saw me."

"A devil? When, where?"

Nolan described the broken ladder and the thing that had rushed at him from a side passage, and its palpable awareness of him when he had climbed away into the shaft above it. "*Their* awareness, it felt like."

He stood up, in careful stages, and looked out the dusty window at a recessed doorway in a white wall, no more than twenty feet away across some narrow street.

He turned back to her. "You said once that you didn't know where this place is."

"I still don't." She waved at the window. "That view is no help. You and I moved more or less north, down there, and we certainly didn't go under the river. So—maybe near the Gare d'Orléans railway station."

Nolan looked around at the room, and he tried to imagine couches, a table, children. "Was it ever . . . pleasant, here?"

She looked at the cartoonish camels on the faded mural. "Sometimes. I had friends, until they changed and I didn't. I wonder if my bed is still upstairs." She looked up at him and cocked an eyebrow.

He smiled and shrugged. "If you like. Maybe there's running water somewhere—you've got blood on your face."

"Maybe. I believe they maintain several of these nurseries, and use them in rotation." She led the way down a hall to a set of wooden stairs. She paused, looking at faint grime streaks low on the walls. "I'm back here again," she said quietly, then started up the stairs. "But everyone's gone."

At the first landing she stepped into another hall and began walking hesitantly past a row of empty doorframes with screw-holes in hinge-shaped patches on the jambs. The hall and the rooms echoed with her footsteps and Nolan's, emphasizing the absence of children's voices.

At the entrance to one of the rooms she stopped, and touched a hinge-patch on the doorjamb. "The doors had been taken away even then," she said, then added, "I slept in here."

Nolan followed her into a long room lit by a row of tall windows, several of which were shaded by vines growing across the outsides of the glass. No furniture at all stood on the long bare floor.

Vivi crossed to stand by one of the windows. "My bed was right here." She turned to the window, which was one of those partly obscured by ivy. "It was out this window that I watched *gendarmes* paddle in boats down the flooded street."

Nolan tried to imagine four-year-old Vivi kneeling on a bed, one of a row of beds, peering out.

"Why do you suppose only a couple of those *sauteurs* reacted to the Scriabin?" he asked. "The others didn't seem to have earplugs."

"Those would have been the newest," Vivi said as she stepped away from the window. "Their parasites would still be a bit wobbly." She rolled her head and rubbed her shoulder. "Like mine.

"Water," she said, and she led him back into the hall and walked to the end, where faucets and a sink were mounted in an alcove. She twisted a faucet, and exhaled when a weak stream of rusty water trickled into the sink.

After catching enough of the water to fill her cupped hands, she splashed her face and wiped it on the collar of her coat. "You too."

Nolan obediently splashed a handful of the water on his own face and ran his fingers through his hair.

"Now we—" she began. Then her eyes widened and she hurried out of the room and back down the stairs.

When Nolan caught up with her she was in the downstairs room on her knees, looking around uneasily at the scattered skull fragments. She looked up. "I was afraid they might have started to crawl away. But they do move, when I try to sweep them together."

Nolan grimaced. "They're pointing toward *you*, as best they can. When I lifted the skull off the shelf down there in the repository room, it twisted around to face you."

"Good God." She wiped her hands on her shirt. "I shouldn't have broken it. But we've got to gather them up. It's too bad the rucksack is gone."

Nolan pulled his arms out of Stein's coat and kicked a stray tooth aside to lay the coat on the floor. "We can bundle them up in this."

"I don't know if Miss Stein will want it back now. Harry, we've got to pulverize these pieces *today*. What time is it, do you think?"

Nolan looked out the window again, but with the other building so close on the opposite side of the street, he could only tell that it was not yet dusk. He tried to remember how long they had spent in the catacombs. To his surprise, he concluded, "It's probably only about noon."

"I don't want to feed him to pigs. They're alive—I don't want him occupying a pig."

"I'd mix the ground up pieces with gasoline—"

"And some holy water!"

"And then burn it in a pan, and toss the pan into the river. Holy water's a good idea."

She was picking up the twisting pieces of bone and tossing them onto the red silk lining of Stein's coat. "I'm getting more Catholic all the time." She paused and looked up at him, frowning . "Oh—and Pagan, somehow."

"A bit," he agreed.

Nolan knew Cybele was real, and it seemed that Moloch was too. One was drastically preferable to the other, but in some sense both gods were on one side of a fundamental line.

He shrugged, and thought of the ladder out of the catacombs, "Follow any spots of white paint, I guess."

She shook her head. "I hope they're visible."

When they had gathered up every scrap of bone, and swept the dusty floor with their palms to catch the tiniest splinters and shaken them onto the coat lining, Nolan bundled up the coat like a big tweed bag.

"Let's not forget your gun," he said.

"Oh," said Vivi. "Right." She picked up her revolver and handed it to him. "You should keep it. If he comes back on, the first thing he'll want to do is kill you."

Nolan nodded and flipped out the cylinder. Three of the brass shell casings showed dimpled primers, but there were three other rounds in the cylinder, still live. He closed the cylinder and slid the gun under his belt.

He hefted Stein's coat carefully and turned to the street-side door. "It's sure to be locked," he said.

Vivi managed a smile as she pulled from her pocket the two metal strips she had used to pick the lock at the Church of Saint-Jacques du Haut-Pas this morning.

The pins of the old lock yielded to her jiggling, and Nolan pushed the door open. They stepped outside, into breezy fresh air, and Vivi began walking toward a cross street a hundred feet away. Nolan followed, carrying the bundled-up tweed coat like an eccentric sack.

At the equally narrow cross street, Vivi looked left and right and nodded. "This is the Rue des Saints-Pères. The river's just to our left." She looked back down the street behind them. "I think I've walked past that door a dozen times, without recognizing it." She shrugged. "The only time I would have seen it from the outside was when I was escaping, and then I was looking the other way."

They trudged between close apartment buildings whose top-floor windows shone with reflected sunlight, then blinked in the glare when they reached the wide noontime lanes of the Quai Voltaire, crowded and noisy with traffic.

After a pause for restorative hot coffee at a street vendor's cart, they pushed on and crossed the Pont du Carrousel, stopping several times to lean on the concrete abutment and just watch barges slide past on the river below. At last they made their way to the offices of *Le Fouisseur* on the Rue de Rivoli just east of the Louvre, where Nolan was able to get a hundred francs in cash by signing a forfeiture of the more substantial amount the editor owed him for several drawings.

Late afternoon found them sitting on the north embankment below the span of the Pont Neuf, staring at a smoking iron pan on the pavement. The concrete embankment sloped down to the river at this point, and Nolan got to his feet, ready to kick the pan into the river. None of the passersby had done more than look curiously at the pan when it had been flaming, evidently supposing it to be an ill-considered attempt at cooking some sort of supper, but Nolan was afraid a *gendarme* might happen by and object to the smell of burnt gasoline.

"Wait a moment," said Vivi, leaning over the pan to shake a few drop into it from an emptied Coca-Cola bottle. "May as well use every drop of holy water."

After leaving the *Le Fouisseur* office, they had embarked on a tour of shops along the quai, and had bought the pan, a big canvas bag and a small leather one, a bottle of Coca-Cola, and a gallon can half full of gasoline. Everything had gone into the canvas bag except for the pieces of Cadieux's skull, which they had carefully picked out of Stein's coat and dropped into the leather bag. Nolan had put on the coat.

Then they had walked up and down the streets, darting into lanes to tuck the leather bag under the momentarily paused wheels of one bus or truck after another. Motorists and pedestrians had shouted questions at them as the vehicles rolled over the bag, but no one had tried to interfere, and after twenty minutes they had retreated around a corner to a table at a sidewalk café, where Nolan ordered a beer while Vivi drank the Coca-Cola. They could feel no lumps in the bag, which had by now been run over by heavy wheels a dozen times.

There had been one more stop: at the Church of Saint-Germain l'Auxerrois, where they had filled the empty Coca-Cola bottle with holy water. Vivi had made the sign of the cross, in apology for the probable sacrilege.

On the embankment pavement, they had turned the leather bag inside out over the pan. No piece of Cadieux's skull had been bigger than a fingernail, and most had been rendered to little more than jagged gravel and coarse sand. Nolan brushed and shook every bit into the pan.

They had splashed it all liberally with gasoline, shaken the holy water onto it, and then Nolan had struck a match to it.

Both of them had stepped back as the gasoline flared up. It burned for several minutes, and when the flames subsided, they had both sat down, a comfortable yard away from the still-radiating pan.

Now Vivi set the thoroughly shaken-out Coca-Cola bottle on the pavement and stood up. "Okay," she said, stepping back.

Nolan kicked the pan, and it skittered down the concrete embankment slope into the water. A splash and hiss and a brief wisp of steam, and it was gone.

Vivi had exhaled sharply in the moment the pan sank, and Nolan stepped forward to catch her if she should fall; but she caught her balance and straightened. For several seconds she stood motionless, and Nolan watched her carefully.

At last she stretched her fingers, looked out across the water to the trees on the western end of the Île de la Cite, then pinched up the hem of her coat with one hand and did a brief jig on the pavement.

She laughed softly. "I felt him go. Like having a tooth pulled." She hopped up and down twice. "A tooth with a really long root." She gave Nolan a wondering smile. "Thank you, Harry. Beyond words."

Nolan smiled back at her. "I'm happy we did it."

Thinking that some bone fragments might still be clinging to the interior of the leather bag, Nolan tossed it too into the river. He put the bottle and the gasoline can into the canvas bag and dropped it into a nearby dustbin. Vivi took his arm, and they began walking east along the embankment.

Their shadows stretched away in front of them. The arches of the Pont au Change shone in afternoon daylight a quarter of a mile ahead, and Nolan recalled a ramp that would take them up to the Place du Châtelet. A few minutes later they had arrived there, and were sitting on the low wall around the fountain.

An old woman in a threadbare shawl sat on the wall a few yards away, shivering and holding the beads of a rosary. Nolan got up and took off Stein's coat, then walked to where the old woman sat.

"*Un cadeau de Gertrude Stein,*" he said, handing it to her. *A gift from Gertrude Stein.*

The old woman laid aside her rosary and slid her thin arms into the coat sleeves, which were the right length for her. Looking up, she quavered, "*Merci. Bénédictions sur elle.*" She picked up the rosary and resumed her prayers.

Thank you, he translated mentally. *Blessings upon her.*

Nolan nodded and went back to sit beside Vivi.

She stretched and yawned, then leaned forward to look past Nolan at the old woman.

"I'm not sure if that counts as a corporal work of mercy or not," she said. When Nolan gave her a puzzled look, she added, "You know, feed the hungry, clothe the naked, shelter the homeless. I don't know about *give away someone else's coat.*" She sighed and got to her feet. "There's a bath at my building. Two francs. And then—I'm starving."

The bath in Vivi's building was up another flight of stairs from her flat, and before she went off to find the *concierge,* Vivi offered to let Nolan bathe first, and then use the same water herself; but Nolan assured her that he could afford to spend four francs for two baths. She got the concierge to agree to three francs for two baths, and Nolan was pleasantly surprised to find that there was enough hot water for both.

An hour later they were seated at an indoor table at the Café Reggie in the short Passage Sainte-Avoye, three streets south of Vivi's flat. Vivi was wearing her brown corduroy skirt and a fresh white blouse under a black sweater. After her bath she had brushed her hair, and curly blonde bangs covered the bruise and cut on her forehead. Her hazel eyes shone with renewed vitality. Nolan was still wearing his gray woolen trousers, his once-white shirt, and a secondhand coat they had bought on the walk here.

Their table was at the back of the café, under a very old-looking brick arch. The air was steamy, and redolent with a smell of garlic that Nolan guessed had not abated here in centuries. A new electric lamp mounted on the arch overhead kindled a warm golden gleam in the bottle of white wine that stood between them.

Vivi insisted that Nolan tell her everything that had happened in the catacombs after her consciousness had been pushed down by Cadieux's, and when he had finished his account, and she had pressed him for every detail he could recall, she looked at traces of white paint still visible under the fingernails of her right hand.

"I guess that was some leap," she said.

"To that broken-off ladder?" Nolan tried to laugh, but just shook his head and poured Sancerre into the two glasses on the table. "If you—he—heard that thing in the side passage, I bet you could have leaped even higher."

She picked up her glass and took a deep sip of the wine.

Nolan raised his own glass. He breathed deeply, and it seemed to him that he had not been able to take a deep breath since Friday night, when he had pointed his .45 at a little girl on the embankment beside the Pont Saint-Michel.

"These three days have been a big leap," he said. I've leaped right out of my old life, he thought.

She gave him a rueful smile. "I'm sorry I jolted you into it."

He thought about the closed circuit his life had been during these solitary last four years—he travels the fastest who travels alone!

"Not before time," he said.

She cocked her head and gave him a serious, curious look. Then she nodded, as if having formulated some questions to bring up at another time.

A waiter walked up and set on their table two steaming plates of the roasted chicken and mashed potatoes they had ordered. They both began eating hungrily.

The chicken breasts had been marinated in oil and vinegar and garlic, and the skin was broiled nearly black, and Nolan doubted that he'd ever enjoyed a meal more. "We've got to come back here," he said.

Again she looked at him curiously.

Nolan had begun to think of coffee when Vivi frowned and put down her fork. She turned her hand over and lightly tapped the tattoo on her wrist. She looked up. "It's hot."

Nolan frowned. "Cauterizing itself?" he hazarded. "Now that the soul it was linked to is gone?"

Vivi bit her lip. "Could you see if they have ice here?"

Nolan got up and hurried toward the street entrance, and within a minute he was back at the table with a wooden bowl of ice cubes. Vivi quickly rubbed one of them on her wrist.

"That helps." She waved her hand in the warm air. "It seems to be wearing off."

"Maybe you just burned it on that pan, by the river."

She nodded and picked up her fork again. "Stay at my flat tonight?"

Nolan thought about the *sauteur* children, and Achard's damaged Stutz. "Yes, thank you."

She gave him a wry, tired grin. "Of course keeping Saint Genevieve in mind."

"Of course. Yes. I remember the statue at the Pont de la Tournelle."

"The little girl made of stone."

"... Yes."

"Will you go back to your flat tomorrow?"

"Not tomorrow. I'll find another place for a while." He poured wine into their glasses. "I can get a fresher copy of my passport from the American Consulate tomorrow, and I'm sure I can withdraw money from the bank without actually going in. I think I'd be wise to leave Paris."

She had picked up the bottle and was studying the label. "Back to the United States, then?"

"No. I tried that five years ago." He swirled the wine in his glass. "What are your plans, now that you're ... alone in your mind?"

"I'm very glad to finally *be* alone ... in my mind," she said carefully. "I never thought that would happen. But—"

Nolan spoke quickly, interrupting. "The thing is, Vivi, I don't want to say ... *goodbye forever,* to you."

She nodded, still not looking at him. "Likewise. But I've never been out of Paris."

"There are other places. Nantes, La Rochelle."

"I suppose. For a while."

Nolan wondered if she meant she would eventually return to Paris, but her tone had been muted, almost mournful. Did she imagine she was fated to die young?

Before he could think of anything to ask her, the waiter returned, carrying a piece of paper which he laid on the table in front of Vivi. The man looked back toward the entrance.

"A child, *mademoiselle*," he said, "run away weeping now, wrote this and said to give this to you."

Nolan's chest had gone cold at the words *a child*. To the waiter he said, "Boy? Girl?"

"A boy, *monsieur*. Perhaps eight years old."

"*Merci,*" Vivi told the waiter firmly, and when he had walked away she passed the note to Nolan.

The words on it were clumsily scrawled in pencil: *Une année vous une année moi grande richese longue vie.*

One year you, Nolan translated mentally, *one year me great wealth long life.*

"This is from *him*!" Viv looked back toward the street entrance and started to stand, then sank back in her chair. "Eight years old—the boy's parasite soul couldn't have been firmly attached yet."

"Him?" Nolan stared at her. "*Him?* Vivi, it can't be, we burned him up and dropped him in the river—"

"Oh, Harry, no, we didn't! That wasn't *him*, his *soul*, that was just his soul's hook in my mind. We broke *that*, thank God. Hush now." She closed her eyes for several seconds, frowning. "Yes," she said finally, opening them, "he's definitely gone from my mind. The ... *space* where he used to be is empty. That tooth *is* pulled." She scratched her tattooed wrist. "But obviously he can still sense me, even from outside. This shared mark must be how he can do that." She scratched harder. "I wonder how deep in the skin it is."

"But—" Nolan too threw a harried glance back toward the street door. "How can he—"

"Let me think. His soul has no body at all now, but it's obviously still in the *sauteur* web. He pushed out that boy's own parasite just now, and—for a few moments—took over the boy's body."

Nolan thought about it and gloomily decided she was probably right. He sighed. "And he still wants yours," he pointed out. "To share, at least. *Une année vous une année moi.* A year for you and a year for him—as if he'd ever let you back in. Is that even possible?"

She shook her head. "No. He's got no foothold in my mind now. *No,*" she added emphatically. "He's dreaming." She drank the rest of the wine in her glass and set the glass down firmly.

Nolan picked up the note and looked again at the penciled scrawl, but Vivi snatched it out of his hands. After a moment she dropped it and sat back. Her face was expressionless.

Nolan saw now that a single word had been penciled on the back of the note: *kykeon.*

Nolan looked up at her cautiously. "That's some kind of drug, you said yesterday."

"What? Oh—yes." She yawned and rubbed her hand across her mouth. "Yes, they gave it to us at the nursery." For a few seconds she was silent, then added, "Disorientation—you don't know who you are. Your identity floats away from you. Loose." She yawned again. "Ordinarily it settles back down to its proper place after a few minutes."

She leaned back in her chair and looked at the ceiling. Her skin had paled, and Nolan could see the shallow cut in the side of her neck where the *sauteur* bullet had nicked her two nights ago. "This building used to be a convent," she said. "The Sisters of Sainte-Avoye. Maybe I should become a nun. 'Get thee to a nunnery.'"

Nolan understood that her last sentence was a quote from something. He wondered if the café served hard liquor.

"He's *not* dreaming," she said softly. "It's possible that he *could* do it, if he was in some body—even just for a few moments—and we both took a dose of *kykeon*. We'd be disattached, he might be able to switch places." She gripped her shoulders and rocked in her chair, hugging herself. Nolan recognized it by now as her reaction to stress.

He pushed the note away from her. "But—no—if he could shove himself into that kid's body just now, why won't he just do that again, and keep the body? Instead of trying this *kykeon* trick to get yours?"

Vivi lowered her gaze and frowned. "No, Harry, don't you see? The boy ran away crying. Cadieux wasn't able to maintain his hold in it for long. The boy's mind wasn't... *shaped* for him."

"Shaped," echoed Nolan.

"Yes. *My* mind *is* shaped for him. They did it in the nursery. Like—like clay folded tightly around a wax figure, for lost-wax casting, you know? You and I melted the wax and poured it out, this afternoon." She tapped her bruised forehead. "But the Cadieux-shaped cavity is still there."

Nolan hoped she hadn't considered the rest of her casting metaphor: the filling of the cavity with molten metal, and then, when the metal cooled and solidified, the breaking away of the now-superfluous clay.

She tapped the note, and then her wrist. "This was a prelude. He'll get in touch again."

Nolan clenched his fists on the table. "So let's get to Nantes before that. La Rochelle—hell, Rome, Cairo! There can't be a lot of imperfectly moored *sauteur* folk for him to occupy in those places."

She touched her face hesitantly. "Tomorrow. We'll need money, and I can't win at the races anymore. Miss Gertrude said she'd give me traveling money, for Beltran's sake." She looked over her shoulder toward the restaurant entrance. "Let's not hang about for coffee."

Nolan laid some francs on the table and stood up. Vivi took his arm as they walked out into the narrow Passage Sainte-Avoye and made their way, anxiously, back to Vivi's flat.

At one point during the night, Nolan was awakened by a whisper from Vivi and her grip on his upper arm; she had got out of her bed and was crouched on the floor beside him in the darkness.

"My tattoo," she whispered. "Woke me up. Burning again."

They waited tensely, without moving, and after a couple of minutes Nolan heard confused mumbling from outside her bolted door, then uncertain footsteps descending the stairs. The footsteps seemed very light.

Vivi released his arm. "He fell out of control before he could knock. I think that was the original child, just now."

Nolan quickly got to his feet and unbolted the door, but when he stood on the landing outside, he could see nothing in the darkness, and the only sounds were distant music and the wind in the eaves. Thinking of a child suddenly finding itself on a dark stairway on a cold night in the Marais—*run away weeping now,* the waiter had said, *perhaps eight years old*—Nolan called, *"Enfant! Venez et soyez en securite!"* Child, come and be safe!

There was no response. He blundered down the lightless stairs to the alley, and called again. There was no use in groping his way in one direction rather than the other, and after waiting a full five minutes, and calling several more times, he gave up and climbed the stairs back to Vivi's flat.

She was waiting at the open door. "The child's intended possessor took control again pretty quickly, I imagine," she said quietly as Nolan stepped in and she closed the door and re-bolted it. She was rubbing the back of her left wrist. "But—for the sake of the lost child that was once me!—thank you for trying."

It took Nolan a while to get back to sleep, and he was sure from her breathing that the same was true of Vivi.

CHAPTER FIFTEEN:
What Purpose?

Sunlight and a cool breeze through the partly opened window woke Nolan, and he was sure the hour must be getting on toward noon. He rolled over on the floor and stretched; aches in his knees and elbows brought back the memory of his feverish climb up the ladder in the subterranean shaft, the day before.

He sat up carefully and looked across the room at Vivi, who was still asleep. She had made that climb too, at least her body had. Her fair hair, no longer a tangled thatch, was feathered across her forehead, covering the bruise she had sustained at the Cybeline temple two days ago. He didn't want to wake her.

I'm very glad to finally be alone... in my mind, she had said last night. *I never thought that would happen.*

Nolan yawned, soundlessly.

Beltran Iglesias—*a sort of father to me,* she had said—was dead, murdered three years ago. And Elodie—*mother and sister to me*—was gone, broken up and dissolved in the Seine... after one last, fleeting contact with Nolan, under the water. A vision of Vivi as a child.

And now there's me, he thought.

From where he sat he could see his passport and the depleted bundle of franc notes on the floor below the window, along with the revolver that she had carried up from the catacombs yesterday.

So we're off to La Rochelle, he thought, or somewhere. I can get work illustrating, and Vivi... He smiled. Vivi can be a pool hustler. We—

She sat up in bed, blinking around. She was scratching her wrist. "Good morning," she said gruffly. She rubbed her eyes. "I'm sorry—my tattoo is burning again."

"*Ach*." Nolan frowned and got to his feet. "We'll be leaving Paris soon. I don't think he can do much in the meantime, besides make impossible offers." He didn't mention *kykeon*.

"Not do much? Harry, what if he commandeers a *sauteur* child long enough to get hold of a gun?"

Nolan recalled her saying that Thibaud Cadieux's evicted spirit could not hold on to even a very young *sauteur*'s body for more than a few minutes. The boy who had written the hasty note at the restaurant last night had apparently run away weeping immediately after handing the note to the waiter.

And the person who had stood outside Vivi's door in the middle of the might a few hours ago—who had almost certainly been Cadieux in a briefly held *sauteur* child—had fled without making any contact at all.

Nolan tried not to sound as if he were humoring her: "Vivi, even if he could grab a gun in the few minutes he'd have—the last thing he wants to do is shoot you. And why would he waste one second of his slippery hold on a kid to shoot me?"

"Oh—" She scrambled out of bed, wearing an undershirt and socks and white briefs, and hurried to the closet alcove. For a moment he had glimpsed raw scrapes on her bony white knees.

"He wouldn't shoot you *fatally*, at first," she said as she pulled on her twill trousers. "If he could somehow get hold of a bottle of *kykeon*," she went on breathlessly as she yanked at a flannel shirt, "as well as a gun, he would *threaten* to *start* shooting you, unless I did what he asked."

"Oh."

"You see?"

One sure way to prevent that unlikely development would be for Nolan to leave her, go away on his own. But it was fantastic—and in any case they'd be leaving Paris shortly.

"That's impossible, Vivi. We—"

"You know what's possible and what's not?"

Nolan let himself imagine it happening. "Well, even if he did, you'd be crazy to—you'd never—I mean, he'd certainly kill me anyway. After."

He waved toward her. "And you'd be gone forever, in spite of whatever he'd tell you. You know that."

She was buttoning her shirt and looking around the floor. Almost inaudibly, she muttered, "Wouldn't matter." More loudly she said, "Do you see my shoes anywhere?"

Her sotto voce remark had startled him, and touched him, deeply. "Vivi," he began, with no idea how he was going to continue, but she interrupted him with, "There they are!" and snatched her shoes up from where they had been lying in the corner. She sat down on the bed to put them on.

Her hands stopped moving when there was a knock on the door.

She gave Nolan a startled look, then hurried to the window and picked up the revolver. She sat down on the floor, pointing the gun at the door.

"Open it," she whispered.

Nolan crossed to the door, hoping it wasn't the concierge, about to find a gun pointed at her.

He twisted the knob and pulled the door open, standing to one side. Bright daylight spilled across the threadbare rug.

Silhouetted in the doorway stood a little boy perhaps eight years old, wearing the same knickerbocker trousers and short collarless jacket he had been wearing two days ago. Nolan recognized him, and knew that his red hair was cut short in front because it had caught fire when he had involuntarily fired a pistol in front of his face, in Achard's automobile. The boy's hands were empty, and, seeing Vivi at the far end of the room, he turned in a circle with his arms out, clearly to show that he had no weapon.

Nolan's heart was thudding in his chest. He recalled that the boy's name was Robin, and he wondered if the mind in the boy's body knew that.

"I'll wager that was your own nursery," the boy piped, nodding to Vivi. "Your memories jumped up and crowded me straight out!"

The moment seemed stretched, almost twanging. In spite of the events and revelations of the last three days, Nolan's mind rebelled against this new demand: to believe that this child was the current host of Thibaud Cadieux's spirit; and that Thibaud Cadieux—who was killed fifteen years ago—had inhabited Vivi's mind until Nolan kicked a frying pan into the Seine yesterday!

Nolan gripped the edge of the door to restrain himself from simply slamming and bolting it, and then resuming his conversation with Vivi as if there had been no interruption.

The boy was sweating, and Nolan noticed a couple of dots of imbedded gunpowder in his forehead. To Vivi, the boy called, "Oh, lay it aside, *chica*, of course that me-a-year-you-a-year idea would not work. It was my thought that you are as foolish as this young man gaping at me from behind the door. I see you are not. But—"

"What do you want?" asked Vivi, her voice tight with tension. "You can't have much time."

Nolan stepped carefully from behind the door and crossed to stand beside Vivi. It occurred to him that this was the first time Vivi had ever been able to actually converse with her *sauteur* parasite, and she clearly found it disorienting.

The boy tapped the side of his head and smiled. "My feet are firm in the stirrups of this one. The proper *caballero* must have been thrown recently, and not yet got firmly back in the saddle. I feel him pushing, but I am secure here for a time yet." He let his little hand slide lightly over his face. "Powder burns!" His tone was light, but sounded forced as he went on, "I suspect he tried to shoot himself, but his hand wavered!"

Proper *caballero*! thought Nolan bitterly. You mean another *sauteur*, the one I whistled out of this hijacked body in in Achard's automobile two days ago.

Nolan noticed some ink marks on the boy's hand, and the boy caught his glance.

"My birthdate. *My* noted birthdate, to stake my claim on this body." The boy looked past Nolan at Vivi. His voice softened: "I see you at last, *chica*! All the years I lived in your head, I could only imagine what our body looked like. Thin!" He looked around at the sparsely and poorly furnished room. "Is this the place where we lived? I should have helped with more horseraces."

"What do you want?" Vivi repeated.

Nolan was achingly aware that Cadieux's hold on this boy's body might slip at any moment, and be replaced by the *sauteur* who had held a gun on him in Achard's automobile; and that person must not learn where Vivi lived.

"We talk somewhere else," Nolan said.

The boy gave Nolan a mocking smile. "Ah, the *amante* speaks! None of this has to do with you, *niño*."

"It has everything to do with him," said Vivi. She didn't elaborate, and the boy gave Nolan a more careful look. "And," Vivi went on, getting to her feet, "he's right. Let's all go for a walk."

The boy looked worried, than shrugged. "I can always find you again, if I fall out of here."

He turned and started down the stairs. Vivi found an old cloth purse in the closet alcove and dropped the revolver into it, then she and Nolan followed the boy.

In the alley, Nolan took the lead and guided the other two out to the narrow Rue du Temple. He waved to the right, then walked between Vivi and the boy—who was walking slowly, with his arms slightly out to the sides, as if for balance. The street was in shadow even at this noontime hour, and they made their way at a measured pace past parked bicycles and stacked crates. Vivi kept her hand in her purse.

When they had walked out onto the sunlit lanes of the Rue de Bretagne, the boy waved ahead, toward the clustered trees in the Square du Temple.

"If I were as accustomed to this body as I am to yours," he said breathlessly to Vivi, "I could walk ten miles and not be out of breath. But in this—walking is too up and down. We must sit."

The square was certainly far enough from Vivi's flat, and Nolan slanted their course across the street to the entrance gate. Once inside the gated square, the boy hurried across the packed dirt to a green wooden bench and sat down. The toes of his shoes only brushed the ground.

Vivi and Nolan stood in front of the bench, as if to block the boy from running away; though in fact he seemed exhausted.

"Call me...Thibaud," the boy said, with the air of choosing the name at random. He spoke quickly, evidently fearing that in spite of the inked marks on his hand he might at any moment lose control of Robin's body. Looking up at Vivi, he said, "The Cybelines tried to kill you, you know. They will try again." He looked past her for several seconds, then went on, "At their temple you spoke about how the Moloch bull might be killed. There is an old fable concerning that." The boy paused again, thinking. "If they catch you, tell them you know where the mirror is."

"What mirror?" asked Vivi, frowning in convincing puzzlement.

"Ah, you do not know that story. Never mind—the man who killed me made a thing that's described in this fable as a mirror. They will know what you mean." Even sitting down, his breathing was labored. "They will not kill you then."

"No," said Vivi, "they'll just force me to take them to this... this *mirror*. Where is it?"

Thibaud shook the boy's head. "I think it is destroyed, and in any case must not be found. But they will want it, and not kill you. Be clever. Delay, escape."

"Why do you care if they kill me? We have no attachment anymore."

Having led Thibaud away from Vivi's flat, Nolan now simply wanted to get rid of him. No attachment, he thought—perhaps not, Vivi, but you said your mind is shaped for him, like clay folded around a wax figure. And *kykeon* exists.

Vivi still had her hand in her purse. She glanced behind her at the overhanging trees—at two old men huddled over a chess game, and a well-dressed woman sitting on a bench beside a baby carriage—as if to reassure herself that a normal world did exist.

Thibaud leaned forward. "I will have a body of my own. You can do things I can't presently do—I need to renew talks with a certain architect—"

"You mentioned him," Nolan interrupted, "in the Cybeline temple." He cast his mind back to the conversation that had led to Vivi's head being slammed against the temple's marble floor. "Charles-Édouard something."

Vivi gave him a blank look.

"Charles-Édouard Jeanneret," said Thibaud. "Yes. I cannot approach him as a child. And there are things I need to know about the *apaches*—"

The boy looked up and saw the expression on Vivi's face. "I have seen the future, remember," he told her. "And I know many dire secrets. I can quickly make you wealthy beyond your present ability to imagine." He frowned and cocked his head. "You understand? Wealth, riches? Yes? A palace, servants..." Vivi's expression hadn't changed, and he went on, a bit desperately, "Good food in plenty, you understand? Warm clothes..."

He coughed and spit, then looked around at the square in evident alarm. Nolan and Vivi took a step back. The boy squinted up at Nolan and Vivi, and his eyes fixed on Nolan. His small hand touched his raggedly cut hair.

"Harry Nolan," he said.

"Robin," Nolan said, and gave Vivi a nod of confirmation.

The boy took a deep breath and let it out. "Okay, pal, who was just here?" He glanced at Vivi. "Cadieux? You're the Chastain girl?" He slapped at his clothing, perhaps to see if he carried a gun; he shrugged and went on, "They say you two shot up one of the repositories, took his skull. Did you *evict* him?" Vivi had taken another step back, and was staring at him impassively, her purse slightly raised. Robin went on, "Or was it Tremblay? His head's gone dead and nobody knows where his hands have got to."

Robin started to get to his feet, then sagged back onto the bench. His face kinked in a very adult expression of annoyance. "Damn. Whoever it was must walk like an *ourang outang*. All the wrong muscles. Are we even still in Paris? I feel like I've walked for miles."

Maybe you have, Nolan thought; this body, anyway. He caught Vivi's eye and jerked his head back toward the gate. She nodded, and they began backing away from the boy on the bench.

"Achard will find you!" he called after them. "He loves that car!"

Back on the wide Rue de Bretagne, Nolan and Vivi hurried west, by unspoken agreement heading farther away from her flat. Vivi was hardly as tall as Nolan's shoulder, but he had to take long steps to keep up with her.

After they had crossed several streets, she slowed to a halt. "You heard what Cadieux said," she burst out. "We need to talk to...the man who killed him!"

That was Picasso, Nolan thought, on the Quai de Passy in 1910. He recalled Picasso's dark, shabby studio. *He works,* Stein had said, *halfway between the cemetery to the west and the church to the east*; and Toklas had added, *He faces west, but fears it.*

"Why?" Nolan asked.

"Why? Because he has the mirror, the mirror that's the baby's face, in Beltran's story! He *made* it. It must be a painting."

"Thibaud said it was destroyed. And anyway—"

"He said he *thought* it was destroyed. I'm sure that's what he was told. But Picasso sold his soul for the ability to paint—I can't believe he would destroy *any* piece of what cost him so dear." She nodded. "But I don't think he'd want to keep such a thing near himself either."

"He didn't sell his soul. He—what did Stein say? He made a bargain with God—he'd give up painting if God would save his little sister—"

"And God didn't keep His part of the bargain. Near enough." She resumed walking.

Nolan fell into step beside her. He was unfamiliar with these streets north of the river, and when he and Vivi came to a wide six-way intersection he blinked around at the tall old apartment buildings that stood like ships on the wide sea of pavement. Picasso's studio was a good two miles away, and he supposed Vivi meant to go there now.

"It would have to be a—a portrait of Moloch," he said, "wouldn't it? To act as a mirror?"

"It would have to be a portrait of what Moloch is, even if Picasso didn't know that's what he was painting."

"Why would he—" But Nolan paused, remembering their conversation with Gertrude Stein and Alice Toklas on that first night. *His sister died,* Stein had said, *and now he paints.* Vivi had replied, *Ugliness,* and Toklas had said, *Say nihilism, rather.*

Nolan went on, "Nihilism is a portrait of Moloch?"

"Oh," said Vivi, waving ahead, "nihilism, or anti-growth, or... *anti-life*. Moloch lets his people see the future, sure, a narrow version of it, but... sacrifice the children! You saw that painting of his that I touched—that was anti-life."

Nolan had only noticed that it was hideous.

They passed the arches of a long building Nolan thought was a church, but which Vivi explained had been converted to a museum during the Revolution, and shortly he saw a cluster of blue-painted chairs and tables in front of a wide doorway ahead. He guided their steps toward it and sat down at one of the tables.

Vivi looked farther down the boulevard, then sighed and took a chair on the other side of the table.

"Have to eat," said Nolan. When she shrugged, he stretched and said, "What would we say, to Picasso?"

Vivi clanked her purse down on the table. "He needs to give the painting—I'm sure that's what the mirror is—to the Cybeline priestesses. According to Beltran's story, they'll need it to kill Moloch."

A waiter appeared and handed them book-sized slates with menus chalked on them. When he had walked back inside, Nolan said, "They'll kill you. Again."

"I'm sure they'd like to. But Picasso can bring it to them."

Nolan smiled tiredly. "If we convince him to."

"Miss Stein would help, I think." She peered at the slate she held, then laid it down on the metal tabletop. "I just want coffee."

Nolan and Vivi both jumped then, for a bright white light was suddenly shining on the café wall, projecting the shadow silhouette of a great cat crouching as if to spring. Both chairs rutched around, but their squinting eyes saw no horizontally laid searchlight—automobiles and pedestrians were visible in plain sunlight, their ordinary shadows distinct beneath them.

Nolan turned back to the wall, but the sourceless light was gone. Vivi was looking the other way, and in that direction he saw a black cat standing on a vacant table closer to the street. Had it cast that huge shadow? In what momentary light?

Le Lion de Cybele," whispered Vivi.

Nolan had slid his chair back and begun to get to his feet when a woman halted beside their table. His eyes were already dazzled by the glare moments earlier, and he squinted up at a hat and a narrow coat with a high collar.

"What is the answer?" said the woman, and Nolan recognized Alice Toklas. Cars growled past on the boulevard, and a wind from the east blew leaves across the sidewalk.

"What is the answer?" Toklas repeated.

Vivi sighed, glanced at Nolan, then returned Toklas's stare. "There is no answer," she said.

"Then there is no question," Toklas finished.

Again the exchange reminded Nolan of Catholics making the sign of the cross—a pagan equivalent, perhaps—though it seemed to express a stoic hopelessness.

The black cat leaped from the farther table, and its legs flexed as it landed on their table between Vivi's hands. The cat laid a paw on Vivi's right hand.

"Marechal," she whispered.

"Stand up, child," said Toklas, "against the wall."

When Vivi didn't move, Toklas waved a black box about the size of a pocket cigar case. Looking more closely, Nolan saw that it was one of the new Leica 1 A 35 millimeter cameras.

"I need to take your picture," said Toklas.

Vivi shrugged and slowly got to her feet. She shuffled over to the white café wall and squinted toward Toklas.

"Straighten your coat," Toklas said, peering through a little viewfinder on the top of the camera. "And open your eyes wider."

Vivi complied, and Nolan heard a click.

Toklas was twisting one of the knobs on the camera. "You too," she said to Nolan. Vivi resumed her seat and stroked the cat as Nolan stood up.

Mystified but not alarmed, he walked to where Vivi had stood, and pushed his dark hair back from his forehead. He was looking into the camera lens when he heard another click and Toklas stepped back, winding the knob again.

"Sit," she said, and Nolan resumed his seat. "What have you done with Gertrude's coat?"

"I gave it to the poor."

"It's true," said Vivi solemnly.

"Well," said Toklas, "so did she."

Another woman walked up to the table, and Nolan's chest went cold when he recognized the smooth, vaguely Arab face of Kirenli. Today she wore a long skirt of flower-figured silk, with a broad-brimmed straw hat over her cropped black hair. The relaxed urbanity of her manner two days ago was gone, and her eyes were unreadable pits of darkness.

Nolan reached across the table and lifted Vivi's purse. Its angular weight was obvious.

Vivi looked up at Kirenli. "I'm not going near any body of water with you."

Kirenli nodded, acknowledging Vivi's point, but said, "I must ask you to. The Canal Saint-Martin is only minutes away. There is a boat, and we must talk surrounded by water."

"I'm afraid we've got plans," Nolan said. He slid his hand into Vivi's purse and took hold of the revolver's grip; he was sure these two women would not attempt a kidnapping—or a murder—on this busy street, but he recalled Kirenli pointing his old .45 at Vivi and himself.

"We can tell you—" Vivi began, but Kirenli cut her off with an abrupt wave.

"Tell me nothing here. It seems I was wrong, before, in arranging your death. The two of you getting together was indeed an unlikelihood that changed the charted future." She gave Vivi a piercing stare. "For a purpose."

"I'm sorry—" Nolan began, but Vivi held up a hand to stop him. She was staring into the cat's golden eyes. Nolan recalled Toklas saying on Saturday night, *Trust the cats, the* matagots. *They see past fate.*

"What purpose?" Vivi asked.

"A purpose that will banish the Phoenician god from the world," said Kirenli, "as Cybele did two thousand years ago. Leave his perverse followers to truly die."

Nolan opened his mouth to ask, *How?* But again Vivi raised her hand. "This can happen?"

"My sisters and I have a task to accomplish first, for you—but yes, I am sure of it," said Kirenli. "With your unique participation."

Vivi cocked her head, again staring at the cat. "Unique, you say."

"No one else has been as variously prepared as you have been."

"Prepared," said Vivi softly. "For a purpose!... Outside their charted future. Yes." None of the others spoke, and after a few seconds she went on softly, as if talking to herself, "It could be. From the nursery to Elodie to Beltran to Harry. Yes. All the way from when I painted a rainbow on the nursery wall."

"You are ours," said Kirenli.

Vivi looked up at her. "No, not yours." She touched Marechal's head, and the cat rubbed against her hand. "But I've seen the goddess, and she has seen me."

Kirenli waited for what Vivi might say next. Nolan was reminded of a fencer, poised to parry in any line.

"I'll go with you," Vivi said finally.

Nolan burst out, "No, Vivi! We can go anywhere, Nantes—hell, Hong Kong, Buenos Aires—" He stopped when she gave him a distressed look.

"Oh, can't you see the direction of it, Harry? I—I think I must release you from your protector role."

Nolan sat back and wished he had a cigarette. "I don't think you can release me," he said with a sigh, "at this point." He met Kirenli's hot stare. "Her death is not part of your present plan, I gather."

Kirenli shook her head and held out her arms. Nolan was baffled by the gesture until the cat sprang to her chest. Without any further comment she turned and began walking away.

"There's an automobile," said Toklas, quickly raising one palm in a *get up* gesture.

Vivi took her purse back from Nolan. "The cat led you to me?"

"Of course," said Toklas impatiently.

Vivi stood up, so Nolan did too. He looked around at the massive buildings, widely separated by the intersecting streets, and now they reminded him of the timeless striated buttes in Arizona's Monument Valley—truncated towers of lifeless stone; but he shook his head and made himself notice the endless busy fretwork of windows and balconies.

A big maroon Pierce Arrow pulled up to the sidewalk. It was an American automobile, but with a right-side steering wheel, and Kirenli waved from the driver's seat. Toklas walked around the headlights to get in on the passenger side, and Nolan opened the rear door. He got in first, sliding across the seat, for he could imagine Kirenli driving away without him.

Vivi got in beside him and closed the door. Her purse was in her lap.

"'Push off,'" she whispered, "'and sitting well in order, smite the sounding furrows. It may be that the gulfs will wash us down; it may be we shall touch the Happy Isles.'"

Nolan gathered that it was another quote from something. "That's one way of putting it," he muttered.

"Tennyson," she said.

The automobile moved forward almost silently, and soon they were coursing through traffic around the broad square of the Place de la République. On the far side of it, Kirenli sped northeast and then turned left into a narrow lane with a hedge and a railed walkway on the left. They passed a high arching footbridge and canal-lock gates on that side, and then Nolan could see a hundred-foot-wide canal, glittering in the sunlight. The railing had ended back at the bridge and lock, and now only a brick-paved sidewalk and a long, low bench separated the street from the canal. Kirenli brought the automobile to a halt in the shadow of a building at the right-side curb.

Toklas was holding the cat now, and with one hand opened the door. She stepped down to the street, and Kirenli slid out after her.

Nolan followed Vivi out on the other side, onto the narrow sidewalk. Looking across the street, Nolan could now see a long rowboat halted at the near edge of the water. A hooded figure sat in the middle by the oarlocks, and Kirenli and Toklas hurried between moving cars in that direction.

Vivi was looking to her left, at the one-way traffic on this street, and after a few seconds she stepped around the back fender and was sprinting through a gap between a cab and a bus. Nolan was right behind her.

Kirenli had already crossed the brick sidewalk and stepped into the bow of the rowboat. Toklas, standing back, waved Vivi and Nolan toward Kirenli.

"You're not coming?" Vivi asked her.

"I've facilitated the meeting," said Toklas. The cat in her arms was staring at Vivi in what Nolan thought was a peremptory way. "They don't mean to kill you," Toklas added, then turned and began walking away north along the brick sidewalk.

The water was only a few inches below the coping in this section of the canal, and there were no boats visible upstream; the lock below the footbridge wouldn't be opened to lower the water level for at least several minutes. Vivi stepped into the boat and sat down on a thwart at the bow, opposite Kirenli. She was holding her purse in both hands. Nolan settled beside her.

The woman on the central thwart pushed away from the canal edge with one oar, and the boat shifted out across the sunlit water.

"At present," Kirenli began, "you are bound to another, a man who died—"

"No," Vivi interrupted. Kirenli blinked but didn't resume speaking, and Vivi looked from one side of the canal to the other. The breeze had blown a fringe of blonde hair across her eyes; she pushed it back and said, "Yesterday, Harry and I went down into *les carriéres*, and found the skull of the *sauteur* who was attached to me—who hoped to displace me. We destroyed it. The bond between him and me is broken."

The woman at the oars smothered an exclamation.

Vivi touched her own forehead. "He's not in here anymore. His name is Thibaud Cadieux, and now he can only occupy *sauteurs* whose hold on their hosts is loose. And even then only for short times."

Kirenli's dark eyebrows were raised. "You did this? The two of you? This is true?"

Vivi smiled tiredly. "At that temple you were able to sense him, in me. Look again."

Kirenli stared into Vivi's eyes, and Vivi's head rocked back, again as if the woman had prodded her forehead.

At last Kirenli sat back. "You are alone," she said wonderingly, and she sighed in evident relief. "We had decided that we must find his skull ourselves, in the next day or two, and free you."

Nolan recalled her saying, *My sisters and I have a task to accomplish first, for you,* and he huffed out a short scornful laugh, remembering his and Vivi's travails in the catacombs. "You couldn't have done it," he said.

Vivi frowned at him, then said to Kirenli, "Cybele helped, at one point."

"You are a priestess," Kirenli acknowledged. "This is a gift from her. Today we had hoped only to find you and take you into our protection. But now we can proceed more quickly."

The woman behind Kirenli had let go of the oars and turned around to openly listen.

Vivi said, "You remember the story of the goddess and the bull? The infant effigy with a mirror for a face? We know what the mirror is."

Kirenli's face was expressionless. "We have," she said, "what we believe is the mirror described by Pausanias in his *Hēlládos Periēgēsis*, from the temple of Ceres at Patmos."

"No," said Vivi. "The mirror the story refers to was made by a painter named Pablo Picasso, who killed Thibaud Cadieux in 1910. I'm sure it's not a literal mirror—I'm sure it's a painting."

Kirenli said nothing, so Vivi added, "Only an hour ago, in a hijacked young body, Cadieux told us that the man who killed him made the mirror. He didn't know I'd seen his memory of who that was, and recognized Picasso."

Kirenli was slowly shaking her head. "You say your occupier was Thibaud Cadiuex? Once of the National Assembly?"

"The very."

Kirenli exhaled through pursed lips and looked out at the water. "You *spoke* to him, today?"

"He spoke to us. He imagines he can find another body to keep."

"Be assured he still wants yours," said the woman at the middle thwart.

"Of course." Vivi smiled mirthlessly at her, squinting in the sunlight. "He's out of me, but I'm still fitted to him."

Kirenli looked downstream, toward the footbridge and the canal lock gate. "Cadieux," she said. "I remember him. It was his goal to reestablish the immolation of babies, to placate Moloch. Long ago he tried to recruit an architect to design new Carthage-style temples."

"Charles-Édouard Jeanneret," said Nolan.

Kirenli gave him a startled look. "Yes. He goes now by the name of Le Corbusier, and we have spoken with him. He would not entertain the idea, and will not."

For nearly a minute none of the four in the boat spoke. The wind rippled the water and sighed in the trees along the streets on either side of the canal, the hum of automobile engines rose and fell, and voices of pedestrians were intermittently audible.

"The *sauteurs*," Kirenli went on at last, "have set into motion a... convergence."

"Say final battle," put in the woman sitting on the center thwart.

"Yes," said Kirenli. "A dreadful conjunction, to occur on Midsummer Day, in Spain. The *sauteurs* will call up their god there, incarnated in one of them."

"Not a bull?" asked Nolan. Kirenli glanced at him, frowning, and he said, "Why not in a bull?"

The woman at the oars snickered. "Bulls can't talk."

"No," answered Kirenli. "They hope to gain access to a power they can *deal* with."

Vivi shifted on the thwart beside Nolan. "In Tarragona."

"As you say. The *sauteurs* have the mad idea that their god might be persuaded to make a... a *truce* with Cybele, uniting against a dominant common rival." She shook her head. "It is folly. The gods could no more unite than two magnets could cling together at the wrong ends. And the rival is indomitable."

"Christianity," said Vivi. "The Church." She nodded firmly.

Nolan recalled Beaufroy saying, *Moloch and his creatures have* révulsion *to Christianity.*

Kirenli did not contradict her.

Vivi was trailing the fingers of one hand in the water. "You said I've been prepared," she said, "for a purpose." She looked hard at Kirenli. "Tell me—what purpose?"

Kirenli sighed. "You are a virgin," she began, then hesitated and squinted from Vivi to Nolan. "Still?"

Nolan scowled at her and Vivi hiccupped.

"Yes," Vivi said. "My body is. My mind is not. I think that's what makes me... unique, isn't it?"

Kirenli blinked at her in some surprise. "That's right." She exchanged an unreadable glance with the woman on the central thwart. "That and being a priestess of Cybele."

"Which you made her," said Nolan, "in order to kill her."

"You," Kirenli said to him, "may very well figure in the accomplishing of this priestess's purpose, but I don't see that you must be privy to a conference among us." Over her shoulder she said, "Bring us back to the street, Sarkaya. Mr. Nolan is—"

"Not going anywhere," said Vivi, "without me."

"Damn right," Nolan put in. "And what did you do with my .45?"

Kirenli closed her eyes and said, "Keep us where we are, Sarkaya."

Nolan saw that Kirenli was deferring to Vivi; her standing, relative to Vivi's, had evidently changed.

After several seconds, Kirenli opened her eyes. "Genevieve, your mind is indeed no longer virginal. It was broken open when you were a child, for occupation by a thief—whom you have somehow managed to evict! Our order could never have committed the violation of your mind that you suffered at the hands of the *sauteurs*. But now, being opened—"

Kirenli hesitated, then said clearly, "—it may lawfully be occupied by another."

The hundred-foot-wide canal seemed to separate from the rest of Paris. Nolan could hear automobile engines and voices, but distantly. By another? he thought incredulously. Who, a ghost of your own this time?

He opened his mouth to protest, but Vivi spoke first.

"By the goddess," she said. "By Cybele."

Nolan exhaled sharply. He recalled the vision of Cybele that the two of them had endured at the Cybeline temple only two days ago; and Vivi, unlike himself, had met the goddess's direct gaze.

He turned his head to look at her now, sitting beside him in her baggy coat and twill trousers—perhaps five and a half feet tall, weighing hardly more than a hundred pounds—and her big hazel eyes blinked back at him from below her tousled straw-colored bangs.

He nearly said, *That's ridiculous,* but he didn't want to risk a quick, decisive contradiction from her.

Kirenli said, "Of course the *sauteurs* are all broken in that way already. Any one of them could, and one of them will, serve as the corporeal host of their god."

"A *big* fellow, I would think," said Nolan, grasping for some reasonable objection to what Vivi had said. "to contain a god."

"A big mind," Kirenli said. "Yes."

"And we'll find the mirror," Vivi said, "Picasso's painting." Nolan knew she was forcing her voice to be steady. She met his eyes again. "To kill Moloch, Harry. To use my life for something. No more *sauteur* nurseries like the one I grew up in—and no children burned in Moloch's furnace." She clasped his hand, reminding him of the first time she had done it, at the café across from his flat on Friday night. "Harry—it's what God has made me for."

He burst out, "To be possessed by a . . . a *pagan goddess*? Vivi, you're Catholic, or nearly! Find this painting, sure, give it to these people, but—"

She squeezed his hand. "Hush."

Kirenli reached back toward Sarkaya, who now passed something small to her. Kirenli extended her hand and dropped it in Vivi's lap. Nolan saw that it was her old watch, which Beltran Iglesias had given her years ago.

"Awareness of time," Kirenli said.

Vivi released Nolan's hand and pulled her left sleeve back, then looped the watch around her wrist, covering the Moloch tattoo. He knew he was on the point of losing her.

Abandon nineteenth-century ideas of time, Gertrude Stein had said, but a priestess of Cybele would gain an aeons-old idea of time. And Nolan recalled the dismembered timekeeper in the catacombs, perpetually facing a clock with no hands—*set undying before a clock that shows no duration.*

With a chill, he wondered what sort of duration Vivi's watch might end up measuring.

"Vivi," he said, "I love you." It was a desperate throw of the dice, but as he said it he knew it was true. "Marry me—today. Step down from the statue of Saint Genevieve."

Until then it hadn't been clear how tightly Vivi had been maintaining control of her expression and responses.

But the watch dropped from her wrist unfastened, and she lowered her face into her hands. After several long seconds, "Harry," she gasped without raising her head, "how can we?" She looked up, and tears streaked her cheeks. "Can't you see it's impossible, no matter what we might want? How could we... have children, knowing that other children..."

Nolan switched his gaze to Kirenli. "Will it kill her, being host to the goddess?"

Kirenli returned his stare for several seconds, then said, "I don't know." It was clear to Nolan, and probably to Vivi too, that she believed it was almost certain.

Nolan took a deep breath and let it out. "Genevieve will do what she chooses to do," he said. "She and I will be where she chooses to be on Midsummer Day. She—"

"She must come with us," said Kirenli, "stay with us."

Vivi cuffed away her tears and sat up straight. "I'll host Cybele," she told Kirenli. "I'll be in Tarragona, virginal, on Midsummer Day, and I will probably die there. But—Harry and I have to get the mirror painting."

Kirenli shook her head. "You will help us get it. Your place now is with us."

"My place," said Vivi, bending to pick up her watch, "is where I decide it is." She looked past Kirenli at Sarkaya. "Take Harry and me back to the street." She flipped the watch onto her wrist and buckled the strap.

Kirenli opened her mouth, then closed it, frowning, and Nolan was sure that his guess a few minutes ago had been correct—Vivi's standing among the Cybelines now eclipsed Kirenli's.

Sarkaya was already rowing back toward the canal edge.

"Wait, we need to be in contact with you," said Kirenli, speaking rapidly now. Her voice was higher, almost shrill. "The lion—the *matagots*—it is capricious, and there are only eight days until Midsummer Day, the Roman festival of Fortuna. Alice Toklas has taken photographs of you, passports will be prepared. But we *must* have this painting, what you say is the mirror, immediately!"

Vivi was already on her knees on the thwart, clutching her purse and watching the approaching pavement. Over her shoulder she said, "We can leave messages for one another at a bookshop called Shakespeare and Company, at Twelve Rue de l'Odéon, on the Left Bank."

CHAPTER SIXTEEN:
My Own Peace with God

"Eight days," said Vivi after she and Nolan had walked south for several minutes without speaking. The canal was on their right, but flowed underground here, beneath rows of trees in a long narrow park. Nolan wondered if Kirenli and Sarkaya would follow its subterranean course through all the locks down to where the canal flowed into the Seine at the Morland bridge.

"We'll need money for travel," Vivi went on. "A train, a hired car... donkeys, for all I know." Her shoulders were hunched as she strode along, one hand shoved in a pocket and the other swinging her heavy purse. She squinted up at Nolan, clearly precluding any more personal topics. "I think Gertrude Stein will provide it."

"We'll need it," Nolan agreed. "I have about enough in my pocket to get us to the Quarter in a cab."

"Better than walking. I don't want your friend Robin stopping us again."

"No," Nolan agreed.

In his mind he kept hearing her say, *I'll be in Tarragona, virginal, at Midsummer Day, and I will probably die there.* He ached to argue, but knew that her replies, spoken aloud, would only solidify her resolve.

Maybe we won't find Picasso's damned painting, he told himself; and then he winced to realize that the thought was disloyal to her.

At the Boulevard Voltaire she flagged down a horse-drawn cab. "Keep an eye out the back window," she said.

✣ ✣ ✣

In front of the street door at Twenty-seven Rue de Fleurus, Nolan paid the driver with his last francs. When he and Vivi were standing on the sidewalk, he looked from the stone head of Bacchus above the glass-and-wrought-iron door to the door handle, and he forced away the hope that it would be locked, the flat empty.

In fact, it was pulled open even as he and Vivi stepped toward it. The short, stout figure of Gertrude Stein stood on the courtyard walkway beyond, her round face creased in worry.

"Vivi!" she said quietly. "I'm very glad to see the two of you alive, but I can't receive you now. Pablo is here, and he's just had a very upsetting visitor at his apartment." She reached out and touched the watch on Vivi's wrist. "I'm sorry, child, but I can't risk a...a *dual personality* of your sort here with him."

"I'm not that any longer," said Vivi. "Harry and I banished my other." Stein cocked her head as if to hear better, and Vivi went on, "We found his skull and destroyed it." She touched her forehead. "I'm alone in here."

Stein's eyebrows were halfway up to her short-cropped gray hair. "The two of you did this? In the catacombs, yesterday?"

"With a bit of help from a pagan goddess," put in Nolan.

"Cybele, no doubt," said Stein. She frowned and peered at Vivi. "This is true, child? You are sure?"

"It has been proven beyond doubt," Vivi assured her; and Nolan nodded, remembering Cadieux's visit in the Robin body. "I swear it on the soul of Beltran Iglesias," Vivi added. She scratched her nose. "And in fact we need to talk to Picasso."

Stein hesitated, leaning out to look up and down the street.

"About an old painting of his," Vivi went on. "We think he hasn't destroyed it."

"An old painting." Stein frowned for several heartbeats, then stepped back. "Perhaps you do need to talk to him," she said. "Alice is out, but I can serve brandy."

Nolan was wondering whether or not to mention that Toklas and Kirenli had approached them earlier, when Vivi said, "We spoke to Miss Toklas not an hour ago. She was with a priestess of Cybele. A *matagot* led them to me."

"Really!" Stein turned around and began walking back toward the door of her studio. "Ah, Alice is secretive, but we may rely on her."

She opened the door and stepped in. "Pablo," she called, "it's Iglesias's orphan, but she has shed her *sauteur* Siamese twin. She is one person only, now. I know this for a fact." She glanced back at Nolan and added, "And Mr. Harry Nolan, whom you also met Saturday night at your Bateau Lavoir." Nolan recalled that Bateau Lavoir was the name of Picasso's run-down studio in Montmartre.

He and Vivi stepped into the long room behind Stein. The tables and chairs were lit in sunlight reflected through the windows from the building on the other side of the courtyard garden. The many paintings, higher up on the walls, were in shadow, but Nolan could make out the three pictures over the couch in the far corner: his own pencil sketch of Vivi, the cubist portrait of Beltran Iglesias, and Picasso's stylized portrait of Gertrude Stein.

Picasso now stood up from one of the chairs near the couch. Today, in contrast to the worn denim overalls of four nights ago, he was wearing a three-piece suit in herringbone tweed, and his gray hair was oiled and neatly combed. From a table he picked up a flat foot-and-a-half-square package wrapped in brown paper, and, after cocking his head at Nolan and Vivi, he reached inside his coat with his free hand.

"I cannot stay longer," he said to Stein. "Thank you for holding it."

He had started toward the door, but Vivi stepped in his way. She looked from his dark eyes to the package he was now holding under his elbow. "You've had years to destroy it," she said. "Too late now—we need it."

Picasso gestured for her to move aside, but she stood still and pointed at the package. "You must let us have that painting." Nolan wondered how she could be sure it was the mirror painting, or a painting at all; but she caught his eye and muttered, "Who do you suppose his upsetting visitor was?"

Picasso's dark eyes darted from Vivi to Nolan, then past them at Gertrude Stein. "Tell your small friend to let me pass."

Stein shook her head.

"We'll have it," said Vivi.

Picasso pursed his mouth as if he might spit. He drew his free hand from under his coat, and he was holding a pistol, pointed at the floor— it looked to Nolan like an MAB semiautomatic, French made, probably .25 caliber. "You know nothing," he said. "I am leaving."

Vivi held up her cloth purse and gave him a bright smile. "Who was your visitor, earlier today? A little boy, a little girl? Well, the body wouldn't matter, would it?" She let her purse fall to the carpet, and her right hand was clasped around the grip of the .38-caliber revolver she had brought up from the catacombs yesterday. Like Picasso, she held her gun pointed at the floor.

Gertrude Stein crowded between them. "You are both my friends," she said firmly. "I won't have you killing each other. Put them away."

Vivi shrugged, then bent down and picked up her purse. Picasso slid his pistol back under his coat, and Stein stepped away to stand beside Nolan.

"Do you know who your visitor was?" Vivi asked Picasso as she dropped the revolver into her purse.

Gertrude Stein was no taller than Picasso, but her broad, seamed face was indomitable. "Do you, Pablo?"

Picasso retreated to the couch. He sat down heavily, and laid the package on the nearest table.

"It was a *sauteur*," said Vivi.

He sighed, and nodded. "In the body of a little girl. No name."

"It was Thibaud Cadieux," Vivi told him. "The man you killed in 1910."

Picasso shook his head. "Not that one," he said. "Cadieux is gone. And who says I killed him?"

"I do," Vivi said. "I saw you shoot him, on the Quai de Passy. Cadieux was the *sauteur* who inhabited me, until Harry and I banished him from me yesterday."

For several seconds no one spoke. Picasso was staring at the floor. "Impossible," he muttered at last. "He fell into water—the overflowing river. *That* banishes them."

"Did you stay and watch him fall," Vivi persisted, "or did you turn away right after you pulled the trigger? His memory of it, which I experienced, ended at the moment the bullet hit him." When Picasso didn't answer or look up, she crossed to the couch and sat down next to him, setting her heavy purse on the table beside his package. "The *quai* was flooded, but it was shallow water. And there were wooden frameworks for the raised plank walkway." She touched the sleeve of Picasso's jacket. "I *know* he did not fall into the water."

Picasso opened his mouth as if to object, then just shrugged. "Maybe."

Gertrude Stein sat down on a chair near the couch. "What did... this child... say to you?" she asked.

Picasso rubbed both hands over his long face, then let them fall into his lap. "She thought that I was one of them, an ally, at least." He looked up. "Adrien Achard has thought this, that I might yet one day join in them."

He yawned, and blinked around at the room.

"The child said I made a painting that could summon the god. She said she believes I still have it, and I should give it to the *sauteurs*, for that purpose." He gave Vivi an empty look. "If she was Thibaud, as you say, this was all a lie. He did not believe I am an ally."

"Not after you killed him, no."

Picasso grimaced in reply. "Achard buys my paintings, has me as a guest at his villa. He does not know it was me who—yes!—wiped Thibaud from the picture... or," he amended, "tried to.

"And," he went on in a defensive tone, "I did take Hemingway's story from Achard's house, and gave it to Barbier at *La Prosodie*. I have done what I can to impede them. It is enough."

"You mean now to destroy the mirror," said Vivi, "because of what Cadieux told you today."

Picasso frowned. "Mirror?"

"You read Hemingway's article," Vivi said patiently, "and crossed out his name and address on it. You know the story of the winged bull and the straw child with a mirror for a face." She nodded toward the package he held. "That painting is the mirror."

"In an old fable," said Picasso quietly. "Perhaps. Whoever the child today was," he went on, "my part in all these things is finished."

Vivi was frowning and shaking her head. "But in Beltran's story the mirror was a part of *killing* the god. Cadieux *wants* you to destroy it."

Picasso shuddered. "Was that little girl truly him, an hour ago? If what you say is true, I'm glad I did not know it was Thibaud! I could not have faced him. In many ways he was a friend, and I killed him.

"But I think," he went on, "I think the child was right, that in any case this painting—call it a mirror if you like—might enable the summoning of the god." And he repeated, as if it were an article of faith, "My part in all these things is finished."

He got to his feet and picked up the package.

Vivi stood up too. She pointed at the portrait of Beltran Iglesias on the wall behind Picasso. "Beltran would not have passed the fable on if there weren't some truth in it."

"Pablo," said Stein, in a gentler tone. "The bargain you made with God—your sister's life, or your paintings. You chose your paintings, and she died. You might redeem that choice now, with *this* painting of yours."

Picasso shot her an angry look. "I will make my own peace with God."

"When?" spoke up Vivi. "What peace, what redemption, after Midsummer in Tarragona? It will mean nothing after that. The *sauteurs* can call up their god, make it incarnate, without your mirror. But the Cybelines need the mirror to *kill* Moloch. So..." She cocked her head and gave him a quizzical look. "Your choice is your own, but it is now."

"All time is present in now," said Stein.

Picasso's swarthy face had emptied of all expression while Vivi and Stein had been speaking.

Slowly his hands opened, and the package fell to the floor. "Take it," he said, "and spare me your blessings."

He strode to the door, pulled it open, and was gone.

Stein walked to the door and closed it. She looked back with raised eyebrows at her two visitors.

"We have to leave Paris," said Vivi, looking tired and older than her nineteen years. "For Spain, God help us." She turned to Stein and nodded toward the portrait of Beltran Iglesias. "You said on Saturday that you might give me traveling money, for his sake."

"Yes," Stein said, and sighed. "Though at the time I thought it was so you could get *away* from trouble. Excuse me." She walked back across the room to the hall, and a few moments later Nolan heard her heavy footsteps on stairs.

Vivi picked up the package Picasso had dropped and sat down on the couch with it. She began unfolding the brown paper.

Nolan crouched beside her and caught her hand. "You want to *look* at it?"

"I need to be sure it is a painting. We can't hand Kirenli a blank canvas."

She had folded back one edge of the paper, and Nolan could see tan and red brushstrokes. "Okay, cover it up," he said.

But Vivi freed her hand from his and lifted the entire paper away. What she held was a painting of a bullfight in drab daylight—a matador and bull in the foreground, and an arena in the background with spectators indicated by little blobs of color.

It seemed entirely unremarkable. Nolan squinted at the proportions and the composition of shapes, trying to see any portentous pattern—but it remained simply a typical picture of a bullfight, not substantially different from dozens that could be seen on sidewalk easels around Montmartre.

"This can't be the mirror," said Vivi. She looked across the room at the door, as if considering going after Picasso.

But Nolan had noticed that the paint on the canvas had an unusually matte, almost powdery, texture. He licked a finger and rubbed one corner of the picture.

The color was wiped away, exposing a glossy black surface, streaked with yellow, beneath.

"The bullfight scene is camouflage," he said, "watercolor over varnished oil paint. The real mirror is underneath."

Vivi folded the paper back over the canvas and laid the package back on the table. "Good enough. We don't need to actually *look* at it."

"No," agreed Nolan emphatically.

Gertrude Stein could be heard descending the stairs now, and Nolan and Vivi both stood up. Stein appeared in the hallway, breathing hard, as if she had had to move some furniture upstairs.

She handed Vivi a bulky envelope. "A priestess of Cybele."

Vivi shrugged. "Just so they could legitimately kill me. But yes, I am, now."

"I think," said Nolan, closing his eyes for a moment, "Miss Stein meant the woman we saw today with Miss Toklas."

Stein nodded. "I did, yes; but it was wise of that sisterhood to consecrate you—if foolish to then decide to waste what you are. I gather they see that, now?"

"Yes," said Vivi.

Stein went on, "What did Alice and this priestess today tell you?"

"They said I have a purpose."

"I see." Stein looked past her at the door, biting her lip. "Do you... have some idea of what that purpose might be?"

Vivi sighed. "Yes."

Stein nodded, then pointed at the envelope Vivi held. "There's enough there for both of you to go to America, instead of Spain. I have friends in New York. I could give you letters of introduction."

"Thank you," said Vivi. "You're very kind! But—if I don't do this, I don't know what I was ever... *for*."

Nolan sourly recalled his offer of marriage. And he imagined the little stone girl beside the statue of Saint Genevieve not stepping down from the concrete plinth, or even remaining where she was, but falling into the river to join Elodie in oblivion. This afternoon she had said, *I think I must release you from your protector role.*

But he had answered, *I don't think you can.*

He spoke up. "I'd like one particular letter of introduction, if you don't mind." And when Stein gave him an inquiring look, he pointed at the wall. "The drawing I did of her."

Both Stein and Vivi looked surprised, but Stein stepped to the couch, stood on her toes, and lifted down the framed drawing. She turned to Nolan, holding it out.

"Thanks," he said, taking it from her. He sat down, flipped it over and began prying up the bent staples that secured the cardboard backing.

He looked up. "It's Vivi, as *I've* captured her."

He turned the picture over and pushed up on the glass, and his drawing slid out. He laid the empty frame aside, unfolded the brown paper from the Picasso painting, and slid the drawing in behind it.

"I'll bring it back," he told Stein gruffly as he refolded the paper, "if I can."

Stein's face was grave. "Will you stay for brandy? Alice should be home soon."

Vivi didn't look as if she wanted to see Toklas. She slid the envelope into a pocket and picked up her purse from the table. "I'm afraid we've got a message to deliver, and time is short." She held out her hand, and Stein shook it, holding on for an extra second.

"God be with you," she said, releasing Vivi's hand.

Vivi started to speak, then just nodded and turned to the door. Nolan picked up the paper-wrapped painting, gave Stein an awkward bow, and followed Vivi. Together they walked out to the street.

It must have been about noon, and the sky between the high rooftops was clear blue.

"A message?" he asked.

Vivi's purse swung from her hand like a pendulum. "At Shakespeare and Company, for Kirenli. We'll say we've got the mirror, and see if there's a message from her yet." She looked up at him from under her tousled fair hair. "You're mad, you know. To come along."

He shrugged and forced a smile. "I blame you."

She nodded and said, "Yes," very quietly. Then she quickened her pace and he had to hurry to catch up.

CHAPTER SEVENTEEN:
I Trust God Will Take That Into Account

There was no message yet from Kirenli at Shakespeare and Company, but Sylvia Beach agreed to deliver a note from Vivi to "a tall, black-haired woman who will ask, possibly Alice Toklas."

From the bookshop, Nolan quickly led Vivi on the remembered zigzag course he had taken three days ago: through the courtyard gate across the street and the back door of the restaurant kitchen, and through the restaurant to the next street east. They paused to catch their breaths, and no one at all followed them out of the restaurant's front door. Vivi led the way then, south, past the columned portico of the Odeon Theatre.

Having delivered the note and eluded any pursuit, her pace was slower. She looked around at the trees and the buildings in a mood that Nolan recognized as preemptively nostalgic. The gun in her purse and the package Nolan carried seemed for the moment forgotten.

Across the broad lanes of the Rue de Vaugirard, the tall black-iron fence bordering the Luxembourg Gardens stretched from the three-story Luxembourg Palace on the right and around a curve of the boulevard to the left. Its gold-tipped pickets still looked forbiddingly like upright spears, but a small gate was open, and Vivi took Nolan's free hand and crossed the lanes to the sidewalk in front of it.

They stepped through, and the arches and windows of the palace were on their right while a tree-lined lane stretched ahead of them. After a few minutes at Vivi's unhurried pace, they passed the corner of the palace, and then they were looking out across the lawns and wide, gravel-paved paths and flower beds of the gardens. Chairs and benches stood along the border of a grassy square to their right, and on their left a terrace sloped up to the waist-high stone railing of another lane. The breeze was warm, scented with rose blossoms.

Together they walked forward, past strolling couples and scampering children and women pushing baby strollers, and Vivi paused beside the Grand Bassin to watch toy sailboats scudding across the blue water. Tables and chairs stood at wide intervals beside the basin.

"It's as if no time has passed," said Vivi quietly, "since Elodie and I used to come here." She was blinking, smiling faintly. "I half expect to see the two of us, over there on the other side of the water, like two young sisters strayed from their mother." She huffed. "And if we were to try to walk around and meet them, they'd disappear."

She had let go of his hand when she crossed to stand by the basin. Now she looked up at him and took his hand again. "I doubt we'll be here again. Either of us." She led him away from the water to a path that curved below the shallow terrace.

They came to a set of white marble steps and walked up them to the terrace path. A lane straight ahead between groves of trees led out of the gardens, but Vivi was tugging him to the left, toward a marble statue at the edge of the path thirty yards away.

As they trudged closer, Nolan could see that it was the figure of a woman in a long, layered dress, her hands crossed at her waist. There was no statue of a little girl with her, but Nolan knew who this must be.

Vivi stopped a yard in front of the statue. "I hoped I'd get to show you to her," she said softly.

Nolan looked at the calm stone face, and wondered how many times the child Vivi had stood here, with her scarcely older protector Elodie, and he remembered his first glimpse of the skeletal, porcelain-masked thing that Elodie had become, and of his fleeting final encounter with her in the depths of the Seine.

Above him, Saint Genevieve's marble eyes seemed to gaze with remote sternness into his own. I'll stay with her, he mentally told the saint. I'll do what I can. That seemed inadequate, so he amended it: I'll do what can be done.

Vivi leaned forward and touched one of the statue's hands, then released Nolan's hand and turned away. "Come on," she said. "There are other places in Paris I want to say goodbye to. You too, maybe."

Not many, he thought. I believe, now, that I've spent most of these four years here waiting for something, which turns out to have been this, and you.

It wasn't until that evening, when they were back in Vivi's tiny flat in the Marais, that Vivi was willing to talk about the days ahead.

They had spent the afternoon walking. In the Church of Saint-Sulpice, Vivi had lit a candle and knelt silently for several minutes in one of the back pews. Nolan had stood in the entry arch behind her, reflecting that this was the third time in the last three days that they had been in a Catholic church, but the first time it had been their own idea.

When she had stood up she'd been facing the altar, and though her arm moved he hadn't been able to see if she made the sign of the cross. He didn't ask how she reconciled praying to the Christian god while at the same time being an active priestess of Cybele.

They crossed the river on the Boulevard du Palais in a fast motor cab, then wandered through the old Marais district, pausing to gaze at several unremarkable buildings or squares that evidently bore some memories for Vivi, though she didn't explain. In the early evening they'd had dinner at the old hangarlike Compas d'Or before walking the half mile of narrow streets back to Vivi's flat.

Six black cats were perched on the rickety stairs that led up to her door. "The lion is watching over us," Vivi muttered. She unbolted the door and stepped in, and a moment later a match was struck and the gas jet on the wall illuminated the bed and armchair and bookcase.

Nolan followed her in and laid the wrapped painting against the wall by the little stove, then sank into the armchair while Vivi set her heavy purse beside the painting and perched on the bed. She opened a fresh pack of Gauloises, lit one, and tossed the pack to Nolan.

Her words were puffs of smoke. "Have you ever been to Spain?"

"No." He leaned his head back and looked at her. He knew there was no use right now in trying to dissuade her from going along with Kirenli's plan.

"I haven't either." She nodded thoughtfully, staring at the ember of her cigarette. "Have you read Cervantes's *Don Quixote*?" Nolan shook his head. She went on, "Don Quixote was a fair madman. He imagined shabby inns were castles, he thought a barber's basin was some legendary helmet—but he did actually free a dozen galley slaves along the way."

Nolan imagined that she was thinking about children who were now in *sauteur* nurseries. In the catacombs, they had passed three other NID ladders, besides the one that had led up to the nursery in which she had spent her earliest years.

"I've seen the Doré illustrations at least," he said. "Don Quixote attacking a windmill."

"A fair madman," Vivi conceded. She leaned back against the wall with her hands behind her head, staring now at the cobwebbed ceiling. "Passports! And Midsummer Day is now only eight days off. Tarragona is probably very far away."

Nolan still hoped it was a fantasy, but felt bound to play along. "I expect we'll take a train," he said, "at least partway, and then maybe hire a car. Two or three days altogether. We'll have time."

"We, yes." Still looking up, Vivi said, "A convergence, Kirenli said. A dreadful conjunction, a final battle. Both gods present, in the flesh, with the *sauteurs* imagining that a truce might be made between them."

Nolan nearly added, *In somebody's flesh*, but Vivi was apparently willing to accept the appalling idea that Cybele would occupy her body, and he didn't want to needlessly reinforce it.

Vivi went on, "Against Christianity. And Kirenli and her Cybelines—especially including me—will oppose the truce, and kill, or at least banish, Moloch."

If that painting is the fabled mirror, Nolan thought unhappily, if old Iglesias's story has any validity. If this proposed course wouldn't just be the waste of your life.

"So—I'll be defending Christianity." She looked at Nolan with her eyebrows raised. "Right?"

In a sense, thought Nolan. "Sure," he said, "if it happens."

"I trust God will take that into account."

Vivi turned her eyes again to the ceiling. "Elodie and Beltran," she said quietly, "were both murdered—one by the *apaches* and one by the *sauteurs*." Without looking down, she said, "I would be unhappy if one lot or the other were to murder you."

Nolan looked at Vivi, and after a moment she nodded and stood up, letting the revolver point at the floor. "Miss Stein trusts you," she said. "Come in. How did you find this place?"

Hemingway stepped over the threshold in a draft of beer and automobile exhaust, and blinked around at the sparsely furnished room. "You're both still alive, so I guess you didn't get very far in the catacombs."

"Far enough," said Vivi. "How did you find this place?"

He crossed to the window. Peering out at the rooftops and the alley below, he said, "What's the answer?"

"What? Oh." Vivi sighed. "There is no answer."

"Then there is no question." He turned back to the room. "A very old recognition exchange, did you know? Shared by so many weird old groups that it's not much use anymore. Still, it means... important, not to be repeated." He nodded at Vivi. "You said a lot of crazy stuff the other night at Gertrude's place, but you had got beat up somehow—and shot, you said!—and the ladies were taking you seriously."

He shrugged out of his coat and laid it across the back of the wooden chair by the table. "Not that that necessarily means anything. But you got me wondering about that bull-and-goddess story, and I went to the café where I met Beltran Iglesias three years ago—the Café des Amateurs, in the Rue Mouffetard."

Nolan wrinkled his nose, remembering his own visit to the unsavory café five days ago.

"After I bought them drinks," Hemingway said, "a couple of the old rummies there remembered Iglesias, and you. One of them told me you still visited the place, after Iglesias was killed."

"Sometimes," said Vivi cautiously. "I know those chaps."

"He said he got sick last year, bad fever, and you brought him here and took care of him for a week, soup and brandy, till he was well again."

Vivi nodded. "He's an old friend."

"He remembered this address." He gave Vivi a direct look and said, "I haven't passed it on, and I wasn't followed today. But yesterday I talked to Adrien Achard."

Nolan closed the door. "I hope you were very careful about not being followed."

Hemingway looked critically at the chair, then sat down on it. "As a matter of fact, I was. Several motor cabs, every which way. Cost me what I was going to spend on lunch."

Marechal, or another black cat, appeared on the windowsill. Hemingway reached across to scratch behind its ears, and it rolled its head contentedly. A good sign, Nolan hoped—the Lion of Cybele likes him. Immediately he dismissed the thought as foolish.

"What did Achard say?" Nolan asked.

Hemingway ignored him and spoke to Vivi. "When you found me at the Closerie on Saturday, you drew that three-eyed bull symbol in my notebook and you talked about the *sauteurs*. Gertrude once mentioned the *sauteurs* to me, described that symbol. She said they were a crowd it'd be best to steer clear of—some occult thing, I gathered. I didn't know you, but you seemed lost, and you did return my manuscript. I figured she could give you some advice."

Vivi nodded, clearly willing to let him unfold his story at his own pace.

"I've stayed at Achard's villa in Cap d'Antibes," Hemingway said. "Like a lot of artists and writers." He shrugged. "He's a generous host, buys everybody's paintings, subsidizes writers who need money. I've never taken it. And in fact he's dropped hints that there's some sort of elite group, or club, that he belongs to. I didn't know it was the *sauteurs*.

"A couple of times he's pretty much said he could get me in, waiving the fee, which I guess is pretty big." He hesitated, then looked up with a slight frown. "Even accepting his lavish hospitality, his generosity, seemed a bit...what, demeaning? Subservient? So I let his hints go right by me. Nice cat," he added, stroking Marechal.

"But at Gertrude's place on Sunday night," he went on, "she said he had offered it to her, and she turned it down, and"—he shook his head—"she said he'd have had to *kill* her if she'd accepted it. Apparently Picasso told her that. Said she was too *mundane* to accept the terms, which you said involved killing children."

He held up his hand. "Picasso is too excitable, and Gertrude is gullible. So are you, I think." He stood up and moved to the window again. "But! Yesterday morning, Achard sent a car for me. Driver was a woman, took me to an office on the Champs-Élysées, and Achard was there. He didn't hint this time. He told me that the *sauteurs* offer immortality—by way of *directed reincarnation*. Said the *sauteurs* can see the future too." He gave a short, deprecating laugh, which to Nolan sounded forced. "Seems I'm fated to die in a plane crash in Africa in 1954, but if I join up I can then start a new life in 1955. See the twenty-first century."

Vivi closed her eyes for a moment, then gave Hemingway an impatient stare.

"My wife and I," Hemingway went on more quickly, "have plans to go to Spain with some friends, leaving next week. We do it every summer—fishing, bullfights. Well, Achard told me he'll make me a member of his *sauters* club, *gratis*, if I help out at a ceremony—a sort of... *congress of cults*, that's going to be held at a ruin outside of Tarragona." He huffed another syllable of a laugh. "Something like the Knights of Columbus and the Freemasons!"

Vivi's set expression didn't change.

"He wants me to catch the last train to Marseille today," Hemingway said, "at three p.m. My wife could follow later with the others, and I'd meet up with them all later."

He pursed his lips. "A few days ago I bought a painting, a Joan Miró." He nodded at the statement, as if he were partly talking to himself. "It cost five hundred francs, and my wife isn't happy about it. Achard says he'll give me five thousand, for travel expenses."

"'What shall it profit a man,'" said Vivi, "'if he gain the whole world, and lose his soul?'" She cocked her head. "But for five thousand francs?"

Hemingway laughed softly. "That's from one of the gospels, isn't it?" He looked away. "Yes, there's the money." He ran his fingers through his brown hair. "But that's not the payoff. Damn it, he also mentioned my stolen manuscripts—they're everything I wrote, before 1923. He said he was aware they'd been lost, and... he could find them for me. If I meet him in Tarragona."

"Sure," said Vivi. "He's got them already. It was his people who stole them." She leaned forward. "Mr. Hemingway, his gifts are back-door coercion. He wants you there in Tarragona so you'll be committed, complicit in what will happen." She gave him a bleak smile. "Alice Toklas isn't the only one who tests people. You have a choice."

For several seconds no one spoke.

"Yes," said Hemingway finally, "join his group and go along with him to this meeting, get my manuscripts back—and get money—"

Vivi interrupted sternly: "And a new life, one day? The *sauteurs* do worship Moloch, as I said at Miss Stein's studio. They steal children's bodies. At Tarragona they will call up the god, in the flesh! They hope to establish a truce between Moloch and Cybele, on Midsummer Day."

Hemingway looked at the cobwebbed ceiling and yawned. "Kind of a forced truce, actually, is the idea I got." He shook his head. "Gods and goddesses! Achard did say there's a rival group that has to be overruled—your Cybelines, I take it—but he's got an agent among them to undermine any objections, and they'll have to fall in line with his group's agenda."

Nolan glanced at Vivi. She was staring at Hemingway.

Hemingway met her gaze for a moment, then sighed and got to his feet. He picked up his coat from the chair. "I know. There is no question, right? I won't accept his *gifts,* or ... or anything else." His hand moved up, then dropped, and Nolan thought he had been about to make the sign of the cross. Hemingway went on quickly, "No. I won't be in Spain until a week after his party is over—whatever it is—and I won't be anywhere near Tarragona." He gave Vivi a direct look. "I like you—you took a bullet for this guy here, and I saw the picture he drew of you. You won't be in Tarragona either, if you have a brain in your head."

Nolan didn't speak. Vivi already knew that he believed this was sound advice.

Vivi didn't speak either, but steadily met Hemingway's stare.

After a few seconds he looked away and put on his coat. He hesitated, then said, "Come see me at the Closerie sometime." He walked to the door and pulled it open. To Nolan he said, "Take better care of your girl." Then he was gone, and Nolan heard his heavy footsteps clumping down the stairs.

Nolan closed the door and looked back at Vivi. "Lunch. Coffee. Then ... where to?"

"We should buy some clothes. And then the bookshop. Kirenli may have left a message."

"Hemingway said there's a traitor in her camp."

"Can't be helped."

"The *sauteurs* are likely to be watching the bookshop."

"So we'll be agile. Do some more in-the-back-door-and-out-the-front moves afterward. Look out the back windows of some fast motor cabs."

She stood up and went to her closet to fetch her coat.

✤ ✤ ✤

Nolan didn't see any children at all in the narrow Rue de l'Odéon as he and Vivi climbed out of a cab by the green front door of Shakespeare and Company.

"I never really looked through this shop," said Vivi sadly, squinting up at the sign hung over the door, with Shakespeare's enigmatic face painted on it.

Nolan's reply was firm: "We will come here after all this business is done. We will buy books."

She nodded and squeezed his hand without looking at him, then opened the door.

As he stepped through after her, Nolan himself found that he was looking at the shelves and tables and framed photographs with what he had thought of yesterday as preemptive nostalgia; as if what he saw was a receding memory as much as it was immediate perception. He inhaled the mixed aroma of book paper and tobacco smoke as if it were incense.

"Genevieve!" came Sylvia Beach's voice from the far corner of the shop, and a moment later she straightened up from behind a low shelf. "A woman did stop in and pick up your message, not an hour ago." She handed a book to an elegantly dressed old *boulevardier* and walked to the back room. When she emerged she was carrying a small leather valise. "She left this for you."

Vivi took it from her and sat down in an easy chair by the fire.

"She read the message you left," Beach went on. "She seemed anxious. Asked me twice if I was sure you hadn't left a painting for her as well."

"It'll work out," Vivi told her. Beach smiled uncertainly, hesitated, then stepped away.

Nolan pulled up a chair beside Vivi. She unsnapped the strap of the valise and they both peered into it. Nolan saw a packet of French franc notes and another of Spanish pesetas, alongside a cloth-wrapped bundle and a thick Manila envelope.

Vivi looked around at the customers in the shop—the nearest was a young woman hunched over a magazine at the big table, probably a student from the Sorbonne—and lifted out the envelope. She opened it and handed Nolan one of a pair of passports. It was a new style that Nolan had not seen—a little booklet bound in brown leather, its cover stamped with THE UNITED STATES OF AMERICA. Vivi's was a similar booklet, with green leather covers and stamped REPUBLIQUE FRANCAISE. He flipped open the cover of his, and saw the photograph Alice Toklas had taken of him yesterday. His expression in it was wary. The Cybelines had worked fast, and had even presumed to sign *Harold Nolan* below the photograph. He reflected sourly that he would have to practice the new signature.

He reached into the valise and started to lift out the cloth-wrapped bundle. It was heavy, and he let go of it when his fingers recognized the shape of his .45 semiautomatic.

Along with the passports, Vivi slid out two folded documents that proved to be *première classe* tickets issued by the Paris-Lyon-Méditerranée railway, for travel from Paris to Marseille, leaving from the Gare de Lyon railway station on Sunday the twenty-first, three days off. Paper-clipped to the tickets was a handwritten note: *Automobile from Marseille to Tarragona—Sister—meet sooner than this departure, please—but you MUST be there with a mirror at dawn on St. John's Day—if not sooner—in the name of the goddess who knows you.*

"Three days from now," Nolan said. "Why do you suppose Achard wants Hemingway to leave today?"

"Some kind of initiation, first?" said Vivi. She looked again at the date on the tickets, then looked up and called to Sylvia Beach, "When is Midsummer Day?"

Beach walked to a bookshelf and pulled down an almanac. She flipped through the pages and said, "Traditionally it's June twenty-fourth, that's . . . seven days from now. St. John's Day. The Catholic churches will probably have special Masses."

"Traditionally?" said Nolan. "Not literally?"

Beach turned back a couple of pages. "No. Astronomically speaking, the actual summer solstice—the longest day, the shortest night—will be on June twentieth this year. Three days from now." She smiled, then put the almanac back on the shelf and walked to the front of the shop.

Vivi gave Nolan a stricken look. "The . . . my sisters . . . are acting on the historical date, the Roman festival of Fortuna. But the *sauteurs* are going to summon . . ." and even though she was whispering, she said only, ". . . *their god* on the astronomical date—four days earlier. That's why Achard wants Hemingway to leave today." She tapped the tickets. "We'd be too late with the mirror."

"We," said Nolan cautiously, "*would* be?"

Vivi slid the passports and tickets back into the valise and closed it. She got to her feet. "Would be if we used these tickets. We'll have to exchange them or buy new ones." She glanced at her watch and clicked her tongue, then reached down with her free hand and tugged urgently at his shoulder. "Today's the seventeenth. We've got to get new tickets and leave tomorrow, first train, to have any hope of being in Tarragona by dawn on the twentieth."

"You—good Lord, Vivi! *Tomorrow?*" Nolan raised his eyebrows and exhaled. "You should leave a note for your fellow—your sisters, telling them, so they'll know to be there too."

"They have a *sauteur* agent among them!" She scowled at the doorway. "I bet if we tried to use these tickets on Sunday they'd have some of their damned children watching for us at the station. With bad intent."

"But," said Nolan, "your old parasite can still track you, in newly taken bodies. How can we—"

"We won't be slow. Get up!"

Nolan got to his feet. The cat had jumped down from the shelf and now stood at the window, its tail curled around a white oval in a little stand on the windowsill. As he and Vivi started to walk past it, he saw that it was one of the widely reproduced casts of the face of *l'Inconnue de la Seine*—the anonymous girl who had drowned in the Seine decades ago.

He paused, and the cat stared intently into his eyes until he lifted the plaster face away from her tail.

He turned back and called to Sylvia Beach, "We need to make a purchase." And as he and Vivi walked back to the big table he muttered, "And we've got to buy a good-sized doll somewhere too."

PART FOUR:
Tarragona

CHAPTER EIGHTEEN:
Their Plan Is Moot

Looking out the automobile window at the sunlit Mediterranean Sea, Vivi shook her head. "Well, Beltran told us what to do, didn't he? The goddess—in me!—will lure the golden bull to the effigy and the mirror, then it gets attached to its mirror image, and we break the mirror."

Nolan kept his eyes on the narrow curving road. In as kind a voice as he could muster, he asked, "How"—he didn't add *exactly*—"is this to happen?"

She sat back and rubbed her eyes. "I don't know! As in billiards, I imagine it will depend on where the balls stop rolling."

The Paris-Lyon-Méditerranée train for Marseilles had left at 9:00 a.m. from the Gare de Lyon station the previous day, less than a mile up the Seine from where the temple of Cybele had fleetingly stood four days earlier. There had been no difficulty in exchanging the tickets Kirenli had given them, and Nolan and Vivi had carried their valises and the packaged painting along a wide platform crowded with noisy travelers and stacks of luggage, past the enormous Mountain 4-8-2 locomotive with its eight big, connected driving wheels, to the line of Wagon-Lits coaches that stretched behind it. They had soon found their compartment, which proved to be a suite with two couches that could be opened into beds, along with a private *cabinet de toilette*. When the train had got underway, Vivi had already been kneeling on one of the couches and peering out the window with anxious excitement.

For the next several hours the train had rolled south, and had soon been passing between fields of poppies and ripening barley. A stop at Dijon had been long enough for them to venture out and get a hasty lunch of sausages and Chablis, and then through the afternoon the train's course had continued south, to Lyon in the Saône valley. They hadn't left their compartment at Lyon, for by this time Vivi had fallen asleep in her bunk; and night had long since fallen when the train steamed through Avignon and arrived at last in Marseille. Nolan had roused Vivi and they had disembarked at the Marseille-Saint-Charles station, and trudged from streetlamp to streetlamp down the long Saint-Charles grand staircase to the nearest hotel. Vivi had refused a separate room, and she and Nolan had both slept in their traveling clothes.

Early the next morning, Nolan had bought a map and laid down a substantial security deposit to rent a four-year-old Citroën with a hand brake and three-speed transmission, and after breakfast he and Vivi had set out on the 370-mile drive along the road that curved around the Bay of Marseilles below the eastern foot of the Pyrenees. The Citroën's steering wheel was on the right, and along several stretches Vivi was able to peer to the left, shivering, straight across low brush at the broad blue face of the Mediterranean Sea—the first unbounded body of water she had ever seen.

"Where the balls stop rolling," Nolan said, echoing her. Vivi just settled more deeply in the seat and didn't look at him.

At noon they arrived at the Spanish border, ten miles south of Perpignan, and Nolan's new-style American passport raised no comment. In Spain now, he kept driving south on the coast roads, and at dusk they stopped in Barcelona to eat and refill the fuel tank. By Vivi's returned watch it was eight p.m. when they finally reached Tarragona.

Nolan soon found the town's main avenue and drove slowly past many whitewashed houses separated by plane trees, and a hotel, the Centro. Reasoning that the *sauteurs* would probably be occupying the hotel, he steered the automobile south, past several narrow, ill-lit streets and a square in which citizens apparently cooked over open fires, and on a side street found a shabby two-story hotel called the Continental.

Nolan parked the Citroën under a glowing lantern beside the hotel wall, and they were carrying their luggage to the entrance steps when a rising roar overhead made them look up. The sky was clear, and for a few moments the silhouette of a big biplane was visible, with a long fuselage and smoking red lamps on its lower wingtips, flying west at an altitude of hardly a hundred feet. When it had passed out of sight and the roar of its three engines faded, Vivi turned to Nolan.

"A flying boat," he told her, "a seaplane. One of the Curtiss NCs. I saw several of them during the war." He sighed and picked up their two valises. "The map shows a breakwater at the south end of town—they'll be touching down in the lagoon."

Vivi lifted the packaged painting in both hands. "Nothing to do with our concerns," she said with mock confidence.

"Of course not," agreed Nolan dryly.

Wary of the censorious look of the *dueña* at the lobby desk, they took two adjoining rooms, but Vivi picked the lock on the connecting door and wedged it open. When the hallway doors were closed and locked, Nolan lit the gas jets in his room while Vivi began unpacking one of the valises on his bed.

"The *sauteurs* must be here already," she said. She took out the .38 revolver and laid it on the bed, then hefted the cloth-wrapped bundle that was his .45 semiautomatic and handed it to him.

"Most of them, certainly," Nolan said, taking it. "That might have been Achard on the seaplane." A table with a ceramic pitcher and basin on it stood by the window, and he sat down on the floor beside it. He unwrapped the pistol and slid the magazine out of the grip, noting that it was fully loaded now. He laid it aside and began field-stripping the pistol.

Next Vivi lifted out a ball of string and the ornately dressed doll they had bought at a toy shop in the Boulevard Saint-Michel, and she fitted over its porcelain face the plaster cast of *l'Inconnue de la Seine*. She unwound a yard of the string and tied the plaster face over the porcelain one.

"A good lure, I think," she said, laying the doll on the bed and hoisting up the Picasso painting in its brown paper wrapping. "Now the mirror."

She unfolded one end of the paper. She gave Nolan a wide-eyed look, then slid the canvas out, and in the dim gas light they both stared dubiously at it.

The dark patch in the corner of the painting, where Nolan had wiped off the watercolor, made the banality of the surface bullfight scene seem sardonic.

Vivi laid the thing on the carpet and fetched a sock from the valise, then stepped over the painting to the table. She poured water from the pitcher into the basin, dipped the sock, and crouched beside the painting. She took a deep breath, then began gently scrubbing its surface.

Nolan could see that her eyes were on the moving wet sock rather than the emerging oil painting. When she was just smearing the dissolved watercolor paint, he stood up and carried the basin over to where she sat.

"I can take over."

She rolled away, leaving the wet sock on the painting. "Take it."

Nolan sat down, wrung out the sock, and dipped it in the basin again to resume the work. The underlying oil painting was heavily varnished, and the watercolor paint came off easily. He too avoided looking directly at the painting they were exposing, but from moment to moment he got peripheral impressions of a contorting animal, or a mountain poised against a turbulent sunset, or a burning tower.

When his sliding hand felt only the smooth varnished surface, Vivi tossed him a fresh sock and he wiped the thing dry. He slid the painting back into the folded paper beside his drawing of Vivi.

Vivi took it and leaned it against the door. "We've got to get to the old arena early tomorrow," she said, "in that village Hemingway mentioned."

"Sant Salvador." Nolan resumed his seat below the window. He pulled the slide off the pistol and lifted out the barrel. He peered through it, shook it, and peered again. "Have you got a pencil?"

Vivi rummaged through her valise and tossed him one. He slid it into the barrel and jiggled it around, then pulled it out.

"A squib load," he said. "There's a solid obstruction in the barrel. I think one of your sisters fired a round through it with no powder in the shell, just the primer." When Vivi shook her head, he said, "The bullet is stuck halfway down the barrel. If I tried to fire one through it now, it might shoot both bullets—or do nothing—or blow up and take off my fingers."

Vivi frowned at the steel cylinder. "Why would Kirenli—?"

"Hemingway said one of her lot is working for Achard, remember?"

He broke two inches off the point end of the pencil and took off his shoe. Setting the barrel upright on the wooden floor, he pounded the heel of his shoe on the splintered end of the pencil—several times, with increasing force, until the pencil split. The obstruction in the barrel hadn't moved.

He sat back. "It's good and stuck," he said. "I need a better wooden dowel, or ideally a brass rod." He sighed. "And a hammer. And a vise." He pulled the pencil out of the barrel. "For tomorrow, I'm afraid we rely on the revolver." He fitted the barrel back in the slide and began reassembling the pistol. "In a pinch we might at least be able to threaten somebody with it."

He stood up and gave the pistol to Vivi. "I'm going to go downstairs and ask that old lady where Sant Salvador is."

At dawn the next morning, Nolan and Vivi stood on the unpaved street in front of the hotel, both of them wearing clothes they had bought in Paris: khaki jackets and cargo trousers, and sturdy leather boots. The cold breeze smelled of fish and the sea.

Vivi was holding the paper-wrapped painting and Nolan carried a valise, and both of them were blinking mistrustfully at a short wooden wagon that stood behind a donkey in the street. The vehicle had two big wood-spoked wheels and a canvas roof, and its white-bearded driver sat on a plank at the front, puffing a stubby clay pipe.

Last night, the *dueña* had assured Nolan that their Citroën could not possibly negotiate the road up to the old *capea* arena by Sant Salvador. She had offered to provide this *tartana* carriage for transport, and she had asked for payment in advance—five hundred pesetas, which Nolan estimated to be about twenty francs. He suspected that the elderly driver was a relative of hers.

Vivi turned to Nolan. "This can go where your automobile can't?" Her breath was steam on the chilly morning air.

"In a pinch we can walk. Three or four miles, she said."

"*Capea?*" called Vivi to the old man. "*Sant Salvador?*" She waved north.

He took the clay pipe out of his mouth and answered in Spanish.

"I believe he said, 'yes, with the others,'" Nolan said.

"And *ayer* is yesterday," said Vivi. "Others have been there since yesterday."

"I bet they have."

Nolan stepped forward and dropped the valise into the bed of the wagon, then carefully put one foot on a wheel-spoke to climb in over the side. The floor of the wagon proved to be a rectangle of old carpet laid over a rope mesh. Vivi handed him the wrapped painting.

"Step flat," he told her as he caught her wrist and hoisted her in, "or your foot will go through the floor."

They sat down on opposite sides, while the old driver tried to rouse the donkey with loud imprecations; but it wasn't until he slapped its flank with a rope that the animal lifted its head. And then it began galloping at such a clip that Nolan and Vivi were tipped against the back planks. The cart shook across four luckily empty streets and past some low buildings that might have been stables, and then it was barreling along a dirt road between stony fields, heading north. The sky was pale blue, but the sun had not yet risen over the mountains to the east.

After two miles the road became a path up a rocky valley studded with short, spiny palm trees. The little wagon was moving slowly now, but it tossed in all directions as its two big wheels rotated over protruding stones and slid into deep muddy ruts, and Nolan and Vivi had to grip the sides and brace their feet on the ropes under the loose carpet floor.

At several points the road descended briefly, and the driver yanked on a brake lever. The wooden brake shoes sent a shrill squeal rebounding among the rock outcrops on either side. The wind down the valley was cold, scented with wild rosemary.

When the blue sky outlined a crest ahead, Vivi jumped as if stung, and struggled to the front of the wagon bed. "Much farther?" she asked the driver. "Uh...*mucho mas?*"

In answer, the driver held up a thumb and forefinger close together, indicating that their destination was very close now.

She slumped back onto the disarranged carpet. "We should walk from here," she told Nolan, then called to the driver, "Far enough! *Suficiente aquí!*"

The driver seemed happy to terminate the ride. Nolan climbed out and took the painting and the valise from Vivi. When she was standing beside him, watching the driver trying to get the wagon turned around, she raised her left hand and said, "My tattoo is hot."

Nolan stepped back and stared at her. "What, here?"

She just stared at him.

"Sorry, right, okay." He rubbed his eyes. "So he's here, with them."

The driver had the wagon facing back toward Tarragona, and the brake screeched some more as the donkey began tugging it away downhill.

Watching its unsteady receding progress, Vivi said, "I doubt Achard meant to bring him along. More like a ... a rat hiding in a grain shipment. But of course they'd have brought several of their newly grafted members, the ones that aren't firmly set in their latest bodies yet."

Nolan raised a spread hand, and she added, "To be sure of having a sacrificial offering, see? At least one whose identity can easily be displaced by their god." She shivered. "Volunteers, maybe."

"Oh." Nolan was glad she hadn't pronounced the name *Moloch* out loud here. He nodded. "And Cadieux has hitchhiked along on them, among them. Well, he can't trespass in a *sauteur's* body for long."

"Not at any one time." She was looking nervously at the rocky hills on either side. "But he wants me. And they'll certainly have brought some quantity of *kykeon*, to float one of their offerings out of his body—make room for their god."

She took the valise from Nolan and crouched beside it on the ground. When she unstrapped it and opened it, she peered in at the doll with the plaster *l'Inconnue* face tied over the front of its head. The rough wagon ride had not dislodged it.

She closed and buckled the valise and gave it back to him. "'Here's a sigh for those who love me,'" she said, standing up, "'and a smile for those who hate.'" She sighed and shook her head.

For once he recognized the quote—it was from a poem by Byron that he had learned in high school. "'And whatever sky's above me,'" he said, recalling it, "'here's a heart for every fate.'"

"Well now, Harry!" For a moment a grin lit her urchin face, and she looked very young. "*Two* hearts."

"Two hearts," he agreed.

The sun was just clearing the hills to the east, and it occurred to Nolan that when it set, he might be alone, or dead.

Vivi might have had the same thought. Her expression was again watchful and intent.

They picked up the paper-wrapped painting and the valise, and began making their way over the stones of the valley crest. Soon they could hear distant calls and shouting, and the wind carried a faint smell of roasting pork. They set down the painting and valise and moved forward on their hands and knees to crouch behind a boulder that overlooked the descending slope beyond. Nolan edged his head around the boulder.

"We should have brought binoculars," he said.

At the bottom of a long rocky slope lay a circular flat area, about fifty yards wide, ringed by upright plywood panels and curved segments of an old stone wall. On the far side, a couple of dozen men in white shirts and trousers and straw hats—presumably amateur bullfighters here for the *capea*, without the elaborate costumes of big city *toreadors*—milled around open fires, laughing and playfully shoving one another. Beyond the arena, a road curled away, presumably toward the village of Sant Salvador. On this side, three or four people wearing variously dark jackets stood beside a couple of big black Ford trucks. Nolan squinted, trying to focus past the glare of the rising sun on his right. Beyond the trucks was a platform with a big gold-colored chair on it. A throne? he wondered.

Motion on the left side of the ring caught his eye, and he saw a wide wood-fenced enclosure; Nolan discerned that the shifting shapes within it were easily a dozen massive black bulls.

"They can't usually need that many bulls!" he said quietly.

"This isn't an ordinary *capea*."

Vivi was lying prone beside Nolan, and she pointed at a thirty-foot-long tan canvas tent partly hidden by the trucks. A flap on one side had opened and been secured, and now a line of children in what seemed to be school uniforms trotted out, each carrying in one hand some small black object swinging on a handle. Nolan counted ten of the children when they separated; each hurried to a different spot on the perimeter of the circle.

"We can't get down there unobserved," he said.

The children around the circle now all crouched, and when they stood up, the black things they had carried stood on the dirt, with bright red flames flaring at the tops. The children raced back to the tent.

Nolan whistled soundlessly. "Railway flares—are they setting up landing lights?" He glanced at the closely surrounding hills. "But they can't land a—"

"No, not for a plane—they're calling the god!" Vivi rolled back and picked up the painting. "Get the doll out!" she said. "And the gun! We've got to do it up here."

Nolan reached behind him and took hold of the valise—but a rattle of gravel made him look to his right.

Several figures had appeared on the close ridge. They were silhouettes against the rising sun, but he could see that they were three adults and a child, and at least two of the adults held handguns.

As the four came sliding and hopping down toward the path, Nolan sat up. There was no hope of getting the revolver out, but he took hold of a baseball-sized rock in his left hand, out of view of these intruders.

One of them, a man in khaki shorts and a bush jacket, paused in his descent to smile and point his revolver straight at Vivi. "We want her alive for a later event," he called to Nolan in a pleasant tone. His accent was French. "But you could cost her a leg. Both of you stand up."

Nolan let go of the rock and got to his feet, followed by Vivi. Her face was pale and expressionless under her wind-tossed blonde bangs.

"Grab their litter," said the man with the revolver to his two adult companions.

The child hurried down to the path, and Nolan recognized the short-cropped red hair. It was the body of Robin, and Nolan wondered whether it was Robin or Thibaud Cadieux occupying it. "Wound her only slightly, if you must!" the boy piped.

It was Cadieux.

One of the men behind the boy waved Nolan and Vivi back, then hurried down to the path and picked up the valise and the paper-wrapped painting.

"Qu'est-ce que c'est que ça?"

"Some Cybeline fetish, I expect," said the first speaker. "Be quick."

The man partly unfolded the paper and peered in at the painting; then he hastily refolded the paper and picked up the painting, gingerly. Nolan noticed that his little finger was missing the top joint. The *sauteurs* weren't bothering with gloves today.

"Now," said the first speaker to Nolan and Vivi, "down to the tent." He waved his revolver toward the slope in front of them.

"Carefully!" said Robin. "Don't break a leg that will soon be mine!"

Nolan saw cuts on the back of his hand, and recalled that the boy had inked his Thibaud Cadieux birth date there, when he had come to Vivi's flat three days ago—*to stake my claim on this body*. He had now apparently *cut* the date into his hand.

Vivi shot a quick glance at Nolan, but he just shook his head.

With their captors following several yards behind and clapping their hands from time to time, Nolan and Vivi climbed over the crest and began picking their way down the slope toward the circle and the trucks and the tent. The cold wind was from below, and the smell of roasting pork mingled with the reek of the bulls.

They soon reached the level ground, and as they trudged across the packed dirt toward the tent, Nolan looked around at the arena. The curved segments of wall were eroded by centuries of weather, but he could see bumps and grooves in them that hinted at long-lost bas-reliefs. This was where Hemingway had seen a weathered example of the horned, three-eyed symbol. Filling the gaps between the wall sections, the plywood sheets were painted garishly with Spanish words and crude images of bulls. The crowd of amateur bullfighters outside the arena on the north side were increasingly noisy, impatient for the *capea* to begin.

The tent flap opened again and three boys in black robes stepped out, escorted by two women who seemed to be dressed as nuns. Nolan recognized one of them as Gabrielle, the woman who had accosted him outside his bank and taken him to see Adrien Achard. She gave him a look of startled recognition, but marched past without speaking.

"Trot along now," growled one of the men at Nolan's back.

Nolan and Vivi walked more rapidly, but were still pushed into the tent. Nolan caught his balance and looked around.

The tent's interior was lit by oil lanterns at the four corners, and the stale, smoky air led Nolan to believe it had been occupied all night. A table and several folding chairs stood at the far end; a man and a woman sat at the table, while another woman sat off to the right, against the rippling canvas wall. Two of the men who had captured Nolan and Vivi stood just inside the entry flap. The diminutive figure of Robin stepped past them and walked across the canvas floor to stand beside the table.

Squinting in the relative dimness, Nolan's sweaty face was chilled to see Adrien Achard behind the table, getting to his feet. Nolan didn't recognize the woman in the chair beside Achard until after he had looked at the one seated against the wall: the Cybele priestess Kirenli, her arms stiffly folded behind her. Nolan switched his gaze back to the table, and now he could see that the woman there was the one Kirenli had called Sarkaya, who had been at the oars of the canal boat three days ago. *Achard's got an agent among them,* Hemingway had said. Both women wore fur-collared leather jackets, and Nolan was sure it was these two who had arrived last night on the seaplane.

Achard was leaning forward, one hand flat on the table and the other, missing the top joint of the little finger, resting on an ornate lidded gold chalice. His tie was loosened over his rumpled white shirt, and his blond curls were spiked up, as if he had recently run his hands through his hair.

He clapped his hands. "Genevieve!" He waved toward Robin, but his eyes were on Vivi. "I didn't believe Thibaud when he said you were close by." Robin smiled and folded his arms. Achard glanced down at Sarkaya and added, coldly, "We have people who will be waiting for you, pointlessly, at the Gare de Lyon tomorrow."

"That's when we meant them to leave Paris," Sarkaya said. Her voice was steady, and she shrugged. "You've got her now, in any case."

"Yes," said Achard, "where she shouldn't be, today."

In her chair against the wall, Kirenli tossed back her black hair. Her arms were obviously bound behind her. To Sarkaya she said, "And after they've used her to summon our goddess—late, subordinated, preceded by their detestable god today!—do you think this man will have any further use for you?"

Sarkaya gave her a cold smile. "I have assurances..."

"Assurances!" said Kirenli. Her voice was scornful.

"Don't squabble, *mesdames*. You'll all be moved out of range before we begin here, and you can quarrel at leisure." Achard glanced past Nolan. "Henri, what were they carrying?"

One of the men by the entry now stepped forward and set the flat paper-wrapped package and the valise on the table.

Robin pointed at the lidded chalice. "There's enough *kykeon* there for your three young hosts to have a sip each and still leave enough for the Genevieve Chastain girl and me."

"No, Thibaud," said Achard, opening the valise. "It's true your illicit presence here led us to early acquisition of the girl, but now you withdraw. I need Robin's counsel." Looking up at the boy, he added, "You've lost her, Thibaud. Face it. She *exorcised* you, broke the old connection. Let Robin come back up, take the next step—there's a bed at NID.3 for you."

Robin's mouth opened in surprised protest. "*Et comment cela peut-il arriver?* How is that to happen? My sequence is ruptured, I could never come back. No, Adrien—I can restore the connection, now, with the *kykeon*. Her mind is still shaped for me."

"I'm sorry, Thibaud. I'll speak plainly: you were always a reactionary voice, agitating to restore the outmoded Carthage-style immolations—and I need Robin. Lose graciously."

Achard clapped his hands again, then reached into the valise and lifted out the doll. He peered at the plaster *l'Inconnue* face attached to its head, then laid it on the table near the gold chalice. Next he took out the .38 revolver. He opened the cylinder and glanced at the brass shell casings before closing it and putting the gun down. He groped in the valise again, and came up with Nolan's .45 semiautomatic. After checking the magazine and working the slide, he dropped it beside the revolver.

He looked up. "In the old story there was a mirror." He nodded toward the package. "Is that it?"

"Yes," said Sarkaya, "it's a painting. I know their plan!"

"Their plan is moot," said Achard.

Nolan was watching the short figure of Robin. The boy's fists were clenched, and his narrowed eyes were fixed on Achard.

The boy opened his mouth, but whatever he meant to say was drowned by a roar from outside. Nolan shuddered—below the sudden noise, the air had abruptly become heavy with a subsonic pressure, and his thoughts were momentarily scattered.

"The bulls have broken loose," called the man by the tent's entry flap. His voice was hoarse. "All of them. It's starting."

Achard looked up in alarm. "Already? Damn me! Go get the hosts in position beside the throne!" The man quickly left the tent.

Achard picked up both guns from the table and hurried out from behind it. He paused beside Henri and threw a quick, worried glance at Vivi.

"The girl is opened to Cybele," he told Henri. "We can't have her here *now*, for *this*." He rubbed a hand across his mouth, then made a chopping gesture. "Kill her. Kill them all, then bring the *kykeon* out. *Rapidement!*"

Henri was still holding a revolver, and now raised it, pointing it squarely at Vivi.

Nolan threw himself against her shoulder as the shot hammered the air and lit the tent's interior, and she tumbled to the canvas floor beneath him—but she was lying on top of another struggling body.

It was Robin. He thrashed out from under Vivi and stood up. His right arm swung limply, and blood was already blotting his shirt. Clearly he had blocked Henri's shot.

He lurched to the table and with his good hand he grabbed the chalice; the lid fell off, and liquid spilled across the table. "You don't kill *her!*" he shouted after Achard. "She's mine!" He lifted the chalice and took a gulp of its contents.

Henri stolidly aimed the gun again at Vivi, who had got up onto her hands and knees.

Nolan sprang directly at him. With a long, desperate reach he slapped the gun aside in the moment it fired.

Robin had rushed up too, and tripped over Nolan's leg—a gout of spilled liquid splashed into Henri's face, and Nolan smelled mint and quinine as he hopped forward and drove the heel of his hand up with all his strength into Henri's chin.

Henri's head snapped back and he toppled away, the revolver dropping from his limp hand. Still gripping the chalice, Robin darted for it, but as the gun bounced on the floor Nolan kicked it toward Vivi.

Achard had stopped and turned around. "Halt!" he shouted. Both of the handguns he held were now raised, the revolver pointed toward Sarkaya and Kirenli, the .45 at Nolan and Vivi. "Damn you, Cadieux, give me the chalice!"

Vivi had crouched and caught the revolver, and Robin lashed what remained in the chalice into her face. She reeled back, coughing and spitting.

"I said *halt.*" Achard's voice was not as loud this time, but it vibrated with lethal promise. For an instant everyone was poised between actions.

And Nolan raised a fist and took a deliberately distracting step toward Achard. He was achingly aware of the .45 caliber muzzle aimed at his chest—*it might shoot both bullets*—and his mind stuttered in wordless prayer.

Behind the trigger guard, Achard's finger tightened.

Then the air shook as the gun in Achard's hand exploded in a spray of shrapnel and blood. Achard fell to his knees.

Vivi was shaking her head. Her eyes unfocused for a moment, then cleared in a glare of rage. Robin started toward her, but she got the revolver up and yanked spasmodically at the trigger. The gun flared and jumped in her hand.

Nolan didn't see where the .38 caliber bullet struck, but the boy spun and tumbled to the floor. The chalice rolled away, emptied.

Vivi rubbed her mouth with her free hand. "I got a mouthful! He would have tried to switch..." She broke off, staring in shock at the gun in her right hand.

Achard had dropped the other gun and fallen over sideways. Blood ran down his face from a shrapnel cut on his forehead, and he was gripping the spurting wrist of his shattered hand. The windy roar from outside was louder, punctuated now with the hollow knock of several gunshots.

Vivi leaned over the table and grabbed the paper-wrapped painting. "Get the doll!" she shouted to Nolan, and then she hurried past him, leaped over Achard, and ran out of the tent.

Nolan's heart was still pounding after the chancy misfire of the .45. He kicked Achard aside and picked up the dropped revolver. He glanced at the sprawled body of Henri, who didn't appear to be breathing, and stepped quickly to the table.

He reached for the doll, but paused; the lid of the chalice lay upside down next to the painting, and he saw that some quantity of *kykeon*, perhaps a couple of tablespoons, had splashed into it when Robin had knocked it off in grabbing the chalice.

Ignoring a shout from Kirenli, he carefully picked up the chalice lid and drank off the mouthful of *kykeon*.

His nose stinging with fumes of mint and quinine, he tossed the lid aside and took hold of the doll with his free hand. From the corner of his eye he saw Robin, his shirt drenched in blood but somehow on his feet again, hobble with surprising speed across the floor and vanish outside.

Sarkaya had got up and was bent over Kirenli. One of them called something to Nolan, but he tucked the revolver into his belt and hurried out of the tent after Vivi and Robin.

CHAPTER NINETEEN:
A Mirror

The scene outside hit him like a blow. The sky had been bright morning blue ten minutes ago, but it was now darkly overcast with visibly churning clouds, and a hot wind tossed his hair. The three boys in flapping black robes were clustered around the empty elevated throne, scowling in evident confusion, and two or three *sauteur* adults with drawn handguns were running toward the tent.

In the red glare of the widely spaced railway flares, the arena was a dust-blurred chaos of plunging bulls and leaping, shouting men. The clothing of at least one of the men had caught fire, but it had not stopped him from capering in front of the bulls.

Nolan's head was full of *kykeon* fumes, but he squinted around desperately for Vivi. He didn't see her anywhere, but a small lurching figure caught his eye; the red hair and bloody shirt told him it was Robin, making his rapid, suffering way toward a four-foot-tall section of the old wall.

Nolan ran after him through the stinging clouds of dust, and caught the boy by the shoulder a few feet short of the wall.

The boy's head swiveled around. "She's in there!" Robin croaked, nodding at the tumultuous crowd in the arena. "She must not die!" He fell back against the wall, panting wetly.

Nolan climbed up onto the broad surface of the wall and crouched there, clutching the doll. The cacophony of shouts and wind and bulls bellowing made it impossible for him to call to Vivi, so after a couple of the amateur bullfighters collided with the wall near him and sprinted away, he dropped to the packed-dirt floor of the arena.

He was dizzy, and the ground seemed to tilt and rotate like a carnival ride under his feet, but he saw Vivi. She was kneeling beside an upright sheet of plywood to his left, only a couple of yards closer than one of the bright railway flares, and Henri's revolver lay beside her knee. He hurried over and crouched at her side. She pried the doll from his clutching hand and looked up at him. Their eyes met.

And then he was looking at a man's haggard, red-lit face, and recognized it as his own. The viewpoint lowered to the *l'Inconnue* face of the doll, and a memory intruded: the porcelain face of Elodie in the moonlit river, palpably gazing up from the eye holes in the gleaming white face. It was a memory of Vivi's.

The viewpoint shifted, and two blood-streaked young hands hoisted a pain-racked torso up onto the wall. Visible on the other side, below and to the left, Genevieve Chastain and the Nolan fellow were huddled over the doll and the wrapped-up painting. The bloody hands gripped the edge of the wall and pulled the body over it.

Nolan was brought back to his own identity when his shoulder thudded against the packed dirt. He looked at his hands, but saw no blood.

Kykeon! he thought, and he remembered Vivi's description of its effects: *It made us see visions, and forget which of us was which.* And he realized that for a moment he had been Vivi—and then, horribly, Robin.

He spat out the remembered taste of Robin's blood and touched the revolver tucked behind his belt buckle.

Crouched over the doll on the dirt, Vivi had now slid the dark painting out of its paper sheath, but she looked up in alarm, past Nolan.

Nolan turned around. The short figure of Robin had shambled up to within a few feet of them, and now paused, swaying. The boy's blood-slick hands were clasped to his sopping red shirt. One of the amateur bullfighters dived past behind him as a big black bull crashed its horns into the stone wall, but Robin paid no attention, staring at Vivi.

Vivi shivered, then sprang to her feet. She looked wildly from Nolan to Robin, then looked at her own hands.

To Nolan's right, the bloody figure of Robin wailed, "Harry, feed the cat!"

The hot wind chilled sudden sweat on Nolan's forehead. Loosened from Robin's body by the *kykeon,* Thibaud Cadieux was in at least precarious possession of Vivi's.

Vivi had started to turn away, but Nolan drew the revolver from his belt, and with his free hand he gripped her arm and spun her back to face him. His chest felt hollow as he raised the gun and pointed it directly at her forehead. Over the surrounding clamor, he shouted, "Don't move!"

Her mouth opened. "What are you doing? Surely you—"

"Shut up." He stared directly into Vivi's hazel eyes—and in spite of the close tumult of bulls and men skidding on heels and hooves and kicking up dust, he excluded everything from his attention except her narrowed eyes. With the bitter smell of *kykeon* still in his head, he thought forcefully, *Get out of her.*

Her eyes clenched shut and for a moment her teeth were bared in an effortful grimace; then her eyes opened wide, and she whispered, "By Marechal and Elodie!"

Quickly, before their personalities could switch again, he turned and fired the gun directly into Robin's face. The boy's ruptured head snapped back and he toppled away—

—and, in induced mimicry, a new viewpoint intruded: Nolan found himself in a stilled body lying on the canvas floor of the tent, and he remembered that Robin had inadvertently flung a splash of *kykeon* into Henri's face, a moment before Nolan had struck Henri very hard under the chin and sent him arching backward. Nolan could feel no heartbeat in the body, and Henri's dead eyes showed him only a dimming and unmoving view of the canvas ceiling.

Henri's body was killed—but his brain had not yet entirely died, and Nolan was unable to stop it as, in its final automatic reflex, it called on Moloch. The prayer of the dead man radiated away.

Nolan fell out of the terminated mind, and he clenched his own hands and deeply filled his own lungs.

Vivi rushed to him and tightly clasped his free hand in mute thanks. Then she knelt again beside the painting and the doll. Nolan dazedly slid the gun back behind his belt buckle.

But the dead man's prayer was answered from the roiling charcoal sky. The bellowing of the bulls underscored the shouts of the ragtag bullfighters—but now a deep vibration shook Nolan's bones, a more profound roar, grinding out of the unnaturally close and shifting dark clouds. For a moment his frail awareness was pushed aside by a momentous presence that loomed over this corner of Spain.

The sound rumbled away into the surrounding hills and the earth. Nolan's thoughts trickled back into his mind, and he realized that he was lying face down in the dirt. He struggled up onto his hands and knees, and looked to the side.

Vivi was pushing herself up and crawling through the windblown dust toward the doll and the painting. And though their identities didn't shift again, his palms felt the gritty sand as her hands pulled her along.

She fumblingly picked up the doll, and in the flickering light the plaster *l'Inconnue* face seemed alive, about to open its eyes. Vivi looked away and waved toward the painting, and Nolan walked on his knees to it and squinted down at the glossy canvas.

Only after cuffing away dust was he able see that the image in the painting was a sort of face, rather than a burning tree or a view down a fiery chasm. The brush strokes were slashes, but he could make out three gleamingly black vortices that were apparently eyes, above a mouth like a stormy sunset viewed between peaks in Hell. The whole visage was distorted in an angular whirlpool of demonic geometry. The image was crude, necessarily crude, but deep in Nolan's mind it shook memories that seemed far older than his individual lifetime.

He forced himself to look away. In the arena's melee he saw a man tossed cartwheeling through the air by a rearing bull, and another man crawling toward the wall, his trailing leg blackly gleaming with blood.

Now Nolan saw a flickering patch of refraction darting back and forth over the turbulent arena. He was squinting to keep it in sight against the churning clouds, but a cry from Vivi made him look down.

One of the bulls, a plunging black animal that must have weighed two tons, was galloping heavily toward them. Its massive head was down, extending its spread horns, and its hooves pounded the dirt.

Vivi was scrambling to the left, holding the doll, but not fast enough to get out of the bull's way.

Nolan got his feet under himself and sprang to the right with a shout at the oncoming beast. It swerved toward him and he sprinted away from Vivi. After a few running steps, when the thing was only a couple of yards away and closing with terrible speed, Nolan skidded to a stop, hoping the bull's momentum would carry it past him on his right—but it dug in its hooves and turned, fast as a fencer changing lines. The horn on the left rushed directly at his chest.

He leaped straight up and clamped both hands onto the curved horn, unable to get his fingers all the way around it, and the bull flung its head up powerfully. Nolan's knees collided with its long forehead and then he was flying through the air over its back.

He struck the dirt on his hands and rolled as the animal swung around for another attack—but Vivi had had time to stand up, and now called, *"Cybele! Magna Mater!"*

In the next moment, Nolan found himself blinking in sudden white light, and for a few panicky seconds he couldn't see Vivi or the bull. The world seemed to shift under him as he struggled painfully to his feet.

Now he saw the bull shaking its head in the glare and backing away. Turning to look behind, Nolan saw a very tall black-haired woman standing where Vivi had been. The white light was on her—emanating from her.

This corner of the arena had been cleared by the white glare of Cybele, and in that radiance the spot of moving diffraction that he had noticed moments earlier was more visible—as it raced back and forth over the tossing heads of bulls and men, it looked like a twisting crab made of smoky glass.

It dived down and touched Robin's devastated body, and quickly recoiled; and before Nolan could get to his feet, it darted to *him,* and disappeared into his eyes.

Then it was in Nolan's mind, like a groping hand, and he saw its imperatives, felt its furious impatience. Its ancient enemy, Cybele, was present here, and Moloch was unable to take physical form to confront her. The summoning rite had been performed, red flares lit at the temple site, the prescribed Phoenician throne stood beside three black-robed, offered hosts—but the hosts' minds had not been opened, and Moloch had only been able to rush from one end of the area to the other, searching for a body to occupy.

And the god had seized on Nolan's *kykeon*-opened mind.

In horrified revulsion Nolan resisted it, and in response it found and threw at him altered fragments of his own memory: he found himself helplessly reexperiencing the night in La Rochette Wood when German artillery shells were exploding in the trees overhead—but now it was Moloch's immense claws tearing the trees apart to get at him. He was underwater in the Seine, below the Pont de l'Alma bridge, but in this changed memory it was not Elodie's ghost that found him in the cold green depths, but the hungry spirit of Moloch.

Nolan desperately searched his violently stirred mind for a memory to counter these, and he raised an image of Vivi in his flat a week ago, sitting in the chair beside the window and holding the cat Marechal in her lap. And now another power, not Moloch, changed that memory: the remembered Vivi smiled at him, and Marechal leaped to him and laid surprisingly heavy paws on his chest. The cat's eyes bored into his, driving Moloch's claws out of his mind.

When Nolan's vision cleared, he was lying on the packed dirt of the arena, his shadow sharply distinct in the white light from behind him. The last memory had vanished, but Marechal had not.

The black cat stood thirty feet away, but it was huge now, bigger than the plunging bulls beyond it, and a shaggy mane flared around its head and its big glossy shoulders. The bull that had attacked Nolan was gone—just a few scraps of fur and half of one eroded horn lay where it had stood.

The patch of glassy refraction, forced out of Nolan's mind, again raced to and fro over the clamoring crowd. It was clearly searching for any other physical host—then, evidently perceiving at least some kinship, it dove and disappeared into the nearest living bull, which had just thrown a man to the ground.

A dozen of the battered, reeling bullfighters nearby fell down in the same moment; their bodies on the dirt shriveled, and their clothing darkened and tore to windblown shreds that flew to the bull Moloch had taken.

That black bull shivered violently, then to Nolan's astonishment it swelled in size until it was fully eight feet high at the shoulder, and its massive boulder of a head swung toward him.

Nolan got hastily to his feet. The revolver that had been in his belt lay a few yards away, and he hurried to it and picked it up.

Then another black form, big as a locomotive, swept past him, and he nearly lost his balance in the wind of its passage. He glimpsed the radiant figure of Cybele riding the enormous lion, holding a long spear extended straight at the bull. From off to the right he saw the comparatively tiny figure of Kirenli, running toward the bull through the glare-lit dust, her open leather jacket flapping in the wind.

Cybele's spear struck the Moloch bull in the shoulder, and flexed with the force of the impact. The bull fell back, and Kirenli stopped and waved her jacket over her head. The priestess called something Nolan couldn't hear, and the bull turned toward her. In that moment, the lion lunged forward, driving the spear deeper into the bull.

From Nolan's still-jumbled memories came Kirenli's voice from five days ago: *The* taurobolium... *we would have killed a bull with the goddess's sacred spear...*

The bull sank heavily onto its haunches as the spear dug further into its shoulder—and then its massive hind legs flexed and it leaped to the side, breaking the spear and flinging Kirenli sprawling across the dirt.

The light changed—Cybele's radiance still shone bright white, but now a red glow suffused the arena, as if the number of railway flares had increased a hundredfold. Blinking around in bewilderment, Nolan saw that the surrounding wall was no longer low and broken, but extended upward on all sides to a vaulted stone ceiling high overhead. The horned and three-eyed symbol stood out in high relief at regular intervals on the walls.

In a rushing return stroke, the bull's head swept back and struck the lion's head with jarring force. The lion thrashed over onto its side, and the goddess's white light dimmed. The figure that rolled away from the lion was just Vivi.

She scrambled to her feet and picked up one end of the massive broken spear in both hands, then began dragging it back toward where the doll and the painting lay. The Moloch bull started toward her, but it was moving unevenly now, its right foreleg dragging.

Nolan knew the two remaining rounds in the revolver he was holding were useless to stop the oncoming injured monster. He looked back toward Vivi and saw Robin's body lying a few yards away from her, the boy's ruined head in a puddle of black mud, and he remembered how Moloch's darting patch of refracting attention had recoiled from it.

He ran to Robin's body and crouched to shove the revolver's muzzle into the blood-soaked dirt. Death mud, he thought dizzily.

Cybele's black lion was on its feet again, and bounding after the Moloch bull. Nolan gritted his teeth, then made himself hurry forward and step into the path of both of them.

The bull slanted its off-balance drumming course toward him. He stood still in the red light, and at the last moment he dropped to his knees below the scooping horns and fired the revolver directly up into the bull's gaping mouth.

The bull's massive chest knocked him off his feet as it slid to a halt and reared back, nearly standing. Nolan rolled and scrambled away to the side, choking in the close bestial reek. Behind him he heard the cracking collision as the lion struck the bull—and a moment later the floor shook as the two supernatural beasts fell together some dozen yards away from him.

When Nolan was able to look around, gasping for breath, he saw that the huge black bull was back up on its feet, with the lion clinging to its back. Strings of smoking black blood now swung from the bull's slack mouth, and the lion's claws and teeth were buried in its shoulders, but the bull plodded indomitably on toward where Vivi crouched by the wall.

But Nolan and the lion had bought her time—she had dropped the heavy spear and picked up the doll. Her fair hair sparkled and stood out from her head in waving locks, and the white Cybele glow shone again in her face. She was facing the burdened Moloch bull, and even with the lion on its back it was plunging ever closer to her like a ship in heavy seas.

She raised the doll, then laid it on Picasso's painting and leaped to her left along the wall. The white glow stayed on the doll like a spotlight, and Vivi was tumbling away in shadow.

The bull's hooves plowed the dirt as it slid to a halt, and the lion was flung off its shoulders to the side.

Hungrily, the bull lowered its head and drove its horns at the glowing and almost animate *l'Inconnue* face of the doll. The doll was speared and lifted away, and then the bull was at last staring directly down at Picasso's painting.

The bull's high sides flexed in and out like luffing sails, and its nostrils blew out gusts of hot wind.

The painting flexed responsively upward on the dirt, gleaming in the red light, and the sheet of paper blew out from under it. Without taking his eyes off the bull for more than a split second at a time, Nolan hopped painfully to the paper and caught it in his fist.

The light on the Moloch bull was changing—no, the bull itself was changing: in the red light that illuminated Moloch's temple, its black coat became the harsh gleam of bronze. Its form rippled, and it was suddenly much bigger—when it sat back, its horned bronze head towered high above Nolan. Three eyes gleamed like obsidian in its broad saurian face. Massive metal arms flexed and spread wide, and a triumphant bellow rang out of its massive bronze chest.

As Beltran Iglesias's story had foretold, the mirror's reflection had evoked to physical presence the god's material form. The possessed black bull of a few moments earlier, even increased in size and power, had not been Moloch. *This* was Moloch.

Its high three-eyed gaze swept the southern horizon from east to west, and Nolan felt a sudden heaviness in himself and the earth beneath him, as if the very world were being fixed in a determinist mosaic. *Nihilism,* Vivi had said, *anti-growth,* anti-*life.*

The god's head swung down, and Nolan clenched his eyes shut as its withering attention passed across him; but for a moment he had felt again its ancient hatred and insatiable hunger. It had not focused on him this time, but the moment rocked him, and he shook his head and exhaled sharply before he looked back.

Pressed against the wall of Moloch's temple, the whitely glowing figure of Vivi had made its way back to the painting, and in her right hand she now carried one of the flaming railway flares.

She crouched, and in the mixed light it was recognizably Vivi who laid the flare on the gleaming canvas. The canvas burst into flame, and the colossal figure of Moloch reared back, its bellow dropping to a guttural echo.

Vivi straightened—and grew taller, far beyond her own height, and her form was nearly lost in white glare, for she was again fully Cybele. The goddess bent and lifted the broken spear—drew it back over the high promontory of a shoulder—and hurled it.

For an instant, Nolan saw the spear in flight, gleaming in the goddess's radiance, its splintered end rotating, and then it had plunged half its length into the high third eye of Moloch.

For several tense moments neither of the giant figures moved, and even the lion paused, as the red light gleamed on the spear and

Moloch's extended bronze arms, and shouts and bellowings echoed distantly from the dark farther reaches of the temple floor—

Then Moloch was leaning back. The bronze god toppled through the smoky air, slowly at first and then faster, and the earth jumped under Nolan's feet when the god crashed full length to the packed dirt. Its bronze torso broke into glittering shards and fragments that spun away in all directions, exposing a twisting, smoking mass that might have been snakes; they curled and shrank, and Moloch was still. The spear stood up from its face like a bare flagpole.

A cold wind swept across the arena, and then Nolan was blinking in daylight under a cleared blue sky. The high walls and ceiling of Moloch's temple had vanished.

A hundred feet away to his right, Kirenli had rolled onto her back. The ordinary bulls and the ragtag bullfighters were milling around dazedly at the far side of the arena, and Nolan turned toward Vivi.

She was standing beside a low section of the old wall, swaying in the fresh wind. She was once again her normal height, and the sun was shining on her and gleaming in her tousled hair; but she appeared to be in comparative shadow because behind her stood the inhumanly tall, radiant figure of Cybele. The goddess was motionless. The lion was gone.

Vivi was looking toward Nolan with alert recognition, and he dared to smile as he began plodding across the dirt toward her, still holding the crumpled sheet of paper.

But her face contorted and she pointed past him. He spun on one heel, nearly falling over, and squinted against the new sun glare.

Something was moving out there, on the broken bronze head of Moloch. Below the upright spear, a spiny black shape was emerging in unfolding stages from one of the two wide lower eye holes—and a similar shape was climbing up out of the other.

The tentative smile sagged from Nolan's face, and he tucked the sheet of paper into his shirt. He had no idea where the revolver had gone, but he was bleakly sure it would have had no effect on these things in any case.

The black creatures leaped to the ground on either side of the broken bronze head and straightened. The sunlight seemed to dim around them in smoky auras.

And though he had perceived one of their kind only for a few moments in the vertical shaft in the catacombs, Nolan knew in his spine that these were *Shaydim,* the Canaanite demons Alice Toklas had spoken of. They were hunched creatures appreciably taller than a man, with segmented bodies, multiple spidery limbs, and membranous wings. Their heads were eye ridges above black snouts, swinging from side to side.

Nolan knew that their attention would in the next few moments fix on motionless Cybele—who could surely take care of herself—but also on Vivi, who was standing over the smoking remnants of the Picasso mirror. He forced down the primal horror that the sight of the creatures woke in him, and resolutely began walking diagonally to his right, toward the spot where a five-foot wedge of Moloch's exploded bronze body lay on the sand. His heart was pounding and he was breathing deeply through clenched teeth.

As if they were extensions of one entity, the two *Shaydim* simultaneously swiveled their black heads toward him, and broad wings unfolded away identically from their bodies. Their glittering black eyes were palpably fixed on him.

Nolan began running.

A shrill insectile chattering broke from the creatures, and they stepped into the air and were flying toward him, their spider legs swinging below their spread, climbing wings.

Nolan slid to a stop beside the bronze wedge, and he crouched and lifted the heavy thing with both hands. The metal was cold and sharp-edged, and it cut his hands as he set the base of it firmly in the dirt and lifted the narrow end.

The eerily synchronized *Shaydim* had quickly closed the distance to him, and now dived. Both were reaching forward with extended claws, but it was the one on the right that rushed directly down at Nolan. He ducked his head and raised the pointed end of the wedge.

Even as its claws raked his back, its body jolted to a stop above him, impaled on the upright piece of Moloch. The base of the wedge rutched across the dirt, but Nolan held it up, and he could feel the cold bronze quiver in his bleeding hands as the point of it slid by inches deeper into the struggling creature over his head. Its leathery wings beat around him, reeking of sulfur and hot iron.

Exorcism, Nolan thought. What are the words? He drew in enough air to shout: "Die—you bastard—in the name of the Father—and of the Son—"

The *shayd* threw back its long black head and howled; and its companion, now lying on its belly in the dirt a couple of yards away, was howling at the sky in unison with it.

"—and of the Holy Ghost," Nolan rasped, emptying his lungs.

The length of bronze tipped sideways, and the *shayd* fell heavily to the dirt, lying now between its fellow and Nolan. Its clawed limbs folded in around the protruding metal, as if to pull it free, but its dying gaze bored into Nolan's eyes.

And for a few moments his identity shrank to insignificance. He was looking through a hundred eyes: in memories or immediate perceptions, alien awarenesses raced through endless tunnels, soared over domes and towers amid palm groves, surged through phosphorescent subterranean seas... but after a few taut seconds they all bent away into darkness, the multitudes of them echoing the death-wail that still rang in Nolan's ears...

His own identity rebounded and filled the ringing emptiness, and he was looking across close scuffed sand at something like a dry and heavily cobwebbed tree branch. He hiked himself up on an elbow and saw another lying directly behind it.

Blinking past them at the broken head of Moloch, he saw two more webbed angularities half emerged from the bronze eye sockets—motionless and inert.

He glanced toward Vivi, and was relieved to see that she still stood by the wall, with the tall, motionless radiance that was Cybele behind her.

He got to his feet in painful stages, aware of hot wetness on his back and cold wind through his torn jacket and shirt.

Halting footsteps behind him made him turn, and he saw Kirenli limping toward him, still a dozen yards away. Streaks of blood crisscrossed her face under her tangled black hair, and her left arm was bent, cradled in her right hand.

"They were one being," she called, and when she had hitched her way closer, "The destiny you spoke of, in the temple. You and Genevieve." Her voice for some reason was bitter.

Nolan walked to within a couple of yards of her, and she halted, panting. "You used Moloch himself, a fragment of him—to kill them."

And a Catholic exorcism invocation, he thought. *Moloch and his creatures have* révulsion *to Christianity.*

He gestured behind him, toward the two dry things on the sand and the wreckage of Moloch's form. "I know," he said. "I was there."

Kirenli inhaled deeply, coughed, then said, "No, fool. You don't understand." She nodded to the north. "*All* of them. The name of each of them was Legion."

Nolan recalled the passage in one of the gospels when a demon had been asked its name. *My name is Legion,* it had answered, *for we are many.*

Nolan found himself looking north toward the Pyrenees, and far beyond them toward the Loire Valley and Paris. He remembered looking down the shaft in the catacombs at the *shayd* below him, and sensing a multitude in its attention on him; and, only minutes ago, he had helplessly partaken of hundreds of experiences—which had closed in a vast, shared death-cry.

"*All* of them?" he whispered.

"Even so," said Kirenli. "As Cybele through Genevieve has killed Moloch." Her blood-streaked face contorted in something like envy, or grief. "The old fable is fulfilled."

Nolan hitched around to look back, and his scalp tightened in alarm. Where Vivi and the motionless radiance of Cybele had been standing was now only a tall white column whose brightness dimmed even the morning sunlight. He squinted and shaded his eyes, and was able to make out a slumped body at the base of it. He recognized Vivi's straw-colored hair.

He darted a quick glance back at Kirenli.

The woman's face now just showed resignation. "The goddess has taken her spirit into herself," she said, "and will now depart."

I'll host Cybele, Vivi had said, in the boat on the Canal Saint-Martin three days ago. *I'll be in Tarragona, virginal, on Midsummer Day, and I will probably die there.*

But Cybele is still here, Nolan thought, and his pains were forgotten as he began running as fast as he could toward the towering brilliance that stood above Vivi's body. As he ran, he tugged from inside his shirt the crumpled sheet of paper.

He covered the last few yards in a flailing headlong sprint and threw himself onto his knees beside Vivi's lifeless body.

The white fire shape that was the goddess's head inclined, looking down at him—and he was powerless not to raise his head. He saw again the sculpted planes of its face, and its star-bright eyes. The goddess's attention battered his mind, but at least some small part of that attention was perceptibly Vivi's, quivering with recognition and concern. He clung to it, and was able to retain consciousness.

He forced himself to look away, and he held up over his head the crumpled paper—the drawing he had done of Vivi in Gertrude Stein's studio.

"*A mirror!*" he screamed up at the goddess. As forcefully as he could, he projected the thought, *Reflection of you—a part of you, now.*

He bent down, and with shaking fingers pressed the paper onto Vivi's lifeless face. In the goddess's radiance, Vivi seemed to be looking up at him from the penciled lines.

The paper rippled in his bleeding hands and he sat back, letting go of it. The light around him intensified and focused on the drawing, so bright that the pencil lines couldn't be seen and the paper itself seemed to be Vivi's face.

Then the light dimmed, moving away.

The radiant figure above Vivi's body straightened to enormous height and lifted from the ground. It rose through the air above the arena, rotating away and expanding, and faded as it merged with the blue sky. The earth shifted perceptibly under Nolan's knees, realigning.

He looked down. The sheet of crumpled, bloodstained paper had fallen away from Vivi's face.

Her eyes opened, and focused on him. "Harry!" she whispered.

He lifted her in his arms and just rocked back and forth. The morning wind was cold on his wet face and his exposed, bleeding back.

"I think I'm still alive," she said.

"You are," he said thickly. "You are. Through it all."

After some unconsidered time he looked over his shoulder at the arena. The bulls had retreated to stand together against the wall by the opened pen, and the bodies of half a dozen men were sprawled here and there across the dirt. The surviving *capea* bullfighters had climbed out of the arena and were furtively making their ways, with varying degrees of difficulty, north along the road into the hills or around the walls toward the slope behind the tent. Nolan guessed that they would come back to retrieve their dead after the foreigners were gone and the rising sun had cleansed the area of dire magic. And they'd find a couple of guns.

Three men in dark jackets were standing over by the trucks. Nolan couldn't hear their voices, but they were waving toward the arena and the sky.

He wished he still had the revolver.

Only a few yards to his right, the devastated body of Robin lay on its back, facing the sky.

Eventually, Nolan took a hitching breath and asked Vivi, "Can you stand?"

She inhaled deeply. "Of course."

Then he was astonished to see her straighten her legs and stand up easily. Nolan climbed to his feet, wincing and gritting his teeth at a newly noticed sharp pain in his side.

Vivi herself seemed surprised at her effortless limberness. She raised her arms and ran her fingers through her hair, and Nolan saw that her forehead was clear and unmarked, and her throat was smooth—the cut where the bullet had grazed her was gone.

Seeing his amazed scrutiny, she touched her throat, and rubbed a hand across her forehead. She stared back at him wide-eyed and raised her palms in mute question.

Nolan could only point at the crumpled sheet of paper on the ground, and Vivi bent and picked it up. She frowned at it, then looked up at him again, still uncomprehending.

"I used it," he managed to say, "as a mirror. For Cybele." He took a deep breath, and the pain in his side sharpened, but he was still staring at her in wonder. He waved from her head to her feet. "And she saw in it the part of herself that was you, and she—"

He laughed quietly, almost incredulously. "She gave it back. Vivi, she *restored* you!"

Vivi exhaled a wordless exclamation and quickly unbuckled her watch. And after staring at her wrist for several seconds, she showed it to Nolan.

The *sauteur* tattoo was gone.

She looked up at him. *"Merci,"* she said, *"pour ma vie."* Those had been her last words to Elodie—*Thank you, for my life.*

She looked past him now, and her gaze sharpened. "Is that... Kirenli?"

He turned his head to look back. The hunched figure of Kirenli was limping toward them, cradling her arm.

"Yes," he said. "She tried to kill you again."

"No—*deify* me! Harry—" Vivi turned to him, and her eyes were wide and bright. "I was the goddess! I was...vast! Like a living mountain—or a planet—racing through space!—through years, centuries. You can't imagine it. *I* can't imagine it." She looked at the sky, then sighed. "But I'm very glad to be...finite, *small* again." She re-buckled her watch on her now-unmarked wrist.

Kirenli had limped up to within six feet of them, and stopped. "Sarkaya and Achard are dead." She sat down abruptly, wincing and clutching her injured arm. "Achard," she gasped, "had a knife, and managed to cut his own throat. I'm sure he imagined he would be reborn, but—" She nodded out across the arena toward the scattered bronze fragments of Moloch. "All of that is finished. The god's power is stopped. Now the *sauteurs* simply die."

She looked up at Vivi, squinting as if the goddess's light still shone on the girl. "You," she said, and Nolan could hear hatred in her voice, "you were the goddess! And I am no longer even a priestess. Sarkaya—we flew here in an aeroplane, in useless haste, to stop the summoning of Moloch. But she had sold herself to the adversary."

Nolan recalled that the priestesses were forbidden to directly kill one of their sisters.

"Achard's knife?" he asked quietly.

Kirenli nodded. "She thought she could make amends. And so I am simply another *citoyen* of 1925." She began shifting her legs, trying to stand. Nolan moved forward to help her, but she snarled, "Keep away! I will fend for myself." But she gave up and sat back, panting. Grudgingly she said, "You should get out of Spain quickly." She looked over her shoulder toward the tent, and Robin's body. "Murders have been done here today."

Nolan stepped back. He nodded acknowledgment and looked past her toward the tent and the trucks. He saw no one around them now, and exhaust fumes from the trucks were blowing away on the breeze.

"Goodbye," said Vivi to Kirenli. After a pause, she added, "There's still a way."

Kirenli's reply was a harsh whisper: *"Lasciate ogne speranza."* It sounded Italian.

Vivi tugged at Nolan's arm, and they moved away from Kirenli toward the low wall. "Lashyatay?" said Nolan quietly.

They climbed over the wall, and Vivi looked back at the huddled figure of Kirenli. "It's from Dante's *Inferno*," she said. "'Abandon all hope.'"

"Ah. She may speak for herself."

They walked across the flat dirt, toward the slope and the path that would take them back to Tarragona, and the waiting Citroën.

EPILOGUE:
There Is No Answer

Alice Toklas set the tray of little glasses on the table beside the couch, then sat down in a chair a few feet away. The early afternoon sun didn't reach down to the little garden outside the windows, and lamps on tables threw an evening glow over the paintings that filled the walls.

"What," she asked, "is the answer?"

"There *is* a question," Gertrude Stein said. She shifted on the couch and looked at Nolan. "What's become of the children in the orphanages—the nurseries?"

Nolan straightened up in his chair and inhaled, painfully. Cuts ached under bandages on his back, and razory pain flared in his side, but two days ago a doctor had told him that taking deep breaths would aid in healing his cracked ribs and prevent pneumonia.

Vivi answered first. "The *Préfecture de Police* and the Carthusian monks have taken charge of them," she said. "Most of the children are still children. The others pretend to be. The police have arrested Fernand Beaufroy—they hope to use his records to find out who the original families are. But all four of the nurseries are empty and locked up."

Nolan remembered asking Vivi if life in the nursery had ever been pleasant. *Sometimes*, she had said. *I had friends, until they changed and I didn't.* He thought of the mural on the wall of NID.1, with the rainbow that four-year-old Vivi had painted, and hoped it would somehow be preserved.

Two days ago he and Vivi had gone with the monks and the *gendarmerie* to NID.3, in the Rue Dupin, and seen the bewildered children being herded onto a bus—and he had wondered how many might remember when Trochu was president.

"And the *sauteur* forecasts," said Stein, "they're not true, now? Mr. Hemingway will not die in a plane crash in 1954?"

Or you, Nolan thought, after surgery in 1946?

"There is no answer," said Vivi. "He might, or might not. Moloch is banished, the futures are invisible, and the *jalon* bell won't be rung anymore."

She and Nolan had arrived back in Paris two days ago, and she was wearing her corduroy skirt and white linen blouse. Her fair hair was freshly washed, framing her face in gold curls. In contrast to Nolan, she looked almost dazzlingly healthy.

"Mr. Hemingway earned his reprieve," said Toklas. "He took a side."

"Twice," said Vivi. Nolan nodded, recalling the crowbar Hemingway had given them in the Church of Saint-Jacques du Haut-Pas, and his decision to reject Achard's offer of endlessly extended lives . . . and, in the other direction, the return of the lost manuscripts of his youth.

"And the *sauteurs*," pursued Stein. "When they die, will they be reincarnated at random, anywhere, like everyone else?"

"Reincarnation is a wishful myth," said Vivi. She and Nolan had gone to an evening Mass at a Catholic church in Marseilles, across the border into France, three days ago. Vivi had said it was *a spot of white paint to follow*. "They'll go on to judgment—like everyone else." Her gaze swept across the paintings on the walls, and she shivered. "Like the rest of us."

She had told Nolan before Mass that the two of them were not in a state of grace, and could attend the service but not take Communion. Before they could ever do that, she had said, it would be necessary to have their "sins forgiven in baptism."

Nolan had known she was apprehensive about having summoned and surrendered herself to a pagan goddess—and in truth he was uneasy about his own participation in it.

He leaned forward now, carefully, and laid a cardboard portfolio on the table. "I said I'd return this," he said to Stein. "I'm afraid it got a little beat up."

Stein flipped open the cover. Nolan's drawing of Vivi was crumpled and streaked with brown stains.

She looked up at him. "Your blood?"

"It was a stressful morning."

She looked at the bandages on his fingers and nodded. "It doesn't interfere with your work?"

Nolan flexed his hands. "No."

Confident that the *sauteurs* were in hopeless disarray, he had slept in his old flat these past two nights, uneventfully. Vivi had visited him there, and yesterday he had sat down at his drafting table and quickly drawn a couple of good sketches of her and Marechal—who had shown no signs of being anything but a hungry, grudgingly affectionate cat. There had been no watchful children on the street, and the cat had joined them for a long lunch at the Café Lepovre across the street.

Now Vivi took a sip from one of the glasses and put it down. Getting lithely to her feet, she glanced at the cubist portrait of Beltran Iglesias on the wall behind Gertrude Stein. "From Beltran and me, both," she said, "thank you." And she added, paraphrasing what the old woman at the Place du Châtelet had said, *"Bénédictions sur vous."*

Stein had got to her feet. "And on you, child."

The visit was apparently ending, and Nolan stood up too, concealing the effort it took. "Your supplies saved us, in the catacombs," he told Stein, thinking especially of the kerosene lantern. "We're very grateful."

Stein smiled and touched his shoulder. "Do good work." To Vivi she said, "Will the two of you join Alice and me for dinner, at Lipp's this evening?"

Vivi looked at Nolan. "You can go. Today is St. John's Day—traditional Midsummer at last! I've got an appointment." When he raised his eyebrows, she said, diffidently, "You saw me talking with one of the Carthusian monks? He wants to talk some more—he says he could arrange for me to be baptized." She wrinkled her nose. "And not in the river."

Toklas had stood up when Stein did, and now nodded, frowning. "Does he know you've—spectacularly!—broken the first commandment? 'Have no other gods before me'?" She spread her hands. "You're a priestess of Cybele! She healed your hurts, took away the *sauteur* tattoo!"

Vivi gave her a steady look. "He said I would not be the first one to come from paganism to the Church. And the goddess healed me because Harry tricked her with"—she touched the stained and wrinkled drawing—"a mirror."

Stein glanced at Toklas, then turned to Vivi. "I think it's a good idea."

"Wait," Nolan said to Vivi.

I suppose I'm Catholic if I'm anything, Hemingway had said. *Certainly can't take any other religion seriously.* In this last week Nolan had been tumbled into a perilous supernatural world behind the evident world, and all sorts of things might turn out to be true. And he had used the Catholic invocation to finish off the *Shaydim*.

"Would your monk object if I came along?"

Vivi's eyes were bright. "He asked if you would be joining me."

Joining you, Nolan thought. "I'd like to." To Stein, he said, "On another evening?"

She waved toward the door. "Of course."

Nolan and Vivi walked out of her studio and made their way down the path by the garden to the street door. They walked slowly—Nolan had refused to use a cane, but his steps were careful.

Vivi levered open the street door, and they walked outside. To the left, between the tall apartment buildings, the green trees in the Luxembourg Gardens glowed in sunlight, and the afternoon breeze smelled of a hundred flowers.

"I could fetch us a cab," said Vivi.

"The gardens aren't far off." He thought of the statue Vivi had led him to, a week ago. "I'd like to see Saint Genevieve again."

After a few paces, Vivi said, "We both said *Yes,* to Cybele." They walked on in silence for a minute, then she went on, "Cybele was the ... not good ... the *preferable* of the two powers, contending in that fight." She looked up at Nolan. "But she was elemental—merciless."

Nolan recalled the vision in the Cybeline temple, in which the goddess had first appeared as a crag breaking free of a mountain, and he recalled the mind-crushing stress of her inhuman attention.

The day was warm, but he shivered. "May our *Yeses* go back with her," he said, "to whatever sort of Limbo the ... shadows! ... of old gods rest in."

Vivi smiled and took his hand. "You know, I rather think we'll both be baptized."

Nolan sighed. "I think so too."

Her hand tightened in his. "And then," she said, looking ahead, toward the gardens, "if you still want to, I'll ask Saint Genevieve for her blessing, and... step down from her statue by the river."

Nolan thought back to his first meeting with Vivi—when she had come to his door asking to see the goddess-and-bull manuscript, and had walked away when he told her to wait and see the story in print; and to their second meeting, that night, when he had unexpectedly found her in his flat, holding his .45. It had certainly not seemed likely, then, that their lives would become entwined, mutually dependent, mutually protective... and soon, God willing, joined.

"Yes," he said. "I do want that."

Together they walked on, toward the sunlit gardens.